CAPTIVE LIES

VICTORIA PAIGE

This book is a work of fiction. The characters, names, locations, events, organization,
including law enforcement and judicial procedures, either are a product of the
author's imagination or are used fictitiously. Any similarity to any persons, living or
dead, business establishments, events, places or locale is entire coincidental. The
publisher is not responsible for any opinion regarding this work on any third-party
website that is not affiliated with the publisher or author.

Cover Design: Robin Ludwig Design Inc.
http://www.gobookcoverdesign.com
Content Editing: Christina Trevaskis
https://bookmatchmaker.com
Editing : Edit LLC
https://writeeditread.com

PROLOGUE

"I can't do this anymore. I'm sorry."

Grant stared once again at the text message he'd received that morning. Even when Blaire failed to debark from her Boston flight, denial still rallied in his mind and heart. Seven hours had passed. He had since flown from New Jersey to Colorado and, after the countless times he'd willed the words on the screen to change, their weight slowly sunk in. In the ensuing hours when his calls transferred to voicemail and later to a disconnected number, the reality settled like an anvil in his chest.

She had left him.

Expelling a ragged breath, Grant slipped the phone into his suit pocket and drummed his fingers on the steering wheel of the Escalade as he contemplated the log cabin before him—Blaire's secluded sanctuary. The structure was built with locally harvested Engelmann spruce while tall evergreens stood behind it like sentinels. Part of the back deck had a gorgeous view of the Colorado Rocky Mountains—a far cry from the urban setting of his brownstone back in Massachusetts.

"Ms. Callahan's not here," Jake Donovan, his head of security, noted beside him.

"No, she's not." Grant had already arrived at the same conclusion. He got out of the SUV, prompting Jake and his security detail in the car behind them to step out as well. Blaire's old pickup was still under a tarp, covered by a layer of decaying leaves, branches, pollen and dirt. All hinted at the seasons that had passed since he whisked her to civilization nine months before. He hadn't expected to find her here. This was the last place Blaire would go if she was trying to hide from him. But as untouched as the surroundings looked since the last time Grant had been here, he hoped to find clues as to why his woman fled.

It was fortunate Grant had the foresight to have made a set of spare keys to the cabin before they left for his home in Boston. Unlocking the door to the log house, a musty smell greeted his nose. It was dark except for the streaks of sunlight filtering through the slit between the curtains.

"Open the windows," he instructed his men as he walked into the kitchen area where the circuit breaker was located. Blaire had refused to disconnect the utilities because she wanted to be able to come back here whenever she wanted. It was another point of contention between them in the past month. Her refusal to permanently move in with him infuriated Grant to no end.

When the lights came on, he walked into the master bedroom. It was furnished with custom-made furniture that matched the cabin's interior. A wood-burning fireplace was built into the wall across the bed. It was surrounded by a slim couch, two chairs, and a coffee table. His heart squeezed at the memories this room evoked.

"Mr. Thorne?" Jake stood just inside the doorframe. "Liam Watts' house is empty. It appears to have been abandoned for a while."

Just like this property, Grant thought. There was an overgrowth of wildflowers and weeds around the cabin.

"Also"—his security guy's throat bobbed—"there's something else you need to see."

Grant crunched his molars as he followed Jake to the kitchen. The farmer's table and rug had been moved, exposing a trap door to an underground cellar.

"What the fuck?" he muttered as he walked around the opening in the floor. Grant didn't know what was down there, but a troubling premonition told him that everything as he knew it was about to change. He took a deep breath, and just as his foot hit the first step, Jake gripped his arm.

His head of security looked contrite. "I've failed you, Mr. Thorne, and will totally understand if you fire me after this."

"As long as my girlfriend is not a serial killer, you can keep your job." He attempted to smile, but the muscles in his jaw refused to cooperate. He clenched and flexed his fingers but still failed to relieve the compressive tightness that had gripped his body. What the hell was Blaire keeping from him?

He descended the steps and her paintings greeted him. Nothing unusual about those items given she was an artist. It wasn't until he saw the wall on his left that the air was punched out of his lungs.

Jesus Christ.

Grant took a couple of steps closer and saw the open safe and the documents scattered on top. He shuffled through them in disbelief. He could blame his lightheadedness on the lack of oxygen in the cellar, but he'd be lying to himself. He could blame his shortness of breath on the thin mountain air, but that wouldn't be true either. But the truth before him threatened his future with Blaire.

Would there even be one after this?

A future obliterated in the blink of an eye.

1

NINE MONTHS earlier

Blaire

"I THINK that's a body in the snow."

Liam grunted at my statement but guided our vehicle to the treacherous shoulder. Whiteout conditions had grown worse in the past hour so I almost missed the royal blue lump so out of place against the white and gray landscape. The snowstorm that was supposed to hit east of Vail decided to take a turn. Judging from how fast the snow was falling and the wind was gusting, we were in for a blizzard.

I pushed open the door and cold needles assaulted my face. My friend slammed out of the vehicle and went to the back of his Suburban to retrieve the sled he kept there for situations where he needed to haul items across snow. If that were indeed a person, the apparatus would come in handy. I saw tracks from several snowmobiles before spotting the transport twenty yards from its presumed rider.

"The fool." Liam trudged past me as he pulled the sled behind him, reaching the person first. He crouched beside him just as I got near. The man was face up in the snow. He was wearing a helmet with a clear shield and blue ski jacket over jeans.

"Big motherfucker, too," my friend spoke above the howl of the wind. The unconscious man was easily over six feet. The true bulk of his frame was hidden beneath his coat. However, Liam was no lightweight either. For a man of fifty, he was extremely fit, with solid muscles only years of lifting weights could give him.

"What do we do? Take him to Summit County?" I asked.

"Radio says roads are shutting down. We'll never make it." We had been heading into town when the weather took a turn for the worse, forcing us to turn around. Liam started examining the man's body, starting with his pulse. He tried to rouse the unconscious stranger to no avail.

"He has a pulse and is breathing," my friend informed me.

"We need to get him out of here."

"No shit," Liam muttered. "Get his legs."

There was no choice but to move him as I bent and took hold of the man's boots. With the blizzard strengthening, we'd risk getting stuck ourselves and first responders wouldn't be dispatched until the conditions improved. I imagined the 911 call center was already backed up. This man was either going to be dead, alive and paralyzed, or alive with no lasting injuries.

Liam carefully slipped his hands under the man's shoulders and cradled his head and neck under his forearms. We tried to keep his spine as straight as possible as I pulled him feet-first onto the sled, but the board was too short for the man's frame, so parts of his lower limbs ended up dangling. His head, torso, and hips were level on the sled. After securing him with a couple of belt straps, we trekked back to the vehicle, pulling the sled behind us.

"Thanksgiving week brings in the idiotic tourists," Liam grumbled.

"At least he's wearing a helmet." The visor had a crack, so the man must have hit one of the trees. His choice to wear jeans riding a snowmobile was questionable unless he wasn't expecting to stay in freezing temperatures for long.

"Still an idiot."

I smiled. Liam did not suffer fools. He had no patience for them. Unfortunately, Vail attracted the privileged rich and had become an everlasting source of irritation for him with their sense of entitlement.

When we reached the SUV, lifting more than two hundred pounds of dead weight into the back presented another challenge. After debating what to do for a few minutes, Liam stooped over and removed the belt straps. He then raised the damaged visor. I finally got a good look at our injured charge and my breathing hitched. Thick lashes, classic Roman nose, and whatever angles exposed of his face were chiseled granite. But what struck me the most was how much presence the man exuded even in his unconscious state. My friend tapped the man's cheek. "Hey. Wake up."

The stranger's brows cinched together before thick lashes lifted briefly to reveal inky blue irises. "What?" he rasped.

"Thank fuck," Liam grunted. "Can you move?"

The man blinked once as if confused, then, as if belatedly understanding what he was asked to do, he shifted to his side to push up. Liam and I rushed to help him. My friend managed to get the stranger up before the man swore under his breath and started to crash.

"Easy," Liam cautioned. "I've got you." The man passed out again, leaving us to struggle for a few minutes to settle him into the SUV's cargo space. By the time I jumped down from the tailgate, my overheated skin felt like it had withstood the flames of a furnace so I welcomed the blast of cold air.

Liam shut the cargo door and walked to the driver's side.

I got in beside him and stole a glance at our guest. "You think he'll be okay?"

As if on cue, we heard a groan from the back.

"He's alive," Liam muttered and gunned the engine.

"True."

"We more or less confirmed he's not paralyzed."

Again, I agreed.

"Otherwise, I'd have to kill him."

I snorted a bewildered laugh. "What?"

Liam glanced at me. "He'll blame us, saying we caused it by moving him. We don't need that trouble."

"Liam ..."

"I'm already regretting that we had to rescue his sorry ass."

"Do you see any cars on the road at the moment? He'd die from hypothermia if not his injuries."

"Our life is already too complicated, Blaire."

Yes, it is.

"The sooner we get rid of him the better," Liam informed me.

I peeked at our passenger again. *Why do I already feel his loss when I don't even know his name?*

My friend barked a censuring laugh. "No, Wren. He's not one of your injured birds." And that was how I earned my nickname. I rescued a Canyon Wren with a broken wing and kept it for a while.

"I don't know what you're talking about."

"You've always had a soft spot for wounded creatures."

"And you forced me to let them go every single time," I retorted.

"Wild birds are exactly that, Blaire. They belong in the wild," Liam sighed.

And him? I did not say and, instead, looked out my window wistfully.

Grant

GRANT WOKE UP SHIVERING. The orange glow of a fire taunted him with its warmth, and yet he couldn't feel its heat. His bleary eyes tracked a shadow moving closer. A vague figure crouched in front of him and his vision focused.

Hazel eyes assessed him.

"You're awake." The voice, coming from perfectly formed lips, was melodious and soothing.

A warm hand touched his skin and he leaned into it. She smelled of some ethereal musk.

An angel.

"You're not dead, big guy," she chuckled. "You just have a fever."

Grant smiled despite the goose bumps that ghosted over his skin. He tried to tuck into himself, yanking at the blankets covering him.

The angel got up.

"Stay," he said in near panic.

"I'll be back."

He fretted and drew the covers around him. This didn't feel real. Grant had never felt this needy in his life.

She returned, holding a tumbler with a straw. No way was he sipping through that thing like a sissy. He tried to get up, but he was pushed back down.

"I can sit up," he muttered.

"Quit the macho bullshit," the angel admonished. "Just drink this."

Grant gave in and sipped from the straw. Then he spewed everything out.

"What the fuck is that?" he growled, then was immediately contrite because his involuntary liquid expulsion landed on his angel's face.

"Spruce tea. It's an old Indian concoction that's good for respiratory infections." She wiped her face, emitted a long-suffering sigh, and held the straw to him again.

This time Grant obediently drank the bitter liquid, ignoring the urge to spit it up again. When he dutifully finished, he asked, "What's your name?"

"Blaire."

"Grant," he returned. The tea momentarily warmed him, but it didn't take long for his body to quake with chills again. "Feel like shit."

"I've already given you some meds," she informed him and then a crease marred her forehead. "Your fever's not breaking. If the roads were open, I'd take you to a hospital, but the blizzard has shut every-thing down. What were you doing out there anyway?"

Shit, his family must be worried. *Oh, fuck. Val.*

"My sister. Did you see my sister?"

"You're the only person we found."

Grant pushed the blankets aside and attempted to get up. "She's out there. She's ... fuck." He fell back as if a magnet yanked him flat on the mattress. *What the fucking hell?* His muscles weighed like lead and whatever strength he had initially deserted him. He fought to keep his eyes open.

"You need to rest."

"Phone?" he muttered.

"Cellular service is down."

He rallied against the drowsiness but it was a losing battle. "What was in that tea?"

"I didn't poison you if that's what you're asking," came the pert reply.

"Sass," he said. "I want to kiss that mouth." He felt the corners of his mouth tip up. "I'd be fucking an angel."

"You're delirious."

"Cold," Grant murmured. "Sleep with me."

HE WAS SUBMERGED UNDER WATER, *tangled in a net, his lungs close to bursting and he couldn't get to Val. She was right beside him, eyes closed. She had given up the struggle moments ago.*

"Val!" he yelled. Painful spasms followed the gurgling sound of his voice.

He was drowning.

"No!" Grant came awake to darkness and flame.

"It was a dream," a calming voice told him. He tried to rise but hands pressed down against his shoulders as confusion overpowered his foggy brain.

He needed to save Val. She was going to drown.

"Val," he croaked.

"Grant, do you know where you are?"

"Water's freezing," he told the voice.

"Shit. Okay, hold on."

"My sister ... why ... why is there fire in the water?"

No response. There was a rustle of clothes followed by a presence wrapping him in a shroud of comfort.

"Shh ..."

"Save her."

"Grant, sleep."

"I can't ... need to save her."

"You'll be okay."

"Drowning ..." Darkness sucked him back into the abyss, but his thoughts had quieted, pacified by the warmth tightly wound around him and the fragrance of heaven in his nose.

THE NEXT TIME he woke up, he was covered in sweat but no longer shivering. Grant could feel the heat of the fireplace on his right, and on his left, a warm body wrapped around him. A warm, soft body that cleaved to him in all the right places. If circumstances were different, he'd be sporting wood by now, but he was physically spent battling the fever. Contentment washed over him. His hand circled Blaire's arm that was draped across his torso; he clung to it like a lifeline, a buoy that kept him anchored in tranquility. He let himself be drawn into slumber once again.

VOICES.

Hushed whispers.

Blaire was gone from his side and though his fever had abated, his whole damned body hurt as if he'd been run over by a freight train—from the almighty headache, sore throat, aching chest and ribs to the throbbing in his left leg. How much damage did he sustain? Then he remembered why he was in this predicament in the first place and concern for his foolish sister surged to the forefront of his mind. Val had taken off in a snowmobile after a fight with her boyfriend. As for that useless prick, he decided to disappear in the opposite direction, so it was left to Grant to make sure Val came back in one piece. Then he recalled his dream when he was delirious. It was a recurring nightmare from when Val almost drowned. Except in that dream, his sister always died. But something felt different this time and he hadn't awakened to hopeless despair. Instead, his body recalled that moment of soothing calm as Blaire wrapped herself around him.

Shadows moving by the open door pulled him out of his thoughts.

"It was a mistake to bring him here," a man's voice growled.

"Road conditions were treacherous," Blaire replied. "We could have been stuck in a ditch. State Highway Nine was almost shut down by then, remember?"

They must have moved further away because Grant couldn't hear the man's reply. Who the fuck was that guy? He hadn't stopped to think that Blaire might belong to another man. A strange emotion pierced his chest.

Grant didn't know how long he'd been at the cabin, but it was time he found out. Every bone and sinew protested as he pushed himself from the bed. He managed to stand up, his surroundings spinning for a few seconds, and he stood still until he found his equilibrium. Taking a step forward and putting weight on his left leg was a mistake.

"God fucking dammit!" he cursed as he crashed to his right knee. The only reason he didn't fall flat on his face was because he managed to brace himself with his right arm. The jolt wasn't pleasant either, but he swallowed back another curse.

Blaire and a man he didn't recognize appeared at the door.

"Why did you get up?" she snapped. Blaire was about to walk up to him when the man she was with blocked her.

Grant didn't like that one bit and his face must have shown it.

The man before him had a head of cropped salt and pepper hair. Weather-worn lines creased his forehead and the corners of his eyes. But the tight thermal he was wearing did nothing to hide the muscles bunched underneath. He was a fit man who looked to be in his late forties or fifties.

"Who are you?" Grant demanded.

The man snorted. "None of your goddamned business, Thorne."

Grant didn't remember giving his last name to Blaire, neither had he taken identification on him when he took off after Val. He picked himself up from the floor just as Blaire shook off the newcomer's grip. She attempted to guide him back to the bed, but Grant wasn't about to display any form of weakness. He stood tall, his six-three height topping the other man by at least three inches.

Blaire rolled her eyes at the blatant show of testosterone. "Liam and I found you," she explained.

"Yes, we know who you are," her friend said. "It's all over the local radio. Senator Thorne's billionaire son missing. Search teams are organizing as we speak."

"How long since I was reported missing?"

"It's been thirty-six hours since we found you," Blaire replied. "Look, as soon as the roads are passable, Liam here will take you to Summit County Hospital."

"Phones still out?"

Blaire nodded. "Cell service has always been spotty up here and the landline is down."

"Valerie Thorne ... my sister, is there any news about her too?"

"No. There are other tourists missing, but I don't think your sister was one of them," Blaire said, laying her hand on his arm in a show of comfort. Her touch startled them both and she quickly stepped away seemingly flustered. "I'm...I'm going to check on dinner," she muttered.

That gesture of kindness tugged at an unfamiliar muscle in his chest, and he had an odd desire to make her stay when she turned to leave. His eyes followed her retreating form until Liam moved and obscured his view.

"Hey," the other man snapped his fingers in front of his face as if to break Grant out of a trance. "Don't even think about it."

He narrowed his eyes at the older man. "Snap your fingers at me that way again and I'll break them. You saved my life. I'm thankful. But don't get between Blaire and me."

"What did you just say?" Liam growled, taking an intimidating step forward.

Grant didn't back down and, instead, stared down his nose into angry gray eyes. "You're protective of her. I get that. But I'm not some psycho you guys rescued who's gonna hurt her."

Liam snorted.

"You have a problem with me, Liam?"

"Only rich assholes."

"When have I wronged you?"

"I know your type."

"I assure you," Grant replied, gritting his teeth because he was in no shape for extended verbal sparring with this man. "You've never met my type."

"I haven't gotten you to the hospital yet," Liam threatened before he backed away, continuing to hold Grant's gaze, until he reached the door before turning to leave the room.

2

Blaire

A JOLT of awareness shot through me when I touched Grant's arm and, it was so unnerving, I had to leave the room. When his fever spiked, a desire to help him overwhelmed me. It was a simple act of caring—or so I told myself. But I realized I'd left myself open to feeling more. That was one complication I couldn't afford. I had remained clinical when Liam helped me strip our guest out of his wet clothes, but seeing Grant on his feet, towering above me—and even Liam—I couldn't help but recall the searing temperature of his tanned skin and how his corded muscles bunched under my palm.

Chicken and dumplings was perfect comfort food and a cure-all for all illnesses including the temptation of making bad decisions— like getting attached to a stranger who was only passing through. So I turned my attention to the pot of simmering broth and lifted two whole chickens from its depths to let them cool before I pulled the meat off. I'd sautéed the vegetables earlier, so all that was left was to add the broth to the mixture. Drop biscuits were next. Scooping flour into a bowl, I cut in the butter, milk and other spices.

As I shaped the dough, my friend stalked out from the hallway and, judging from his scowl, he and Grant must have had words. He was about to say something to me when the kitchen light flickered more than normal. We'd been on generator power since the night before. It had stopped snowing, but the roads wouldn't be passable for another twenty-four hours. The county took snow removal seriously because businesses around here thrived on ski-resort tourism —two feet of white powder was something they had to be prepared for.

"I'm going to check on the generator," Liam informed me. "If I weren't worried about you freezing, I wouldn't give a fuck if *your* guest turned into a popsicle."

"Liam."

"What?" he growled.

"*Our* guest," I reminded him.

"Whatever," he muttered. Cold air shot into the house as he opened and closed the door.

I sighed. Liam was used to having his way. Even before I knew who Grant was, my instincts told me he wasn't a pushover. And I was right. Battered, concussed, or fighting a fever, he wore his dominant personality like a second skin. And yet, I witnessed his vulnerability when he had that nightmare.

Liam was gone less than ten minutes when I heard a shuffle on the wood floor and then, "Something smells good."

I jumped and spun around. Grant stood there, his hair curling in wet tendrils, looking ridiculous in Liam's smaller clothes. His crooked grin did funny things to my heart.

"You should lie down," I told him.

Ignoring my statement, he limped toward the stove. "Took a shower. Hope you don't mind if I used your ... uh, shampoo. I couldn't stand myself anymore."

"Yes, you were smelling a bit ripe." I leaned in and mocked a sniff to tease him further. "Lemon verbena sure smells good on you."

There was a quick hitch to his breathing and I berated myself for letting my guard down, but before I could take a step back, he caught my elbows and drew me close.

Our faces were almost touching, and I felt a shiver run through me and a strange flutter low in my belly.

"It sure smells good on you," he murmured. I wondered if he could hear my heart pounding. The scent of spicy citrus only enhanced his clean, masculine smell, a heady lure that made it difficult to pull back. I was sure he was going to kiss me and I wasn't sure if I was going to stop him. So, I was baffled when he dropped his hands, moved away, and cocked a hip against the counter. A tremor ran through him as if someone had walked over his grave.

"Are you all right?"

"Yeah," he muttered. He nodded to the pot. "What are you making?"

"Chicken and dumplings."

His slow smile set my heart racing again.

Jesus, Blaire, get a grip.

"I haven't had homemade chicken and dumplings since Miss Lynette passed."

"Miss Lynette?"

"My mother's housekeeper."

When I didn't say anything, he continued. "Mom's from Savannah."

"A Southern woman," I quipped.

"Born and raised," Grant drawled. "Spent my summers on their family farm. Hot as hell, but the food Miss Lynette served up made the oppressive heat worth it. Best fried chicken and chocolate chess pie anywhere."

"Are you hungry, Grant?" I laughed.

His nostalgic expression morphed into an aggrieved look. "Starving."

"Well, let's get you fed then," I said. With my clean hand not covered in biscuit dough, I reached up and touched his forehead. "Good, no fever. But you need to stay warm." I motioned to the living room. "Why don't you sit by the fireplace? Dinner will be another fifteen minutes." My brows drew together and I looked at the door. "Liam should be back by then."

"Does he live here?" There was an edge to Grant's voice as he made his way to the living room. Liam really rubbed him the wrong way.

"No. He has a house a mile down the road."

A thoughtful look came over his face. He must be wondering why we didn't take him there instead. The short of it was, Liam's house wasn't guest-ready. He had shit strewn about that would be a little hard to explain.

I dropped the dough balls into the pot. That would take about twelve minutes. I pulled the meat off the chicken, making sure to leave big chunks and covered it with foil. I washed my hands and dried them on my apron and went to check on my patient.

He wasn't on the couch, but standing by my drawing board near the bank of glass doors that opened to the patio.

"You're an artist?" he asked, turning as I approached.

"Yup."

I linked my hands behind my back as I stepped up to him, suddenly shy at having him perusing my work.

"These are good," he said, referring to the set of four panels of watercolors. "What do you call this type of art again? Three panels are called triptych, right?"

I nodded, "That's a quadriptych."

"Beautiful," he murmured, but his eyes were not on the pieces but were unwaveringly trained on me. The spotlight on the paintings flickered, but no distraction could break the lock of our gazes.

"Blaire ..."

I cleared my throat. "You should be resting." Turning around to walk to the couch, I pointed to the furniture. "Sit."

"Yes, ma'am." There was a hint of a grin on his face that turned into a grimace as he lowered his body to the cushions. "Shit."

I held a lap blanket to my chest. "You okay?"

He blew out a breath. "Yeah."

"It's okay to admit you're in pain, you know." I handed him the blanket which he took but set aside.

Men.

My expression and long-suffering sigh must have given my thoughts away.

"I'm comfortable," he grumbled. "Don't fuss."

I raised a brow. "Men who are sick are usually big babies."

Grant chuckled. "Is Liam?"

"No, he just turns ornery," I replied, remembering the time Liam was sidelined for a month because he hurt his back.

His face sobered. "Can't thank you both enough for rescuing my ass out there."

"Anyone in our place would have done the same."

"I doubt that." He nodded at the space beside him. "Sit. Tell me about your art."

"I'm fine standing," I replied too quickly that I blushed, feeling the heat steal up my cheeks.

His mouth twitched. "You make it so goddamned hard ..."

"I don't understand." I totally understood if his heated gaze were anything to go by.

He gave a shake of his head, his wry grin letting me know I knew exactly what he meant, but he was letting me off the hook with his eyes giving me an explicit "later."

"Do you sell your art?"

I did, but this conversation could be tricky. "Yes."

He waited for me to say more. When I wasn't volunteering additional information, he followed up with more questions. "Where? How?"

"A gallery in Vail." That was true, but I was an anonymous artist only known as Nyuki, which was Swahili for "bee." I dropped off the paintings and I was paid by direct deposit. I never met with clients or did any special orders.

"What's the name of the gallery?"

I was saved from answering when the door slammed open. Liam

stomped his boots at the door to shake off the snow then dragged himself in. "Damn, it's freezing."

He scowled at the sight of Grant on the couch before his eyes shifted to me. "Dinner?"

"Two minutes." I came unstuck and hurried to the kitchen. "You guys entertain each other," I threw over my shoulder.

Grant grunted a non-response and I was sure Liam maintained his glower. Dinner could be quite entertaining. Maybe I should have made popcorn instead.

WHILE CHICKEN and dumplings was the cure to all illnesses, apparently it applied to grumpiness as well. The men followed me to the kitchen and hovered around the farm table which doubled as my center island. I had a bench along the long end of the table, and one chair at the short side. The other seats were scattered around the cabin.

The moment I removed the lid of the dutch oven, the aroma of homey goodness filled the kitchen. The men's expressions brightened as if the weight of the world had been lifted from their shoulders. I smiled inwardly as I transferred the chicken into the soup to heat it through. One man was chilled to the bone from battling generator issues, while the other had not eaten for the past thirty-six hours. I couldn't blame them for drooling.

"Can I help?" Grant asked, coming so close to me, the heat of his body seared through my clothes. His eyes were not on me, though, but on the bubbling liquid. I was oddly envious of the food.

"This will take another minute," I told him and then, "You look famished."

"You have no idea," he whispered, staring longingly at dinner.

I laughed.

Liam cleared his throat. "I'll get the bowls." Then without skipping a beat, he added, "Thorne, you might want to step back from Blaire, yeah?"

Grant turned slowly to face Liam. "You're starting to piss me off." His voice was flat, but there was no question that his patience was at an end.

So was mine. Liam needed to back off.

I waved the cooking spoon between them. "You two, stop it. Anyone who says another word between now and dinner will not be getting any food. Clear?" I felt like a referee between two children but, unfortunately, my dear friend was the bully.

Liam's mouth flattened before he turned away to get the bowls. Grant still had his raptor stare on, following my friend's movements, and making no move to step away from me.

Returning with the bowls, Liam gave Grant a brief glance, before handing me the dishes. I scooped steaming chicken and dumplings into the first bowl and set it on the counter. I had an idea how two alpha males would behave if I gave one his food first. They'd both insist on waiting for me to eat. So, to avoid any awkwardness, I filled the three bowls without handing them out.

I opened the utensil drawer and handed each man a soup spoon and fork, then I picked up my chicken and dumplings and headed to the table without a word. They stood back and I heard terse, whispered conversation, but I didn't pay them any mind. I sat down on the lone chair at the table, took an exaggerated inhale of the ultimate comfort food, and dug in, blowing gently, before I took my first bite.

The two men settled on the bench with their soup, but Grant managed to get to the edge closer to me.

"I believe she's ignoring us," my friend muttered.

"Believe so, Liam," Grant replied.

I looked up from my bowl, slightly annoyed. "Are you two best friends now?"

"Hardly," Liam retorted.

"We called a truce," Grant said, shooting the other man a warning glance. "We apologize if we've ruined your mood for dinner."

I sighed and lifted my chin to his dish. "Eat." I projected nonchalance, but I was sneaking glances at Grant beneath my lashes. He took a spoonful of hot dumpling and closed his eyes. Deciphering his expression was tricky. I wasn't sure if it was enjoyment or agony on his face.

"Did you burn your tongue?"

He swallowed his food without answering and took another bite, and then another. He must be really hungry.

Finally, after his fourth bite, he smacked his lips with enthusiasm. "Damn. Tastiest chicken and dumplings I've ever had."

There was a disgruntled snort coming from the other end of the bench but we both ignored it. I was preening under Grant's compliment and I wasn't going to let my overprotective friend mar the moment. Admittedly, I put a lot of effort into making this soup and it was one of the best I'd ever made.

"Thanks," I said and continued to eat my dinner.

Grant quickly polished off his first serving, got up unsteadily, and went back for seconds. I worried that he was going to feel sick by eating too much when his stomach had been empty for so long. I didn't say anything, though, because his color had improved.

He sat back down and he grinned at me. "What else do you make?"

"Are you planning on staying here indefinitely?" Liam asked.

"No," Grant shot back. "But I plan to visit often."

Oh, shit!

I shot Liam a panicked look, but he didn't catch it because he was glowering at Grant, who seemed more interested in the dumplings and was oblivious that the other man could easily murder him and hide his body. I watched Grant pack away his second bowl and was thankful that I had the foresight to cook two chickens.

"I make a mean seafood gumbo," I said, looking indulgently at his empty dish. Why in the world was I bragging?

Grant's eyes lit up as he gazed at me with unmistakable adoration. "Angel, you have to marry me now."

Angel. My jaw hurt from containing the smile that wanted to break out. Liam's glare was like a laser from across the table. I knew I'd be hearing words from him later, but I also knew my boundaries.

Couldn't I enjoy feeling like a woman just this once—adored and wanted? Sadly, I knew I couldn't afford to indulge in such moments.

"Right," I said, giving Grant a sidelong glance that told him I wasn't taking what he said seriously. He protested when I picked up his bowl and put it on top of mine.

"Let the food settle down," I advised, reverting to nurse-mode. "There's more if you want some. Liam?" I turned to my friend. "Want another round?"

He slid his bowl across the table to me and nodded. I sighed. My friend was brooding. Grant unsettled him. I didn't blame him—our guest unsettled me too. With a sinking heart, I knew Grant would be leaving soon.

3

Grant

DINNER PUT him in a food coma, but Grant woke up feeling a little better than the day before. His head didn't feel like exploding. His throat was worse, but that was expected. He needed something warm to soothe it. His joints didn't hurt as much, but his ankle was swollen. Following Blaire around the house like a lovesick puppy probably wasn't a good idea. He couldn't help it—she was one of the most nurturing souls he had ever met. It radiated from her like a beacon and he was drawn to her. When he saw her standing in the kitchen, he'd immediately pictured her in his own kitchen in Boston. He loved the idea so much that it had spooked him, which was why he retreated initially, but even that didn't last long.

He didn't imagine the spark of interest in her eyes. She was attracted to him but he could see the conflict inside her. Would a quick fling satisfy whatever was brewing between them? As soon as that thought crossed his mind, he dismissed it savagely. The woman saved his life; he needed to leave her alone. His life was on the east coast and he didn't do long-distance relationships.

With that thought, he decided it was time to get up. He had a feeling he'd been sleeping for some time. He swore viciously as he got off the bed. His ribs hadn't liked that. When he limped into the hallway, the smell of coffee hit his nose and he realized he'd not had caffeine in almost three days.

An overhead wrought-iron lamp brightened the kitchen, but the whole house was lit by the reflection of snow coming from the windows. A fire was burning in the living room hearth and, as Grant exited the hallway, he spotted Blaire sitting on the kitchen bench in red plaid pajamas. She had one foot raised on the seat and a sketchpad rested on that bent knee. Her hair was tied back in a ponytail, head tilted as she pulled expert strokes of charcoal across paper. He rubbed at his chest, an odd ache forming there. Grant wanted to commit this unguarded moment to memory so he could take it with him when he left.

But when Blaire glanced up and a smile broke across her face, all of Grant's selfless intentions disappeared. There was no fucking way he was never seeing that smile again.

"You're awake!" Blaire chirped, setting her sketchpad on the table and jumping up. "Twelve hours, Thorne."

"You're shitting me."

"Nope. You passed out at nine," his angel informed him. "It's nine-thirty. Imagine that?"

He grunted.

"How's the head?"

"Better."

"Blurred vision?"

"Nope," he answered, and before she could ask another question. "Coffee?"

"Oh, you're one of those." She raised a brow. "The ones who can't function without caffeine?"

Damn, he wanted to kiss that smart mouth.

"No coffee," she said. "You're getting lemon tea—"

"The fuck?"

"And if you still want coffee, you may have a cup."

Grant was rethinking her nurturing soul. Maybe he'd been hallucinating the past few days. "Do you like torturing your patients?"

"You're better, aren't you?" she sassed as she turned around and presented him with her oh-so-shapely ass. She headed to the stovetop to turn on the burner under the kettle. Grant spotted the coffee machine, limp-stalked over to the stove and switched it off.

"Hey—"

"Coffee, woman. None of that lemon tea bullshit." He started searching the cabinets for a mug. Finding one, he turned around and saw that she had her hands on her hips, her eyes shooting sparks of annoyance at him.

"You're still sick," she reminded him.

"And you made me drink fucking spruce tea," he shot back. "I deserve coffee."

Grant tagged the pot of brew and poured himself a cup. He took a healthy gulp and enjoyed the burn going down his throat but he had to admit, it wasn't as effective as spruce or lemon tea.

Blaire threw up her hands. "You're having oatmeal for breakfast."

He sighed. "I'm really hungry."

"I can put some eggs in it," she offered. "Liam does it and I think it's disgusting, but I guess you'll need the calories to maintain those muscles." Her eyes widened when she caught his smirk "I mean ..."

"You perving on my muscles?"

She scowled. "Do you want breakfast?" She spun around and pulled the refrigerator open with a huff. "And I'm not a pervert," she told the fridge.

"I was teasing, Blaire," Grant murmured. "You're cute when you're flustered."

She didn't say anything, and he began to regret teasing her. She was obviously uncomfortable with flirting. But if her flaming cheeks were anything to go by, she was definitely *not* uninterested. He'd wondered since the night before if, when she blushed, she was pink all over. Grant groaned inwardly. He had felt her bare legs against him, her soft curves against him—maximum body heat. What he would give to experience that closeness again. Except it would end up with him balls-deep inside her. He'd climb over her, wrap her legs around him, shove her panties aside and slide his cock right into her tight heat. And there was his dick rising up to the challenge.

"Grant, are you sure you're okay?" Blaire asked, a frown creasing her forehead. "You look like you're in pain."

You have no idea, Angel.

"Are the phones still down?" he asked as he willed his wayward thoughts to go on a different track.

She nodded. "You're worried about your sister?"

"The radio didn't report her missing the same time they reported that I was. I think she's fine," he concluded from what Blaire and Liam told him the day before.

"You sound pissed at her," Blaire observed, stirring the oatmeal into the pot of water.

He lowered himself to the chair and leaned back. Taking another sip of coffee, he contemplated where exactly his headspace was regarding his sister. "I'm caught in the middle of worry and anger. There's still a chance that something happened to her. Also," he sighed. "Not being able to get word to my parents that I'm fine is frustrating."

"I'm sorry," she whispered.

"Not your fault," Grant said quickly. "You guys have gone above and beyond for a complete stranger." And that was why he tolerated Liam's hostility to a certain point.

"Why were you both out in the snow?"

"Fight with her boyfriend," he said, his blood starting to boil. "Val got so pissed, she took off on a snow mobile. Fucker didn't go after her, so I did."

There was that look on Blaire's face that tempted him to hug her. The closest word that came to mind was "compassion." Her face was so expressive, her eyes—he couldn't even decide what color they were. Dark rimmed around the edges with light brown and green ... no, sometimes they were almost blue. The previous night when she stood before him in front of her paintings, she took his breath away. Blaire by firelight was breathtaking.

Grant cleared his throat. "Where's Liam?"

"Haven't seen him since dinner."

He wouldn't put it past the older man to plow the snow himself if it meant getting rid of Grant.

Blaire turned away from him to check on his oatmeal. Watching her crack the eggs into the porridge and stir it in, he thought about how these moments with her would be perfect if he didn't worry about his parents, half-out of their minds, wondering if he were dead or alive. Suddenly impatient, he got up from the chair and limped to the window. Liam had indeed cleared the snow from the front of her house.

"Getting cabin fever?" she asked from behind him.

Grant turned and noticed her sad smile. "Thinking of my parents and Val." Did she sense that she was at the center of his conflicted emotions as well?

"You'll see them soon," Blaire said softly. "Oatmeal is ready."

A SCRAPING NOISE jolted Grant awake. For a second, he wondered where he was until he saw the fireplace. After breakfast, which had been an excruciating exercise of shoveling the gruel into his mouth while not hurting Blaire's feelings, they decided to play cards and board games. Lunch was leftover chicken and dumplings and then that was it for Grant. He hated getting sick. One minute he'd feel like he had recovered enough, and then his head and lungs would conspire to suck the life out of him. He ended up falling asleep on the couch.

The door flew open, sending him jackknifing on the couch and instantly regretting it. He swallowed a curse at the pain shooting up his torso and glowered at Liam who stood at the entrance with a triumphant smirk on his face.

Blaire rushed out from the hallway, this time in pink sheep-print flannel pajamas. For a moment, Grant forgot the other man and decided that he had become fond of sheep-printed sleepwear. But then the look on her face tweaked a muscle on his chest.

"Get dressed," Liam ordered. "The plows just came through."

"You?" Grant asked Blaire even as a sinkhole formed in his gut.

She frowned. "What about me?"

"Are you coming too?"

"You don't need me anymore," she replied. His mind protested every word of that statement. Groggy from sleep, his brain wasn't firing on all cylinders and scrambled to find a reason to keep her with him.

"They might need information." Grant directed his question at Blaire.

"About what?" Liam cut in. "We found you. You have a concussion, maybe a respiratory infection, bruised or cracked ribs, and a sprained ankle. End of story."

Blaire hugged her biceps as if she was suddenly chilled. "You guys need to get going. Another round of snow is on its way and the roads might not stay open." She turned away and walked into the kitchen.

"Get moving, Thorne," Liam said, coming up beside him and, for the first time since he'd known the older man, concern showing on his face. "I'm sure your folks are worried. The sooner they see you're okay, the better."

How could Grant argue with that?

"END OF THE ROAD, BIG SHOT," Liam informed him when the SUV pulled in front of the emergency room entrance.

"Shouldn't you come in with me?" Grant said, not willing to lose his last link to Blaire. "They might have questions."

"Tell them a good Samaritan found you," the other man said.

"There might be a reward," he pointed out.

Liam's jaw tensed. "Blaire and I were just doing what normal human beings would do." He nodded to the entrance. "Go on. There's another storm coming and I'd appreciate not getting stuck in it."

The older man's expression was flinty; it was obvious that Liam couldn't wait to get rid of him.

Grant couldn't recall a time when he'd taken a person's order, but he felt honor-bound to respect Liam's wishes. For now.

He tentatively stepped down from the vehicle, but nearly retreated back into it when people loitering around the entrance paused, gasped, and started murmuring amongst themselves. It felt as though his face had been on posters everywhere. As soon as he shut the door to the SUV, Liam screeched away from the curb, leaving Grant standing in the clothes he'd been found in.

"Mr. Thorne?" A woman dressed in green scrubs approached him with tentative steps, head tilted to the side with bright eyes taking him in from head to foot.

Grant, still feeling like death warmed over, longed for the coziness of Blaire's cabin, but he wanted to get this over with, so he simply nodded and followed the woman.

AFTER HOURS OF PRODDING, scans, and needles, Grant was ready to check himself out of the hospital.

Within half an hour of his appearance at the Summit County Hospital, his parents—Senator Marcus and Amelia Thorne arrived with an impressive entourage of family, friends, and a security team. It was the Thanksgiving holiday weekend after all, and they'd been keeping vigil at the family residence in Vail.

Grant experienced a pang of guilt. As everyone worried, he'd been selfish in his reason for wanting to stay with Blaire. Seeing his family, he wondered if how he felt about his time with her would change. Maybe the isolation of the cabin had magnified the significance of his moments with her? Grant squashed that assumption. How could he easily forget a woman who had saved his life?

The first person to hug him was Val. He had never seen his sister's face so ravaged before. He found out from his mom that she'd been crying non-stop since they'd discovered his wrecked snowmobile with no trace of him.

"I'm so sorry. I'm so sorry, Teddy," Val cried. She uttered her childhood nickname for him—from his middle name Theodore. She did this when she was highly emotional and that moment qualified as one of those times. Val would have climbed into his hospital bed if the nurses didn't warn of his possible injuries. After about ten minutes of being fussed over by his mother and sister, and to a certain extent, his dad, a series of medical tests commenced.

The final verdict was Grant was battling a respiratory infection, he had two bruised ribs, a sprained ankle, and a concussion but, luckily, no cerebral edema.

"You gave us a scare, son," his dad said while his mother and sister sat on either side of his bed. "A state trooper found Valerie; we had to pick her up from the sheriff's station. Even then it took forever to get to her. The roads were a mess. It was hours after the blizzard hit that we were certain something had happened to you."

"I don't recall much except my snowmobile struck something and I flipped over."

"They almost didn't locate your ride because the snow had come down heavily and covered all other tracks. We had to rely on Val's recollection of her route to find you," his dad explained.

"We thought you were buried under eighteen inches of snow and we'd never find you," Val sobbed. "I wasn't thinking when I took off. I was just so mad at Paul." Grant adored his sister, but he wasn't blind to her faults, especially her choices in men. The siblings often clashed because he had yet to approve of a single guy his sister dated.

"Please tell me your son of a bitch boyfriend is gone." Even in his bed-ridden state, he wanted to wipe the floor with that bastard for putting his sister in danger.

Val nodded. "He left this morning. I'm done with him."

His sister linked her hand with his. "I'd never forgive myself if we lost you." She hiccupped as wet misery trailed down her face.

"Hey," Grant whispered, used to his sister's emotions. Reaching out to her, he drew Val's head to his chest. "I'm here. I'm whole. Don't blame yourself, but, please, for the love of God, no more losers, all right, Val?"

He heard his father grumble in agreement. The problem was both he and his dad were guilty of spoiling Valerie. They'd nearly lost her to a drowning incident when she was five years old and Grant was fifteen. Both men had been with her at that time. She fell off a sailboat, got tangled in some fishing net, and nearly drowned. She had suffered a hypoxic brain injury because of it. This affected her neurological and motor skill function. It took years of therapy, but Val recovered fully with only the occasional tremor. Sometimes Grant wondered if her out-of-nowhere impulsive behavior and adrenaline rushes were side effects of that brain injury.

"What I want to know is whom we should be thanking for helping you," his mom was ever gracious and skilled at changing the subject when it was called for.

Grant smiled, remembering Blaire, but he shook his head. "They're private people and don't want the publicity."

"They don't want the ten-thousand-dollar reward?" The speaker was August "Gus" Lynch, his father's political advisor. He stood at the doorway like a hawk assessing his prey. The tone in the man's voice raised Grant's hackles.

"Doesn't anyone find this suspicious?" Gus continued asking. "Or do they have a problem with politicians."

"Gus, now is not the time or the place," his father reprimanded.

Planting a kiss on Val's forehead, Grant gently eased her away so he could sit up on the bed. He and his father's right-hand man didn't see eye-to-eye on many issues, which was why Grant stayed away from the senator's politics when he could.

"I believe the doctor said family only," Grant said coolly. "Why are you here, Gus?"

Valerie tittered while his mother looked disconcerted.

"Your father's communications director needs a statement from the family," Gus replied even as redness crept up his neck.

"Tell them I'm alive and well."

"They'll want details of the past two and a half days. We need to know the name of your rescuers."

Blaire Callahan and Liam Watts, he thought, but the world and Gus weren't getting their names.

"No," Grant growled, turning to the senator. "The people who helped me want to remain anonymous. That's the least I could do—"

"We're missing an opportunity here, Senator," Gus appealed to his father and, if his mother hadn't been sitting on his right, he would have gotten off the bed and punched his dad's advisor straight across the jaw.

"Opportunity? Fuck you, Lynch," he snapped. "Get the fuck out of my room."

"Grant, language!" his mother admonished, but she glared at Gus.

As for Grant, he was too pissed to care. He nearly died out there. The only reason he didn't reiterate that point was because he didn't want his sister to feel guilty all over again.

"I mean it," Grant said, looking at his father. "We're not turning this into a media circus. This ends here. At the hospital. I walked through those doors and I'm alive. End of story."

His father nodded and turned to his advisor. "You heard my son, Gus. You can communicate to the public that Grant is a bit battered but, otherwise, healthy. He's recovering among family and friends."

Gus' lips flattened, but he acknowledged the orders from his boss and left the room.

Exhaling a sigh of relief, his mother began making plans for his homecoming.

"We never had that Thanksgiving party. Some friends are staying past the holiday weekend," his mother covered his hand. "There's so much to be thankful for."

Grant soaked in his family's presence, and yet his thoughts kept drifting to the cabin. It seemed surreal ... like a dream, a different world. All he knew was he needed to see Blaire again.

4

Blaire

I HEARD tires crunch on gravel and my heart skipped a beat. My eyes swept around the cabin and took in the assortment of flower arrangements covering every available surface. They started showing up a week after Grant left my care. The loss I felt as I watched those red taillights disappear, taking my injured guest away, was different from the times I had to let my healed creatures go. Grant hadn't been with me for even three days, and yet I wanted to keep him. Liam blamed my Florence Nightingale syndrome, but the speed with which he wanted Grant out of our lives revealed that he sensed how my houseguest had affected me.

The week before Christmas, Grant began sending food items. An Iberico ham, complete with a deluxe wooden ham holder, arrived on my doorstep one morning. I read the literature on the gift. It was made from those Spanish, acorn-fed black pigs. A leg of ham this size cost over a thousand dollars!

Footsteps echoed from the porch before three strong raps sounded on my door. This was Grant's third attempt this week. I had ignored his previous visits, not wanting to open the door and get sucked into those slate blue pools of his eyes again.

I laid a palm against the wooden barrier and inhaled deeply, the butterflies in my stomach fluttered madly, causing my heart to pound painfully behind my ribs. "Go away, Grant."

"I'm not leaving this time, Angel." His voice filtered from behind the door with determination.

My fingers couldn't unlock the deadbolt fast enough. Irritation mixed with desire to see him driving my actions. I was still conflicted when I dragged the door open, convincing myself that I wanted to tell him face-to-face to go away.

I wasn't prepared for how his smile transformed the attractive man I remembered into the devastatingly handsome version before me. Full of health, vigor, and virility, my mouth fell open and my words, meant to banish him, clogged up my throat.

"Hey," he murmured and his gaze, imbued with wonder, warmed my skin. "Your eyes are as mesmerizing as I remember them."

"Uh ..."

Caught unaware by his frank appraisal, I wasn't prepared for when he shouldered the door wider and walked right in. "I thought you'd never ask."

"I didn't." My irritation turned to outrage. Although, if I were honest, I was secretly thrilled that he overpowered my resistance. At least I tried, *right*?

His grin grew wider. There was almost a smirk lurking there, and, heaven help me, my hormones were running a charged circuit in my body with a direct line to my vagina. Gorgeous men were not in short supply in Colorado, but Grant Thorne was almost a unique sub-species. I tried very hard not to stare past his face even as I was tempted to look lower. God, I remembered the outline of his cock behind his boxer briefs. It was huge even in its relaxed state and I wondered how a fully erect ...

Stop!

"You're blushing." He wore a full-on smirk, eyes gleaming know-ingly. "I wonder why that is?"

I chose to ignore his innuendo even if I was guilty as hell. "You're a bullheaded man, Grant Thorne," I said as I crossed my arms over my chest. "You've thanked me enough. We saved your life. I know you think you owe us unending gratitude, but have mercy on the delivery guy. You've sent enough flowers, chocolate, and fancy food to last through winter. I don't know where to put them anymore."

Thankfully his gaze left me briefly to survey the contents of the cabin, and a corner of his mouth kicked up sheepishly. "I guess I went overboard."

"Yes, you did."

He took a step forward and I was tempted to retreat but held my ground.

"Let me make one thing clear, Blaire," he said. "I'm indebted to you and Liam forever, that's true. But that's not why I'm here."

"Grant, don't ..."

"All Liam got was an expensive bottle of Scotch." The distance between us diminished and I could feel the heat of his body. And his eyes, good Lord, his eyes were burning so hot, it was as if he'd incinerated every piece of clothing between us. His nostrils flared as if he were scenting me. He had turned very still.

"Grant?" My eyes turned wary. "Are you okay?"

"I want to know you better, Blaire." His husky voice was like fingers caressing all the sensitive places of my body, but I couldn't give in. I lived in this secluded cabin for a reason and Grant represented everything I should stay away from.

His brows drew together as if sensing my regret.

"Won't you give me a chance?" he pressed.

"What's the point?" I answered. "You're not from here. You're a senator's son. You live in Boston. You're a billionaire."

"Is this some kind of reverse prejudice you and Liam have against rich people?" Grant demanded.

"You're missing the point!" I snapped. "Has it even occurred to you that I don't like to be around people? I'm up here living a life of solitude in a log cabin and don't want to change a thing. Your life is an endless string of galas, fundraisers, and dinner reservations at the poshest restaurants. I'm a recluse, Grant. We don't fit."

"I'm not asking you to marry me," he responded softly. "I just want to get to know you. Give me a chance, Blaire. Spend time with me."

"I don't know why you're pushing this so hard."

"Can't get you out of my mind," he said gruffly. His eyes looked at me in earnest, pleading, and yet his jaw was set in determination.

As for me, I was drowning with wanting him, to give myself over and experience this man even for just one night, but I was afraid one night with him wouldn't be enough.

"Is it because I slept with you?" I asked, injecting scorn in my voice even if my heart rebelled against doing so. "You were shivering, delirious with a fever and, on top of that, you were having a nightmare. Maybe I should have asked Liam to cuddle you instead."

"That's a joke, right?"

I had to grin at his mortified expression. "I'm trying to prove a point. You're making it sound like we have a special bond, when it could have been with anyone who took care of you." I was such a liar.

Grant didn't like what I said at all as he moved into my space, his presence so overwhelming, I had to retreat. I hit a corner table just as his body hit mine and pinned me with his hips.

"Back off," I growled. I held on to my annoyance because his erection pressing against my belly made me want to spread my legs and have his hardness move against the ache between my thighs.

"Make me," he taunted.

I pushed against his chest, but he grabbed my wrists and held them on either side of me.

His eyes traveled from my parted lips to my heaving chest where it lingered. I was wearing a thermal, but I knew, with as hard as my nipples had gotten, he could see their outlines. This madness needed to stop. I squirmed and tried to twist out of his grasp, but he was stronger, and he trapped my legs, so I couldn't knee him in the groin.

"I'm tempted to kiss the fuck out of you, but I won't," he said conversationally as if he didn't have me pinned against a table. "We'll try to take this slow. It appears you need some convincing so this is what's going to happen. I'm going to make us lunch from the bread, ham, and cheese I had delivered to you this morning." He paused. "You received the bottle of Tuscan olive oil and sun-dried tomatoes earlier this week?"

I nodded, simply whiplashed by the way he changed tactics when my libido was at full smolder.

"Excellent. I'm going to make you one of my favorite sandwiches," Grant continued to inform me. "We're going to have lunch and talk. I'm going to tell you about my life; you're going to tell me about yours."

He released my wrists and backed away from me. "Deal?"

"You're crazy." *And I was breathless.*

"Never said I was sane."

"And overbearing."

"I'm the head of a multinational corporation, baby. I have to be."

"And very cocky."

Grant raised a brow. "I can show you just how cocky I can be, Angel, but I think you need sustenance first."

My already heated skin burned hotter.

"Lead the way." Innuendo dripped from those words. He meant the bedroom or the kitchen.

I scooted past him and fled into the kitchen before I gave in to the desire to jump his bones.

5

Grant

GRANT PULLED his SUV beside the beat-up pickup truck parked in front of the log cabin. He was half an hour early for dinner, but couldn't cool his heels at the Vail family residence any longer. Not even his company's pending multimillion-dollar deal worked to take his mind off Blaire. Three weeks of nothing but quick lunches or dinners—often with Liam, the cock-blocker, in attendance—resulted in no more than chaste kisses and perpetual blue balls.

Grant couldn't figure out who the older man was to Blaire. There was nothing possessive in the way Liam looked at her, but there was no doubt he was fiercely protective. His first impression of Liam was that of a Colorado mountain man sporting a flannel shirt complete with a rough beard. The times Grant had been around him, he usually smelled of pine, gasoline, and bar oil as if he'd been walking around all day wielding a chainsaw. There was something in the way he held his back straight, how he moved nimbly around the room despite his bulk and size, and how his ever-watchful gaze seemed to catalogue every one of Grant's movements as if storing information for later use. There was more to Liam than a man who gained his muscles by lifting logs or cutting down trees.

That morning, Blaire invited Grant to dinner. He'd forgotten the reason for the invitation because all he heard was that Liam was out of town.

Liam was out of town and that meant Blaire was alone.

Blaire was alone. Therefore there was no Liam to give him the evil eye every time any part of Grant's anatomy brushed by her.

Erotic images swam in his head.

How many times when they'd be having dinner had he imagined Blaire splayed on that table ready for him to have his way with her? He'd kiss up her shapely legs before diving into the sweetness between her thighs. Grant gritted his teeth and willed the discomfort behind his jeans to go away. He could hardly walk in there with a massive hard on. Although sex with Blaire was at the forefront of his mind, he was going to prove to her that he could wait. He wasn't going to take advantage of Liam's absence.

His dick just called him a liar.

Growling at the war between his brain and his cock, he slammed out of the vehicle and marched up the steps. The door opened and he nearly swallowed his tongue. All thoughts of abstaining from sex evaporated. Blaire stood before him in a long-sleeved flannel shirt that hit mid-thigh. Her legs were bare and she had a towel wrapped around her head.

"You're early," she said breathlessly.

Grant took in the flushed look of her skin and the damp curls framing her face before tracking down the haphazardly buttoned shirt to her legs and feet.

"You're going to freeze," he said gruffly, stepping inside and backing her into the foyer. He took his time turning to close the door, his knuckles turning white around the doorknob as he sought to tame the raging desire to scoop her up like a caveman and fuck her.

Fuck her deep.

His painfully erect cock wanted nothing more than to rip through her, he thought savagely.

"Grant?" her tentative whisper brought him out of his haze and he realized he had shut the door but was still facing away from her.

"Sorry if I am too early," he cleared his throat and turned around, careful to keep his eyes on her face.

She cocked her head then shrugged. "I was running late. Had to do some maintenance on the pickup and the time got away from me."

"You need to get rid of that pile of junk," Grant muttered. "It's a death trap and unsafe." If it didn't make him sound desperate and psycho, he'd offer to buy her a new car.

She shrugged again. "It suits my needs, but I do understand your point." She pivoted and headed toward the kitchen. He probably shouldn't torture himself but he let his gaze eat up her retreating figure, zeroing in on her swaying hips.

"The good news is," she continued as Grant unfroze and followed her. "The stew has been simmering for hours, so if you can hang around a bit while I dry my hair and put on more appropriate clothes for company..."

She stopped suddenly and Grant plowed into her. He grabbed her hips and she turned. Her lower belly pressed against his erection and his brain short-circuited. A growl rumbled up his throat just as his lips came down on hers in a crushing kiss. Weeks of pent-up sexual hunger were unleashed. Days of trying to act like a worthy suitor. Hours of living in the skin of a man that was not him. Grant was a man who took what he wanted. And he was taking it now.

Blaire broke off from his kiss. "This is a bad idea," she whispered against his lips.

"I like bad ideas," he growled. His prick was so hard, he was afraid he'd stroke if he didn't get inside her.

"Well, it's a good thing I like them too," she breathed against him. "Fuck me, Grant."

"You got it." Their mouths clashed and tongues tangled. His hands moved from her hips to her ass and squeezed so hard she yelped. He might have murmured an apology but he never let go of her lips for long. His fingers stroked up her side and his thumb brushed over her tit and felt a hard nipple.

No bra.

"You're killing me," he groaned as he continued to flick the tip, her little mewls at the back of her throat sent him into possessive overdrive. Lifting her onto the table, he hooked her legs around him and ground his erection against her pussy. He reached down between them and grazed her panties with the back of his fingers.

"Drenched," he rasped. "Christ."

"Grant ..." she panted against his mouth.

"What do you want, Angel?" He sunk his fingers in her pussy, her muscles clamping at the assault, soaking them with her arousal.

They groaned together. The sheer rapture of finding her hot and wet, coupled with the breathless moans his fingers wrenched with each stroke, fueled the feral beast inside him. She writhed against him, rubbing the top of her pubis against his hand as she eagerly sought her own release. But Grant didn't allow this. He withdrew even as her eyes flashed with unfulfilled hunger. "I'm not finished," she protested.

"First time. You come with me inside you," he muttered as he took a condom from his wallet. "Keep your legs open, baby. Keep your eyes on me. *Watch* as I fuck you."

The sound of his zipper echoed in the room. His cock was painfully erect, jutting right between them and aching to plunge into her. She looked down between her spread legs, her eyes widening at the sight of his arousal.

He needed her naked.

Grant unbuttoned her flannel shirt, controlling the desire to simply shred it to pieces. He inhaled sharply as her tits, crowned with dusky pink nipples, spilled out. The urge to bend forward to suck, lick, and worship them was almost too strong to resist. But Grant was compelled with the single-minded purpose to claim his woman. He eyed her with a hunger unlike anything he'd felt before. Pulling his shirt over his head, he tossed it on the floor. Those tits were going to rub against his skin as he fucked her.

Deeply aroused, he hiked her legs high around him for deep penetration.

"You're mine now, Angel," he growled as he drove hard inside her. Her back arched from the table and he yanked Blaire toward him as he swallowed her cry, digging his fingers into her damp hair which had since escaped the towel. He devoured her mouth, keeping her busy as her body stretched to accommodate him. Grant acknowledged he was a big guy and had to give her time to adjust. Seconds passed, and she circled her hips, eliciting a soft growl deep inside his chest. He released her lips and showered her face with kisses. "Okay?" he asked, his voice was gentle despite the ferocity thrumming through his veins.

She nodded and he withdrew slowly. He set a steady pace at first, watching for signs of discomfort or pleasure, but it wasn't long before she was rocking impatiently against him.

"Faster, Grant," she moaned. "Harder."

That one word unleashed a torrent of carnal greed. He folded over her and clutched her, flexing his hips back only to slam back into her. Over and over, each pounding thrust sought to fulfill their frenzied lust. Wet heat clenched around him and threatened his control. He lifted his head in time to watch her gorgeous eyes slide shut, her forehead crease, and her lips form an "oh" as she cried out her release.

He followed her directly into climax, his need for her overwhelming any desire to prolong the pleasure. It simply wasn't possible. And as he drove into her one last time, shudders ripped up his spine and his mind blanked except for one word.

Mine.

GRANT JOLTED awake to unfamiliar surroundings until the memories of the night before crashed through him.

He'd had sex with Blaire.

On the kitchen table, against the wall, and finally on this bed.

His chest constricted as he reached beside him, his hand encountering cold, satin sheets.

Even without searching the house, he knew Blaire was gone.

IN ALL OF Grant's thirty-five years, he could count only a few times when he'd become single-minded in his pursuit of a female. The most obsessed he'd ever been, was when he'd been in eighth grade and he'd stalked the student lockers for a glimpse of Lucy Quinn and her crown of golden curls. He'd been a gangly teen with a mouthful of braces and his fair share of acne. She broke his heart by publicly rejecting him when he'd gathered the courage to bring her flowers on Valentine's Day. She had accepted them. She did so with such sickening sweetness, Grant knew a train wreck was about to happen and he was going to be its unfortunate casualty. Lucy promptly handed the bouquet to her friend. He'd scrimped two weeks of allowance on those expensive roses.

Then she laughed.

At him.

In the most insulting way.

He learned his lesson early in life that beauty was ephemeral and was a diminishing asset when balanced against the entire package. The next year, he grew almost six inches and started to bulk up, his hormones calmed down and his acne went away. Lucy tried to get with him then, but it was too late because he'd lost interest. There was no desire for revenge either; he simply didn't care. Grant didn't have a type—physically beautiful or average, warm or reserved, CEOs or supermodels. He'd even dated a detective. He'd experienced stimulating company, interesting conversation and, for the most part, great sex. But all of them paled to the euphoria of his pursuit of his next business venture or takeover bid. He'd been accused by his partners of being distracted and that frequently triggered the end a relationship. Admittedly, Grant had never given any of his girlfriends a hundred percent of himself. He'd never had a woman live with him. Stayed for a few days, yes, but not one shared closet space. Valerie used to tease him that he'd been ruined by Lucy Quinn. The story of her rejection of Marcus Thorne's son was like an urban legend given that Grant was now a billionaire and not lacking in looks either.

With Blaire, the rope around his strangled heart unraveled. It unfurled into this connection that nagged him to explore. He wasn't giving up on her. She was his game changer. His gut told him he'd never find another woman who would fire his blood the way she did.

Grant would admit that he might have moved too quickly, but he wasn't known for his patience. Her hesitancy before they fucked, and her statement that they were a bad idea bothered him. He responded in the heat of the moment, thinking it was foreplay, but he was wondering if there'd been real conflict behind her words.

He'd never been in love before, but he felt he was on the cusp of something life-altering. The challenge was convincing Blaire that what they'd shared was special, worth pursuing, and not something to run away from.

The ringing sound of his phone pulled him from his thoughts. He slid the device from his pocket and glanced at the screen. It was his PA. His company almost lost a costly business deal because Grant's focus had been on Blaire. He sighed in frustration and let the call go to voicemail. He couldn't manage the corporation long-term from Vail, but he sure as hell wasn't leaving Blaire behind. A radical idea formed in his head; he was surprised how quickly he wanted to move on it even as he was prepared for her resistance.

Blaire was his woman. He had no qualms of using everything in his arsenal to make sure she was on the same page as he was. As if in sync with his thoughts, his phone rang again.

It was his investigator.

This time, he picked up.

6

Blaire

IT WAS dark when I returned to the cabin—fourteen hours after I left the man who had given me the best sex of my life. I'd told Liam to make himself scarce, that I was going to give in to my one night with Grant, but I would make him hate me in the morning. The plan was to kick him out of bed, but I couldn't do it and, instead, I was the one who left.

If I'd been just another notch on his post, the second he had sex with me, he'd be gone. Apparently, I was right. His Suburban was nowhere in sight later that night.

I felt relief for having avoided a confrontation, but an aching disappointment squeezed my heart. There was that glimmer of hope though, stemming from my understanding of the man I had gotten to know. Grant had been relentless in his pursuit. A man of his stature led a busy life and he still found time to spend with me. We had yet to go on a date, but it was not from his lack of trying. However, he had no problem worming his way into my life and my dinner table.

Sleeping with Grant served another purpose other than physical gratification. Liam was pinged by a friend that some agency was digging into our background. Not surprisingly, it was Grant. That was a disaster on so many levels.

We thought of ways to turn him off. It was too late to use Liam as a lover. After spending time with us, Grant was familiar with our dynamics and a sudden romance with Liam—I shuddered at the thought because it seemed incestuous—wasn't going to be believable at this point. But even Liam thought that wasn't going to stop Grant. Not someone like him who'd survived that cut-throat world of international business.

I realized I'd been sitting in my battered pick-up for almost ten minutes. The truth was, I was too sentimental to go into my bedroom. My sheets would have his smell—that masculine spice and woodsy scent that I loved so much. As my heart dueled with my mind, I fought against the melancholia squeezing my entire being as the consequences of what I'd done that morning crashed around me. I'd alienated the one person who'd painted my gray and mundane existence with the color of a life worth living. When we finally had sex, that elusive bond snapped into place, but I responded with cowardice and ran. Exhaling in self-deprecation, I got out of the vehicle and walked up the cabin. I put the key in and turned, but it was unlocked. Annoyance swept through me. He was too pissed, apparently, to even lock up.

Still fuming, I felt my way through the darkened foyer, dropped my cross-body bag on the side table and switched on a lamp.

I turned.

And then I screamed.

Grant was slouched on the couch, watching me with steely eyes. His expression was impassive, but some predatory energy radiated off him. Like he was a panther about to pounce and I was a gazelle frozen in place.

I glanced at the door.

"Don't even think about it."

"Where's your car?"

"I have people."

Such a simple statement, but it bled power.

"Are you over it?" he clipped.

Not getting him, I frowned. "What?"

Grant stood up and started walking—no—stalking toward me. "Are you over it?" he repeated. "Your freak out."

I laughed nervously. "My what?"

"Don't lie to me, Blaire." His eyes flashed. "You left because you got scared." He'd reached me and we were toe to toe. He lowered his head. "Sex changed things between us."

"Have you never heard of *casual* sex before?" I snapped, my mind still had the power to squash the yearnings of my heart.

Grant chuckled derisively. "Oh, baby, there was nothing casual about last night. Balls-deep in you three times. Came the same number of times on my mouth and twice on my cock. Managed to eat dinner at two a.m. I'd say we're past casual."

I couldn't breathe as an image of his dark head between my thighs with his hands spreading me open, flashed through my head. I leaned against the side table, suddenly lightheaded.

"Glad you remember," Grant muttered.

"You were supposed to lose interest."

Frustration scored his expression as comprehension dawned. He clenched his fists at his sides. "You let me fuck you thinking I'd lose interest," he stated quietly.

"Tell me I'm wrong," he pressed when I didn't say anything.

"You're not," I said softly.

He tipped my face up to look at him. "Why, Angel? If all I wanted was a fuck, I wouldn't have put up with your mountain-man friend cock-blocking me at every turn."

A corner of my mouth quirked up before turning down again. "You were getting too close."

"That's the whole point, isn't it?"

"Our worlds are different, Grant. You live in the public eye while crowds make my skin crawl."

"What happened to you, Blaire?" he asked thoughtfully, my statement leading him to believe something in my past made me this way.

Something had and that was the reason I didn't want him to know, I thought sadly.

Grant took a step back, his gaze unwavering as he contemplated me for long seconds. Rubbing his chin with his forefinger, as if coming to a decision, he said, "Okay."

My brows cinched together in confusion. "Okay, what?"

"It seems all that's preventing us from being together is your aversion to crowds," he explained, resting both his hands on my shoulders. "I'll never force you into a public situation."

"Wait. Back up," I exclaimed. "Together? Did I miss something?"

"Keep up, baby," he smiled. "Last night changed everything. Don't fucking deny it. If you think after you've given me a taste of you that I'm giving you up, that's your first mistake."

"Oh, enlighten me. There's a second?" I invited with sarcasm.

"I don't have a lot of quit in me, Blaire," his nostrils flared. "Your second mistake was thinking if you ran, I wouldn't come after you. If you hadn't come back tonight, I'd have set my entire investigative division on your ass."

Oh shit.

I felt my face blanch. Grant's expression turned concerned.

"Blaire ... fuck ... that sounded psycho, didn't it?"

I just nodded, but my mind was racing. "But all those parties," I lowered my eyes, thinking of other excuses why I shouldn't be with him. "I've looked you up, you know. You're always with someone. You need dates for those events."

"And that's all they ever were," he replied. "Eighty percent of the time, if I'm not in a relationship, those dates end when the event ends. They go home, that's it."

"And the other twenty percent?" I whispered.

"Not lying," Grant said shortly. "I'm no saint, Blaire. I've had one-night stands."

That stung. It shouldn't, but it did. "You need to be with someone who'll be there to support you in—"

"Trophy girlfriend? No thanks." He tipped my face up. "Listen to me, Blaire. I'm not going to force you to go with me to a party or fundraiser. But I need you with me." He took a deep breath. "I need for you to move to the east coast."

I was already shaking my head. "That's impossible."

"I can't manage the company long-term from Vail. Thorne Industries headquarters is in New York, but I prefer Boston living and stay there most days, including the weekends. Think about your art, you'll have lots of inspiration. You can paint anywhere, right?"

"Yes, but, Grant—"

"Hear me out," he interrupted gruffly. "I don't want a long-distance relationship. Never tried it and never will. But this thing between us? I'm willing to do whatever it takes to give it a chance, even stay in Colorado longer if I have to."

"But you don't want to."

"Not lying, Angel, it's been challenging."

I frowned, noticing evasion in his eyes. "Is your, er, company in trouble?"

A slight grimace crossed his face but he schooled his features quickly. "It doesn't matter."

"Grant—"

"Getting off topic, baby," he cut in. His company was obviously a sore topic. "I have a brownstone in Boston and another property outside the city if you prefer wide open spaces," he shrugged. "We could live there instead."

My head was spinning with how fast he was moving. "I need time to think."

"Blaire," he crooned. "Say yes, baby."

I wanted so much to say yes and yet ...

"I need time," I whispered.

IT TURNED OUT, time wasn't on my side.

Three days after Grant asked me to move to Boston, Liam returned. I was at my usual place by the window, painting a flock of bluebirds, when he walked in.

"Hey, Wren."

"Liam," I said, putting down my paint brush. "Good trip?"

"Productive," he said shortly, walking over to my work area and shuffled through my pictures.

"Looks like you've been busy," he mused. Sometimes, I committed scenes to memory to paint later. But that day I fled the cabin after my night with Grant, I had my DSLR camera with me because I needed to occupy my mind in order to avoid thinking about the man I left in my bed.

Liam glanced up at me. "Did it work?"

"I couldn't do it."

"He's still in the picture?"

I exhaled heavily. "He wants me to move to Boston."

His eyes narrowed. Running fingers through his beard as he started pacing, I could almost hear the cogs turning in his head. I was surprised he didn't blow up. Or at least laugh.

He sat on the couch and stared at me. "It might work to our advantage."

"What?"

"We've been on the run for two years. It's time for us to start living our lives again," Liam said. "I want you to do that."

"How? By going to Boston?"

"Yes."

"You forget people are after us and Grant isn't exactly low profile."

"That could be a problem," Liam admitted.

That was a huge problem.

"And what about you? I'm not leaving you here by yourself."

"I won't be here."

"What?" I exclaimed for a second time.

"I've got a couple of leads I need to track down."

"Take me with you."

Liam raised a brow.

"Grant," I muttered.

Liam leaned back. "Thorne has been digging into federal databases for our information. So far, everything is legit on paper. If he follows up on any of those leads like your fake parents, this shit is going to blow up in our faces."

"He did threaten to unleash his investigative division on me if I disappeared," I said, worrying my lips.

"When?" His face darkened with concern.

"Three days ago when I took off for more than half a day."

My friend sprang to his feet and started pacing again. "Yeah, but he started before that. Nosey bastard. So far, from what I've gathered, he's only scratched the surface." Liam stopped pacing and faced me. "How do you feel about him?"

"Not sure I'm following."

"Do you love him?"

"That's kind of personal," I said, all my defenses rearing up in attention.

"But pertinent to where I'm going with this," Liam replied. "I have a hunch that he would stop digging into our backgrounds if you were to move to Boston. I'm not cool with that plan if you don't care enough for him and you end up feeling like a sacrificial lamb."

"It's too soon to tell, Liam," I said quietly.

"You feel something for him?" he asked a less direct question.

"I do," I admitted wistfully. "I'm not sure what it is yet."

"Shit," Liam muttered. "You're in love."

"I'm not!" I exclaimed, a little too quickly.

He barked a laugh. "Well, you're in *something*. Your face doesn't lie."

"You're embarrassing me right now," I grumbled as I felt heat creep up my cheeks.

Liam sat beside me again. "From what I can tell, he's damned serious about you, but what I've uncovered about his past relationships isn't promising." I had a feeling I wouldn't like his next words. "They don't last more than three months. At most, four. If you do go to Boston, it may not be a lasting move."

I laughed without mirth. "So why risk exposing myself?"

"Once I go after the person who has the physical evidence, it could turn ugly—our cover, blown. This cabin may no longer be secure. I may not be able to warn you or protect you in time, but Grant has the resources to provide you security."

"For at least three or four months?" I said sarcastically. "I guess the clock is ticking then."

My friend exhaled heavily. "I've done my own research on Thorne. I couldn't get the data on the type of security he has on his properties for obvious reasons, and he doesn't have personal security teams unless he goes out of the country. You'll need to lay low. Can you do that?"

"I told Grant I'm an introvert, that I don't do well with crowds."

Liam broke into a slow, proud smile. "Atta girl. It's easier to stay anonymous in a city like Boston. Most of my leads are on the east coast, so if you get an inkling your relationship with Thorne isn't working out—give me a heads-up as soon as you can, so I can make plans to extract you."

I shot him an apprehensive look.

"It might take me a couple days ..." he explained. "Maybe a week to make sure I can cover my tracks and get you some place safe if this cabin is compromised."

"Or you can simply take me along," I suggested.

Liam gave me a wry grin, but instead of answering, he asked, "So where's loverboy?"

I rolled my eyes. "He's in Vail. Said the Wi-Fi was faster there."

"Is he coming by today?"

My cheeks burned. "He's been staying over every night."

"You work fast."

I scowled at Liam. "When do I tell him I'm willing to make the move?"

"As soon as possible."

"Tonight?"

Liam looked at me strangely.

"He asks me every night before bed," I explained.

"Persistent son of a bitch."

"That he is," I agreed.

Looked like I was moving to Boston.

7

Blaire

EARLY APRIL HERALDED the arrival of brisk spring weather in Massachusetts. Boston Commons was alive with a sea of vibrant emerald, the grassy landscape a tempting invitation to lay down a blanket and laze the day away. I leaned back under the canopy of an ancient elm tree, the dappled sunlight filtering through the leaves. Knees pulled back, I laid my sketchpad on my lap and outlined the arresting landscape before me. The equestrian bronze statue of George Washington stood tall and proud among an army of tulips in shades of red, pink, orange, and yellow. It was one of Boston's most impressive sculpture with both horse and rider hewn in graceful and natural lines. A ghostly weeping willow served as a backdrop in the distance. The promise of new life in the air inspired my fingers to work the charcoal pencil feverishly over the textured drawing paper.

I moved to Boston at the end of January. Grant took time off from his work at Thorne Industries to show me New England living. The architecture and history provided instant appeal. I also relished capturing on canvas the everyday life of bustling municipalities like Provincetown and other quaint communities that speckled the Northeast corridor. But Grant himself was the biggest selling point of this temporary move.

Three months had already passed, and Grant, instead of losing interest, had become more determined to bind me to him. Last week, he'd been after me to give up my cabin in Colorado. He told me that as long as I had a place to run away to, I couldn't commit to him. He actually used the word "commit."

His success, good looks, and stature in life should have intimidated me, but when he was in my company he had a way of making me feel special, not to mention he'd been giving me the best sex of my life. I exhaled heavily. And yet it was the little things ...

As if my thoughts conjured him up, I saw a tall familiar figure approaching me with easy strides. My heart stuttered, before a bubble of happiness burst inside me. What was Grant doing in Boston on a Wednesday morning? He usually left Monday afternoon for Manhattan and returned on Thursdays. The muscles of my cheeks hurt from grinning too wide as I lowered my sketchpad on the blanket to admire the man dressed in faded jeans and Henley—a far cry from the sharp suits I was used to seeing him in during the week. The nylon cooler he was carrying in one hand did nothing to disrupt the controlled grace of his movements, like a jungle cat prowling its territory with confidence.

"The board called," I hollered when he was twenty paces out. "They said you're fired."

His lips fractured into a broad smile, his teeth flashing as he looked to the side before cutting his glance back to me, eyes crinkled in humor. "I got tired of their squabbling. I told them I had better things to do."

I laughed as he reached me. He lowered the cooler, stooped to kiss me and, before I knew what was happening, I was flat on my back with one hard-bodied male pinning me to the ground. I wrenched my lips away. "Grant! We're in public."

He stared down at me, unrepentant. "Missed you so much," he murmured and captured my lips again. The undisguised yearning in his kiss filled my own heart with longing that was strangled by conflicting emotions.

I love him.

Without a doubt, I love him.

I shouldn't. It wasn't part of the plan. And yet, the way his kiss demanded my response, stripped of control, I articulated my love in the way I kissed him back, in the way I molded my body against his. It might had been a few seconds, it might had been long minutes, but for that fragment of time, we lost ourselves in each other. Grant ripped away from the kiss and swore. He rolled off me, lying flat on his back with his arm across his eyes. I propped up on my elbows, panting, and tried my best to cool off my heated flesh.

He was breathing raggedly, his erection pressed painfully against his jeans, and then in small degrees, I watched him reel it in.

"Fuck." Grant grinned crookedly as he lowered his arm and looked at me. "You little witch."

My brows quirked. "I'm the little witch? Aren't you the one who invaded my little space of tranquility?"

"Yeah, but ..." his face turned serious. "What just happened felt different."

I started at his perceptivity. How could he tell from a kiss that I had let go of my reservations about falling in love with him? Walls quickly slammed up around my heart.

His eyes narrowed. "Blaire ... don't."

Flustered at being laid open, I changed the subject. "Why are you back in Boston so early?"

I held my breath as he regarded me for long moments before he expelled a hiss of frustration. He recovered quickly though, and grinned. "Making a lunch delivery?"

"Okay, be serious," I said, relieved that he didn't force the issue. "I thought you had a lot of meetings and paperwork to get through?"

He shrugged those powerful shoulders. "I do. I had Heather clear my day and move all my meetings to tomorrow. Might as well make use of web-conferencing technology. I brought all the paperwork with me. Most of them are on our FTP site anyway."

"So, you're all mine for the afternoon?"

"I'm yours all day," he paused. "Might have to do some work tonight though."

"I don't like the idea of you working late because you have to spend time with me."

Grant didn't immediately respond. He sat up and scooted back against the elm tree and then dragged me into the circle of his arms. "Blaire, I was successful in business because nothing made me happier than closing that next deal." His fingers combed through my hair. That felt good. I snuggled closer and his arms tightened. "Now nothing makes me happier than being here, exactly this way with you." He pressed his lips to my temple. "You're my new high, my drug of choice. Are you going to deny an addict his fix?"

I took a good look at Grant. His grin supported the levity of his statement, but his eyes spoke of deeper emotions. This was confirmed when his smile faltered and his jaw tightened briefly. We were left at this awkward impasse because we were both holding back.

"Well now, I don't want to be that cruel," I said lightly. "I guess I can put up with your company this afternoon."

"Witch," he murmured.

"I've got a couple of hours of sketching," I warned.

"As I said, Angel, I'll be right here," he gave me a chaste peck on the lips then surveyed the scenery. "Are you going to translate this to oil?"

"Yes. The scenery would be perfect for my Medici colors, but I think I'll stick to Windsor and Newton," I said glumly.

"Why?"

"I'm saving the Medici for Provincetown. You know I can't get those paints anymore." The Medici oil paints were handmade, and the paint maker, Stephen Vasari, had retired. The paints were made from the highest quality alkali-refined linseed oil, free from fillers like wax and chalk. The resulting pigments were vibrant and lush. Each tube was filled individually by hand. It was an artist's dream medium.

"Hmm ..." Grant mumbled, absentmindedly stroking my hair.

I should be irritated that he probably asked the question to make small talk. Every time I talked about painting, he seemed genuinely interested in what I had to say, so maybe he was just tired. After all, he was here when he was supposed to be running an empire.

"So, what's in the cooler?" I asked, deciding to redirect the conversation.

Grant untangled our limbs and yanked the cooler by the strap. He unearthed a bottle of wine, some cold cuts, and cheese. There was also cold pasta salad and roast chicken plus a variety of fruit. I got on my knees and dug through my bag for the wet wipes to clean my hands.

"You know you're making this a perfect day," I said. "Blue skies, calm breeze, tulips in full bloom." Our eyes locked. "Sexy man at my beck and call." I leaned in and teased him with my lips and was gratified when I registered the rumbling of a growl deep in his throat. "You look hungry, Mr. Thorne." I plucked a grape from a cluster. "Have a grape."

He snatched the berry from my hand but deliberately caught the tip of my fingers between his lips and let his tongue lick me. I inhaled sharply and his eyes flashed. We were treading on very risqué ground. His face was a stark canvas of a starved man and it had nothing to do with food.

"Blaire," he said thickly as he swallowed the fruit with difficulty. "I want to fuck you so bad."

"I know," I whispered and my tongue darted over my lower lip, my mouth suddenly dry. "Are you going to pour us some wine?"

"You know you're going to pay for this later, right?" he muttered as he handed me wine in a plastic goblet. "The first thing I'm going to do is lick that pussy and make you come on my mouth so many times you beg me to stop."

Oh dear.

"Roast chicken?" I held out a slice of breast; he accepted without taking his eyes off me.

"Then I'm going to force you down on your knees and fuck you from behind."

I squeezed my legs together as a pulse twitched my pussy. My goblet shook as I took a sip of red wine.

Our banter continued throughout lunch, I'd offer him food and he would describe the ways he wanted to fuck me. By the time we got to the chocolate mousse in shot glasses, he'd taken off his Henley, revealing his fitted white tee. That did nothing to calm my raging libido because I knew how those sculpted muscles looked beneath those last layers of threads. Meanwhile, I'd taken off my spring jacket and I was pretty sure my panties were soaked.

"Maybe we should leave the mousse for later," Grant suggested. "I can find better places to eat this from."

I raised a brow. "I'm sure you can, but I want mine just where it is."

He chuckled, pulling at the collar of his shirt. "We sure worked ourselves up into trouble, didn't we?" He stared mournfully at his hard-on.

"I had nothing to do with it," I returned. "I was busy feeding you."

His gaze softened. "That was sweet, baby."

And my heart just melted into a puddle. Getting scorched by a lust-filled stare was one thing, but when his eyes warmed with tenderness, they were actually more lethal.

I held out a spoonful of mousse to him but he shook his head and instead continued to stare at me.

"You're making me self-conscious," I chided, lowering my gaze to the ground as I felt a blush steal up my cheek.

"I just love watching you," he murmured. "Sue me."

I shook my head in amusement and finished my mousse. Grant told me he'd pack up our lunch and I should finish my sketches.

He laid back on the blanket and closed his eyes. He untucked his white tee to cover his erection. Poor man. I resumed drawing, but I was finding it hard to concentrate.

All I could imagine was Grant fucking me the way he laid it out over lunch. And it didn't help that his fingers were lightly brushing my leg as he relaxed. After an hour, I hadn't really gotten anywhere because I kept erasing what I drew.

"That's it," I fumed.

Grant's eyes popped open. "What, baby?" he mumbled sleepily.

"Let's go," I announced. "I need my man naked."

We couldn't leave that park fast enough.

GRANT HAULED me into the house and kicked the door close. Then his hands grabbed my face and slammed his mouth on mine, stealing my breath. I dropped my things to the floor as his body pushed me deeper into the house and I had no choice but to scuttle backward. His hands left my face and ripped my top from my body, and as he gripped the bottom of his tee, my own hands swept under it, desperate to touch his bare skin.

We were a tangle of frantic limbs and lust. My nails raked down his shoulders even as his fingers worked my jeans. He bore me down to the living room floor, kneeling before me as he stripped me of my clothes, cursing as he encountered a problem removing my boots. I didn't know how he got them off, he might have ruined them, but then my back slid on the area rug as he peeled off my jeans along with my panties. He tore off his belt, dropped it to the floor and unbuttoned his jeans.

Feral eyes roved over my form before he wrenched my legs apart and plunged his fingers in my pussy, growling as my back arched with the invasion. I writhed beneath his hungry gaze, his wicked fingers, plunging and seeking, my breath hitching as he pressed against my sweet spot. Arousal flooded my entrance and then with my legs on his shoulders, he lifted my hips off the floor and buried his face between my thighs.

His tongue tore through me, licking my slit, lapping at my sensitive folds. He sucked on my clit and I came on his tongue, gushing, slicked and slippery, and he ate all of me. I couldn't count the times he brought me to orgasm, all I knew was I was begging for him to stop. That I couldn't take anymore and I needed him inside me.

Grant finally pulled back and his hand gripped my ankle, and with the other on my hip, he flipped me over. His hard chest hit my back, curling an arm under my belly as he pulled me up to all fours. I felt his hand work between us and the sound of his zipper ratcheted up my anticipation. The head of his cock swiped at my entrance once, twice and then he plunged deep, stretching me with the silky hardness of his shaft.

He took me fast and hard. His thrust so deep and powerful, that if he wasn't holding me up, I would have flattened on the floor. Grant's hand moved to my breast, squeezing, then he dragged me upright and my ass was on his lap. His hand shifted to my jaw, turning my head into his kiss as he continued to fuck me. His front to my back, sliding me up and down on his cock, we were reduced to skin stroking against skin, breath and sweat mingling, two people moving to the symphony of grunts and moans. And as our climax crashed around us, we continued our dance until our rhythm turned erratic and the movements ebbed. Grant kissed my shoulder and dropped his head in the crook of my neck, maintaining our connection as if he didn't want us to be parted. Minutes passed before he lifted me off his lap and carried me to the couch. He stretched beside me and tucked me close. Neither of us said a word as we absorbed the aftermath of our intense coupling.

I LISTENED to his steady breathing. Grant had fallen asleep, so I decided to clean up. I freed myself from our naked embrace. Well, I was naked and he still had his jeans on. How was that fair? He mumbled in protest but didn't even open his eyes. I climbed over him and got off the couch, staring at him for a while. No man deserved to look that handsome. A pang of regret swept through me again. I wished circumstances were different, but this thing with Grant wasn't going anywhere unless Liam found a way.

Forcing myself to turn away, I bent over to pick up his white shirt, inhaled his scent like a stalker and decided to put it on. I collected my clothes and padded to the foyer where I had dropped my backpack and sketchpad. Balancing all the items in my arms, I made my way to the room Grant had converted into my art studio. I lowered my backpack on the chair and the sketchpad on the drawing table and that was when I spotted it. A rectangular package covered in brown paper.

Baffled, I picked it up. My name was scripted on the paper in Grant's handwriting. Curious now, I tore off the wrapper to reveal a plain looking box. I flipped open the top and my breath caught.

Tubes of Medici paints laid neatly side by side.

"How?" I whispered to the four walls of the room.

"I tracked down Stephen Vasari," a voice said behind me. Grant stood there, leaning against the door frame, shirtless, with his jeans still undone.

Words congested in my throat and tears burned behind my eyes as the sheer perfection of the day overwhelmed me—this beautiful man before me, this box in my hands that held the breath to my art, this life I desperately wanted to hold on to.

"Grant," I choked as I looked at him through a blur of emotions while trying to keep my face from crumpling.

He straightened and approached cautiously. "I convinced him to create these colors for you."

"I don't know what to say ..."

"You'll be happy to know that his grandson will be continuing his paint making craft, but it won't be available for another year," he continued speaking as if I weren't about to fall apart in front of him. "I hope what's in that box will hold you until then, but he agreed to make you some more if they're not enough."

My jaw was hurting from trying to keep it all in. I gave him a watery smile. "I ..." *I love you so much.*

He pulled me into his arms, his chin resting on the side of my head. "I know, baby. I feel the same."

We had danced to a tune of unspoken words since the beginning of our relationship.

"Thank you." Words weren't adequate anyway to describe what I was feeling.

Grant had smashed through the defenses of my heart and touched my soul.

8

Blaire

MONTHS PASSED, and spring gave way to hot summer days. As much time as Grant and I spent together it seemed I couldn't get enough of him. I lived for the weekends when we spent each waking moment with each other. We could be driving down to the cape, we could be walking around town, or we could just be hanging around the brownstone catching up on a TV series. I knew I was setting myself up for a lot of heartache when our relationship needed to end, but ever since he'd given me those Medici paints I'd been in a free fall. The days he was in Manhattan were the hardest and I started having trouble concentrating on my work.

August brought about a distinct change in Grant's moods. He'd become broody and I knew why. My reticence about my personal stuff, my refusal to give up my cabin, and the ways I deflected conversation regarding the future of our relationship were wearing down on his patience. His scowls lasted longer, and the unspoken words had become more grating in the silence.

He took me to dinner at his parents' a couple of times; Marcus and Amelia were gracious hosts. I had an easy time chatting with them, especially with Grant's mother. His sister Valerie was a different story. I marveled at her ability to cause tension without uttering a syllable. It was in her head-to-toe appraisal of me, or the way she hugged her brother and ignored my presence. After my attempts to make conversation left me speaking to air, I decided it was best to stay out of her way. I sympathized with Amelia as she tried to cover for her daughter's quiet hostility toward me. In some ways, I understood Valerie. Even when I refused to speak about my own life, Grant was the opposite and never held back in telling me stories about his. That was how I knew how he and his dad had spoiled his sister terribly—a by-product of guilt from her near drowning. And now she viewed me as competition for her brother's affections.

Little did I know that avoiding Valerie didn't mean she couldn't cause trouble between Grant and me.

As a way to alleviate my loneliness when Grant was in Manhattan, I decided to take an art class for the summer at a studio near Harvard Square that met on Monday and Wednesday evenings. He'd ask me before if I wanted to go to New York City with him, but I knew I was a distraction his business didn't need. How many times had he worked through the night because he wanted to take me to dinner or spend the afternoon with me? He told me one time that he thrived on very little sleep, and yet I could see the toll it was taking by the shadows under his eyes.

I did mention my figure painting class to Grant, but I wasn't sure he fully understood that I had to attend evening classes. And with some guilt, I continued to let him think otherwise. Aside from his brooding, he'd been distracted lately by a couple of high-profile property deals that were swinging in favor of the competition. I told myself I didn't want to add to his worry.

For my art class, we started with the female nude for the first few weeks, but for the last three meetings, we had a male model, Claude Cluzet—a French exchange student. The man was simply gorgeous. His body was lean, sculpted perfection, but his lips were my favorite feature. On any other face, it would have been too feminine, but it was the consummate pouty lips for a strong angular jaw that made me see why he'd become an instant sensation and an in-demand model for artists and photographers.

Some of my female classmates were definitely enamored outside the realm of art. I got dragged to an after-class social at Hoosier Bar the week before. And it was just my luck, I ran into Valerie who was a law student at Harvard. Grant's sister chose that time to act like we were best friends and interrogated my classmates about the class, but I knew better. It didn't help that Claude was sitting beside me.

So, the next outing, I begged off. Obviously, the bar was a common haunt for the Harvard crowd and I didn't want Val getting the wrong idea.

That Wednesday, when class packed up, I tried to leave as quickly as I could, but my teacher wanted to talk to me. After giving me glowing reviews about my work, I exited the studio, giddy with happiness. I couldn't wait to tell Grant.

Claude and a couple of girls were waiting at the bottom of the steps. The model's face broke into a dazzling smile when he saw me, but it made me uncomfortable because I hated the attention.

"There you are," Claude said as he ascended the steps and tried to grab my portfolio which I angled away from him.

What the hell?

His brows drew together, but my subtle rejection didn't faze him at all. He stabbed his fingers through his thick long hair—one of his other great features and he obviously knew it. My female classmates were staring daggers at me.

Seriously?

"You're not skipping Hoosier's this time," Claude informed me. "You're joining us for a drink." At the bottom of the steps, he put his hands on my shoulders and turned me a quarter so I was facing him. He leaned in suggestively. "And maybe more." Funny how many models looked better when they kept their mouth shut.

I was about to shoot him down when I felt my nape prickle.

"Take your hands off her before I break them," a voice threatened behind me.

Claude visibly stumbled back as I turned around to see Grant directly behind me. His fingers clamped down on my bicep as he deposited me behind him. I dropped my things and clutched at his torso when he didn't miss a stride stalking toward Claude.

"Stay away from her," Grant growled.

"Grant, it's not what you think," I whisper-yelled, appalled at the scene we were causing, especially since our teacher had appeared at the top of the steps.

Claude raised his arms. "We're cool. Didn't know she was taken." Then he smirked. "Beauty like that you need to put a ring on her."

I wasn't sure, but I thought I heard Grant mutter, "I will."

I let him go and grabbed my things and walked away. Belated humiliation hot-wired my system and I was pissed at Grant for showing up the way he did.

"Where are you going?" he snapped behind me before taking my arm and spinning me around to face him.

"Home," I snapped back.

"You use the subway?"

"I always use the subway."

"Today was the last time," he decreed. Before I could challenge him on it, a Black Escalade glided to a stop beside us.

Grant opened the door. "Get in."

"Why are you here?"

A muscle ticked his jaw.

"Val told you," I exhaled in resignation, suddenly exhausted. This was an argument I wasn't going to win. I was supposed to be a recluse and I'd gone to a bar. "Where's your Maserati?" I asked, climbing into the car. This was the first time I'd seen the Cadillac. And when did he get a driver?

Grant got in beside me. "The brownstone, Tyler."

"Yes, sir."

Who was this guy? Grant didn't seem interested in making the introductions as he seemed more intent in ignoring me to scowl out the window. When he was extremely angry, he had a habit of shutting down. Grant said he had a tendency to say hurtful words that could ruin a relationship.

"Hi," I told the driver. "I'm Blaire."

Tyler's eyes met mine in the rear-view mirror. "Pleasure to meet you, Ms. Callahan."

"Have you always worked for Grant?"

The driver shifted uncomfortably in his seat. "Mr. Thorne will explain my role when we get home."

"What do you mean ..."

"Blaire," Grant interrupted in a voice that scraped like gravel. "We'll talk at home."

The street light caught the lines of fatigue on his face and, rather than argue, I kept my silence.

———

THAT NIGHT burst the bubble I had lived in for the previous eight months. When we got home, Grant informed me that his father was announcing his reelection bid. White supremacists had been vocal about their opposition to the Senator's politics to the point of threatening Marcus Thorne and his family. The senator's office had received anonymous mail containing pictures of Valerie walking the Harvard campus and Grant leaving his office in Manhattan. All the pictures had red bullseyes drawn on their heads.

This wasn't the first time Grant's father had received such threats, but there'd been indication from the feds that this fringe group had ramped up recruitment to their militant division that necessitated the hiring of bodyguards. Jake Donovan had always been Grant's head of security, but he specialized in security for their interests abroad, providing executive protection in countries with volatile political situations. This time, Grant wanted Jake to concentrate on personal protection detail and had met with the senator's own security team to outline the new threats and countermeasures that needed to be taken. It was obvious that Grant himself was having trouble with the changes to our privacy. Tyler was to be my bodyguard and driver. I couldn't take off on my own to the park or drive myself to the cape any longer. I considered giving up my art class.

What was more troubling were the questions Jake asked about my family and background. I realized they needed to investigate every possible weak link that could compromise the senator's protection. I was a basket case until I got hold of Liam to tell him what was going on. After cursing Grant quite colorfully, he told me that he would "handle it." I wasn't sure what that meant. Pay someone off the streets to pretend to be my parents? That was another sticking point Grant had with me. He wanted to meet my parents and I had to make up some bull crap excuse that they were always traveling.

Grant and I had not had a private conversation for several days. Most of our exchanges had been brief and impersonal, but I'd sensed a gradual thawing the night before. He'd come to bed early, drew me immediately into his arms and brushed his lips across the top of my head. I welcomed his innate affection and curled into his embrace. Though I wanted to talk about his inability to communicate when he was pissed, I was wary of forcing a confrontation while Jake was doing his background checks.

Oh, to be held captive by my lies.

Two days after the art class debacle, I entered the brownstone and watched Grant walk out from our bedroom in the process of fastening the cufflinks on the sleeves of his dress shirt.

"Hey, Angel," he smiled as he greeted me in the foyer, bending down and kissing me sweetly on my lips.

Uh, what? I melted inside, but I wasn't going to let a kiss sweep our issues under the rug.

"Are you over being pissed at me?" I asked dryly.

He looked contrite, his glance cutting to the side before returning to mine. "I'm sorry, baby. I just ..." he shook his head. "Didn't want to say words I'd regret. I was jealous and I was wrong to let Val mess with my head. Made me question whether you'd been lying to me about being uncomfortable in crowds."

There was a direct jab to my conscience.

"I've thought about it," he continued. "Figured you're acclimating, right? You're doing better in public places? That's why you gave the bar a try?"

He looked hopeful. I simply nodded as my guilt strangled my words.

"We'll talk more later," he promised. "Right now, you need to get your sexy ass in a dress. We've been summoned to dinner by Amelia Thorne."

"Oh, is that why you're looking all dapper?" I said, trying to free the crush on my chest.

He chuckled and nudged me toward the bedroom, telling me which restaurant we were meeting his family so I could dress accordingly. I was relieved that Grant had gotten over his mood, but I couldn't shake the pit of anxiety in my gut.

A pit that only grew as we neared the restaurant. When we arrived, instinct screamed at me not to get out of the car.

"Blaire?" Grant's voice came to me in a vacuum. "Are you okay?"

There were several cars pulling up to the dining establishment with elegantly dressed couples stepping out.

"Restaurant's busy tonight," I remarked inanely.

"Friday, I guess," Grant shrugged. "Shall we?"

Tyler opened my door and I forced myself to step out. Grant offered me his arm and I clung to him tightly. He glanced at me questioningly, putting a reassuring hand over my icy fingers as he led me into the restaurant.

The place was packed and every pair of eyes swung to us and I froze. There was no question this was a private event.

Grant cursed under his breath. "What the fuck?"

Amelia met us at the entrance, her expression apologetic.

"Intimate dinner?" he growled at his mother.

"Gus," his mother hissed. "He invited supporters to formally announce your dad's reelection campaign. I could strangle Marcus for agreeing to this. I forgot to call you because I was swamped getting ready at the last minute."

Grant turned me toward him, resting his hands on my shoulders. "What do you want to do, Angel?"

I wanted to leave. I felt too exposed.

The words wouldn't come.

Someone called our attention. Bulbs flashed, and our picture was taken.

"That's it," Grant muttered. "I'm taking Blaire home." Not waiting for his mother's answer, he wrapped his arms around me and rushed me back to the car, but my heart had already splintered on what I had to do.

Our photographs were splashed in the tabloids the next day.

Game over.

Weeks later, I left him.

9

Present

GRANT STARED at the various documents before him. Passports from different countries—Mexico, Germany, Russia, and Canada. The woman in the picture was undoubtedly Blaire, but with different names and hair styles. With each discovery, the hole in his chest expanded into a chasm. He wanted to roar. Instead, he crouched down and studied the contents of the safe: two gold bars, money in different currencies, two cell phones and a couple of flash drives.

"Mr. Thorne."

Grant stood and glared at the wall before him. "I don't know who she is anymore, Donovan. Is Blaire even her real name?"

"What do you want me to do here, sir?"

"Gather everything, especially the passports and flash drives." He nodded in front of him. "And those."

The wall of guns.

A veritable arsenal of sniper rifles, carbines, semi-automatics and more.

10

Grant

SHE'D LIED TO HIM.

A few days after the discovery at the log cabin, Grant had managed to control his rage enough to function on the low side of normal. He didn't know what he would have done if Blaire had been with him then.

Was she a spy? For which side? Or was she doing something illegal? His blood boiled, remembering the many times he thought about her excuse about being an introvert and he had fallen for it: hook, line, and fucking sinker.

It always baffled him how the few occasions he'd brought Blaire over to his parents for an intimate dinner, she didn't exhibit any social awkwardness at all. She charmed his mother and father. It was in public places where she seemed to withdraw into herself and Grant figured that was why she liked going to the park during the week when it was less crowded. This bombshell blew all his notions to bits.

She wasn't socially inept. Whatever Blaire was involved in, being seen in public would be catastrophic. She couldn't afford to have her picture taken and have it splashed over the tabloids. Being anonymous wasn't a choice—it was imperative for who she was.

The sound of a crash broke the internal war in his head and he realized he'd thrown the paperweight straight across the room and knocked one of their industry award plaques off the wall, leaving a dent in the plaster.

His personal assistant, Heather, rushed into his office, looking concerned.

"I'm okay," Grant muttered. "Just dealing with some shit."

"Is there anything I can get you?" she asked softly.

Feeling uncomfortable under his PA's scrutiny, he changed the subject. "Any word from Donovan?"

She shook her head. "He's still in DC following up on a job you gave him. He said he might be back tomorrow."

"That's good. That'll be all, Heather. Thanks."

When his PA left, he resumed brooding. Logic dictated he should let Blaire go. His father was running for reelection. If Blaire were in some way mixed up in any illegal or clandestine activity that may cause a scandal in their family, he should forget her.

But his heart refused to listen to logic. They'd been happy. That was fucking real. *No.* He and Blaire were not over. Far from it. An underlying fear festered through all his anger, a gut feeling that his woman was in danger. The instinct to protect her roared inside him.

GRANT WAITED at the curb of the Grand Hyatt, watching the limos crawl by. At this rate, he'd be out of here in another hour. He took out his phone and called his driver-slash-bodyguard.

"Mr. Thorne."

"Where are you, Tyler?"

"Still at the parking lot. It's a clusterfuck. Pardon my language, sir."

"I'm heading your way. Instead of circling to get me, just make a right and wait for me at the corner."

"Are you sure, sir?"

"A seven-minute walk versus what could be another hour? Positive." Besides, a walk would be good. He thought about Blaire and how she avoided situations like this. Maybe she had a point. Social scenes were getting old, or maybe he just missed her, and he wouldn't hesitate to trade all the galas and parties just to have another night with her.

After he'd wrecked his office wall, he forced himself to gain perspective, setting aside the bitter taste of betrayal. Blaire had tried her best to avoid getting involved with him, but he was the jackass who wouldn't take no for an answer. So, in some way, he'd brought this down on himself. Whatever Blaire had gotten herself into, she knew she wouldn't fit in his life. Grant hadn't accepted that. He wouldn't give up on her until he understood who she was.

He also knew he had to tell his father and soon. Grant would beat himself up if he ruined his dad's chances for another run at the senate. The dossier he had on Blaire and Liam had been forged. Further digging into their background yielded falsified information. Their fingerprints weren't in the FBI database. There was no record of a Blaire Callahan at the high school in the file. Her parents did not exist. No wonder she put him off about meeting them. As for Liam, he was supposed to be a product of the foster care system, but that was rigged as well. Grant hoped they were in some kind of witness protection, although the guns and the multiple passports nullified that idea.

He'd been brooding so deeply, he didn't realize that two men had flanked him before it was too late. A barrel of a gun poked his ribs.

"Do as you're told, Mr. Thorne, and you won't be hurt," one of the men said. That they knew his name meant this was not some random mugging. Grant immediately thought of his father and their security briefings he failed to pay close attention to. He'd left them mostly to Jake, but he'd sent the guy to DC.

He cocked his head at the speaker on his right and noticed belatedly that he had an accent ... and a pronounced hawk nose. His cohort on his left wore a fedora pulled low that concealed most of the guy's face. Despite Grant's grim situation, anticipation churned inside him. Maybe this had nothing to do with the threat against the senator, but it had everything to do with Blaire. He couldn't alert Tyler just yet because Fedora guy was holding on to his arm where he wore his security watch. They led him into a dark alley just a block from the hotel. Fedora man immediately slammed him against the wall and punched him in the gut. Grant coughed and hunched over, gritted his teeth, and discreetly twisted the dial on his watch to signal Tyler that he was in trouble.

"Where's Paulina, mu'dak?" Fedora guy hissed.

"You idiot, he knows her as Blaire," Hawk-nose corrected and smacked his partner upside the head. Grant wanted to ram their heads together, but keeping them talking was the better option.

"I don't know. She left me," he informed them.

"She was stupid to get involved with you. A senator's son," Hawk-nose cackled maliciously. "Let's see how much she cares for you."

Hawk-nose swung at him and Grant managed to block the blow. Fedora man's ham-sized fist crashed against Grant's cheek and another jab to his stomach sent him staggering. Just as the goon was about to kick him, he grabbed and twisted the other man's ankle and flipped him onto the ground. Hawk-nose drew his gun, but Grant went low and slammed his shoulder against the man's gut, sending both of them crashing to the pavement. Hawk-nose's gun clattered to the side.

Grant recovered faster and went for the other man's weapon, rolling on his back and instinctively pointing his gun at Fedora man who had his own firearm aimed at Grant. Hawk-nose picked himself up from the ground and was in the act of unholstering another firearm from his ankle.

Fuck.

Footsteps rushed from behind him and judging from his attackers' expression, Tyler had arrived.

What followed was a blur of movements and explosion of gunfire.

Grant felt a burning sting to his arm as his assailants fell to the ground. Standing up, he walked over to them with gun still raised, but he lowered his arm when he saw their condition. Grant had put a hole through Fedora man's gun hand, but Tyler had put a bullet between each man's eyes.

Well, fuck.

It would be another three hours before Grant returned to the brownstone with Tyler who grimly walked ahead of him. After getting patched up by an EMT, Grant, together with his bodyguard, made a statement to the police explaining that it was an attempted mugging.

Grant crashed on the couch, grunting his appreciation when Tyler brought him a glass of Scotch that he tossed back.

"You know who those men were?" his security person asked tightly.

He shook his head. "Not really, but they had information."

"About Ms. Callahan?"

Grant nodded. "They're after her. My guess? They're hoping that roughing me up will flush her out."

Tyler emitted a frustrated huff. "I shouldn't have agreed to let you walk."

"Tonight was not your fault."

"You're my responsibility."

"You did your job," Grant muttered. "Quite thoroughly."

His bodyguard's jaw hardened. "You're pissed I killed them."

"It's done, Tyler. Drop it." Grant wanted them alive for questioning, but he could hardly blame his bodyguard for doing his job.

"Donovan's coming back tomorrow," his man told him. "We'll review your security detail including expectations."

Before Grant could reply, his phone, which was on the coffee table, vibrated. It was a blocked number. Both he and Tyler exchanged glances. Grant nodded, giving the signal to have it traced.

"Thorne."

"Grant?" A choked sob. "Oh my God. Are you all right?"

Blaire.

He closed his eyes briefly, letting her voice wash over him. She had cared enough to call. To expose herself. That counted a lot. A whole damned lot. "Blaire," he said simply. All the anger and betrayal sifted away like sand through his fingers.

"Where was your security? How did this happen?"

"I'm all right, baby," he assured her and then, "How are you?"

An irritated sigh hissed through the receiver. "I'm fine. You're the one who got hurt."

"You sound pissed at me," Grant stated incredulously. "I'm not the one keeping secrets."

Silence.

"Are you in trouble, Angel?"

"It's not your problem, Grant. I'll handle this. I didn't want to get you involved in the first place."

"I already am."

"No, you're not. Stick to Jake and Tyler."

"Tell me who's after you, baby."

"I can't," her voice cracked. "It's best you don't know. Forget about me, Grant."

No fucking way.

"Blaire, I know about the guns and passports."

"You broke into my cabin?"

"I had the key."

"I don't recall giving you the right ..." she broke off. "Why are you doing this? You need to let me go."

"Absolutely not."

"Now is not the time to be bullheaded, Grant." There was rising hysteria in her voice. "How did they even get to you?"

His woman was distraught. Grant had yet to look at himself in the mirror, but he bet he didn't look pretty. Fedora man had a solid right hook. There was blood on his Tuxedo from the flesh wound he sustained from a gunshot from Hawk-nose; he was thankful the man was a lousy shot.

"It's not important how," Grant said. "Now, I want you to come home." He looked at Tyler who shook his head. That meant he hadn't traced the call yet.

"Don't do this, Grant. I'll never forgive myself if anything happens to you or your family."

"We'll figure it out." Responsibility to his family weighed heavily in his mind, but he needed Blaire with him to keep things under control. Knowing that dangerous people were after her was driving him insane.

"No, we won't."

"Goddammit, Blaire!" Grant roared, his calm deserting him. "You tell me where the fuck you are, right fucking now, or you can be sure I'll find who those bastards are working for and get the fucking truth from them."

"Don't do that!"

"Your choice, Angel."

"That's blackmail."

"Call it whatever you want. Now," he said in a steadier tone. "Tell me where you are."

11

Blaire

"HE'S OKAY."

I sagged into the motel sofa, its lumpy cushions settling uncomfortably under my tense muscles. My body felt like it had consumed an inordinately high amount of caffeine and I was experiencing a crash.

"You're going back to him?" Liam asked, presumably because he heard me give Grant directions to our location. My friend helped me escape from Grant and he tried to talk me out of it at first, but I threatened to leave on my own. We'd been holed up in a motel in Plymouth, an hour outside Boston. Liam and I used the Dark Web to keep tabs on the criminal underworld, anonymously monitoring common chatrooms to gather information and get a pulse on whether something was about to go down. We knew Russian Organized Crime (ROC) used it and, apparently, they knew we did as well. It was there we discovered that a couple of their associates went after Grant, but failed.

"He's going to get himself killed if I don't."

"Sweetheart, I don't think a man who's made it to the top like Grant Thorne would be stupid enough to get himself killed."

"He said he was going to dig deeper into who attacked him," I snapped. "Why would he do that?"

"He's getting you back, isn't he?"

My relief that Grant was okay trumped my infuriation at his persistence. I looked regretfully at Liam. "I've wasted your efforts to get me away from him."

"I tried to talk you out of it, remember?" Liam reminded me. "My opinion? You're better off with him right now because he has the resources to hire enough security to protect you."

"But it's not about my safety anymore, is it?" I pointed out. "What about his family? His father is a United States Senator, for goodness' sake. Who I am will ruin his family."

"Never talk about yourself that way, Blaire," Liam said. "We don't choose our families and your father tried to do right in the end."

"Grant knows about the guns and passports, Liam."

"Shit. That means he has the flash drives as well. You'll have to tell him something."

"Will you come with me?"

"No," he sighed. "It's been two years. I failed you and your father the first time. You're not hiding from Mikhail Orlov forever." He returned his attention to the piece of wood he was carving. This had been his hobby for as long as I'd known him. He'd make intricate miniature wooden sculptures—animals were his favorite. Right now, he was working on a bear. He'd never given me any of his little masterpieces, though I asked him once.

Maybe when I'm dead and buried was his response, and I never asked again. I think woodworking relaxed him. I wished I could say the same with my painting. I couldn't paint when I was tense.

The months I'd been with Grant, I hadn't seen Liam consistently. It saddened me that the days of driving a mile down the road whenever I needed company were over. He was all I'd known since we'd run from the Russian mob.

"It's my fault we're on his radar again," I said. "We were supposed to be dead."

"He had suspicions we faked our deaths. I told you this. Grant may be our silver lining."

"How so?"

"You'll have someone else to watch over you now."

My heart constricted. "Liam."

"I won't be able to protect you forever, Wren," he said. "But I have a feeling Grant Thorne will."

My throat burned at his words. "We'll figure this out." I echoed Grant's words and reached out to hold my friend's hand. "Please, Liam, come with me."

He smiled sadly. "I'm so close to getting us what we need, but I will contact you. By the way, lose the phone you used to call Grant and use another burner."

Liam had made headway in finding out who had the other piece of evidence that would support what we already had against the ROC. I knew he avoided taking risks because of me. He didn't want me to be alone in this world, but he'd developed a grudging respect for Grant in the past months, especially in the way he cared for me. I was afraid of what was to come, but if there was one thing life on the run had taught me about Liam, he wasn't afraid of anything except abandoning me to the mercy of the Russian mafia.

"Grant may drop us when he realizes how much trouble we're in," I told him in part because it was a strong possibility, and partly because I didn't want him to be suicidal.

My friend appeared to consider this. "Then he's not the man I thought he was. But, my advice? Don't dump all our shit on him at once."

"I'm not lying to him anymore, Liam."

"Then don't lie. Let him know you're not ready to tell him everything."

"This is Grant we're talking about here, you think he'll be contented with piece-meal information given that he'd discovered our stash—"

Liam held up his hand as if to shush me and then cocked his head toward the door. He tossed his sculpture and knife into an open bag.

"What?"

The word barely left my mouth when my friend tackled me across the bed as the door exploded inward.

LIAM HAD ALREADY DRAWN his gun by the time we fell on the other side of the mattress. Bullets flew through the room, lodged into the wall and shattered windows. I crawled to my bed and snatched my weapon from under the pillow. Lying on my back on the carpet, I cocked my gun. I scrambled to my knees and, using the bed for cover, returned fire. But the firefight was short-lived. There was a dead man on the floor and bullet holes on either side of the door frame. Our attackers had either fled or were dead. Liam was rarely caught off-guard. He had an uncanny "Spidey sense."

"Are you all right?" he asked gruffly.

I nodded, but had trouble regulating the surge of adrenaline.

"Deep breaths," my friend ordered as he got up to check on our unmoving attacker. He had prepared me for scenarios like this, but no amount of preparation could substitute for a real shootout. *Oh. My. God.* I couldn't wimp out now. I stood and pointed the gun at the guy on the floor, nodding to Liam that I had his back. I tried to speak but my teeth only clattered, so I clamped my mouth shut.

He leaned against the wall beside the door, then quickly pivoted through the door to clear the hallway. His body relaxed. "They're gone. There's blood on the floor so we got some of them."

"He's dead," I said, pointing to the man in our room. "I don't recognize him at all."

"Neither do I," Liam replied. "He must be a low-level soldier. They're not very experienced. Too eager. Should have used tear gas. The bad news is, it looks like their orders were shoot to kill."

Versus being captured and tortured? Maybe death was preferable.

"We need to move," Liam said as he shoved our things into a duffle. "The cops will be here in seven minutes or less."

"What about Grant?" Given that this place would be crawling with uniforms soon, I doubt he'd think I'd bailed on him again, but how would he find us?

"We'll drive around the block. It'll take him an hour at least to get here."

I nodded shortly. Calling him wasn't an option. Our phone call was the only way these ROC thugs could have tracked us down which meant Grant's phone was the problem. Scant minutes later, Liam and I exited the motel. There'd been tentative spectators, doors slightly open and suddenly shutting as we hastened by. I was wearing a hoodie and had my head down. Liam had on a baseball cap. We both had our guns tucked into our pockets, trigger finger on the barrel, ready to engage if our assailants were lying in wake. Keeping vigilant, we moved in the shadows until we got into our Ford sedan. Liam gunned the engine, backed up, and left the motel parking. Two blocks up we parked at a diner to change clothes. I put on a sweatshirt while my friend donned a NY Giants jacket and took off his cap. Afterward, we got back on the road. It was only then that I noticed my hands were shaking. Cold and clammy with an uncontrollable tremor, I ended up sitting on them.

"You okay?" Liam asked.

"I'm shaking," I gave a nervous laugh. "I'll get it together in a minute. Dead bodies I can handle, just not used to getting shot at."

"You did well back there."

"Thanks."

"I'm serious, Wren. You didn't lose your shit."

"I'll be honest, I feel like throwing up right now."

Liam glanced at me. "Want me to pull over?"

"Keep driving," I said, rolling down the window. "The fresh air helps."

"You're a survivor," Liam muttered and I wondered if he was trying to convince himself that I was.

ALMOST TO THE HOUR, we pulled back to the diner across from the inn. Blue and red lights from three police cruisers strobed and lit the scene. A crime scene investigation van was parked near the law enforcement vehicles. There was a bigger crowd of spectators now than earlier.

Liam swore under his breath. "We're so screwed when they match those prints."

"You fixed it right? It won't link back to us?"

"Our prints have been scrubbed from most databases, but not all. Yours likely won't find a match." Liam hammered the steering wheel in frustration. "My fingerprints are a different matter. I've been with various government agencies for almost thirty years. There's bound to be a record of my prints floating somewhere. If their forensic lab is tenacious in finding out who I am, I'll be in deep shit."

"We'll be in deep shit," I informed him. "I'm not letting you go down alone."

"Blaire ... shit," Liam cut off when two men crossed the street from the inn into the diner property. One was wearing jeans and an Oxford blazer, while the other was in a suit.

"What—"

"My guess are detectives. Let me do the talking."

When the men walked into the parking lot, they made a beeline for us. My heart was in my throat and Liam brought out his gun, but kept it on his right side.

Suit guy knocked on the window. My friend powered it down.

"What's going on over there?" Liam nodded to the motel.

"We're investigating," Suit guy replied. "Did you two just come from the diner?"

"Yes."

"See anything suspicious before the cop cars got here?"

"Can't say I did. Just the regular coming and goings past midnight. Besides, I was entertained by my beautiful companion here."

Suit guy leaned over and looked at me. I didn't like his smirk. I would have smacked Liam later if I didn't know I was a diversion.

"How about you, ma'am? See anything?"

I shook my head.

"Heard anything?"

Again, I shook my head. "The diner was loud." And thankfully still crowded to support my claim. "I hope everyone is all right." I gave my best impression of a concerned, sympathetic citizen.

Suit guy's face tightened. "If you do remember anything, give us a call." They gave Liam their cards and said their goodbyes.

"We can't stay here," Liam said, looking in the rearview mirror. "We'll figure out another way to get you to Grant."

"I'm not going back to Grant," I said. My friend looked at me as if I'd lost my mind. "What if this blows up in our faces? Can you be a hundred percent sure those prints won't link back to Paulina Antonova? They'll have my face and I'll be on a BOLO everywhere for homicide."

"Blaire, you're blowing this out of proportion."

"Am I?" I challenged. "Just look at those flashing lights, Liam. I don't want Grant to see me handcuffed and led to the back of a police car. I can't do that to him. Just ... just get us out of here."

"Listen, sweetheart ..."

"Fucking now, Liam!"

"Jesus, all right. Calm down," Liam grumbled as he turned the engine on. I leaned back in my seat, drained by the roller coaster of emotions I'd gone through in those past two hours. Scared to death that Grant was hurt, hopeful that he wanted me back, fear at nearly getting killed and then, that hope was gone again. I didn't know where Liam and I would go after that. Grant had all my falsified documents. He wouldn't be giving them back without answers ... answers I wasn't ready to give.

Liam swore. "Looks like you have no choice now, Blaire."

In all my self-pitying scramble of thoughts, I noticed we had not moved from the parking lot exit. There was traffic, but not too bad that a driver of Liam's caliber couldn't pull away. It was then I noticed a familiar Black Escalade making a turn from the opposite lane into ours.

"Go, now!"

"Fuck this," my friend said and pulled into traffic.

12

Blaire

"WHAT ARE YOU DOING?" I yelled. I turned in my seat to watch the other vehicle, feeling betrayed by the only person I trusted. "They're right on our tail!"

"You're going to talk to Thorne," Liam told me. "There's no way we could tear out of that parking lot and speed down this road without drawing attention."

I knew he was right. With law enforcement on the lookout for suspicious activity, the less conspicuous we were, the better. I'd give some kudos to Tyler that he didn't try to intimidate us by driving alongside us. I had a feeling if the cops weren't crawling all over the place, Grant would have had him cut us off by now.

Liam turned left into a quiet business park and pulled up to the front of some one-story office buildings. The place was deserted and was ideal for the oncoming confrontation. The Escalade stopped behind our vehicle.

"The son of a bitch blocked me in," Liam muttered. He didn't seem too annoyed, and I bet he would have done the same if the situations were reversed.

Doors slammed and a shadow fell across my window. My door was yanked open and Grant hauled me out of the car. He caged me against the Ford sedan, both arms on either side of me. Whatever objections I had about being dragged out of the car died when I saw his bruised face that was lit by the Escalade's headlights.

"What the hell happened back there?" he growled, his eyes searched mine. "Were you guys involved?"

"Hello to you, too, Grant," I murmured.

"Damn it, Blaire," he released his grip on the car and his hands shook as they cupped my face. "When I saw those flashing lights"—he crushed his lips against mine in a deep but brief kiss—"I thought I was too late ... that they got to you."

"They nearly did," Liam said.

My own hand came up and touched the bruise on his cheekbone. "Oh, Grant."

He grabbed my hand on his face and kissed it. "Come on. I can't wait to get you home. You're welcome to come with us, Watts."

He tugged me in the direction of the Escalade, but I resisted. Grant turned to look at me and his expression hardened. "No, Blaire. Don't even say you're not coming with me."

"I'm a bad bet, Grant Thorne," I said even as my heart yearned for him. "I'm only going to drag you and your family down with me."

He gripped my shoulders. "Listen to me, Blaire. I'm fucking pissed that you have so little faith in me. You think I haven't gotten my hands dirty to get to my position now? I have. I can be ruthless when I need to be. I've dealt with all kinds of organizations. If they start playing filthy games, I'm not above doing the same. Someone had already messed with me and is gunning for my woman. You think the man I am, I'm just gonna let that slide?"

My mouth opened as if to say something but I expelled a resigned breath instead. "Well then."

Grant smiled and kissed the top of my head. "We'll talk, but not here."

"I'm going to ground for a few days," Liam announced. "My number is programmed on your burner, Blaire." He looked at Grant. "I'm not sure what level of security you have on your phones, but if you're going to protect her, you might consider upgrading. Blaire will explain why." He nodded at the Escalade. "I need to go."

"Tyler," Grant told his security man to back up their SUV.

"Not changing your mind?" I asked my friend in one last ditch effort to get him to come with us. "I hate not knowing where you are." There was no use pulling away from Grant because he had my hand locked down tight.

"Sweetheart, I'll be okay," he said. I gave Liam a one-arm hug and he returned the favor. "Now get out of here. Thorne, take care of my girl."

Grant stiffened beside me and, judging from Liam's smirk, calling me "his girl" was a deliberate taunt. Men.

We got into the Escalade. The man beside me suddenly quiet and brooding.

"Hi, Tyler," I greeted Grant's security guy.

"Ma'am."

"I told you to call me Blaire." There was a wariness in the way Tyler looked at me and I had a feeling it was because I was the reason his boss was all bruised up. It wasn't exactly a condemning look, just a feeling of uneasiness.

"The brownstone, Mr. Thorne?"

"Yes." It was a curt reply. Grant was staring out the window, but he hadn't let go of my hand.

"Liam was messing with you." I think I was familiar enough with my man's moods to tell what changed it. He'd always been possessive as hell. I did complain to Liam about this, which was why my moronic friend decided to poke the bear.

He sighed in frustration. "I know. I'm just pissed he helped you leave me."

"At my request." I felt the need to defend Liam. "I'll tell you soon enough who he is to me, but I'll have to start from the beginning."

Grant didn't answer, but he pulled me into his arms and for the first time since I'd ran from him, I felt safe.

"WE'RE HOME, BLAIRE."

I startled awake. I had fallen asleep on the long car ride home, a delayed adrenaline crash of some sort. Grant had his arms around me and my head was on his chest. My heart squeezed. On one hand, I was lucky to have this handsome, caring, albeit intense, man crazy for me. On the other, I felt I was being tortured slowly. Being shown what happiness could be if I was an ordinary girl. But there wasn't anything ordinary about me. I was a woman with a price on her head.

I pried myself away from the hard wall of muscle and took in the familiar brownstone.

"I never thought I'd see it again."

Grant said nothing, just stepped out of the SUV and helped me down. He immediately tucked me to his side and we headed up the paved walkway. Another security guy met us and opened the door, speaking into a wrist radio before greeting us.

"I've stepped up security," Grant told me. "Donovan is due back in the morning." He looked at his watch. "We're reviewing our protective detail." He hugged me closer. "We're going to send a clear message to whoever is after you that you're under my protection."

Oh, Grant, it isn't that simple.

"Wait for me in our bedroom." His mouth touched my ear, causing a shiver to go through me. "I'll be in after a few minutes. I have a couple of calls to return." He pulled back and smiled at me. "Welcome home, baby."

I watched him disappear into his office. I made my way to our bedroom and entered the closet. Grant had showered me with gifts— clothes, jewelry, and expensive shoes. But I didn't take them with me. I could have probably pawned the jewelry eventually, but sentimental fool that I was, I didn't want to tarnish my time with Grant, so I departed with what I came with, except for the Medici paints. I took them with me not because they were rare, but because they were a testament to how much Grant cared about me. I would like to believe that I'd been special to him.

I moved to the dresser and pulled out some soft pajamas and my lips twitched at a memory. Grant bought me sexy lingerie from Agent Provocateur. I'd wear them for his benefit knowing those pieces wouldn't last long on my body. They even wouldn't last long in my lingerie drawer because he frequently ripped them apart in his eagerness to fuck me.

It was not the time to seduce him. I grabbed plain cotton panties and slammed the drawer as anger consumed me at the thought that Grant could have gotten killed.

I stepped into the shower and let the multiple nozzles wash the night away. There was a massage function and I engaged that as well, letting the water beat down on me in a soothing rhythm. I felt squeaky clean when I was done. When I finished and turned off the jets, the shower stall opened and a thick luxurious towel swallowed me up.

"I wanted to join you," Grant whispered as he gently dried my hair. "But watching you through the glass was fucking amazing."

"Pervert," I sassed.

"I missed you," Grant murmured before lowering his head to kiss me. The kiss deepened, his tongue searching and laced with controlled desperation. The towel dropped, his hands slid to my ass, drawing me closer to his jutting hardness. Desire pooled between my legs and I wanted nothing more than to wrap my limbs around him, but there was so much to be said between us. "Grant, we need to talk."

He didn't seem to hear me and went for my mouth again, so I arched away from him. "You need to know who you're letting into your bed, into your life, and who you're exposing to your family."

Grant sighed and stepped back, his gaze piercing and I fought the urge to squirm.

"Answer this," he said. "Are you a spy?"

Caught off guard by his question, I laughed. "No!"

"Are you involved in anything illegal? Are you a criminal?"

"No, but I may be wanted by the law at the moment."

"For what happened at the motel? That was self-defense, don't you think?"

"Why are you so blasé about this?" I was a bit pissed off, because here I was, all worried about telling him who I was, and he was standing there as if he didn't give a damn. I knew better.

"I'm still mad at you," he said, his eyes flashing with something unfathomable. "But after everything I've discovered in the cabin and having time to calm down, I understood why you ran. You should have trusted me, Blaire. It hurt that you didn't and that was what pissed me off the most."

"That's why we need to talk."

Grant shook his head. "Done talking, baby." He bent down and scooped my naked body into his arms. He marched into the bedroom and dropped me on the mattress, then he stood back. In all the months I'd known him, his frank appraisal of my splayed naked body never failed to make me wet. His gaze was devouring, carnal hunger. He climbed on the bed, nudged my knees apart and settled in between. Supported by his arms, his head came down and began to explore my lips again. The teasing articulation of his kiss was the complete opposite of the raw desire I saw in his eyes earlier. His mouth moved to my jaw, grazed me there and then proceeded on a downward quest. His tongue licked my nipple, swirling around leisurely as the muscles of his torso rocked against my damp cove that was only getting wetter by the second. I moaned and moved my head from side to side, my eyes catching his grip on the sheets. He was struggling for control.

"Please," I mewled as the fire in my lower pelvis grew hotter as he took his time worshiping each breast. Then he slid down my body, licked my navel before shifting lower to where I was craving his attention.

"Yes," I undulated my hips, anticipation fractured my breathing. "Yes."

He pushed my legs apart, cocking them to either side, his hot tongue branded my center. My body jerked as he speared my entrance. "You're wet for me, Angel," he murmured, lapping my juices onto his tongue. "So goddamned sweet." He ate at my sensitive flesh, licking and swiping, until I came on a rush of pulses and a breathless cry.

I protested when Grant pulled back, but my eyes hooded with renewed excitement as he exposed his heavy arousal. His knee came down between my legs once more as he lowered himself above me. I expected a brutal thrust as he loved to take me hard but instead his engorged head circled at my entrance.

"Grant, I need you now," I pleaded.

"Never leave me again, Angel," he commanded huskily. He eased inside me and I relished the feeling of fullness. He thrust in a steady pace, unhurried, and savoring. He tormented me, keeping the surge of my second orgasm at bay. I tilted my hips to coax him to speed up, but he weighed me down and compelled me to accept his rhythm. This continued for long minutes, his lips would take mine in an impassioned kiss, and then he would watch my face as if mesmerized by its shifting expressions. When I noticed his breathing turned erratic, his pace also quickened. He surged deep and that elusive high exploded into massive jolts of pleasure low in my belly. He continued pounding until I rode out my wave and then quick successive thrusts brought him his release. He poured inside me, a warm and intimate sensation. We'd gotten rid of condoms long ago when I took the birth control shot. I mentally calculated its efficacy and the anxiety disappeared as quickly as it hit me. I wasn't due for another month.

Grant fell to my side and dragged me against him. After two big orgasms and after the night I'd had, I didn't even care about the sticky spot on the bed. I vaguely remembered getting shifted around, tucked close to a familiar scent and wall of muscle.

I slept.

13

Grant

GRANT LAID WIDE AWAKE. His mind and body were weary, but a lingering unease kept the adrenaline steady in his veins—a fight or flight response that wouldn't be quelled ... a fear that if he slept, Blaire would disappear, her presence beside him all a dream.

He touched his nose to her hair, inhaled the citrus-floral scent of her shampoo and drew her closer. She'd probably complain of all the sweat in between them or sleeping beside a furnace, but Grant didn't care. It meant she was real. He preferred this negligible discomfort compared to the sharp stab in his chest of those times he woke up without her at his side. It had been a hellish few days.

He turned his head to the picture windows. Purple light was breaking through the slats of the blinds, the darkness receding, but he was impatient for the new day to start.

There were things to get done, truths to be heard, and plans to be made. Grant was far from blasé about the whole Blaire affair and that was probably part of his anxiety. He was prepared to accept her past, but how it would affect the people around him like his father's political allies would be a different question. The tabloids speculated whether the woman with Grant at his father's first reelection event was the lady who had finally captured the heart of the senator's son.

He decided to stop brooding and make an early day. He needed to make calls to his real estate investment firm. His buddy from Harvard, Rafael Lopez, headed Thorne Real Estate. They were in the process of acquiring prime commercial areas in several countries, but the ones in Brazil and Russia had been met by stiff competition. He trusted Rafe, but his friend didn't represent the Thorne Industry umbrella, Grant did. The idea of whisking Blaire away from the dangers stalking her was enticing, but he had a responsibility to his company he couldn't ignore.

He eased away from his woman, careful not to wake her, although the sounds of her light snoring indicated she was in deep sleep. Poor thing. He still didn't know whether he wanted to strangle her or kiss her senseless. That was how much she had him twisted up.

After showering, he skipped his facial hair grooming all together. He looked like shit and the bruising had darkened considerably. He'd be working from home for the next few days—that much had appeal. He put on drawstring sweatpants and an ancient Harvard tee. Padding across the black walnut flooring, he headed into the kitchen. If anything, he needed coffee. He pushed the button to make twelve cups and the grinding sound of the coffee station broke through the serenity of the morning. Grant walked over to the living room and tugged back the vertical window treatment—some fancy-fabric accordion-type shit his mother insisted he purchase.

When Grant bought the brownstone, it was for investment. He liked the neighborhood, but the house needed a lot of work. Unlike its typical townhouse architecture, this one was a sprawling bungalow with a basement. One of his companies was a construction firm so it wasn't hard to get renovation started. They tore up the flooring and put down premium hardwood. The plumbing and electrical work were upgraded. The walls were done in shades of brown or taupe, and the furniture was cream-white leather. The kitchen had coffee-colored granite with antique white cabinets and professional stainless-steel appliances. Blaire remarked that it screamed "bachelor pad" so he encouraged her to give it her feminine touch with an unlimited budget. She was an artist after all. His face turned sour. She hadn't touched a damned thing, not even hung any of her paintings. Now he knew why. Blaire hadn't counted on staying. It infuriated him.

The door to the garage opened and Tyler walked in. Above the attached garage were furnished living quarters where the security team stayed.

"Coffee?" Grant offered when his man stepped into the kitchen. Tyler nodded and gave a deep breath. "Donovan called and said he made his flight this morning. He'll be in by nine."

"Any progress report from DC?" Grant asked.

"Yes, I talked with him earlier. He alluded to some information regarding Blaire's background."

"And?"

"I think they have a match and pieced together why and how she ended up in Colorado."

"That's good ... that's good," Grant murmured distractedly as he poured Tyler some coffee. Afterward, he filled his mug and took a sip. Grant grabbed his tablet from the counter to flip through the morning news, but felt eyes on him the whole time.

"I'm okay, Tyler," Grant grinned faintly and glanced up at his bodyguard.

"Donovan is gonna have my ass," the bodyguard groaned.

"I hear you whine about it one more time, Tyler, it'll be me handing you your ass. Cut it out."

"Yes, Mr. Thorne." Tyler's face cleared of emotion.

Now the question this morning was breakfast. Blaire usually did the cooking. Grant could manage basic breakfast items like eggs and bacon. Waffles and pancakes from a box. Cereal and milk. He cringed. His housekeeper, who did most of the cooking, came in only on weekdays. She used to come in on Saturdays but, since Blaire moved in, Grant wanted to laze around in bed and all over the house with his woman and didn't want to chance his housekeeper walking in on them. As he contemplated the cereal choices, he heard Tyler's radio crackle.

"The vehicles of Mr. Thorne's mother and sister are clearing the gates."

Grant groaned inwardly, not ready for company at six-thirty in the morning. He prepared for the inevitable, noting how he looked in the mirror this morning which was actually worse than how he was feeling.

"Where is he?" He heard his mother's panicked voice before he saw her march into the foyer with Valerie.

Amelia Thorne slapped a hand over her mouth, uttered a strangled cry that wrenched at his heart, and rushed toward his son. Grant loathed putting that shocked, anguished expression on his mother's face.

"How did this happen, Grant?" his mother demanded.

"The traffic was bad in front of the Hyatt, so I told Tyler to wait for me at the corner of Main. Two men tried to mug me."

"I hope the cops are looking for them," Val said, outraged.

"They're dead; Tyler shot them," Grant stated flatly.

The two women gaped in shock.

"Are you ... are you in trouble with the police?" Val asked worriedly. "It was self-defense, right?"

Grant nodded. "It was. How did you two find out?"

"A friend called me this morning to ask how you were doing," his mother said, clearly upset. "She saw you sitting on the steps of an ambulance last night, talking to the police. Imagine my surprise when I didn't know what she was talking about. She was also at the gala—an affair I forced you to attend in my place." The last four words were uttered with self-reproach.

Grant hugged his mother. "Hey—none of that now. I'll be pissed if you take any blame for this." He looked into her distressed eyes. "Are we clear?" A troubling feeling nagged him and it had everything to do with the "mugging" lie he'd just told. He didn't expect that covering up for Blaire would indirectly hurt his mother. If he told her the truth, the blame would fall on Blaire. If he didn't, he was sure his mother would continue to harbor some guilt over what happened.

"So, Blaire's not back yet?" Val questioned. "She had to rush off somewhere, right? Changed your vacation plans. That's why you were able to attend in place of Mom?"

He didn't like the accusatory tone in his sister's voice. He knew she didn't approve of Blaire. Hell, Val didn't approve of any of his female friends if they weren't in the required social class in her head.

"She's here. Arrived late last night and she's sleeping."

Val eyed the row of cereal boxes Grant had pulled out. "So, you survived an attempted mugging, and you're the one serving her?"

"Val, it's none of your business," Amelia censured. If there was one person who could attempt to muzzle his sister, it was his mother. "Grant, did you go to the hospital to have a thorough check-up?"

"No."

"Shouldn't you?"

"Nope."

"Grant ..." He was a thirty-five years old and his mother was mothering. He'd once gotten pissed at her for nagging him like he was still a teenager with braces, but she told him until he got married and had kids, he would never understand.

"Good morning," a quiet voice spoke from the hallway.

He turned to Blaire, frustrated that he wanted to be alone with her, yet knowing it wasn't happening soon. Add to that Val's obvious hostility which wasn't helping his woman feel comfortable about being here.

"Blaire," his mother walked toward his woman and gave her a hug. "I'm glad you're back and Grant has someone with him. How's your aunt? Is she feeling better?"

A pained smile flashed across Blaire's face. "She's fine now. Thanks for asking."

"One has to be more careful as we get older," his mother offered. "It's easy to lose balance and fall."

"How old is your aunt?" Val asked. "Maybe it's better for her to stay in a retirement home."

"And it's your business how?" Grant snapped. As much as he loved his sister, he hated her bitchiness and certainly wasn't blind to it.

"What?" his sister replied innocently. "I'm just showing my concern for Blaire's aunt. What if her neighbor hadn't found her."

Bullshit. Grant fumed and judging by the tight expression on Blaire's face, she thought the same.

"I appreciate your concern, Val," Blaire said with saccharine sweetness. "I'll look into it." Walking past his sister, and clearly dismissing her, Blaire opened the refrigerator to take an inventory. "I can make eggs and sausage for breakfast. Anyone hungry?"

Unconcerned that they weren't alone, he approached his woman and brushed her ear with his mouth. "I am."

Blaire inhaled sharply and flicked him a glare even as she turned scarlet. "Grant ..."

"What?" His brows shot up innocently.

"Maybe we should go and leave you two lovebirds alone," his mom suggested, smiling at him slyly. "On second thought, are you sure you should be exerting yourself, Grant, after the night you had?"

"Mom," he growled at his mother's innuendo even if he did bring it on himself.

Blaire, turning redder if possible, grabbed the eggs and sausage from the fridge and moved to the center island. His woman was flustered and damned if he wasn't fucking turned on. His frustration at having unwanted company increased and Grant hoped he could make it through breakfast.

THE MORNING MEAL progressed without much drama or any more embarrassing moments. To Grant's surprise, Valerie behaved and didn't make more snide comments toward Blaire. He was proud of his woman as she turned out to be a gracious hostess. She sent one of his security guys to the bakery at the corner street for some crusty French boule and assorted muffins. She cooked enough for an army and even invited their security detail, including his mother and Val's teams, to the table. They respectfully declined, so Blaire made them a platter to take back to their quarters and sandwiches for those who needed to stand guard outside.

"Your dad is flying up tomorrow," his mother informed him. "He was worried for you. If he didn't have that breakfast meeting with the president's Chief of Staff, he'd be on his way to Boston right now."

"What's the meeting about?"

"Your dad's reelection campaign. The party is discussing the next presidential election." That was three years away, but potential candidates were being scouted and built up early. There were a lot of lessons learned from the tight and controversial race of the last election.

"Is Dad interested?"

His mother sighed. "He's keeping his options open, but I'm not too keen on the idea."

"I don't blame you, Mom. Being a senator is one thing, but president?"

"You know how all these newly inaugurated presidents enter the White House with a head of black hair but when they leave it's all gray?" his mother quipped.

Grant laughed. "You're concerned with Dad's gray hair? It's almost all gray now."

"Pshaw, you know I'm not that superficial," his mother said, her Southern accent more pronounced. "But it's a tell of how stressful the job is. I don't want that for your dad."

"In any case, Mom, you'd make a great first lady." Grant meant that statement wholeheartedly. His mother had Southern charm and warmth that could relate to the people in the Heartland that felt disconnected from their leaders in Washington.

"Well, then you probably need to think about settling down soon," Mom looked pointedly at Blaire who lost all color.

"Uh ..." his woman stuttered, caught off-guard by his mother's comment.

"Less tabloid fodder that way," his mother sighed. "I know you're not the playboy the tabloids make you out to be, Grant. I know my

son better. Your dad pretty much has the senate race locked down."
His mother shrugged. "Unless some God-forbidden scandal happens
to our family, which I hope it won't." His mom looked pointedly at
Val, but Blaire was the one who choked on her orange juice.

"The pressure, Mom," Val grumbled and forked a spoonful of egg
into her mouth.

"It would help if you stayed away from college professors for a
while." Mom didn't specify "married college professors," probably to
spare Val the humiliation in front of Blaire, but Grant didn't think his
woman heard anything else other than "scandal."

This breakfast needed to end soon, he thought grimly as he
watched Blaire swallow a piece of bread with difficulty. He tried to
catch her eyes, but she wouldn't look at him and instead stared at
her plate.

It was with much relief when Jake stepped through the threshold
because he could ask his surprise visitors to leave without offending
their sensibilities. Grant hated the political correctness of it all.

14

Grant

"Don't forget dinner tomorrow night," his mother reminded as he sent her and Val out the door. Grant stood there until they pulled away in the Bentley, their security details following behind them. He closed the door and went to the kitchen to assist Blaire in cleaning up.

She had loaded almost everything in the dishwasher. Looking up, she grinned at him. "I love your industrial-sized equipment."

Grant smirked. "Thank you."

"Is it always innuendo with you?" she laughed.

"I think my mom's to blame for that," he said in a mock-pained tone.

Blaire laughed harder. "Your mom is incorrigible. I like her."

"Yeah, she's all right," he replied deadpan before pulling her away from the remaining dirty dishes to steal a kiss. When he was finished, he kept his lips by her forehead. "Sorry about that."

"About what?"

"The ambush. I knew you were uncomfortable with the senate race talk."

"I'm more concerned that I'm a liability right now."

"I'm getting tired of that argument," Grant snapped as a spike of anger shot through him.

"There's nothing to argue," Blaire leaned against the counter. Grant was getting more pissed because her face was serene. "Because ..." she linked her hand with his. "I'm tired of that argument as well. It's the truth, but it's not fair that you're the only one fighting for us. Whether there's a chance of us making it or not, I'm taking it. I'll fight for us, Grant."

His anger evaporated as he dragged her into his arms, her body pressed to his. "Damn straight you are," he growled and snatched her lips in his. He loved her tiny gasps. They seemed to have a direct line to his dick which hardened in no time behind his sweatpants.

Blaire tried to retreat, whispering his name on a giggle. He chased her mouth and recaptured it, kissing her like they were the only two people in the world. Shit, he wanted to take her right there in the kitchen.

A clearing of the throat sounded behind them.

He'd forgotten Jake was waiting for him in the office. Grant released Blaire who immediately returned her attention to the dishes. He turned to face Jake who was staring at Blaire with an expression that Grant was sure he didn't like on his head of security.

"I will be with you in a minute," Grant said with a curt nod.

Jake lifted his chin in acknowledgment and gave Blaire's back one last look before leaving the kitchen.

"Why don't you leave that for later and join us in the office," Grant told her.

"This won't take long," Blaire said, glancing at the path where Jake disappeared. "I think you and your security team need a moment alone."

"You're right," Grant agreed. "But if you don't show up in ten minutes, I'm coming to get you."

With that statement, he left the kitchen to confront Jake. His security lead and Tyler were already in the office. Grant didn't bother closing the door, because he had nothing to say to them that he didn't want Blaire to hear.

"Let's make one thing clear, Donovan," Grant gritted through his teeth. "I catch you looking at my woman that way again, like she is some threat to be eliminated, you can find yourself another job."

The stubborn set of Jake's jaw reflected the man's struggle to hold back. "Permission to speak freely, sir."

"For fuck's sake," Grant growled. "This isn't the military. Say what you have to say to me now, because if you say anything that would upset Blaire, I'll fucking kick your ass."

"She's entangled with Russian Organized Crime," Jake said.

"So, we're dealing with the Russian mob," Grant stated matter-of-factly.

Jake nodded. "I can't believe she'd put you and your family in danger like that. That they sent someone after you last night meant they're desperate."

"I pursued her," Grant said dryly. "She wanted to stay out of the public eye but I was a jackass. After going through the trouble of forging those documents so she can remain safely in hiding, you think she's just going to 'fess up to a man who can complicate her safety?" Not expecting an answer, he continued, "What do we know of the men killed last night?"

"The ones who attacked you in the alley and the one killed in the motel are part of a Russian street gang here in Boston. Not directly a part of the ROC, but they do business together. Thug muscle and intimidation are part of it."

"Update on security in the brownstone?"

"We're upgrading the motion sensors around the perimeter as well as the fifteen-foot fence, adding trip wires where needed. They're installing surveillance cameras to all street traffic as we speak. We'll be increasing personnel from three to six and adding hourly foot patrols. Interviews scheduled for this afternoon."

"And you think the brownstone is the safest for Blaire?"

Donovan inclined his head. "It's in the city. Boston PD has a five to seven minutes response time to provide immediate backup. It's the only property you have that has a panic room and an armory."

A movement at the door caught Grant's attention. "Blaire, come in."

To his benefit, Jake kept his expression neutral.

Blaire rubbed her hands nervously. Grant extended his arm and pulled her into an embrace. She kissed his cheek and extricated herself from his hold. His brows furrowed as she moved away from him, clasping her biceps as she hugged herself.

"I need to face you all when I tell you my story," Blaire said quietly. She looked at Jake. "Have you looked at the flash drives?"

Jake nodded. "We've decrypted some of them, but I figured they're mostly the same."

Blaire exhaled deeply and looked at Grant. "My real name is Paulina Antonova. My father was Maxim Antonov. He was the cleaner for the Russian Mob."

"Cleaner?" Grant brows drew together. "He's the mob's hitman?"

"The ROC has a couple of assassins. My Papa was usually called to sanitize a crime scene or, if there was no time, he planted evidence to mislead the authorities."

"You said 'was'." He picked up on the loaded word.

"He's dead," Blaire stated flatly. "He took the blame when I killed the Vor's son, Yuri Orlov. I did it in self-defense."

Red hazed his vision for he knew in his gut why Blaire killed the boss's son, but he kept his rage in check so she could get over this difficult part.

"He wanted me to be his wife and, when I said no, he tried to force himself on me. He thought if he got me pregnant, I would have no choice. He already had one of my friends killed because he thought he was my lover. As loyal as Papa was to Mikhail Orlov, he loved me more. He also knew Yuri was unstable. It pained him to start gathering evidence against the Bratva, but it was the only way he could get us out."

"The cleaner of the mob is one of its most trusted members," Grant murmured. "I can see why Orlov wants his pound of flesh."

"That's where Liam Watts, formerly known as DEA Agent Lucas Myers, comes in, right?" Jake asked, opening the folder he had with him. Grant walked over to his desk and picked up a similar binder.

She nodded. "Liam Watts was supposed to be Papa's alias. When I killed Yuri ..." Blaire's face turned red, her eyes filled with tears. "Yuri broke into my apartment in Miami. There was a struggle but I managed to stab him in the ribs. His death wasn't quick, but the wound was fatal. I called Papa. I didn't know then that he was working with the DEA. He arrived with one of Orlov's henchman and I thought ..." Blaire inhaled on a sob. "I thought he chose the Orlov Bratva. My hurt was so deep, I couldn't cry—I didn't even say good-bye to him—I just looked at the ground and accepted my fate that I was going to die by Orlov's hand." Tears were streaming down Blaire's cheeks.

"Do you want to do this some other time, Angel?" Grant asked.

She shook her head and expelled a ragged breath. "I was in shock. I had just killed a man and my father gave me up to the ROC. It wasn't until I noticed we were driving out of Miami that I wondered what was going on. Was the Bratva's soldier going to kill me and dump my body somewhere?"

"It was Liam, wasn't it?" Jake interjected.

"Yes," Blaire confirmed. "He'd been undercover with the Orlov Bratva for three years at that point. His expertise lies in determining who can be turned. It didn't take him long to work on Papa, what with Yuri's interest in me."

"Why do you still have all the evidence?" Grant asked.

"Killing Yuri messed up the DEA's plans. There was no evidence that could be used to prosecute Mikhail Orlov, only his inner circle ... especially his assassins. Liam's boss reneged on his deal with Papa. Liam got pissed. A few days later, his boss and Liam's entire team were found dead."

"I heard about that," Grant said. The news was about three years ago. DEA agents were found in a shallow grave in Ciudad Juarez.

"I can shed light on that," Jake interjected. He handed Blaire a file. "Appendix B. Liam's team had been working in Mexico at that time. It appeared the ROC made a deal with the cartel to have them assassinated in exchange for more business. How about your father, Blaire? Are you certain he's dead? There was no record of his body."

Grant wanted to smack Jake for his insensitivity. His head of security was nothing but thorough and speculations were just that until physical evidence was presented.

"I think she's answered enough," he growled.

"No, it's okay," Blaire whispered. Her eyes turned glassy again. She had just stopped crying, dammit. Grant glared at his security guy who flinched. "You have to understand, Jake, we're talking about Florida. The swamps were used to get rid of bodies."

At that moment, Grant would take pleasure in dropping his head of security in a goddamn swamp.

"Did you ever help your father clean up—"

"That's enough," Grant barked.

"Mr. Thorne—"

"I won't have her incriminating herself without a lawyer," he cut Jake off. "There are certainly more details to be sifted through, but let's focus on the issue at hand—the ROC has put a hit on Blaire and Liam because they don't want the contents of the flash drive revealed and Orlov wants revenge for his son. That's all they're after, right, Blaire? Did you or Liam take anything else from them?"

There was hesitancy on Blaire's face before she shook her head.

Alarm ghosted over his instincts, but he ignored it for now, not wanting to upset the tenuous bond they were trying to re-forge. He turned to Jake. "Find out about the ROC, what their weaknesses are, who their business associates are. I've got billions at my disposal —use it."

"I want to point something out," Blaire spoke up. "We're not simply talking bodyguards here, Grant. They were able to trace your phone last night."

"I figured that," Grant said, motioning to Tyler. "We're upgrading our phone's security with the highest encrypted channels."

"You'll also have to review cyber security at your company." Blaire chewed her bottom lip. "ROC is dealing with drugs, game fixing, and prostitution, but they're increasingly employing hackers to hold company data hostage. They're only going after small businesses for now, for protection money, a way to fund some of the gangs who are also their distributors." Blaire shook her head from side to side as if weary and defeated. "The more I think about it, the more I wished I was back in my cabin in Colorado."

Grant glanced at her sharply. "Don't turn chicken shit on me now, baby."

For some reason, his woman smiled at his provocation.

"Mr. Thorne, as much as we want to keep everything under wraps, Ms. Callahan's past with the ROC may, in some way, affect security for the senator. We need to alert his men about what's going on."

"I know, Donovan," Grant looked at Blaire and held out his hand. "Come here, Angel."

When her hand curled into his, he gave it a tug to bring her close. "Should I call you Paulina?"

She grinned. "No, I'm used to Blaire. Liam and I agreed to use our new identities. The process the DEA used was similar to witness protection."

Grant pressed a kiss against her temple. "It's going to be okay. We'll get through this."

"I trust you," she said, smiling up at him.

A twinge of unease pricked his chest. On this, he would agree with Donovan—he couldn't procrastinate in informing his father about Blaire's association to the Russian mafia. It would be selfish and dangerous should he delay.

It could be deadly.

15

Blaire

THE AIR between Grant and me sizzled when our security team left us alone. The events of the previous night, and the relief that we came out of that alive, temporarily put our other issues on hold. But judging from the working muscle in Grant's jaw, and the awareness needling my skin, my reprieve was over.

I gave him a tentative smile, but his hewn expression was unflinching as he fixed his gaze on me.

"Had you always planned on leaving me?" Grant asked.

The truth was going to hurt, but lies would come out eventually. "I conditioned myself that we were temporary." My voice faltered when Grant's face morphed from stony to furious. He clenched his fists and I imagined them around my neck.

"Was any of this real?" he asked, his tone guttural. I stepped toward him but he backed away with distrust in his eyes. "Tell me, Blaire. Is this"—he pointed between us—"even real then?"

"What do you think, Grant?" I whispered. His lips twisted into a sneer but I soldiered on. "The plan was to live in the moment, to be happy with whatever time we had, but then I started falling for you and I found myself aching for a future."

Surprise lifted the fury from his face to a certain degree. In its stead was wary hope. "Are you saying you feel something for me?"

"I fought hard against it," I admitted. "Each day I was plagued by regret. I'd feel the high of being with you and then I'd feel despair knowing that any moment it could be ripped away."

"Yeah, but it didn't have to be if you had just told me the truth!"

"Would you have stuck it out with me?"

"I guess we won't know now, will we?" he replied disparagingly. "You never gave me that chance. You were prepared to think the worse of me ... that I'd get tired of you. I've shown you for months how much you meant to me. And what did you do? You left me!"

"I cared for you enough to leave you."

"You're saying you left me because you cared for me? That's fucking bullshit."

"Is it? Look at all the security changes you have to make because of me."

"Let's back up a bit," Grant said, the tension in him easing slightly. "I'm not without fault. I should've anticipated the abrupt changes in my dad's campaign schedule, but you shut me out for weeks after that political dinner."

"You shut me out too. After you nearly attacked Claude—"

"Do not mention his fucking name—"

"I bet you had a file on him even before you showed up at the art studio and claimed me like some freaking caveman."

The barest flicker in his eyes told me my statement was true.

I puffed a short laugh and shook my head in disbelief. "You did."

"The only man you should be staring at naked is me," he replied, all surly and grumbly and completely unrepentant.

"I'm an artist!"

"We're getting off topic but, before we leave this subject, it's not gonna happen again. Got me?"

"Grant!"

"Now, in regards to me shutting down, it's because I say shit when

I'm angry but I did not shut you out to break up with you. And after everything we'd been through, I didn't expect you to put me in cold storage for weeks."

"After our pictures appeared in the tabloids I knew our time together was over," I explained. "Liam got delayed in getting me out. The longer I stayed, the harder it got to pretend that everything was okay, so I avoided you."

"You stopped having sex with me and that drove me crazy. We quit talking. You locked yourself up in the art studio," Grant said. "I thought all you needed was space after the political dinner spooked you."

"That wasn't anybody's fault." Not even Gus, who was only doing his job. And yet there were no words to describe the heartache I felt that day when I made the decision to extricate myself from his life.

"A takeover bid took away my focus, but I thought I had time," he muttered. "I thought if I took you back to Colorado, we could recapture our connection that we'd somehow lost these past two months." His tone took on an edge of frustration. "I'm surprised you didn't want to leave before."

"We thought you would lose interest and be the one to break up with me."

"I should be mad at you," Grant said quietly, taking one step forward. "I felt you holding back, you know. At first, I tried to convince myself that you needed time, but weeks turned into months ..." he broke off, gave one shake of his head and looked at the floor.

"You were losing patience," I concluded.

"Yes. And in all that time I gave you reasons to stay, you were planning to leave me," he glared at me. "I should be mad at you," he reiterated. He leaned in, yanked me into his arms, and pinned me to the hard length of him. "I don't know what I feel about you right now. One minute I'm pissed, the next minute I'm hopeful, and then in another minute, I want to fuck some sense into you." His hands dug into my ass and I yelped. "I'm going with wanting to fuck you."

He backed me into the dining room and laid me on the table. He divested me of my pajama bottoms, leaving my panties on, and dragged my butt to the edge of the table. He kissed me, his tongue driving in to tangle with my own. I pushed his chest at the same time wrenched my mouth from him. "Grant, we need to talk."

"No, I need to fuck you," he growled. "I can't think clearly when my cock is begging to get inside you." Two fingers slipped past my panties and penetrated my pussy. I gasped at the sudden intrusion, yet I felt myself gush all over him. "Fuck," he hissed. He continued to pump inside me, angling his knuckles as he spread me wide, his mouth hovered against mine with just enough space between our faces to pant against each other. My eyes grew heavy-lidded and I saw his smile of triumph before he devoured my lips again. His kiss was hungry, desperate, his chest rumbled as he moved to the side, our mouths still locked. I nearly protested until I heard my panties rip as he tore them off my legs. He broke our kiss then and sank to his knees. My thighs were shoved apart and a flat hot tongue stroked up my slit. He lapped at my entrance, spearing in, tasting more. Greedy, sucking mouthfuls sent me soaring into my orgasm.

His fingers took over and I heard his voice. "I'll take your body now, Blaire, but I'll be taking your mind, your fucking heart. All of you," he growled as he sucked hard on my clit. I hadn't fully come down from my crazy release when he hauled me off the table and my back slammed against the wall. My legs came around him, but he was pushing up inside me even before I could register that he had released his cock. His up-thrust was harsh, almost vicious.

"Grant ..." My head shook from side to side as I was still throbbing. I didn't think I could take his pounding and breathe.

"No mercy, Angel, I'm gonna fuck you until you feel me for days," he snarled, driving so deep I felt him bottom out inside me. "Look at me!" he demanded and my eyes popped open to his heated ones. "You will never leave me." Thrust. "Even if you do, you'll remember my cock inside you like this." Thrust. Thrust. "Marking you, stretching you ..."

"Yes ... yes ..." I moaned, feeling another wave building.

"You're mine," he declared raggedly and his voice broke off as he swore, canting his hips to hit me just where I ached the most.

He came on a roar as I blissfully quaked and moaned in the after-shocks. We collapsed in the middle of the living room on the plush area rug with his cock still inside me. He kept us connected, letting his cum seep into me. We were both sweaty, exhausted, and sated.

Our bond was damaged these past two months, but our physical attraction smoldered just as strongly. Whether our passion was hot enough to reforge the frayed strands of our connection remained to be seen, but Grant was right. Knowing we still burned for each other had left me with a clearer head.

16

Blaire

GRANT'S PARENTS had a house on the Back Bay area of Boston. A historic townhouse that was recently renovated with an elevator that serviced all six levels, it still maintained the stately charm of a Victorian brownstone. Sensible shoes for the cobblestone sidewalks were a must. The first time I had dinner at Senator and Mrs. Thorne's house, I wanted to make a good impression and wore three-inch heels with my dress. Grant didn't think to inform me that I was navigating a bumpy path. He also thought parking for an easier exit was ideal and chose not to park at the three available spaces behind the house, because it meant two extra right turns and needing to get around the block to get back on the main road.

Men.

So, on top of the anxiety of meeting his parents for the first time, I had to worry whether I was going to break a heel or my ankle before introductions were made. Grant, to his benefit, was perceptive enough to hold me up while I teetered over the uneven surface.

He kept mumbling apologies and, from the set of his jaw, he was kicking himself for his lack of foresight when it came to women's footwear. I must also stress that living in the mountains for so long, I'd lost practice strutting in heels, so it wasn't entirely his fault. But Grant was a quick study and for successive dinners at his parents', he reminded me about shoes, which really wasn't necessary since I'd learned my lesson the first time. He'd also started parking behind the townhouse.

That night I wore loafers, light wool slacks, and a flowy blouse with ruffles at the neckline and sleeves. There was a chill in the September breeze, hinting of the end of summer, so I wrapped a shawl around me.

Grant opened the door and held out his hand to assist me out. "You look beautiful."

"So you told me earlier," I grinned.

"Never get tired of telling you, Angel."

Le Sigh.

I should really bask in this perfect moment. Grant shut the door behind me and gathered me close, giving me a kiss. "No matter what happens tonight, know I'm on your side, okay?"

I nodded.

I wasn't as nervous as I thought I would be. I think I was feeling relieved that I could finally let go of my secrets and my life could move forward.

FAR FROM AN INTIMATE FAMILY GATHERING, it appeared to be a dinner party of about twenty people. Grant swore under his breath as he tightened his hold around me.

People gasped when they saw Grant. His right eye was still slightly swollen and the bruises had grown noticeably darker. Marcus Thorne's eyes narrowed when he saw his son and stalked toward the foyer to greet us.

"Now what did you do to my son, Blaire?" the senator teased. The amusement in his tone belied the grim look in his eyes.

He couldn't know how close to the truth he was. My expression must have mirrored the guilt I was feeling and effectively wiped any trace of humor—contrived or not—from the senator's face.

"Well, damn, I was just joking, sweetheart," the senator said. I wished I was a better actress but I wasn't.

"Blaire saw me soon after it happened," Grant explained. He left it hanging there because any other excuse would become a lie later.

"Sorry, I overreacted." I forced a smile.

"At least you got the bastards." An unusual savagery crossed the senator's features.

"We'll talk later, Dad."

The senator gave a quick nod, slung an arm around his son, and led us further into the house.

Senator Thorne mixed a most yummy cocktail. I sipped a red-orange drink of Drambuie with a hint of Campari and lime. As with all the times I'd had dinner here, the Thornes were hands-on hosts. The senator mixed some of the drinks himself and Mrs. Thorne was all Southern hospitality in the way she minded the kitchen and made her guests feel at home.

A mild buzz relaxed me enough to mingle and let Grant talk business with some of the guests. Valerie avoided me and I was fine with that. I didn't have time to pretend to be civil with her. A young man I hadn't seen before handed me a martini.

"The Senator sent this over," he said, smiling sheepishly. He had a mop of curly red-brown hair, a pale complexion, and a smattering of freckles. He was dressed in slacks and polo, a man of medium height. "Andrew Spencer."

I placed my empty glass on the side table meant for used glasses and accepted the proffered drink. "Blaire Callahan."

"I know. The senator mentioned I should check out the woman who's finally captured his son's heart."

I emitted a nervous laugh, and took a healthy sip of the martini. "I think the senator is jumping to conclusions. And why would he send you over?"

The smile faded. "I'm one of his political advisors."

My lips paused on the rim of the glass. "Ah ..." So it began, the grooming and coaching, making sure I didn't embarrass a potential first family. They were definitely jumping the gun; they had not even heard the best part of me. I couldn't help it and snickered.

Andrew's mouth quirked into a wry smile. "Just to make it clear, it wasn't really the senator's idea. He couldn't care less who his son dated."

I didn't offer anything, just waited for him to explain further.

"It's my boss, Gus," he admitted. Of course, the senator's main political strategist would take an interest in me. I was surprised he hadn't sent out PIs to check out if I really graduated from Swift River High School or if I went to the Reynolds Community College or if my parents were Mike and Beth Callahan. He probably didn't think I'd last as Grant's girlfriend given my aversion to public engagements and thought Grant was just keeping me as a fuck-buddy. I wasn't related to a Rockefeller, Koch, or a Kennedy. I didn't have the right pedigree.

"And so far, am I passing the bar?"

"If you ask me, I think you're perfect." He grinned at me.

"Are you softening me up for the kill?" I laughed.

"Baby." Grant appeared by my side, drawing me close. He was frowning at Andrew, but I wasn't certain why. "I see you've met Mr. Spencer."

"Andy, please," the senator's man offered. "Your father sent me over with a drink for Blaire. Looks like we all need to get acquainted since the campaign meetings are gearing up."

"I'd appreciate it if you don't approach Blaire when I'm not around."

"Grant," I chided. "Andy here is just being friendly. It's fine."

"I'll decide what's fine, Blaire," Grant answered. I bristled at his tone, which was only further exacerbated when Andy's brows shot up in response to my man's highhandedness. I didn't want to cause a scene, but I had a strong urge to stomp on Grant's shoes and regretted not wearing stilettos.

"All right, folks!" Mrs. Thorne's voice rang through the room. "Dinner will be served in ten minutes. Please take your seats in the dining room." She paused. "Also, there are new faces around and it would really please me if you don't do the couples thing but, rather, mix it up."

"What's the matter, sweetheart, you don't want to sit beside me?" Senator Thorne's baritone interjected.

Everyone laughed as Amelia shot her husband an exasperated look. She clapped her hands to facilitate the migration of the crowd from the parlor area to the dining room.

Andy, unfazed by Grant's hostility toward him, offered me his arm. "I guess, we should acquiesce to Mrs. Thorne's wishes. Blaire?"

Grant's grip tightened on my waist. I looked up at him, but he was staring Andy down.

"Andy, save a seat for me," I said before turning to face Grant.

"What the fuck are you doing?" he growled.

"I'd like to ask you the same," I returned calmly. "What you said to Andy earlier was uncalled for. You're making me sound like a doormat."

His expression softened. "Blaire, that's the last thing I want to make you feel."

"Well, I didn't like it," I retorted. "Look, Andy seems like a nice guy."

"He was hitting on you."

"There's hitting on me and there's harmless flirting. He's practically a kid. Don't tell me you're jealous."

"What if I am, Blaire?" Grant challenged. "You know how hard it is for me to leave Tyler alone with you? I'm jealous of every man who has the privilege of breathing your air."

"Okay, my man," I cupped his face between my hands. "This is a good time to chill. We're going to walk in there like civilized people. You're going to let me sit beside Andy. I hope to have decent conversation with your father's political strategist and promise not to embarrass you."

Grant scowled at me and jerked his face out of my hands. "How could you think you'd ever embarrass me? That's uncalled for, Blaire."

"So was your highhandedness earlier."

"Okay, I get it," he grumbled. Grant took my hand and led me to the dining room and walked me to where Andy stood to hold the chair out for me. It didn't escape me that some alpha-male posturing came from Grant's side, but Andy was surprisingly good-natured about it. After all, he did work for Grant's father. It was best not to aggravate the son too much.

When I sat down, Andy leaned in close and whispered, "I hope I didn't cause trouble between you and Mr. Thorne."

"No, but you were very brave to offer to be my dinner partner."

"Your boyfriend is scary," Andy said. "But I think Mrs. Thorne is scarier."

I burst out laughing. I wasn't meaning to because, even without looking, I could feel the weight of Grant's glare behind me.

"Shit," Andy murmured. "Maybe your boyfriend is scarier."

"He's glaring at us, isn't he?"

"Yes," my dinner companion sighed dramatically. "Should I be worried about walking to my car later?"

"I'm not sure." I was surprised that it was an honest reply.

17

Blaire

I'D NEVER HAD A MORE relaxed dinner in the presence of this political crowd—maybe because I wasn't sitting beside Grant who drew everyone's attention. It was fortunate that he was engaged in conversation on both sides of the dinner table. It seemed Andrew Spencer turned out to be closer to my age of twenty-nine. He had the look of a college freshman. He lamented his boyish features, saying that people frequently underestimated him and it had been difficult to find work out of college. He'd been lucky to land a position on the Florida governor's campaign and managed to turn a beleaguered politician's career around. That was how Gus Lynch discovered him and offered to be his mentor.

"I've admired August Lynch since college," Andy said with obvious hero-worship. "I can't believe he called me a few weeks ago and offered me a job."

"You mean he called you out of the blue?" I asked.

"No. I sent in an application when there was an open position," he said. "I had these alerts that notify me of available openings with lawmakers I admire."

I was careful not to reveal too much of myself to Andy. I knew his affable behavior could be a smoke screen for a cunning political mind. Why else would a shrewd man like August Lynch hire him to be his aide. I immediately felt guilty when I thought about it. No harm. No foul. Andy was a consummate dinner companion and conversant.

When people started to rise from the dinner table, I saw Grant make a beeline for his dad.

Shit. This is it.

All my nervousness from earlier returned and that last bite of chocolate pie seemed to have lodged in my throat. I gulped some coffee.

"Hey, you okay—?" Andy started. "Hmm ... looks like I'm needed. Uh-oh, I hope your boyfriend's not complaining to the senator about me." For the first time that night, Andy looked unsure of himself as he pushed back from the chair. "Excuse me, Blaire." He smiled, though it didn't reach his eyes. "I enjoyed your company at dinner."

I wanted to assure him that Grant's call for a meeting with his dad and political advisors had nothing to do with one of them hitting on his girlfriend. Even Grant wasn't that petty; he would've handled that situation himself. I kept my mouth shut though. Andy would find out soon enough that fifty percent of what I told him over dinner was fabricated.

THE GUESTS HAD STARTED to leave. Amelia and Valerie were busy chatting them up on their way out while I sat in one corner of the parlor, pretending to show interest in the latest issue of Elle Home. I'd made some acquaintances, mainly women who were curious as to who had managed to hold Grant Thorne's attention for months. As for the men, they wanted to find out how they could win favors with my man. I wasn't delusional to think it was my sparkling personality that attracted their interest. I snickered inwardly.

The door to the senator's office opened and a stone-faced Grant emerged, heading straight for me. *Uh-oh.* Not sure those forty-five minutes that they'd spent holed up was a done deal. When he reached my side, he held out his hand. "They want to talk to you."

"Of course," I replied, but it didn't mean I was going to tell them everything.

When we entered the senator's study, Marcus was perched on the edge of his desk, Andy was sitting in front of it and Gus was pacing the length of the room. The collective gazes that zeroed in on me when we stepped through the doors nearly had me retreating, but Grant's firm hand on my elbow was all the courage I needed.

I smiled tentatively.

Gus Lynch was about to open his mouth when Senator Thorne held up his hand to stop him. "Blaire, please sit," he said.

Grant guided me to the chair. He walked back to the entrance, closed the door, and leaned against it.

"I'm going to be cliché for a second," the senator led in. "To say that this was a big surprise is an understatement. I thought Grant was going to tell me he was getting married."

I glanced at Grant, but his expression was unreadable, he didn't even crack a smile. Okay, this wasn't reassuring. My initial bravado deserted me, and I felt like a lamb being led to the slaughter.

"This link to Russian Organized Crime is troubling," the senator admitted. "But we don't choose our families. What we want to know, my dear, is if you have participated in any way in that business."

I remembered how Grant had stopped Jake from asking me the same question. This time he remained silent by the door, but not a muscle twitched on his face except for a subtle darkening.

"My father brought me along sometimes when I was too young to be left alone, and when there was no one to look after me. The calls mostly came late at night or early in the morning."

"Jesus, how old were you?" the senator asked while Grant cursed. Gus stopped pacing and watched me intently. I couldn't look at Andy.

"My mother died when I was two." I shrugged. "I went with him until I was thirteen." This explained my relative calm around dead bodies.

"And you didn't assist in anyway?" Gus asked.

"What? Like hand him the pliers so he could extract their teeth?" I asked.

"You think this is a joke, Blaire?" Gus snapped.

"I'd watch your tone if I were you," Grant warned his father's aide.

"You asked me if I assisted him. I remember handing him stuff because he was busy trying not to leave evidence behind," I retorted. "You think it's a picnic for me recalling the childhood I had to spend among the casualties of the ROC?" I tapped my temple. "I see it in my head. I hear my father's voice explaining to me why blood is spattered the way it was or how the person was killed. I had to cope, so my father made it into a science project. But as I got older, don't think I didn't see how wrong it was." I took a deep breath. "I was eight-years old when I was pissed at the dead because they made me miss school and I had to skip art class. Years later, when I think back to how I felt, I realized how this had fucked me up so bad."

Andy, who was fidgeting on his phone, looked up. "It said here Yuri died of heart failure."

"They didn't want the police looking into it, probably because they also killed my father."

"You're safe from getting prosecuted for his death," Gus concluded.

"It was self-defense," Grant barked, walking across the room to put his hands on my shoulders. I put my hand on one of his to reassure him I was fine.

"It *was* self-defense," I said. "My conscience is clear on that point."

"That's good," Gus said. "Look, Grant. I have to play devil's advocate here. Blaire is on the run from the Russian mafia and, as much as we want to distance your father's campaign from your relationship with her, it's impossible. Your relationship with her ... is your family's relationship with her. She's not some first or second cousin. She's your girlfriend and, through you, she has direct access to the senator."

"The ROC is not a top priority for the FBI," the senator said. Marcus Thorne was the Vice Chairman of the Senate Intelligence Committee. "It'll be challenging to pull resources to investigate them. Mobs are just hard to dismantle, especially since they've blended so well into the community."

"I'm having my men look into them," Grant said.

"I'd be careful poking into their business, son," the senator replied. "The Russian mafia is known to have ties to the Kremlin. In fact, the Russian government and the oligarchy have used the mafia to do its dirty work. Your business interests in Russia could become vulnerable."

Grant shrugged, as if unconcerned. "I'll tell my men to be careful. If I have to pull out of the Russian market so everyone feels better, I'll do it. I'd just hate to give those fuckers the satisfaction."

"As long as they exist and want Blaire, they could be a threat to this family's safety," Gus said, turning to me. "I'd like to help you, my dear, I really would. We don't want the Thorne family to be a target of the Russian mafia."

"They're nothing like the Italian Mob, though," Andy interjected. "They prefer to do things low-key. The last thing they want is to go after a high-profile target."

"They should have thought about that before they went after my son!" the senator snapped, momentarily losing his cool.

"I'm sorry," I said. I heard Grant mumble something to his dad.

"Grant said you have several flash drives that have a collection of evidence regarding the crime scenes," Gus said. He looked doubtful. "What's on it?"

"Photos, voice recordings, and some videos," I said. "A witness list."

"Okay, that's a start," Gus said. "But what of the other evidence, Blaire? The physical evidence that a forensic lab can process? Without that, photos and recordings are not much to work with."

Of course you'd expect a lawyer to always think like a lawyer in evidentiary support. I was hoping I wouldn't have to mention the self-storage unit yet.

"There's a storage unit ..." my voice trailed off. Grant's hands dropped from my shoulders.

"You didn't mention that to me," he stated flatly.

"It didn't come up," I offered. It was a lame excuse, but that was a big piece of what the ROC was after, their history of crime and violence was stored in an eight by ten space in an industrial lot in Miami.

"So, where is it?" Gus asked.

My lips thinned. "I'm afraid I can't tell you right now." Liam and I didn't know the exact location either, but he was working on it.

There was a smug look on Gus's face. "Grant, I thought you and Blaire were on the same page. What else has she not told you?"

I couldn't look at Grant, but I wasn't even sure he could look at me right now and I was right. He moved to the window of his father's office, probably to stare outside and contemplate his woman who was full of secrets.

"Come on, guys," Andy said. "The poor girl has been on the run for two years. She grew up with the Russian mafia, where it's ingrained at an early age that discussing mob business gets you killed."

I was startled to find an unlikely ally in Andy. With the way Gus turned to glare at his protégé, I was afraid he was going to get himself fired.

I quirked a smile at Andy, barely controlling the urge to grin broadly. He winked at me as if saying, "I got you, girl."

Grant was instantly at my side, but I refused to look at him. As much as I understood where he was coming from, I felt he abandoned me when I needed his support, and it had taken someone I barely knew to give me what he should have.

"When did you suddenly become an expert in the mob, Spencer?" Gus demanded.

"The Godfather and Sopranos," Andy said, deadpan.

"I don't believe this," Grant growled. "You got this clown as my father's political strategist?" He was looking at Gus.

I wanted to smack Grant upside the head. I wanted to yell at him that at least Andy—a total stranger—stood up for me. I was about to get out of my chair and give Grant a good talking to when the senator intervened.

"Grant, Gus. Both of you, stand down," Marcus ordered. "I can't believe that you two couldn't see what was happening here." The senator shook his head. "Andy is right, we can't expect Blaire to tell us everything. I know enough about 'need to know' working the Intelligence Committee." He looked at Andy. "Well played, my man."

Grant shot his father an incredulous look. His father returned his scowl and said, "I'm disappointed in you, son, but that's conversation for another day." Then the senator's eyes landed on me. "Blaire, I'll respect your wish to keep some of your knowledge private. I presume it's to protect someone involved, but the sooner we address the threat to you, the better I'd feel about my family's security."

"Understood, sir," I said.

The meeting broke up soon after that.

Grant and I walked out of that room with a wall between us. It was as if we'd withdrawn to our own corners. The drive home was quiet. He was brooding; I was still smarting from his perceived desertion. When we entered the brownstone, he went directly to the bar and poured himself a drink, then headed to his office and shut the door. I gave him time to stew at whatever it was I did that made him angry. I did not regret omitting the storage unit from my initial interview with Jake Donovan because Liam was on the trail of the person who had access to it and it would be a disaster to have another party involved. After I completed my nightly rituals and Grant had not shown up for bed yet, I decided enough was enough.

I marched directly to his office and flung open the door. His scowl did nothing to faze me; I stepped up right to his desk. "I find a lot of things attractive about you but sulking is not one of them."

"I have nothing to say to you right now, Blaire."

"Is this about the storage unit?"

"No, it's about you keeping things from me that could hurt my family," Grant replied levelly. "I know you're only trying to protect Liam, but how long will you prioritize him over me, Blaire?"

"It's not about who's more important!" I yelled. "It's more about doing the right thing."

Grant shook his head in disgust. "Keep telling yourself that, honey."

Somehow the endearment sounded like an insult and I realized we weren't going to be dissuaded in our beliefs. I got him—I really did—but it wasn't that simple.

He wasn't even looking at me, just typing on his computer. When I hadn't budged, he spared me a glance. "Anything else?"

I wanted to grab the paperweight and launch it at his head. Instead, I said, "I should have known better than to believe your words and promises."

He frowned. "What are you talking about?"

"'No matter what happens, I'm on your side?' Ring a bell?" I scoffed. "Just because your ego was bruised that I didn't tell you everything, you try to punish me with this closed-off version of you. Don't make me regret coming back here."

"That sounds like a threat, sweetheart."

"Yes. Keep telling yourself that, *honey*," I repeated his statement with equal mockery. I didn't wait for his response and left his office.

18

Blaire

I DIDN'T KNOW what time Grant came to bed, but when I woke up, he wasn't beside me. Maybe I was pathetic to feel relieved at seeing the indentation on the pillow and the rumpled sheets that indicated he'd slept beside me. I might have also dreamed the kiss on my forehead, but I was clinging to hope that it was real.

I changed into yoga pants and a sports bra. Working out alleviated stress and Grant was definitely stressing me out with this uncertainty between us. I needed a blast of endorphins. When I shuffled into the kitchen, Collette was taking a tray of biscuits from the oven that smelled heavenly. I mentally rearranged my workout routine. Fat-burning cardio was more effective on an empty stomach, so I was ditching that for lifting weights because I was going to eat first.

I parked my ass on the kitchen island stool as I snuck a piece of bacon in my mouth. I grabbed a still-hot biscuit and dropped it on a small plate. Collette was Grant's French housekeeper and she was a domestic goddess who could give Martha Stewart a run for her money.

"Where's Grant?" I asked, sounding nonchalant.

Collette frowned as if surprised by my question. "He's in New York. He called me early this morning to tell me to be sure to prepare breakfast for you and your security detail."

"Oh." I stared at the steaming biscuit. I knew it was Monday, but he usually left in the afternoons for Manhattan.

"Grant said it was an emergency," the housekeeper explained. Her gentle tone only made me feel worse. Sure it was an emergency. He needed to get away from me. *Being left behind doesn't feel too good now, does it?* A taunting voice said. Karma definitely was a bitch.

I looked up at Collette and forced a smile and then forced myself to take a bite of the biscuit. It burned my tongue, so I swallowed it, but it burned my throat instead. The housekeeper slid a glass of orange juice toward me. The look on her face wasn't exactly pity, but I hated that look, so I continued to stare into space.

I lost the desire for small talk. Tyler and the other security folks came and went from the kitchen. I nodded when they greeted me, but that was all I could muster. I quickly ate my biscuit and more bacon, then I went to the gym in the basement to work off my angst.

ALMOST TWO HOURS LATER, I was done. I killed myself on the squat rack and finished off on the stair machine. I would feel this later. Bent over, leaning on my thighs, my sweat dripped from my forehead to the mat. I felt euphoric. Grant who?

The Fray blasted in my earphones singing *Over My Head* and I bobbed my head to its catchy rhythm. My eyes caught Tyler tapping on the glass door and holding a phone. I didn't have one except the burner Liam left me. My heart jumped. Who else would be calling me?

I wiped the perspiration from my back and walked toward the door. Tyler walked in and handed me the phone. "It's Mrs. Thorne."

"Thanks, Tyler." It looked like today would be a day of forced smiles as I tried to hide my disappointment.

"Amelia, hi."

"Blaire," she said. "Marcus told me."

"Oh." I didn't know what to say.

"I'm also disappointed in my son," she continued. "Why is he in New York?"

"It's Monday and business as usual," I replied.

"Oh, Blaire," she commiserated while calling Grant some names I hadn't heard before. And then she started making excuses for him, as if trying to convince me not to give up on him. "Men can be so funny about their pride, especially these Thorne men. Sometimes you have to have the patience of a saint. They usually get out of their funk in a day or three. Marcus was the same way when he was younger."

"I have to commend the senator for being open-minded yesterday."

"Well, Marcus took a lot of work in the beginning," Amelia confided with a smile in her voice. "Tell you what? Why don't we meet for coffee and shopping?"

"Amelia, I'm kind of on lockdown."

"We've got my security and yours, we'll be fine."

"Amelia, I don't think—"

"Listen, Blaire. If I let every security threat dictate how I live my life, I'm letting the bad guys win."

"My situation is different. Something already happened to your son and people have come after me. It's not a threat, Amelia, it's become a reality."

"Hold on, dear," Amelia started talking to someone else. After a few minutes, she said, "Morris, my bodyguard, said they have vetted several restaurants in town. And by vetted, they know the background of every employee working there and will do a sweep before we walk in."

Wow. It was almost like security for a president.

"So, lunch?"

I was actually looking forward to some kind of normal.

"I'll tell Tyler."

I EMERGED from the gym and handed Tyler the phone. "I'm meeting Amelia for lunch. They're still working out which restaurant." Not waiting for his reply, I made my way up the steps to go to the main house.

"Does Mr. Thorne know?"

"Grant? He's in New York. I don't see why this should concern him."

"He left specific instructions that you weren't to leave the house."

I ignored Tyler, feeling a twinge of guilt because he was only doing his job, but pissed at Grant that he could think to tuck me away somewhere and go his merry way.

"Ms. Callahan," Tyler called when I was halfway through the kitchen. I exhaled a long-suffering sigh so I didn't end up yelling at the poor guy. It wasn't his fault he felt like one of my captors.

"Work it out with Amelia's security team and then contact Grant and Jake," I told him. "Agreeing to be held a prisoner in this house wasn't a part of any deal I struck with your boss." Maybe if he'd hung around and discussed it with me, I'd be more reasonable.

"We're on radio-silence right now," Tyler informed me in turn. "That's why Mr. Thorne hasn't called you. He's working with a security specialist regarding our servers to make sure they're compliant to the highest encryption and protection."

"He couldn't give instructions from here?"

"Mr. Thorne is a hands-on guy with certain things," Tyler said. "The majority of our servers are in New York."

"What are you not telling me?"

My bodyguard cut a side-glance before looking straight at me. "It's not my place to say and, in my personal opinion, I think Mr. Thorne should have talked to you himself. I think he's foreseeing this business with the Russian mafia getting ugly and he's shoring up his defenses where he could."

"Because I couldn't tell him everything," I concluded.

"Not judging, Ms. Callahan," Tyler said. "But we need to be on the same page and soon. We need to know everything that the mob wants from you so we can protect it and use it for leverage."

"I understand," I said. I would talk to Liam soon. "I'll see if Amelia will take a rain check."

———————

IT TURNED out Amelia Thorne was a force to be reckoned with when she showed up at Grant's house and whisked me away to a tiny Italian restaurant, Pepito's, in Boston's North End. It was a family restaurant and the owner was a childhood friend of the senator. Our security was camped out in the back alley and the entrance. Tyler and Morris, a member of the senator's security team, were sitting at a table beside us.

Pepito himself took our orders and suggested a bottle of Barolo to go with our meal. After our bread basket arrived, Amelia gushed about the grassy and peppery notes of our olive oil dip. When our server was out of earshot though, she assessed me with a thoughtful look and asked, "How are you holding up, dear?"

"Surprisingly well." My conversation with Tyler helped alleviate some of the angst Grant caused me when he left for New York without a word to me. That was an issue to settle face-to-face with him.

"When Marcus told me this morning about the late-night meeting in his study, I immediately called Grant," Amelia said. "I know my son. It took a lot for him not to relieve me of my guilt for sending him to that gala and getting him mugged."

I blanched. "Grant never told me that you sent him to the gala."

"He knew I would learn the truth soon enough, he didn't want you to harbor guilt over letting me feel responsible, knowing he'd clear it up soon."

I buried my face in my hands. "Oh, my God. I'm so sorry, Amelia."

Her hand peeled mine away from my face. "Look at me, Blaire."

"I don't know why you're so nice to me," I said when I finally returned her gaze.

"People have short memories, but I don't," Amelia said. "And neither does Marcus. You saved my son's life once upon a time, Blaire.

It was barely nine months ago, but it seems Gus has forgotten that. What do you think Marcus would prefer? To win the senate race or to have his son alive and well?"

"But I've put your entire family in danger."

"Ever since Marcus entered politics we've received all kinds of threats," Amelia said. "Don't get me wrong, I can be very protective of my family, but I know Marcus and Grant are too alpha to be coddled. It's Valerie I'm most concerned about since she keeps eluding her security team, it's a wonder Marcus has not restricted her movements."

"Has she been made aware of the new threats from the ROC?"

"Yes," Amelia replied. "She's not happy." She sighed. "I know she's giving you a hard time, but don't think it's you. She's possessive of her brother."

"Grant said he spoiled her."

"Did he tell you what happened when she was younger?"

"The near-drowning? Yes."

Amelia's face sobered. "Thorne men take responsibility seriously and they carry guilt for a very long time."

I merely nodded. Besides that time at the log cabin, there were two other times I'd awakened to Grant's nightmares of Val's drowning.

"Did he tell you he'd been mad at his sister right before she fell off the sailboat?"

My brows furrowed. "No. He just said they'd encountered rough waters and everything went wrong after that."

"Grant wanted to help his dad secure the boat, but Valerie wouldn't stop crying. He lost his temper with his little sister as only a fifteen-year-old boy could. Grant admitted to me he had said pretty hurtful things, ordered his sister to stay in the interior cabin, and left her to help control the sailboat. Val followed him right up, lost her balance, and fell overboard. The waves ripped the life jacket off her."

"Grant said he was the one who put the vest on her," I murmured, feeling a surge of compassion for the boy he had been, for the guilt

he'd harbored all these years. And for Val—what a traumatic experience for such a young girl.

"That's why his guilt is three-fold," Amelia explained. "Val barely
remembers anything, but for Grant, everything—including the
scathing words he said to his sister—is forever etched in his
memory."

A thought occurred to me. "Is that why Grant shuts down when
he's angry?"

Amelia sighed. "Yes. Grant has my grandfather's Irish temper.
Very passionate and quick to anger. After that incident with Valerie,
Grant found a way to keep it all inside but the result is avoidance and
shutting people out which, unfortunately, is a trait he got from
Marcus." She sighed again. "It's a good and a bad thing. Good in that
he won't say words that can never be unsaid. Bad that unless that
anger dissipates on its own, it will only build and the explosion could
be just as bad, if not worse."

"Marcus told me that Grant wasn't happy when he found out
you'd left out information." Amelia pursed her lips. "And now he's off
to New York when you've just returned. He's shutting you out,
isn't he?"

I didn't answer. I was sure Amelia meant well, but I felt she was
getting too intrusive into my relationship with Grant.

She must have sensed my uneasiness and laughed. "Goodness,
I'm getting too meddlesome, aren't I?"

I smiled wryly and nodded.

Her eyes sparked merrily. "Oh, well, I understand. I promise I
won't be a troublesome mother-in-law."

"Amelia," I groaned. "Stop. You're making me nervous."

"All right," Grant's mother relented. "We need to get you and
Valerie together though."

My eyes narrowed warily.

"Grant means well, but he's going about this the wrong way,"
Amelia explained. "He needs to take himself out of the equation."

"Are you suggesting Val and I spend time together by ourselves?" I
asked incredulously. That was a terrible idea.

"Well, not exactly. I'll be with you at first," Amelia said. "I'm not blind to my daughter's shortcomings. She's headstrong and willful, not to mention an adrenaline junkie, and has given us a heart attack one too many times. But one thing I can't deny is how much she loves her brother. She's convinced that no woman will be good enough for Grant. It's unfortunate she thinks that every woman is just after her brother's money."

"And you think spending time with me will convince her otherwise?" I challenged.

"Do you know why she's especially hostile to you?"

I shook my head.

"It was her fault Grant nearly died in that snowstorm and you saved him."

"Shouldn't she be thankful instead though?"

"Maybe she would have been if Grant had not fallen for you," Amelia tried to explain her illogical assumption. "But Grant nearly dying because of her has righted the scales in her mind. Not that she had ever pulled that guilt card on her brother, but it has always colored the way their relationship has developed ever since her near-drowning. Now comes this woman who has saved her brother's life. How can she compete with that?"

"But it's not a competition!"

"That is why both of you need to spend time with each other without Grant."

I was still doubtful, but there was a bigger priority. "I think I need to figure out my relationship with your son first."

She smiled warmly. "Of course. I do have one more question and I want you to be honest."

"Okay." My tone was tentative.

"Do you love my son?"

I did, but Grant deserved to know first before anyone else. The server brought out our food, which gave me some reprieve, but Amelia continued to look at me expectantly and made no move to serve, so I knew it was no empty question.

"I care for Grant very much, but we haven't discussed our feelings yet," I replied as honestly as I could. "You see, I never thought he could be mine. I do think I love him, but whatever we feel for each other, it's between him and me."

Grant's mother nodded, but there was a tightening around her lips that told me she wasn't satisfied with my answer. "I've never seen my son behave this way around a woman before, so I'm very hopeful that he's found the one." Amelia scooped a healthy serving of pasta alla vodka onto her plate and urged me to do the same, handing me the fork. "I like you a lot, Blaire." She sniffed. "But if you hurt him in any way, you'll see the wrath of this southern momma."

I had to grin at her last statement.

"I'm not kidding." She glared at me, but it held no heat. She smiled and shrugged. Oh, the threat was there and I didn't doubt it, it was only softened by her southern charm.

The rest of our lunch progressed to less sensitive, but no less important topics.

Like shoes.

19

Blaire

"WHERE ARE YOU?" I asked Liam when I got hold of him later that afternoon.

"What's going on, Blaire?" My friend ignored my question, so I knew he wasn't comfortable revealing his location.

"I had to tell them about the storage unit." I heard a muffled curse, crackling, and then sounds of shuffling like he was moving to a different position.

"Why?" Liam asked after a while and the signal was clearer.

"The senator's political advisor questioned the evidence we had and said we had to have supporting physical evidence for it to stick."

"True, but even that's no guarantee. A good lawyer can have all the evidence thrown out. I know the inner workings of Orlov's mind. You killed his son. He wants you executed in front of him, which tells me the people who went after us in the motel were acting on orders of someone who didn't want the evidence leaked. There's also been chatter that Orlov executed one of his lieutenants for defying his orders, which supports my theory. That failed mugging of Grant had brought the Boston Russian gang unwanted scrutiny and in turn, the ROC. Either they'll back off or move quickly."

"Shit," I muttered. "We need to get to that storage unit fast."

"I'm working on it."

What I had not told Grant that although we knew the general location of the self-storage facility, we weren't sure which exact unit it was. My father was careful not to put his eggs in one basket so to speak. For two years, we thought the evidence in the flash drive was useless because Orlov destroyed all the physical evidence after he'd executed my father. It was only in January when Liam had been tipped off that we might have been misled. It turned out that my father managed to give the storage unit key to another federal agent who was working undercover unbeknownst to Liam. He'd gone rogue as well after all those DEA agents had been assassinated in Mexico.

"So you got a lock on your target?" I asked.

"I have him."

A chill skated up my spine. "Do we know which agency he used to work for?"

"He wouldn't say. I don't care at this point."

"Liam," I cleared my throat. "Don't do anything irrevocable."

He grunted. "Listen, Blaire. I need to go."

"Liam ..."

The line went dead.

I stared at my phone, frustrated with my inability to help him. We were a good team. We survived on the run. Liam had trained me on guns, physical combat, and how to work surveillance. I was supposed to be helping him, not sitting in a luxury brownstone twiddling my thumbs, stressing about my relationship with my boyfriend. I hated that my existence had been reduced to this. My love for Grant had turned me into this helpless person surrounded by bodyguards. This wasn't me.

"NOT HUNGRY?"

Colette's voice broke through my riotous thoughts. After my conversation with Liam, I'd been fighting a push-pull with my conscience. On one side was everything I had with Grant including my talk with Amelia about not hurting her son, and on the other was my loyalty to Liam. Even if my friend insisted I was better off with Grant, I knew I could help him. I didn't like how Liam sounded in our last phone call. He sounded reckless.

"I had a big lunch." This was partly true, but I felt bad that I was pushing around the aromatic Coq au Vin that Colette had prepared. I forced myself to eat a forkful. The flavor burst in my mouth, but my stomach was so twisted in knots that it prevented the food from going down well.

"Oh, that's unfortunate," the housekeeper said as she polished the countertop, the last chore she usually did before she went home. I could feel her gaze on me, so I put another piece in my mouth. "Blaire, if you need to talk to someone, I'm here."

I gave a shaky laugh. "Do I look that pathetic?"

"No, not pathetic," Colette said gently. "Lost, maybe. That day you left. The day you were supposed to meet Mr. Thorne at the airport, you have that same look right now. I'm glad you came back because Mr. Thorne wasn't doing well without you. He was functioning, but not living, you know?"

Shit! Colette was only making my already confused mind more confused.

"Don't leave him again, Blaire. He needs you." With a sad smile, as if she knew the war in my head, she left.

Not five minutes after, the door to the garage opened and Tyler walked through and he was smiling. He had a device in his hand.

"Our secure phones just arrived via courier," he informed me. "Boss wants to talk to you."

A whoosh left my lungs and, with it, the slew of negative emotions that had taken root since this morning. I took the phone from Tyler and held it to my ear.

"Grant?" I said softly.

"God, baby, I'm so sorry for leaving the way I did this morning," he muttered.

"Yeah, it was kinda shitty."

"I didn't mean to put you through that shit," he said. "I fully expected our new phones to be ready by the time I got to New York so I could have them couriered over immediately. I had a communications expert look at the configuration and she found some vulnerabilities. She installed the fixes, so we're kosher."

"Grant, are you not coming back tonight?"

A deep breath exhaled from his end. "No. There's been a snag with several real estate acquisitions in Brazil and Russia that was only brought to my attention this morning. We're at a crucial stage of negotiations right now and I promised the board I was giving it my full attention. I should wrap up in a few days."

"Okay," I said, deeply disappointed.

"I miss you, Blaire," he said. "I wish you were here, but I couldn't spend any time with you and ... I can't afford the distraction." He chuckled ruefully. "When you're near, all I want is to bury myself deep inside you."

I shivered at his words.

"Look," he continued. "I was still mad at you this morning. I also didn't want to wake you because I enjoyed those few moments of peace watching you sleep when we were not at odds with each other."

"You can't just freeze me out when you're pissed at me."

"That's how I deal with ... stuff."

A female voice spoke in the background and I tensed.

"Hold on," Grant said as he talked to the person in the background. There was a hearty laughter and then he returned to the phone. "I need to go, baby. A couple of us are heading out to dinner and then we're getting back to work for a late night. I'll call you again tonight if I can."

I berated myself for feeling suspicious of my man. Of course he was an equal opportunity employer and he had female employees working for him, but the woman who spoke did not sound like his

PA, Heather. Isolation was making me suspicious, and what was that they said about an idle mind?

Now would be a good time to pick up the paintbrush again.

THREE HOURS AFTER DINNER, I stopped painting and put down my brush. My memory of Cape Cod held no inspiration to put on canvas. I stared at the varying shades of pigment on my palette. My colors were prosaic, the blue of the ocean, flat.

THE SUMMER when I was twelve, a man named Sergei stayed in our house. He was an artist who used the impressionist technique. School was out and I was his shadow as he mentored me on the pros and cons of using different mediums, but his specialty was oil. We became good friends. I imagined him as the master and I was his protégé. He returned the same time every year and would stay for three months at a time. When Sergei returned the year I turned sixteen, he'd become gaunt and seemed to have aged ten years. We still painted together, but he seemed pre-occupied with something else. One night, I couldn't sleep and saw light under the door to his room. I heard him working furiously. I knocked. The brush strokes stopped, then he opened the door and sighed in resignation.

"Come in, Paulina, we have a new lesson."

I stared at the familiar artwork propped against the wall of his room and on his easel. "Is that a Picasso?" I asked incredulously. He was painting over it! There was also what looked like a Jackson Pollock drip painting.

For the rest of that summer, he taught me how to camouflage paintings with different mediums, particularly with watercolor, given that they were easy to wash off. I wasn't naive. I knew those paintings were from a heist and they planned to smuggle it somewhere. My Papa wasn't pleased that Sergei had taught me that craft. That was the last summer that I saw Sergei.

I MULLED over whether I had committed a crime when he taught me to how mask a painting over a painting. After agonizing it over for twenty minutes, I decided it was no different than if I googled it and learned it on YouTube. He didn't actually give me the brush to paint over the artwork, but I'd practiced the technique over my own paintings, fascinated by the process. Did that mean I had the blood of a criminal in my veins? Troubled, I walked over to the garage to make better use of my uninspired time. Before I even made it to the stairwell leading to the security team's quarters, Tyler was hastening down the steps.

"Anything wrong, Ms. Callahan?" he asked, worry creasing his forehead.

"I need a sparring partner."

"Come again?"

"I couldn't sleep. I need to work off this excess energy."

"It's ten."

"So?"

"You spent two hours in the gym this morning."

"If you're afraid to spar with a gal like me, maybe some of the other guys will," I taunted. In my assessment, Tyler was six feet and two-hundred pounds of solid muscle compared to my five-seven, one-hundred and thirty-pound frame, but Liam had taught me moves to even the odds. For me to defend myself successfully, it was about speed and using my opponent's momentum against him.

A ghost of a smile stole over Tyler's mouth. "Wait for me at the gym."

I wore shorts and an exercise bra. Barefoot, I started warming up by doing kinetic stretches. Afterward, I tested my speed by doing a series of fast kicks. Tyler walked in with a smile on his face.

"You sure about this?" he asked.

I hopped from foot to foot and held out both hands and signaled him to come and get me. His smile turned into a smirk and I couldn't wait to wipe it off his face. We put on some head protection.

Tyler's first mistake was hesitating. He chased me around the mat, and threw out a punch, but I ducked and moved closer and hit him with my elbow, then I sprang out of his reach. Tyler shook his head and came at me again. For the second time, he hesitated and when he threw a left jab, I turned so my back was against his front and his left arm was over my right shoulder. I grabbed that arm, and using his forward momentum, I bent and flipped us over with me landing on top of him.

"Fuck!" Tyler choked out. I leapt up and away from him and bounced on the balls of my feet.

"Had enough?" I asked sweetly.

"You're in for it now, sugar," he murmured as he dropped all formality, sprang to his feet, and went after me.

Tyler put his mind to it and he kicked my ass, but I got in my fair share of punches and kicks. I even managed to throw him over my hip once. We started to get tired and I started laughing. It was hard to laugh and spar, especially when you were almost out of breath. Tyler and I were in an armlock, with me clinging to him like a monkey and him trying to shake me off when one of the new security guys walked in.

We broke apart, still laughing and breathing heavily.

"What's up, man?" Tyler asked.

"Boss on the phone for Ms. Callahan."

"Thanks," I accepted the smartphone then turned to Tyler. "Had a great time, Tyler. We need a re-match." He chuckled and gave me a wink.

"Hey," I spoke into the phone. I was still panting and it felt like my pulse was in my throat.

Silence.

I looked at the phone to see if we got disconnected. The seconds were moving.

"Grant?"

"What were you doing with Tyler?" The tone and manner of his question left no question that he was seething.

"We were sparring."

"Sparring," he repeated.

"Yes, I was practicing my self-defense skills."

"He had his hands on you?"

"Jesus, Grant, how am I supposed to throw him over? With my thumb?"

"Did I or did I not tell you that I had problems with Tyler being near you? I had no choice because you needed a bodyguard and now you let him touch you?"

"He's a bodyguard, Grant. Get used to it. *He guards bodies*," I stressed those last three words with sarcasm. He needed to rein in his unfounded jealousy. "If he had to protect me, his hands will be on me to push me out of danger." Then I caught myself. *Why am I explaining this?* "Are we actually having this ridiculous conversation?"

He sighed. "I wanted to talk to you earlier tonight, but Rafe, the manager of Thorne Real Estate needed me on some bullshit meeting. The company selling the commercial property is playing games. We're at a stalemate and I was so frustrated because I could have been talking to you. I called Tyler instead, and this new guy answered saying he was in the gym wrestling with you."

"Ugh, we weren't wrestling. We were doing mixed-martial arts."

"Tell me at least that you were wearing ugly sweats."

My sigh was answer enough.

"What are you wearing?" Grant growled.

"You know, with the mood you're in, I'm taking the fifth."

"With the mood I'm in, I have half a mind to drive two hundred miles tonight, fuck you until morning, and then drag you all the way back with me to Manhattan."

"Grant, you need some sleep. You're tired and cranky."

"Blaire, answer the question."

"Shorts and an exercise bra okay?" I yelled, exasperated.

Grant swore softly.

"Well?" I prompted, my adrenaline still fueling my annoyance. "Cat got your tongue?"

He chuckled, but I had a feeling it wasn't from mirth.

"Yeah, my tongue wants nothing more than to be buried deep in your pussy."

"Ahhh, gahhh!" I exclaimed. "Grant Thorne, I'm hanging up now. Go to sleep and take a chill pill."

I swiped to end the call, left the gym, and marched to my bedroom. Taking a long hot shower, I barely had the arm strength to dry my hair. My muscles were achy from all my workouts that day. Ugh, what it took to manage my Grant frustrations. I didn't even change out of my robe. I dropped into the mattress face first and fell blissfully asleep.

SOMETIME BETWEEN MIDNIGHT AND DAWN, I awoke with a start. I felt eyes on me, and I almost screamed when I saw a shadow rise from the couch at the foot of the bed.

"It's me."

Grant.

My relief was palpable. "How?"

He didn't say anything but slipped into bed beside me. He drew me close and started touching me, kissing me. I hungrily returned his caresses. I missed him. I missed us.

"You're so wet for me," he grunted against my mouth as his fingers brushed against my core. "You make me lose my mind, Blaire. I can't function with this distance between us." He made me come on his fingers before he hauled me up and took me hard against the headboard. When I climaxed a second time, he released inside me, groaning my name with an ache in his voice. I could barely raise my head when he eased me down from the headboard. He tucked me under the covers and left the bed.

Drifting off to sleep, I heard myself ask. "Where are you going?"

I didn't hear his answer.

20

Blaire

IF IT WEREN'T for the evidence between my legs, I would have sworn Grant's pre-dawn visit was a dream. I wasn't sure either if the soreness I felt was from my exercise yesterday or from the roughness with which he fucked me. Maybe it was a combination of both.

Taking in the state of the sheets, one would think a wrestling match occurred on the bed. I forced myself to get up and stripped off the bedding. A piece of paper fell to the floor. And like an old woman who was having trouble moving, I bent to pick up the paper.

On it, six words were scrawled.

"Never hang up on me again."

Anger ratcheted up inside me. I crumpled the note and hurled it into the trash bin, then I walked into the shower to wash Grant off me.

When I got to the kitchen, Colette had breakfast ready as usual, but I was surprised to see Jake drinking coffee and reading the newspaper. Had Grant not left for New York? I was hopeful, but at the same time I was ready to have a knuckle-dragging match with him.

"Where's Grant?" I asked his head of security.

"He's in New York," Jake told me. At my confused look, he added. "He took Tyler with him." His face was bland, so I wasn't sure what his thoughts were. Well, he could be sure of mine.

"What. The. Fuck?" I cried, startling Colette. I yanked out my phone and started to call him when Jake fished it out of my fingers. "What the fuck?" This time this was directed at him.

"Cut him some slack," Jake said coldly. "We drove from New York to Boston at midnight. That was a three-hour drive that should've taken us three and a half. It was a wonder we didn't wreck. He's in the middle of a security upgrade, which, by the way, is because of your issues and is also in the midst of a multimillion dollar deal the company could lose because Mr. Thorne's focus is elsewhere."

That threw water over my anger, but didn't quite eliminate it. I exhaled heavily. "Okay."

"I don't know what happened between you two, but I tried my best to calm him down before he entered the house," Jake said. "He hasn't had any sleep because he insisted on driving last night. At least he let Tyler drive him back to Manhattan this morning. He needs to keep a clear head for these next few days, Blaire. Can you give that to him?"

There was only one word I could push through my teeth that morning. "Okay."

THE NEXT THREE days was an exercise in keeping my cool. Liam was still off the grid. I agreed not to leave the house, so I'd been working out my frustration in the gym because the restrictions stymied my creativity as an artist. With nothing to do, I'd become an online stalker. I was thirsty for news of him, for glimpses of him, and how he was coping with the Galleria development that I've heard was a big story on Wall Street. Instead, I found photos of Grant sitting in various Manhattan cafes and restaurants with the same woman—an ex-girlfriend.

The headlines were screaming of a reconciliation.

> Tech genius, Kylie Peterson, found cozying up to ex-boyfriend, business magnate Grant Thorne. For the fourth day in a row, the couple have been seen together at some of the trendiest Manhattan restaurants. Ms. Peterson, the brains behind KP Computing—a subsidiary of Thorne Industries, said their relationship was purely business. However, sources say Ms. Peterson was seen leaving Thorne's penthouse late yesterday evening. Could they be negotiating a more personal relationship after hours?

"You should stop reading that garbage," Jake said behind me. "Ms. Peterson is testing the security of our servers. She's been working round the clock on it and had to drop all her high-priority projects to do that."

Not even embarrassed at being caught, I left the screen where it was and turned to face him. "He has time to have lunch and dinner with her, but he couldn't spare five minutes to call me?" Or send even a single text?

"You know that call isn't going to last only five minutes," Jake said. "You two have a lot to work out. And I sure hope Mr. Thorne can wrap up his business today because Tyler said he's been hell to work for."

"Is Tyler okay?"

Jake smiled. "He'll be fine. Just needs to get a thicker skin."

"He didn't do anything wrong," I argued. "*We* didn't do anything wrong."

He sighed. "I know, but Mr. Thorne is still figuring out what to do with you."

"What do you mean?"

"You're a game changer for him, Blaire. At the moment, I think you're bad for business." Jake chuckled when I scowled at him. "But the times I see him with you, I think you're the best thing that ever happened to him."

"Why, Mr. Donovan, is that actually a compliment?"

He smirked. "It is, but don't let it go to your head."

THAT EVENING, I dressed with excitement. Grant was coming home. He was flying in at seven and Jake had already left to pick him up. We were meeting him at a trendy restaurant in the Boston North End to celebrate the successful acquisition of a five-hundred-million-dollar property in Moscow—the Galleria Development. Amelia was picking me up first and then Valerie. The senator would join us at the restaurant since he had a late afternoon meeting with his advisors that was running a little over.

Colette had already left, and I was pacing the living room waiting on the car. There was a fluttering in my stomach, an anxiety I couldn't quell. I chalked it up to almost three days of not talking to Grant or Liam. I needed some closure on one of the unknowns plaguing my life.

I heard a car pull up the driveway and one of the new security guys called me on the intercom.

I left the house and saw Morris holding the door open to the Bentley. Amelia was inside, smiling at me.

"You look beautiful, Blaire," she said, noting my red lace over black satin sheathe number. The Spanish-influenced dress dipped in the back, exposing enough skin without being tacky. I wasn't wearing a bra and I felt no guilt that I was using all my assets to blast through the wall Grant erected between us.

Getting in beside his mother, and grabbing my seat belt, I smiled. "Thanks, and you look gorgeous as usual, Amelia."

"Now that we're done with the mutual admiration," she paused and smiled widely. "Are you looking forward to seeing Grant?"

"I am," I said. Amelia had been a great source of support during Grant's radio silence. She'd come over for tea in the afternoons, making excuses that she liked Colette's teacakes, but I think she was trying to distract me while her son had to do whatever was needed in Manhattan. I enjoyed her company, and she managed to keep my mind off this festering issue between Grant and me, which I was determined to resolve before the night was through. Now if only Liam would call me.

The vehicle pulled into traffic and headed to Harvard to pick up Valerie.

"It's been a crazy few days," Grant's mother observed.

"Yes, it has." I had googled news of the deal and there were a lot of speculations about the different entities interested in acquiring the mixed-use properties included in the real estate deal. A powerful Russian oligarch was the lead competitor against Thorne Real Estate.

"I'm glad that's over." The words barely left Amelia's lips when the bottom of the car jolted.

An explosion deafened my ears, yet screams pierced my head.

The world tilted on its axis, until it didn't.

Pain pounded all around me, and then I felt numb.

I stared confused at all the blood covering Amelia's face, while horror set in.

21

Blaire

I ESCAPED WITH A FEW SCRATCHES ... not even a bump on the head. But Amelia, *oh my God*, Amelia was in terrible shape. She hadn't been wearing her seatbelt and got tossed around when the Bentley flipped. No one could explain what had happened. The security vehicle following us mentioned seeing an explosion, and I was sure I heard one. But aside from a flat rear tire, there were no signs of a device. It was as if a strong wind lifted the Bentley and pitched it. The majority of the damage to the car appeared to be from the rollover.

I watched them load Amelia onto the gurney and into an ambulance. Morris got in beside her, and I wanted to as well, but the EMT blocked me. They said they were taking her to Massachusetts General Hospital. I nodded, still in a daze. The driver of the Bentley had a concussion and was loaded into another ambulance. Only Morris and I were unscathed. The rest of the senator's security team followed the ambulance and seemed to have forgotten me.

I stood there, looking lost, and realized I didn't have my wristlet. It was somewhere in the mangled vehicle. A Boston cop put an emergency mylar blanket around me and asked if I needed anything.

"Can you take me to the hospital? Where they took Mrs. Thorne?" Most of the first responders had recognized Amelia and were quick to give her assistance. None of the cops even bothered asking me questions about what happened. Morris did all the talking.

The cop smiled at me. "Sure, lady. Come on."

I'D BEEN SITTING in the emergency room waiting area for more than twenty minutes. Morris sat across from me. I could feel the rage flowing off him in waves and they were directed at me.

"Did you manage to call the senator?" I asked tentatively.

"What do you think?" he snapped.

"Morris—"

"This happened because of you," he said in a low accusing voice.

"I don't ..." my voice faltered. I didn't know what to say. I was frightened for Amelia.

The ER doors slid open and the senator, Grant, and Valerie entered in a rush, followed by Gus and Andy and a host of other men in suits. Their security details, I presumed, because Jake was among them. Morris stood and headed for the senator who went straight to triage. My eyes were glued to Grant and I saw relief in his eyes. I got up from my chair, my legs wobbly, but I managed to move toward him. But something changed from my one step to the next. Grant's eyes turned flat and his face shuttered.

"It's all your fault!" Valerie shrieked as she charged me.

Grant hooked his arm around her waist, holding her back. "Val!"

"No. You brought her into our lives," she screamed, still trying to get to me. "And now Mom is dying!"

I could only shake my head. "I'm sorry." I looked at Grant, but his eyes were dead, even as mine filled with tears. "Grant—"

"You need to leave." His words cut right through the heart of me.

"You heard him. Get out of here!" Val continued squirming in her brother's arms, her fingers clawing out like they wanted to tear me to pieces. There was no need—I was already shredded inside.

"Christ," Grant muttered. He handed Val to Jake and stalked toward me. There was only anger on his face and I wanted the ground to swallow me up. He grabbed my bicep. "You can't be here, Blaire." He turned to Jake. "Find Tyler and tell him to take Ms. Callahan home."

"You'll let me know as soon as—" I started.

"Dammit, Blaire, I can't do this right now," Grant growled. "Look at Dad." He pointed to the senator who had collapsed into a chair; his face buried in his hands. "My family is falling apart." *Because of you* was unsaid, but I could feel the condemnation in his words. "Now leave!"

He let me go with a shove toward the exit and turned his back on me, heading to his father. I stood there, unsure of what to do. *Do I wait for Tyler here?* I fidgeted from side to side and flinched when I caught Valerie's glare. She had calmed down, but Jake was still holding her back. I could feel eyes on me and all of them were hostile. All, except one pair—Andy's. He walked to my side and cupped my elbow.

"Let's go, Blaire."

I left the ER and I left Grant behind.

Only that time, he'd asked, no, told me to leave.

———

"Are you sure you don't want to wait for Tyler to take you home?" Andy asked. We'd been walking along the perimeter of the hospital. I felt so suffocated inside the ER, I needed to walk for a while and Andy kept me company.

"I couldn't take all the accusing eyes anymore," I whispered. "We're over—Grant and I. I could feel it. What happened to Amelia was the final straw."

"Don't jump to conclusions," Andy advised. "It could be white supremacists. Emotions are high and raw right now and you are an easy target for the blame."

"I know, and I can't fault any of them for feeling that way, but I didn't ask for this. I told Grant I was a bad bet. I know I don't have the right to be mad at him. His mother is in critical condition." I suppressed a sob that threatened to escape. "But he made me hope," I choked. "He gave me hope that we were going to make it."

"Hey," Andy nudged me. "Stop that. There's always hope, Blaire."

I wiped the tears from my face. Looking up the night sky, I shook my head. "Every hope I have is for Amelia to make it. I keep none for myself," I turned to look at my one and only friend at the moment. "Can you take me back to Grant's place?"

"You're leaving, aren't you?" Andy said.

I understood what he meant. I was packing my things and leaving Grant for good.

"Yes," I answered. "Even if it turns out to be white supremacists, I can see now how my link to the ROC will always come between us." Misery burned my eyes again. "I'll need your number, so I can find out how Amelia is doing. God, I hope she'll be fine."

We walked to the parking lot and reached Andy's car. "It's okay to change your mind, you know," he said, glancing at the ER entrance.

"I shouldn't have come back," I said with regret. "Now I'm sure of it."

We were about to get into the vehicle when a black van screeched behind us. The side door slid open and three men in ski masks jumped out.

"Run!" I screamed as I kicked the first man who came at me. My damned dress restricted my movements and I only caught his thigh.

"Blaire!" Andy yelled as he tried to punch the man who confronted him.

My assailant was huge and as he reached toward me, I scooted under his arm and elbowed him. He grunted and shook off my strike. "Run, Andy!"

I heard a muffled pop and, to my horror, Andy crumpled to the ground. "No!" I couldn't have a death on my conscience in addition to Amelia's injuries.

I gave up the struggle.

On everything.

Just take me and kill me.

I'm already dead inside anyway.

Everyone will be better off.

"Time to go home, Paulina." My captor spoke in Russian. I felt a needle prick my skin and I welcomed the drug. Maybe I wouldn't wake up.

I'm tired of running.

These were my last thoughts before blackness claimed me.

22

Grant

GRANT WATCHED his father sink to a chair as the neurosurgeon left them. His mother was out of surgery. She was going to be fine. Their group had been moved to a special waiting room away from the general one because reporters started showing up. They'd been in their own private hell for four hours. *Christ.*

The epidural hematoma was not as serious as first diagnosed although they did have to perform surgery to relieve pressure to the brain.

"Thank God. Thank God," the senator muttered. Grant had a hand on his father's shoulder and his other arm around Val who was quietly crying in relief. He had to be the rock for his father and sister, so he had blocked out Blaire's anguished face. He could imagine the guilt she was carrying, but he couldn't go to her, not when his family needed him more. He didn't even remember his words to her in the ER. He'd been lost in the horrifying possibility that he could lose his mother because he had chosen to fall in love with Blaire. He couldn't deal with her too.

"Hey, she's going to be okay now, Val," Grant murmured as he kissed the top of his sister's head.

"Oh, Teddy, I thought we were going to lose her for sure."

"She's a fighter," the senator said, reaching out to Val. Grant handed his sister to his dad. His mother was not out of critical condition yet because of the probability of complications, and there was a possibility she may require a secondary operation. She was in recovery right now. As they waited to see her, he knew he needed to call Blaire and let her know his mother was out of surgery and the prognosis was good. It wasn't a smart idea for her to come to the hospital just yet, not when he had no clue where his father's head was regarding his woman. Val—he knew without a doubt how she felt about Blaire, but he'd handle that soon enough. They weren't sure if it was the ROC or the neo Nazis who were responsible. It could even have been a freak accident.

He frowned when he stepped into the hallway to see cops crawling about in the waiting room. His dad's security detail was guarding their private room, but his men were nowhere in sight.

"Morris, what's going on?" *All those cops can't be here regarding Mom's accident, can they?*

"There's been an incident in the parking lot. Andy was shot."

"What? How?" *Goddammit. Why?*

Morris nodded to where Jake was fast approaching, face grim.

"Donovan, what the fuck is going on?" Grant met his head of security halfway. "I heard Andy was shot." His eyes zeroed in on Tyler who was talking to a Boston cop and his blood iced. "What's Tyler doing here?" he growled. "I told you to have him take Blaire home. Who's. With. Blaire?"

"Mr. Thorne ..." Jake hesitated.

Grant backed away from him, the distressed look on his man's face sent a riff of foreboding up his spine. "No," he whispered. His mind balked at what Jake's eyes were telling him. "Fuck! No." He swallowed hard. "Tell me."

Jake blew out a breath. "Morris saw Blaire leave with Andy, so when Tyler came into the ER to take her home, he went outside to look for them. He was too far away when he saw what happened. A black van stopped behind Andy's car. Three men jumped out. One of them shot Andy."

"And Blaire?" Grant asked, his chest tightening as his breathing fractured.

"They took her, Mr. Thorne," Jake said. He sighed heavily. "I'm sorry."

Grant leaned against the wall, blood draining from his head as fear for Blaire coiled in his gut. However, something wasn't adding up. "When did this happen? Just now?"

"Three hours ago."

"Blaire was taken three hours ago and nobody told me?" Grant roared, grabbing Jake by his shirt. "What the fuck, Donovan?"

"What's going on?" the senator asked, stepping out of the room.

"Blaire was taken," Grant threw over his shoulder before returning his glare at Jake. He gave his head of security a shake. It was either that or slam him against the wall. "Why the fuck wasn't I informed immediately when it happened?"

Donovan's jaw hardened. "You were sequestered in a private waiting room and August Lynch was its gatekeeper. He told us that you and your family were not to be disturbed."

An anguished roar echoed in the hallway and it was only later that Grant realized it had come from him. He shoved Jake to the side when he spotted Gus. He stalked over to his father's political advisor, hauled back, and punched the bastard across the face.

GUS LYNCH WAS lucky the Boston PD was in the ER waiting room or Grant would have killed him. When he learned that his mother had been attacked and was in critical condition, he managed to keep it together for his dad and Val. But when he found out that Blaire had been abducted and that fact had been kept from him for three fucking hours, Grant completely lost it.

Rage. Blinding rage gripped him and despair tore at his guts. His girl was gone. His woman was taken and it was his own fault.

What Grant wanted to know was why Andy removed Blaire from the ER. If the man wasn't all drugged up, he'd have subjected him to an inquisition. Rather than wait for the Boston PD to obtain a warrant for the surveillance video, Grant used his influence with the hospital administrator to obtain a copy of the footage. Being a major benefactor of the institution had its advantage.

Grant saw how he'd treated Blaire in the waiting room and his heart twisted at how lost she looked. Andy said she'd been planning to leave him. After the hostile reception she'd received from Grant and everyone else in the ER waiting room, he couldn't blame her. There was a lot he needed to make up for but, first, he needed to get her back. What slayed him the most was the point where she'd given up the struggle after seeing Andy go down. The footage was grainy, but it was obvious she just stopped fighting. It was as if she'd given up. Grant took the blame for that too. *I'll find you, Blaire. Don't you dare give up hope on us. Don't you fucking dare.*

"Mr. Thorne, your mother is awake." A nurse approached his huddle with Tyler and Jake.

"Thanks, I'll be right there." He looked at Jake. "Find Blaire's burner. She didn't have a purse with her at the ER. We need that phone to contact Liam."

Grant made his way to his mother's room. He took in a deep breath and schooled his features before he opened the door. Bandages obscured his mother's head. There was bruising beneath her eyes, but she smiled weakly when she saw him.

His father was standing at the foot of the bed and Val was sitting by her side.

"I thought my son had forgotten me." Her voice was low and scratchy.

"Had to deal with an issue, Mom."

"It's always one thing or another, isn't it?"

Grant forced a chuckle, but it sounded so hollow, he grimaced.

"Now," his mother said. "No one will tell me how Blaire is." She paused, as if she was having difficulty talking. "Is she okay? Was she injured? Where is she?"

The look on Grant's face said it all.

"Oh no," she whispered and closed her eyes as if pained. "Where is she?"

"Amelia," his father said gently. "You must rest, sweetheart."

"No." There was steel in her voice. "Why isn't she here, Grant?"

"She was taken, Mom," Grant said quietly.

She didn't even ask by whom. His mother's lips pressed together as if holding in a well of emotions and then held out her hand. "Oh, Grant..."

He went to her and clutched her hand in his. Her grip was strong. At that moment, she knew her son needed her strength.

"You'll find her," she whispered.

He gave a tight nod. "I'm not accepting any other outcome."

SOON AFTER LEAVING his mother's side, Grant left the hospital with Tyler and Jake. He left one of his men at the hospital just in case the Boston PD had additional information.

"We've recovered the senator's car," Jake said, getting off the phone. "They're bringing it into Lowell's." Lowell's Forensics was an independent laboratory used by many federal and investigative agencies. "Are you sure about this, Mr. Thorne?"

"The Boston PD is going to drag their asses on this," Grant said. "Didn't they want to rule it as a tire blow out?"

"Yes."

"I'm not wasting time convincing them otherwise."

He pulled out his phone, scrolled through his contacts and thumbed a number. "Hey."

"Hey," Kylie answered. "Grant, how's your mom? I just heard the news."

"She's out of danger but still in ICU."

"Do you know what happened?"

"We're trying to piece things together," Grant said. "Listen, Kyls, I need you to do me a favor."

"Anything, Grant."

"Tyler is going to send you a video. I need you to try and get the number off a license plate."

"Okaaaay?" Her voice was hesitant.

"And I need you not to ask any questions."

Silence.

"Are you in trouble?" she asked finally.

"No questions, Kylie. Can you just trust me on this? The less you know, the better. I assure you. What you're doing for me is not illegal."

"But you're going to use the information I give you to do something illegal."

Grant sighed. "Honestly? I'm not sure at this point. So, are you going to help me?"

"Tell Tyler to send it over."

"Thanks, Kyls. I owe you."

He ended the call and checked his messages. "Tyler, send the video footage to Ms. Peterson. I'll text you her secure FTP site and the credentials."

No response.

Grant looked up from his phone and felt the sudden tension in the vehicle. "Tyler, did you hear me?"

"Yes, boss."

"Good."

"I don't think it's a good idea," Tyler replied.

"Why the hell not?" he frowned. "Kylie is the best in her field."

"So is Lowell's lab and it's their specialty. They're already processing the Bentley, they can process the video," Tyler said.

"I'm not taking any chances. I know Kylie can do it, so do as you're told," Grant ordered. *What the hell?*

Tyler's jaw tightened and Grant caught his glare in the rearview mirror. "Do we have a problem, Tyler?"

"I think this is the problem," Jake broke in as he handed Grant a tablet. "Scroll through the bookmarks."

A series of tabloid articles featuring he and Kylie stared back at him. "What the fuck," he muttered. "This is bullshit." Then a more troubling thought crossed his mind. "Tell me Blaire didn't see this."

"She searched for news about you when you stopped talking to her," Jake derided. "Of course, she saw it."

"And you did nothing to discourage her?" Grant snapped.

Donovan turned in his seat to face him. "It isn't my place to restrict Blaire's access to the internet. If she was messing with the Dark Web, then maybe. I explained to her that Kylie was helping secure our servers. You managed to have lunch, dinner, drinks, and coffee with Ms. Peterson without giving Blaire five minutes of your time."

This was worse than he thought, Grant groaned inwardly. "I've fucked up so bad," he admitted, and even without his men's assent, he could almost feel them nodding in agreement. "That Galleria Development needed all my attention." The only time he could touch base with Kylie regarding the security patches was during those times over a meal, coffee, or drinks. The majority of his time was spent in the suffocating confines of the office and boardroom, but he could see how those tabloid pictures could be misinterpreted.

Grant brought up Kylie's number to call her back and tell her he didn't need her help.

23

Grant

GRANT WATCHED the swinging spheres of the Newton Cradle sitting on his desk. The gadget usually relaxed his mind while he was waiting on results of an acquisition, merger, or expansion, but this time he was waiting on the results of the forensic lab. He'd thrown enough money at them that Jake had to stop him from paying more, since he'd already tripled the expedited rate so they'd have first priority.

It had been fourteen hours since Blaire was taken. He couldn't sleep; he'd barely eaten. Coffee was his friend. He didn't touch alcohol. If decisions needed to be made, he'd need a clear head.

His phone buzzed and he snatched it up to see who was calling. It was Rafe. He'd been avoiding the calls of his managing director since the night before. He knew what he wanted to talk about. They'd been gearing up for an even bigger acquisition. The Meridian Shopping Center in Moscow would be the biggest mixed-used commercial property deal, not only in Russia, but for Grant's company.

And he asked himself again—when would it be enough? But he

couldn't leave Rafe hanging. Before the call went to voicemail, he picked up. "Thorne."

"Grant!" Rafe exclaimed and he could hear the relief in his voice. "I know it's a bad time, man. How's your mom?" He'd received several voicemails from friends and business associates expressing their concern. He hadn't called any of them back.

"She's okay."

"I totally understand if you're staying in Boston over the weekend, but are you coming back on Monday?"

"No."

"Grant, we're kicking off the acquisition of the Meridian to the board."

"You'll have to do it on your own."

"It's a one-point-two-billion-dollar deal, Grant. Without you in the meeting, the board's gonna get nervous."

Jake appeared at the open door of his office. He was holding his laptop and had a binder under his arm.

"I gotta go."

"You can't do this, man!"

"If you need me, contact Heather. She's been instructed to summarize all the business transactions that need my attention." He ended the call and motioned for Jake to enter. "Any updates?"

"We've got the license plate number. It's from a rental company in Miami. The lab is trying to hack into its GPS to locate it. From the company's POS, the vehicle hasn't been returned yet."

"We also have a report on the explosive device used in the car."

"So it's a confirmed explosion?"

"Yes. They found residue consistent with a tripto-blast explosive."

"A what?"

"It's a relatively new technology using a triptinum core, similar to the effect of lighting a hydrogen and oxygen mixture. The resulting explosion is big and fast. Happens in a blink of an eye."

"Triptinum ... sounds familiar," Grant murmured.

"It's a recently discovered metal."

"I remember now. Kazakhstan, right?"

"Correct."

"I don't like where this is going." Grant said, mulling over this information. "We need to know which companies are mining the metal? Who does the refining, and, more importantly, which companies manufacture these types of explosives?"

Jake ran a finger across the stubble on his jaw. "See that's the thing. This is not typical military-grade or commercial issue. As far as I know, only special-ops personnel have this technology and it ain't cheap. It could also be the ROC trafficking these weapons to certain interest groups like ISIS."

"Yeah. Shit," Grant rubbed a hand over his face. "I want to know how that device got into the Bentley. Dig deep into the backgrounds of everyone who had access to it."

"That's going to take some time," Jake said. "Your father's office has stringent security screenings of all its people."

"Unless the person who has the final say is involved."

"Are you saying August Lynch might be involved?"

"Not discounting him," he said grimly. "Everyone is a suspect. The priority right now is finding Blaire. What do you have on that front?"

"Mikhail Orlov has several properties in Miami."

"That's assuming they're taking her to Miami. How long before we can track them?"

"If they haven't disabled the GPS? Within the next hour or two."

A door slammed from the outside and rapid footsteps approached his office. Out of breath, Tyler walked in and handed Grant a phone.

"There's only one number on Blaire's burner that she has called repeatedly."

Jaw clenching tight, Grant held it to his ear. It rang until it went to voicemail. He didn't expect Blaire's friend to answer, but he was still disappointed. "Liam, this is Grant. Call me at this number as soon as possible."

Thumbing the screen to end the call, he looked at his men. "Get ready to leave. Buy anything you think we might need to rescue Blaire. Guns, ammo, vests, hell, a grenade launcher, get it."

"A sizable one-time purchase will raise red flags in the system, not to mention we need paperwork for some of those."

"That stash that we got from Blaire's cabin," Tyler said. "That's a veritable arsenal and I couldn't trace any of those."

"Use it," Grant decided. "Have our pilot fuel up the Gulfstream. Jake, do you have contacts near Florida that we can hire for extra muscle?" He didn't need to say mercenaries.

"I've already made a shortlist of men we could use," Jake said.

"Excellent."

TWO HOURS LATER, Liam called.

And Liam was furious. "What the fuck happened?"

In clipped, succinct statements, Grant told Blaire's friend everything.

"That's a serious breach of security, Thorne," Liam said.

Grant swallowed hard. He wanted to ask Liam about the chances of them finding Blaire alive and unhurt, but the words wouldn't come. He didn't want to know. Didn't want to think that at that moment, his angel was being hurt and brutalized. It had taken all his energy to keep the images in the back of his mind, but here was the one person who knew Orlov best.

He released a shaky breath as their line crackled with charged silence.

"Don't go there," Liam ordered. "Don't ask me either, because at this moment I want to punch through this phone and shoot you."

"Fuck. I'm sorry—"

"Don't fucking apologize!" the other man roared. "Not even a week, Thorne, and you lost her. I should have known better than to trust a pansy-assed businessman to take care of Blaire. I should have listened to her. She said she was a bad bet for you, but I think you're the bad bet."

"I know," Grant agreed. Every word out of Liam's mouth was like a nail crucifying his guilt against his heart. Self-recrimination was bleeding from him, but he refused to wallow in regret. Not when his woman needed saving. "Can we cut the shit for now because, from where I'm standing, it's not helping get my woman back."

Liam barked a short scornful laugh. "Your woman? Gotta hand it to you, Thorne, for having the balls to say that. We get Blaire back, she's mine. Not trusting you after this."

Grant bristled but didn't say anything. The more they argued on the phone, the longer it would take to get to Blaire.

"My men and I are ready to get where you are," he told the older man.

"You and your men need to stand down."

"The fuck!" Grant swore. "I'm not sitting on my ass and waiting for news."

"Stay out it."

"If you think we can't help, then we'll stand down. We'll be where you are and not interfere." Unless they had to. "Need your own men to back you up? Fine. Get the best for the job. I don't care how much it costs."

"Well, shit, at least you're good for something," the other man muttered. "Two million dollars. Cash. Think you can swing that?"

"No problem," he said. "Where do we meet you? I can get the money within the hour and have my plane ready."

"Miami. Call me when you land."

Liam hung up.

IT WAS four hours later when they were wheels up. Grant visited his mother first, but he didn't give any indication that he was leaving town. He didn't say anything to his dad either—just that they were following up on leads. Someone was trying to undermine his relationship with Blaire, and it looked like that someone was working with the Russian mafia. He couldn't help but get suspicious of Gus. It had been obvious that he was against Blaire since the beginning and Grant recalled how he was told of his mother's accident.

It was Gus who called him. *"There's been an accident, Grant. Blaire escaped without a scratch, but Amelia is critical."*

Those two statements set the stage for how he reacted to the entire scene at the ER. Gus set him up, planted the seed that it was Blaire's fault, and his mother was paying the price. And he fell for it.

But it didn't make sense that Gus would collude with the Russian mafia.

He'd get his girl back. He'd do his damnedest to convince Blaire to take a chance on him again—not that he was giving her any choice. So yeah, fuck Liam. He wasn't taking his woman. Grant fucked up. He'd own it. He'd grovel if he had to.

One thing was for certain. When they got back from Miami, there'd be a rat to trap.

24

Blaire

DRIP.

Drip.

The sound of water droplets helped me keep my sanity and kept fear at bay. It muted the skittering on the wet ground, the sighs and groans that echoed around the stone structure of the level that housed my cell, and the creaking floorboards above me. I was in a dungeon, dark and damp, that smelled of bleach and death.

I knew where I was—the mansion of Mikhail Orlov near the Everglades. He didn't take me directly to his solarium. That was where he did his executions. Here in this dungeon basement, he kept his guests to taunt or torture, or leave them to die a slow death. I wasn't sure what he planned for me yet. I was lying on a steel-framed cot with a lumpy mattress that made my skin itch. I didn't even want to see its condition. The pungent odor of copper, mixed with every imaginable bodily excretion from sweat to urine, was enough to make me gag, but my other choice was to lie on the floor with Lord knew what scuttling around. The darkness was a blessing and curse. Mercifully, I was given a t-shirt to wear over my dress so at least there was more barrier between the filth and my skin.

A heavy door clanged. I had not seen Mikhail, but I was sure that was about to change.

A white glow lit the gap between my door and the flooring. An army of footsteps approached. The small window on the door slid open and someone peeked in. As if I could go anywhere when my ankle was shackled to the concrete wall. There was only enough slack in the chain for me to go to the bucket in the corner to do my business and wash up at the drippy faucet.

The door swung open and the man himself stepped in. He was flanked by his trusted second man, Stefan. I didn't know who the other three men with him were. The height and frame of one of them could have been the man who'd drugged me.

Orlov reminded me of those doting uncles you had as a child. He wasn't tall and had a stocky build with a slight paunch. He had dark hair, a receding hairline, and a friendly smile—until his eyes darkened with malice and the smile became a sneer. Then he'd become the bogeyman of your nightmares.

I'd seen it happen before but, at that moment, he had on his doting uncle face.

"My dear, Paulina, it's been almost three years," he said as he stopped short of the bed.

I pushed myself up. I felt a bit nauseated, probably from the drug. "Mikhail."

Stefan set one of those rechargeable lamps on the floor and illuminated the gray cinderblock walls of my room. The cement flooring was uneven, as if the house was built upon a slab of rock. The bucket and the faucet that I had to feel my way in the darkness for, sat in the corner of the room. A groove was carved into the length of the flooring and led into a hole in the ground.

"You're looking well," he said. "I'm sorry for your accommodations." He gave my room a cursory glance. "But you and Maxim broke my heart. He died in here, you know." Orlov shrugged. "It took a few days."

Papa. I tried not to think of him, but images flashed in my head—of him drinking coffee while I finished my milk, of how he'd look over the edge of his newspaper and chided me to hurry up or I'd be late for school. And now I'd picture him in this dungeon...bloodied, dirty, and dying.

I knew what Orlov was doing ... he was trying to play on my grief and my fear. Even as I tried not to give him that satisfaction, an anguished sob broke through my lips as emotions filled my chest.

"Just tell me what you want and get it over with," I choked.

"The thing that bothered me all these years," Orlov began. "Was not knowing how my son died."

"Didn't my father tell you?"

"Maxim told me my son attacked him and he stabbed him in self-defense."

"It was self-defense," I whispered. "You're blind to the monster your son was."

"He took the blame for you, didn't he?" Malevolence darkened his eyes and his lips curled into a snarl. "You're the one who killed Yuri."

"He was a monster," I repeated. "He murdered my friend and you had my father cover it up. You sent him away to Moscow for a year hoping he'd change, but how can a sociopath change when the sickness is in his blood? Your blood."

He ignored my jab. "He was obsessed with you. If you'd accepted him, none of this would have happened."

I laughed without humor. "And here you are still trying to justify his actions. Let me explain to you"—I got to my feet so we were face-to-face—"Yuri tried to rape me! I did what you should have done a long time ago, Mikhail. I put him down."

Orlov snapped. I heard his roar just as the back of his hand struck me. I fell back on the bed, but something else hit me. A cane. Mikhail's preferred method of torture. He hated blood and usually left messy kills for Stefan.

I curled into a ball and protected my head.

He cursed in Russian, chanting like a madman, and I cried when he struck my torso. The beating suddenly stopped as I heard Stefan and another man pull him back.

"We can't kill her, boss. We need the information and—"

"I know!" Mikhail shouted. Fingers dug into my hair and he yanked my head so I could look into his eyes. "Where's the storage unit?"

"I don't know," I whispered. "Ahhh..."

He pulled at my hair again and gripped my chin hard. "Do not lie to me, *suka!*"

"I'm not! We never knew where it was. Papa gave the key to someone else. I swear."

He asked me again and again. He hurt me again and again. This went on for several minutes until he was convinced I knew nothing.

"You're lucky I'm not allowed to kill you," He let me go in disgust. "Stefan?"

In my haze of pain, I registered his strange statement. Why wasn't he allowed to kill me?

"Boss?"

"Make her bleed. Take a picture of her and post it in that chatroom. The one where that traitor Marco will see."

Marco had been Liam's undercover name.

"Tell him he has twenty-four hours to comply."

Mikhail turned and left the room; the three men followed him. I was left with Stefan. Orlov's second looked at me with regret in his eyes.

"You don't have to do this, Stefan," I pleaded. He wasn't exactly a friend, but he was more than an acquaintance.

"Just tell us where it is and the pain will stop," he said gently.

Was this why Liam kept quiet about the location of the storage unit? Did he suspect I would break and, when they got what they wanted, they would kill me? Would I have broken by now if I knew?

"I don't know," I mumbled, closing my eyes.

"I'm so sorry, Paulina," he said and I believed in the sincerity of his apology. Stefan was a good soldier.

I let my mind escape my body. I tried to think about happier times with Papa, but my heart only hurt. My thoughts wandered to my happier times with Grant, but all I remembered was the contempt in his voice when he told me to leave. My heart cracked in two. All those condemning eyes closed in around me until I suffocated.

I coughed and choked.

My hand came away from my mouth.

Stefan did as he was told.

He made me bleed.

25

Grant

VAL!

Grant fought against the tangle of the fishing net. The dark embrace of the turbulent waters stifled his lungs. He broke free and swam to his sister but a burst of white bubbles momentarily blocked his path. His hand pushed through the watery barrier, baffled at the sight of the woman floating in front of him, her face obscured by a mane of chestnut and gold. His fingers dragged away the curtain of hair to expose her face. Blaire's hazel eyes stared at him, unseeing, and a silent roar clawed up his throat.

THE GULFSTREAM TOUCHED down in a private Miami airfield owned by one of Grant's business associates. Their plane taxied straight into a hangar. Out the window, he could see Liam standing in front of two Hummers. Grant didn't waste any time, and, as soon as the pilot gave the go ahead, he was up from his seat and heading toward the exit.

"Mr. Thorne!" Jake growled after him.

"See to our cargo," Grant threw over his shoulder. He heard Jake pass the order to Tyler, but his security lead stuck to him like white on rice. He descended the steps of the plane and saw Liam heading straight for him.

Aggression was evident in every line of the man's body. Jake picked up on the hostility and stepped in front of Grant, but he pulled his man back. If there were a score to settle, he'd rather get that over with so they could focus on finding Blaire.

"Stand down. No matter what," Grant put a hand in front of Jake's chest. "I mean it."

Jake's eyes passed briefly over Grant before narrowing at Liam in warning.

When his bodyguard stood back, Grant turned to Liam who was upon them. Pain exploded at the side of his jaw and he staggered back.

Grant threw a hand out reminding Jake not to engage.

"Mr. Thorne," Jake gritted out.

He faced Liam again and the man threw a second punch and jarred the other side of his face.

Grant swore, shook off the pain, and glared at the older man. "That's all your gonna get until you tell me where Blaire is."

"I should kill you," Liam said hoarsely. His face was contorted in ravaged lines that set off alarms in Grant's head.

"Is she alive?" he asked the one question he didn't want to ask, and yet it was the one question he needed answered.

Liam nodded with difficulty. "But those fuckers hurt her. Bad."

A tide of fury ripped through his body, but Grant reined it in. "As long as she's alive, nothing else matters." And that was the truth. Just before their plane landed, he woke up to a nightmare that had shaken him to the core. Grant wasn't a religious man but he'd found himself bargaining with God. Blaire could return to him a damaged woman ... all he wanted was for her to be alive and breathing. If he had the ability to absorb her pain for her he would. He didn't care if it took a lifetime to make her whole again. He would always stand by her. His face must have shown his determination because Liam's face softened to a degree.

"She's a fighter," Liam said gruffly and then he turned to Jake. "The contents of the storage unit are in that crate." He nodded to an eight-by-eight pod beside the Hummer.

"You had it all along, you son of a bitch," Grant snarled, getting into the other man's face.

"Calm your shit, Thorne," Liam snarled back. "You don't know what I sacrificed to get this. While you were busy playing real estate mogul in Manhattan, I had to make decisions whether to let a person live or die. To save Blaire, there was only one choice. If she dies, I'm coming after you."

"You'll have to come through me first," Jake snapped, this time shoving himself between his boss and Liam.

"Easy, Donovan," Grant said grimly. "I'll face your kind of justice, Watts."

Jake turned his head and glared at him. "Respectfully, sir? You're a pain in the ass to work for."

Liam smirked. "I like this guy."

Grant exhaled in exasperation. "So what's the plan? What are we going to do?"

"Not we. My men and I. You guys stay here. This could get messy, and Blaire will have my ass if I involve you in this shit."

"I'm already involved in this fucking shit," Grant gritted through his teeth. "I go where you go."

"Boss ..." Jake started, frowning.

"Have you ever killed anyone, Thorne?" Liam mocked.

"No, but I'm a pretty good shot," he returned. "You say it like taking a life is equivalent to a badge of honor."

"There's nothing honorable about taking a life, but if it comes down between them and us, there's no time to hesitate," Liam turned his eyes on Jake. "How about you, Donovan, ever killed anyone?"

Jake's expression turned to stone. "I don't talk about it." Jake Donovan had been a marine in the last Iraq war. Grant was sure he had his kills.

"See, that right there is a soldier," Liam approved.

"Look, are we doing this or not?" Grant snapped. He was getting tired of Liam's insults and his barbs cut deep. Because of his inexperience in combat, Grant knew he couldn't take an active part in rescuing his girl, even if he desperately wanted to. They needed the best men for the job. "I want my team to be within striking distance. I'm fully capable of defending myself, so Jake and Tyler can help you if needed."

"We're not leaving you unprotected, Mr. Thorne," Jake protested.

"If Liam needs backup, Donovan, you are ordered to help," Grant declared. He narrowed his eyes when Jake looked ready to argue. "Understood?"

His head of security's mouth tightened in a flat line.

"What's your specialty, son?" Liam asked.

"Sniper," Jake answered.

"Your skills up to par?"

Jake stepped back, crossed his arms, and stared at the other man.

"Guess they are," Liam muttered. "Okay, here's the plan."

26

Blaire

AFTER STEFAN TOOK THE PICTURE, a woman came in to sponge me down and gave me a change of clothes. She left some kind of porridge and water. I didn't think Orlov had anything to do with it. My jaw was painful and swollen and I felt a couple of loose teeth. I bled from my nose, but it didn't feel broken. I wasn't hungry. I couldn't even open my mouth, but I was thirsty, so I just drank the water.

I laid as still as possible and closed my eyes. I hurt less that way.

I heard the creak of the door and realized I'd fallen asleep. My eyes shot open and the fluorescent light blinded me. My visitor was one of the men who'd accompanied Orlov.

"Get up," he ordered. "Marco made contact."

He stood motionless while I struggled to get to my side, then I propped my upper body with my elbow. He removed my ankle shackle, and I swung my legs to the floor, tentatively levering myself up to my feet. My body felt liked I'd ran a marathon, and my brain felt like it wanted to burst out of my skull.

The man whistled. "Let's see your rich boyfriend want you now. Even I wouldn't want to fuck you looking at that face."

I was thankful speaking hurt, because I would have told this bastard that I wouldn't fuck his ugly face either. So, with as much dignity as my beaten body could muster, I marched—okay—limped out of that room. I almost cried when I saw how far I had to walk, although I was sure the cavernous hallway intimidated me because every step was an effort. Orlov's goon got impatient and shoved me ahead. I tried so hard not to stumble, but fell to my knees anyway. I was yanked up and dragged along, so I had no choice but to force my aching limbs to move.

When we got to the first floor, it was like a meeting in a mafia movie. There were about twelve men; I recognized many of them. Some because they'd worked with my father, and the others because I'd recognized them from the files. They were looking at me with a mixture of satisfaction and anger. Many of them were cracking their knuckles to intimidate me. I didn't think I could take another beating, but I doubted they'd be merciful and just shoot me.

One of them approached me. I didn't remember his name, but I remembered my papa saying he was one of the sadistic ones who liked to torture his victims.

"You think you're getting out of this alive, *suka*?" he sneered. "We're going to have fun with you. Don't think that old man can save you. We'll take him too, if not kill him first, but you...?" His mouth lifted in a cruel smile.

"Kiril, stop that shit," Stefan ordered. He walked toward me. "Come on, Paulina, the car is waiting."

The others walked ahead of us while Stefan kept pace with me.

"I don't get you, Stefan," I mumbled through my aching jaw. "How could you hurt me and still be nice to me?"

"I follow orders," he shrugged. "Don't imagine any compassion where there isn't, Paulina. If Orlov orders me to kill you, I will."

I flinched at the bluntness of his words, so I shut up and bowed my head. Orlov met us at a Black SUV. He got in first. I was sandwiched between him and Stefan.

If by some miracle Liam and I got out of this alive, we could start fresh somewhere. I wasn't sure what he told Orlov, if he was bluffing that he had the physical evidence that could link almost all his top level men to their crimes. I was tired of holding on to Papa's legacy like an albatross around my neck. If any of the evidence amounted to anything, that was for the FBI and the DOJ to decide. I was done with it. We needed to get far, far away from the mafia so they couldn't touch us, and far, far away from Grant so I could forget all the heartache.

MY FOGGY BRAIN didn't understand why I was gagged until two SUVs of our four-vehicle convoy broke away. I started to panic. We were meeting Liam and they didn't want me to warn him that there were others in covert positions. Knowing Liam though, he would have prepared for every scenario. I had to trust him.

I recognized the part of town we were in. It was an industrial area that was quiet on the weekends. I'd accompanied Papa several times when the assassins of the ROC did their business here. I wanted to laugh. If Papa hid the physical evidence right in Orlov's own backyard, that would be ironic.

The sign for the self-storage came up and our Suburbans turned into the facility. I wasn't surprised that Orlov had a keycard to the place. He probably had several units here himself. The SUVs slowed to a crawl, I heard the driver communicating with the other cars, looking for signs of an ambush or if there were any suspicious vehicles around, but so far Orlov had gotten the all-clear. After a couple of right and left turns, my heart leapt to my throat as I spotted my friend.

He was standing nonchalantly against one of the units. Liam was wearing a white tee with a Kevlar vest and khaki military cargos. I was sure he was armed, but no apparent weapon was in sight. Orlov stiffened beside me as he and Stefan gripped their guns.

"Marco has a lot of balls," Orlov muttered.

"You should've stayed at the mansion, boss, and let me handle this," Stefan said.

"The men are restless. They need to see that I'm not merely a figurehead," he replied. Translation: Orlov was having trouble maintaining the loyalty of his men.

Our now two-vehicle convoy stopped a few feet from Liam and both turned off the engines.

"I'm not opening the gate until I see Blaire," Liam called out without moving a muscle.

"I have her. You stay in the car," Stefan told Orlov.

Stefan opened the door and pulled me from the vehicle. A flash of fury crossed Liam's face, but he quickly masked it.

"You shouldn't have hurt her," my friend said softly.

I cut my head to the side and brought it back center. Liam tensed. It was our signal that all was not what it seemed.

"Open the gate," Stefan ordered.

"Before I do," Liam said conversationally. "I'd like to point out that there's a grenade launcher aimed straight at your vehicle. Orlov's side actually."

"You're bluffing," Stefan replied. "We'll all be dead."

"If you're going to kill me, why would it matter?"

"You don't want Paulina to die."

"If I'm dead, you think I'll leave her alive for you motherfuckers to torture?" Liam looked at me. "Would you want to live, Blaire, if these assholes kill me?"

I shook my head. Liam was a crafty mind manipulator. Kudos to him. There was nothing scarier than someone with nothing to lose.

Orlov slammed out of the vehicle with a gun pointed at Liam. "Open the motherfucking gate!" he shouted. His men in the other vehicles exited as well with guns drawn. Including the drivers, it was ten against one.

Liam was nuts.

"Now, is this a fair fight?" Liam asked. To his credit, he brought out a card and swiped the slot beside a keypad. The device prompted for a code and my friend punched it in. He bent forward and shoved the gate up. Orlov's men fidgeted from side-to-side with their eyes darting around the area.

When the gate fully opened, the lights came on automatically. Orlov stepped in with one of his men, while the other one kept his gun trained on Liam.

Stefan's grip tightened around me.

Boxes were shoved around.

"What the hell is this?" Orlov roared.

"Now!" Liam shouted.

I stomped Stefan's foot and shoved my head up to his chin. Gunfire erupted amidst another gate rolling up. Stefan grunted, his arms slackening around me as I surged toward Liam who tossed me a gun. I caught the weapon and fell on my back, unloading the cartridges at Orlov's goons advancing on us. They were trying to get to their boss who had taken refuge in the first storage unit.

A couple of the ROC men fell as Liam grabbed my collar and dragged me to an open storage unit where two men in military gear covered us.

Who are they?

"Shooting from the left. Not friendlies," one of the guys muttered.

I yanked the gag from my face. "Two of the SUVs broke off. It must be them."

"You okay?" Liam asked, grim eyes searching mine.

"Fine." I said. "You have a plan getting us out of here?" I grimaced as my earlier escape effort was causing my already-battered body a world of pain.

The shooting ruckus stopped.

"Marco, you son of a bitch! You think you're getting out of here?"

"Take cover!" One of Liam's men yelled.

The rattle of a carbine sprayed into our storage unit.

"Fuck!" Liam hit my crouched body and flattened me.

It lasted a few seconds when that too stopped.

"Shooters on the right!" Stefan yelled from outside as the gunfire resumed.

My friend felt heavy on top of me. "Liam, I can't breathe," I mumbled.

"Goddammit!" Someone yelled.

Noises rang through a vacuum and all I could hear was my breathing.

Liam's groan sounded so far away and a sinking feeling roiled my gut as he rolled off me to the ground and on his back.

Blood pooled under him.

"Oh my God," I whispered as I got to my knees and searched for the source of the bleeding. Eyes closed, his chest heaved with each breath.

I unzipped Liam's vest.

"Armor-piercing," he said, choking on a gasp.

"Oh, please, no!" It must have nicked the brachial artery on his shoulder. I pressed hard. "Stay with me, Liam."

"Sweetheart," he mumbled. "It's okay."

"Don't you dare give up."

"It's gonna be okay."

"How, Liam?" I cried as the blood geysered out. *How is it going to be okay?* I glanced frantically around for something to staunch the bleeding, ignoring the gunfight and the bullets ricocheting crazily inside the storage unit that was rapidly becoming a death trap.

Somehow, Liam found the strength to sit up and we managed to get his vest and shirt off. I wrapped the bleeder with the shirt.

"Fight back." He grabbed my gun and threw it at me. "Leave me be," he growled.

I took one last look at him as he found purchase against the wall before I rejoined the fray.

"Dammit, where are they?" One of Liam's men yelled.

I didn't know what they meant, but I prayed it meant help was coming.

THE END CAME in a split second.

One of Liam's guys was reloading and he got shot in the head. Liam's second man glanced at his comrade and got hit right in the neck.

In the split second I had taken my eyes off Orlov's remaining men who were using the SUV for cover, Stefan materialized in our storage unit. He grabbed my wrist holding the gun and squeezed. The pain was excruciating as I gave a soundless cry. He grabbed my weapon and handed it to Orlov, who was holding his gun at our two men down on the floor.

Stefan glared over my head at Liam. I scampered back to shield him—he was pale and slumped over.

Sporadic gunfire echoed in the distance.

Stefan's smile was cruel. "I told you I have no problem killing you, Paulina." He pointed the gun at me. "Boss?"

"Make sure Marco is dead. We need Paulina alive," Orlov ordered in Russian.

I heard a whistling sound and Mikhail Orlov fell to the ground like a puppet whose string was cut.

Stefan spun around and the blast of a bullet slammed into him, the impact throwing him on the concrete flooring.

Grant walked in, arm outstretched with a gun fixed on Stefan's head and shot him again.

I couldn't believe my eyes. Even as I saw Tyler follow his boss with a frustrated look on his face, I thought my mind was playing tricks on me.

Then I remembered Liam. I got down on my knees in front of him, my aching wrist cradled against my stomach as I touched him lightly with my left hand.

"Liam?" I whispered brokenly. There was no rise and fall in his chest. My lips trembled and my eyes blurred as I touched my fingers to his pulse.

No pulse.

"No!" I screamed. The sinking feeling in my stomach expanded until I couldn't breathe. "No! No!" I fought the arms that wrapped around me.

Tyler crouched in front of Liam and felt for his pulse. I stared at him hopefully. His sad eyes met mine before looking to the person holding me. He shook his head.

"No!" I shouted as I struggled again. "He's not gone. He's not dead!"

"Blaire," Grant's voice whispered. "Let him go, baby."

Arms tried to pull me away from my friend but I clung to his arm. I cried for Liam to wake up. I cried for him to get up. I cried until my voice was hoarse and there was no strength left inside me.

"You can't do this to me, Liam," I sobbed brokenly. "I can't start a new life without you."

My hand fell away from his lifeless body and I felt someone lift me.

I'd given up the fight for good.

27

Grant

"SHE'S ASLEEP."

Grant nodded at the paramedic who'd treated Blaire at the scene. He flinched as he remembered the sobs that ripped from her chest. She had fought him, screamed at him, and called him names, but he held onto her until she collapsed in his arms, exhausted.

His own body shook with anger. The sight of Blaire, beaten and broken, was like a knife through his heart. Her anguished cries twisted that knife and he bled with her, but he had to hold on to his control even as the desire to empty his gun into an already-dead Orlov was overwhelming.

Liam was dead, and it was up to Grant to face the authorities. The storage facility had cameras, but Blaire's friend had a plan and Grant himself had already set things in motion, knowing that things could go FUBAR in a heartbeat. And they had. Liam's backup team got ambushed by Orlov's men. Jake was tasked as the sniper, but after taking out the guy with the carbine, his position had been exposed and he had to find another vantage point. At that time, hearing that

Liam had been shot and they were pinned down in the storage unit, Grant decided to move in with Tyler. They were in communication with Jake, who managed to shoot the last of the Russian goons before taking out Orlov himself. Grant now knew he had shot Stefan. At that time, all he saw was a man pointing a gun at Blaire and Grant fired his gun at him twice. Unlike in the alley where he aimed to disarm, this time he unleashed kill shots with no hesitation.

"Mr. Thorne?"

Grant turned to face the fed in charge of the case. It was fortunate that with pre-planning, the Miami PD had been tasked with only assisting the FBI, because, from what Jake had told him, several of the cops were on the take from the ROC. Since Blaire's abduction had crossed state lines, it had become a federal case.

"I'm Agent Wilkes," the man flashed his badge. "I believe you mentioned this was a case of kidnap and extortion?"

"Yes," Grant replied. "They kidnapped Ms. Callahan and asked for a two-million dollar ransom."

"I see," the fed said. "And you decided to pay it instead of contacting the authorities?"

"I hired K and R professionals hoping to get her back without paying the ransom," Grant replied scratching his jaw. "I didn't trust the local police."

"Your actions resulted in the deaths of thirteen people, Mr. Thorne."

"And three of them are mine," he gritted through his teeth. "Have you seen Ms. Callahan? What they did to her?" If it weren't a felony to assault a federal officer, Grant would love nothing more than to wipe the floor with this asshole. Maybe he was in the ROC's pocket as well. Tyler called his attention that the ambulance was ready to leave. "Look, I need to get to the hospital."

"We may have more questions. Don't leave town."

Grant gave a mirthless laugh. He rarely used his connections to intimidate people. "Look, Agent Wilkes. You know who I am." He didn't need to say that he was the son of the senator who controlled the Intelligence budget. "You know I'm not from Miami. I'm taking

Ms. Callahan to Boston as soon as she's cleared to travel. So it may be this evening. Or it may be tomorrow morning. I will be unavailable at that time. My girlfriend needs me. You want to talk to me, set an appointment with my PA."

"Now, look here, Mr. Thorne—"

"No, you look here," Grant snapped, losing all patience. He didn't have time for this shit. "These are criminals. Thugs. They kidnapped my woman and may have planted the bomb that nearly killed my mother. This might not even be your case tomorrow. I get you need to do your job, but the way I see it," he swept his arm at the carnage around them. "We just did it for you."

"You can't take the law into your own hands, Mr. Thorne."

Grant was already walking away from the fed. "Then do your job."

GRANT POUNDED AWAY on his laptop, catching up with work. In the time since the Gulfstream had left Miami, he'd had several panicked voicemails to return. His dad had called, having caught wind of what happened to the Orlov Bratva. With the death of their Vor, the organization was in disarray and its effect was felt all the way to Russia. There was enough of the inner circle left to run the ROC, but with the evidence Grant was bringing back with him, their days were numbered. His father made a comment that even if this Bratva collapsed, another would rise to take its place. Grant didn't care, that was the problem for the FBI. All he cared about was the threat against Blaire.

A sound from the bed grabbed his attention. He put his laptop aside and crawled under the covers with his woman. He was glad he brought the Gulfstream because it had a sleeping cabin and Blaire would have a comfortable journey home. She had a sprained wrist and two broken ribs. She had cuts on her lips and brows but no facial fractures. It had been a miracle. The swelling and bruising on her face made her features unrecognizable, but her eyes remained quintessentially Blaire. He'd know them anywhere. A tightness in his chest and burn behind his eyes reminded him of how he'd lost it at the Miami-Dade hospital the previous night.

When they took the gurney carrying Blaire away, a noise that suspiciously sounded like a sob rose in his throat. Tyler was startled and didn't know what to do. Grant took a deep breath, excused himself, and headed for the stairwell. He pushed the door open and went down a flight, and then leaned against the wall and simply lost it, letting emotions bleed down his face. He bent over and rested his hands on his knees. His poor Angel. That someone would hurt and brutalize the woman he loved gutted him. He didn't know how long he stayed in that stairwell, but in the end, after he'd regained his composure, fury against the people who'd hurt her dominated every fiber of his being. He wished Orlov was alive, so he could kill the bastard himself. Grant had crossed that line and he could say, without a doubt, that he'd kill for Blaire. He'd annihilate anyone who'd try to harm her.

Liam, my man, wherever you are, I promise I'm going to take care of her.

He stared at her now, wanting to kiss away all her bruises. He wanted to put his ear against her heart and listen to it beat. He wanted to tuck her into his arms and never let her go.

Her eyes fluttered open.

"Blaire," Grant whispered.

At first he saw joy in her eyes, but, when she blinked, grief ripped it away and tears rolled down her cheeks. She turned her head and stared at the wall of the plane.

"Blaire, look at me," Grant pleaded.

"Where am I?" Her voice was flat.

"You're on the Gulfstream. I'm taking you home, Blaire."

"To Colorado?"

Fear pierced his chest. "No. To Boston, then to Manhattan with me."

Still not looking at him, she said, "I'm not going back to you, Grant."

"Baby, let's not talk about this right now." He wasn't giving her a choice. This might end up being a kidnapping, but he'd be damned before he let her out of his sight.

Her gaze shifted to the ceiling. "How's Amelia?"

"She's fine, Blaire," Grant said. "I'm sorry—"

"Don't," she cut him off and then finally looked at him with glassy eyes. "Amelia got hurt because you chose to be with me."

"Blaire—"

"And when I chose to be with you"—the tears flowed freely as she inhaled a ragged sob—"Liam got killed."

"No, dammit! What kind of reasoning is that?"

"Your words, Grant," she said softly. "You told me your family was falling apart. You didn't have to say it was because of me."

"I told you I say shit when I'm angry and that's why I choose to keep my mouth shut when I am."

"You were angry at me."

"No. I was angry at the situation."

"It doesn't matter now. Liam is still dead."

"Listen, Blaire—"

"I'm tired, Grant." Her words, said in a gentle tone, made him more anxious. "I want to be alone."

"Okay, you need your rest," Grant forced himself to say, and then forced himself to move from the bed. He picked up his laptop, looked back at Blaire longingly, but she had already closed her eyes.

He could be patient, he told himself.

28

Grant

ONCE THEY ARRIVED at the brownstone, Grant lost all patience.

Blaire refused his assistance when she got out of the vehicle. He balled his fists in frustration, but allowed her to walk without him, thinking she wanted to preserve her dignity. She refused help from Tyler and Jake as well, so it wasn't personal. But what Grant realized as he walked into their bedroom and saw Blaire packing a suitcase was that she was preparing to live without him.

"What the fuck are you doing?" he demanded as he stalked into the room.

"I'm leaving. I thought that was obvious," she said as she limped into the closet to come back with an armful of clothes.

"Don't be a martyr," he growled, grabbing the items from her left arm and throwing them on the bed. "Look at yourself. You're black and blue. You can't even walk without a limp. Your wrist is sprained. Now is not the time to leave."

"And just exactly when is the time to leave, Grant?" Blaire's eyes flashed at him, defiance mixed with pain. "When someone else gets hurt? Killed?"

"Blaire, it's not your fault. Mom's accident. Liam dying," Grant said with a sigh. "Orlov is dead, baby. We're getting the evidence to the Justice Department. Pretty soon, you'll be free and clear of the Bratva."

Her lips trembled as she grabbed the clothes he discarded and continued to fold them into the suitcase.

"Don't waste your time packing, Angel."

"I need to get away from this place."

"From me, you mean?" Grant felt a spike of his temper.

"I can't take it," she said. "When you shut me out when you're angry, it drives me crazy. Those three days you didn't bother to call or text me made me insecure. I didn't like the person I had become. I stalked you online, for God's sake," she laughed without humor. "I think ..." She shoved more clothes into the suitcase. "I think if we'd been okay—if you'd given me any indication we were okay—I could have accepted your actions in the ER. I wouldn't have left with Andy and would've waited for Tyler instead." Her eyes widened. "Oh God, is Andy okay?"

"He's fine," he grated.

"Okay ..." Blaire whispered. "Okay," she repeated. It was as if she had suddenly lost focus on what she was saying. She walked into the bathroom and swept all her toiletries into an open train case.

Grant strode in after her and put his hands on her shoulders but she jumped, so he dropped his hands at his sides. "Baby ..."

"I can't," she whispered. "I'm not strong enough to be with you, Grant. I'm too messed up here." She tapped her head. "I went back there."

His brows cinched together. "Back where?"

"In that dungeon." Haunted eyes stared in the mirror. She reached out, tracing the lines of her reflection, but her eyes were unseeing. "He beat it out of me. Orlov."

Grant's body stiffened.

"When Andy was shot, I'd given up, but there was that spark ...."

some fight left in me. Orlov ... he tried to beat it out of me, but it was Stefan who buried it. Seeing Liam brought back that fight, but it died with him, Grant. It's gone." Her eyes filled with tears. "I can't find it."

How he wanted to take her into his arms but her whole body language right then screamed "hands off."

"You're grieving right now," he told her. "The pain that monster inflicted on you, we'll get through it. We'll get that fight back in you, baby."

She gave a shake of her head. "No, Grant. You can't help me." Her eyes met his in the mirror. "Because around you, I wish I never existed."

Her words sent him reeling with physical pain as if a battering ram was driven into his chest. Her once enthralling hazel eyes stared back at him as lifeless as the dead. They weren't even sad, there was just nothing in them. Blank.

She was back in that dungeon and he wondered with growing horror and panic if his presence was only making her retreat into those dark memories.

Still, he had to try and reach her. "Blaire," he choked hoarsely. "Don't do this. Please?"

She lowered her eyes and wiped a single tear from the side of her cheek.

"Come back to me, baby," he tried again.

"It's over, Grant," she said. She smiled but it was full of pain. "It's been over since you sent me away."

Blaire wasn't in the headspace to see reason, Grant realized then, but, if he let her leave, he wouldn't have the chance to prove to her that what she was feeling was just a collective effect of what had happened to her. It was unfortunate Grant was the idiot who had started her into her downward spiral.

"You're not leaving," he declared. "If I have to keep you locked in this room, so be it."

"Then you're no better than Orlov," she whispered, eyes blinking in disbelief.

He inwardly flinched at being compared to that son of a bitch, but hope flared seeing a reaction other than indifference.

"Yes, you've made that clear," he jeered. "I'm one of the people who've started you on this self-pitying journey."

This time her face blanched. "Self-pitying? LIAM IS DEAD!"

"Yes, so hate me for it." Grant threw over his shoulder as he exited the bathroom without looking back. He felt Blaire chase after him. When he got to the door, she yanked his arm.

"You're a heartless bastard!" she screamed at him.

"So hate me!" he roared. "Hate me," he repeated, pounding a fist on his chest. "But you're not fucking leaving, Blaire. You're going to live with me, you're going to endure my very existence—"

"I'm not sleeping with you," she cut him off.

"I'm not fucking you until you beg me," Grant shot back. "You're going to New York with me on Tuesday. We'll spend the next few weeks there. We're not living apart. Not for a single day, and you will accept that I am it for you."

"I want my own bedroom."

Grant's chest rose and fell with difficulty. This woman tested every bit of his patience. She always had. His jaw worked convulsively as he stared at her. It was going to be torture not to have her in his arms while they slept, but it was probably a good thing, given her injuries. The temptation to be inside her was always strong. "Done."

Her eyes widened in surprise and Grant inwardly smiled. She wasn't expecting him to agree so quickly.

"Anything else?" he inquired with a quirk of his brow and was pleased to see that old fire in her eyes.

She shook her head and spun away from him.

He watched her retreat to the bathroom and heard her put stuff back on the counter.

The pressure weighing heavy on his chest lifted as he left the bedroom, but the work of winning Blaire back had only just began. He saw Tyler and Jake hanging around the kitchen, peeking down the hallway as he emerged from her bedroom.

"Tyler, keep an eye on Blaire. Do *not* let her leave the house for any reason."

"Mr. Thorne?" His bodyguard's brows drew together in confusion.

"She has it in her head to leave."

"Are you saying I should physically restrain her if she wants to leave?"

"Yes, but if you harm a single hair on her head, I'm going to kill you." He looked at Jake who was trying to control a grin. "You won't think this is so funny after I talk to you. Let's go to my office."

When they reached his office, he motioned for Jake to close the door.

His security lead had a wary look on his face. "Are there problems, Mr. Thorne?"

"Who did you task to bring back Liam's body?" Grant asked.

Jake told him that one of Liam's crew took responsibility and promised to let them know when the feds would release his remains. Since the shootout at the storage facility was under investigation, Grant had no control over the evidence collected, but he was going to do his damnedest to make sure Blaire's friend got the burial he deserved. He saved his woman when he couldn't. Grant owed him everything.

"I have another request, Jake," Grant said. "I want you to put a tracker on Blaire."

"On her purse? Her phone already has one."

"No. On her person."

Jake grunted a laugh and shook his head. "Does she know?"

"She wants to leave me. You think I'd tell her?"

"Mr. Thorne, with all due respect, that violates too many privacy laws."

"Fuck privacy," Grant growled. "I'm not going through that shit again of not knowing whether she's alive or dead. I could take it when she left me voluntarily, but to have her taken from me, Jake? That fucking killed. The image of her beaten up and broken with a gun pointed at her head is forever seared into my brain. I'm obsessed with her safety. So either you do what I tell you or I'll find someone who will. Would you trust someone else with this job?"

Jake glared at him. "I don't like you forcing my hand, Mr. Thorne, but in the interest of Ms. Callahan's safety, I'll do it."

"Good."

Jake pivoted to head out the door and Grant could tell from his head of security's rigid back that he was pissed at him. When Jake's hand was on the doorknob, he called his attention. "Donovan."

His man paused and turned his head slightly.

"Thanks for taking care of Orlov."

Jake nodded. "My pleasure, Mr. Thorne."

29

FOUR WEEKS later

Blaire

GRANT WAS BREAKING down my walls. It was getting increasingly diffi-cult to ignore his presence and his gestures of sweetness. Oh, there'd been a moment three weeks before—a few days after arriving in New York when he'd exhibited his insufferable, arrogant self. In fairness to him, I did elude my security and had almost gotten on a bus to Denver. Grant showed up at the Port Authority bus terminal murderous with rage. He immediately spotted me in line to get on the bus and headed straight for me. He gripped my bicep and hauled me from the line as I thwacked him with my big heavy hobo bag filled with my essential stuff. I'd left with no suitcase. I still had clothes in my cabin.

It didn't work to Grant's advantage that he looked furious and I still bore bruises from my time in Orlov's dungeon and my wrist was in a splint. My whole look screamed abuse victim. Grant got tackled by a guy who had the physique of a linebacker. Another man kicked him while he was down. I screamed for them to stop hurting Grant and tried to pull the giant off him, but Grant, blind with fury and fighting back fiercely, yelled at me to "stand the hell back."

It was fortunate that Jake, Tyler, and a few port security officers arrived at the scene before anyone got seriously hurt. Grant was bleeding from the lip. I couldn't help but approach him to cup his jaw.

He smiled. Actually smiled at me and said, "Can we go home now, baby?" He said it as though he hadn't just gotten into a brawl. I huffed in irritation. The port authority officers didn't release Grant and I until they made sure he wasn't holding me against my will—which in reality, he was.

He put an arm around me and said it was a "lover's spat." I said my bruises were from a car accident. It didn't look like the authorities entirely believed our story, but with me not the least bit afraid of Grant and me yakking at him for his high-handedness, it appeared that he was the recipient of the abuse and not me. We went back to the penthouse and that was when I made another discovery.

I PAUSED RIGHT *outside my bedroom door as a thought hit me and I spun around and headed back to the living room where the men were gathered. I tossed my hobo on the coffee table. "Remove it."*

The men tensed.

"Remove what, Angel?" Grant asked pleasantly.

"You found me too quickly," I said. "I left my phone here at the penthouse. The Port Authority bus station is massive. How did you find me so fast, Grant, if you don't have a tracker on me?"

All three men were quiet.

"Take it out."

"We can't," Jake said.

"Can't or won't?" I snapped. "I swear if you guys stitched it into the leather and ruined the purse, I'll ... I'll ..."

"You'll what, baby?"

I narrowed my eyes at Grant. "Take it out!"

He crossed his arms, bit his lower lip as if he was controlling a grin and rocked back on his heels before he pinned his gaze on me. "We can't. It's inside you, Blaire."

"It's a tracker using nano-technology," Jake explained. "When you swallow it, it diffuses and binds into your bloodstream. The effect is long-lasting."

When I could speak again, after my shock and horror morphed to rage, I yelled, "You've got to be fucking kidding me! How? Who makes this shit?"

"The military," Jake shrugged.

I had to rein in my temper for a full thirty seconds. Otherwise, I would have beaned all three of them with my heavy purse. "And how did it get inside me?" I asked through gritted teeth.

"I may or may not have slipped it into your orange juice," Tyler coughed.

"Unbelievable," I muttered. "You guys are unbelievable. I could sue you for this."

I grabbed my bag and marched into my bedroom and slammed the door.

TWO WEEKS after my attempted escape, we went to Atlanta for Liam's funeral. Tyler did a search for relatives of Lucas Myers—Liam's real name—and discovered he had a daughter who was about my age. I learned that he and his ex-wife had divorced when his daughter was seven years old, but he had been in her life until he accepted his undercover assignment with the Russian mafia. Liam's daughter wanted custody of her father's body. His daughter was married with two children under the age of eight. My heart broke for his family. The sacrifices Liam had made for his job, for me ... especially for me, had been extreme. Grant, Jake, and I watched the service from afar because the funeral brought a resurgence of overwhelming guilt for having taken away this great man from people who loved him.

But I loved him too.

What the past few weeks had taught me was to gain perspective.

The evidence had been brought to the U.S. Attorney General and they had begun prosecution proceedings. Liam didn't die in vain. He had spent almost six years of his life to bring down the ROC and it was finally happening. Orlov's death had left a power vacuum, so it had made it easier to round up the members of his inner circle. It pained my heart that Liam wasn't alive to see the fruition of his sacrifices.

Grant had taken time out of his busy schedule to accompany me to U.S. AG office in Brooklyn. He also convinced me to go to a therapist to work on what happened to me in that dungeon and to come to terms with Liam's death. As I stepped out from my third appointment with Dr. Jones, drained and having cried a bucket of tears for the loss of my friend, I was expecting to see Tyler at the reception area when, instead, I found Grant waiting for me.

"Grant, what are you doing here?"

"Taking you to lunch. You haven't been eating much lately. You're starting to hurt Colette's feelings."

"My lack of appetite has no bearing on her cooking skills," I retorted. Grief and oral surgery to repair my loosened teeth sustained from the beating didn't exactly stimulate my appetite.

"I know, baby." He smiled at me indulgently and my belly fluttered. No. No. No. I was not falling for that Grant Thorne charm again. Apparently my heart had a short memory.

I couldn't deny that without Grant's quiet support these past few weeks, I'd be a mess. Therapy helped where I could just cry, get angry, feel sad, and not be judged. Sad moments and those flashes in the dungeon had become infrequent and, instead, Grant's thoughtful gestures for that day would occupy my mind. I received flower arrangements almost daily; he'd call me at random times of the day or text me just to find out what I was doing. I'd received all kinds of baked goods, although Colette had something to say about that and Grant had to stop sending me sweets. I had no idea why he was keeping me with him. We weren't having sex and, although he'd asked me out to dinner a couple of times, I'd refused. I didn't want him to get the wrong idea that I was agreeing to a date with him. I told him several times once I was done with my twice a week therapy sessions that I was moving out, and he couldn't stop me. Other than the tightening of his jaw, he had no comment, and he'd often change the subject. But I had a feeling he was reaching the end of his patience with me.

Grant took me to lunch at a French Brasserie in SoHo. It was October in New York and there was a definite chill in the air, but the autumn sun was enough to make outside seating comfortable. I didn't know where Tyler and Jake were, but I knew our security detail were somewhere nearby. Grant had become unusually paranoid when it came to my safety, but at least he allowed me to leave the penthouse as long as my three-man security team was with me. I'd gotten used to them shadowing my excursions around Manhattan as they weren't intrusive. It was usually Tyler who was by my side; the other two either checked ahead or protected the rear.

"Anything particular you like with the specials?" Grant asked after our server left us with the menu.

"Hmm," I mumbled, looking intently at the list of specials. I was suddenly very aware of how he filled his suit. As if it was tailored especially for him. He exuded such raw masculinity and power that it made every female of all ages and color turn their heads for a double take. I congratulated myself for taking extra care that morning to cover the bruises on my face that were fading to yellow.

"Moules-frites," I said finally and looked up, surprised to see Grant glaring at a man at the next table. The man was stealing glances at me, but when he caught Grant's eyes, he muttered to himself and returned his attention to his plate.

"What was that, Angel?" he asked, a bit distracted as he narrowed his eyes at someone else over my shoulder.

"If you're done glaring at people," I said dryly. "I would like the Moules-frites."

A disconcerted look crossed his face, and then he tried to smile, but it ended up looking funny because his jaw was tight. "Sorry, can't help it. I hate it when men look at you like they're undressing you."

The same way you look at me? I didn't say. "I'm sure that's your imagination."

"Believe, me, Angel, I know the look." Grant leaned back in his chair when our server arrived with our drinks. "Moules-frites for the lady. I'll have your Bistro Burger."

"Good choice as always, Mr. Thorne," our server said as she entered our order in her tablet, took our menus, and left.

"So, how are your sessions with Dr. Jones? Are they helping?" Grant asked with genuine concern as he took my left hand in his palms, his warmth searing my skin. I tried to yank it away, but he held firm.

"Grant," I sighed in mild irritation.

"Give me this, Blaire," he said quietly. "I miss this physical contact with you."

"This isn't a good idea," I muttered. "Lunch is not a good idea."

"Why? Because it's like a date?" he questioned, his eyes glittering with impatience. "Of course, it's a date. Get used to it."

I yanked my hand away. "I don't like games."

"You're denying what's between us," he shot back, staring at me intently.

Three weeks ago, I could say that his family's safety and Liam's death were between us, but somehow those words didn't seem to hold much weight anymore. Did I still feel guilt? Sure, I did, but Dr. Jones thought it was survivor's guilt. First because my Papa died covering up my killing Yuri, and then Liam, who had been my protector for two years, died trying to save me. Liam and I had forged a bond that went along the lines of *fight together, die together*, but then Grant happened, and Liam pushed me to have that chance at happiness.

"I'm not."

The irritation on his face faded. "What are you saying, Blaire?"

Ugh, I hated the hope in his voice. "I'm saying that I'm still attracted to you, but I still think we're a bad idea."

He exhaled heavily, mild disappointment in his eyes. "You're so aggravating."

I raised a brow. "So, why are you putting up with me? You're spending money on security, on feeding me, on flowers, on chocolate. I got a bracelet from Cartier the other day and earrings from Tiffany this morning. Yet you get nothing in return except 'aggravation'."

"Mom would call that courtship," Grant returned with a maddening grin. "And the aggravation only makes me want to kiss some sense into you." His eyes traveled down my body. "And other things."

I blushed to the roots of my hair and for the first time in weeks I felt a heat below my belly. *Oh, hell no.*

"The sessions are very helpful," I said, desperate to change the subject.

"What about your nightmares?" Grant cut in.

"How did you ...," I frowned.

"I hear you, Blaire, when you cry in pain," he grated, his eyes darkening. "I hear your pleas for him to stop hitting you, that you don't know where it is." Grant took a swig of his beer, his knuckles turning white around the mug. "Several times I was tempted to unlock your door and go to you, but just when I couldn't stand it anymore, your cries would stop."

"I wasn't sure if I was having nightmares," I mused. "I've been startling awake for the past four weeks. It is less now, but I don't remember my dreams."

"Let me back in your bed," Grant said softly. "If only to hold you."

"I'm not ready."

Grant nodded. "At least unlock your door at night."

I looked at him dubiously. "I'm not sure that's a good idea either."

Before Grant could answer, someone called our attention. We looked, and then to my chagrin, a paparazzi took our photograph. "Mr. Thorne, are you back together with Blaire Callahan?"

Grant didn't say anything, because Tyler and another bodyguard materialized to confront the photographer who took off rather than have his camera or flash card confiscated. But I knew better. The photographer wouldn't have gotten through Tyler if he hadn't been allowed to.

I narrowed my eyes at Grant who stared at me in all innocence. "You planned that scene, didn't you?"

"It's about time those tabloids got the story straight," he said with not an iota of repentance.

"What story? We're not together," I hissed.

"Yet."

"Your overconfidence is aggravating," I retorted.

Just then, our food arrived and I had the childish urge to flick one of my mussels at him and wipe that wide, self-satisfied grin off his face.

I huffed and decided to concentrate on my meal, taking the meat out of its shell, and dropping it into the broth. I preferred to de-shell all the mussels first. Grant always found it amusing as he did now. Although, I'd say there was an indulgent look in his eyes that caused my heart to skip a beat. He took a healthy bite of his burger, chewing thoughtfully. I enjoyed spoonfuls of succulent mussel, alternating it with bites of garlic toast that had been drenched in the briny liquid.

We ate in silence for a while, drowning our senses in the chatter of the brasserie patrons and the aroma wafting from the kitchen. Butter and garlic—a heavenly combination.

"I'd like for you to attend an art exhibit with me," Grant said, putting his half eaten burger aside.

"An art exhibit?" I asked. "You have time for that?"

He looked affronted. "I have time for you. Actually, the gallery is displaying some of the artwork I've inadvertently acquired in my recent property deal." A smug expression crossed his face. "Apparently, one of the buildings in that acquisition was sitting on almost a billion dollars worth of lost art."

"What?" My fork dropped into my bowl. "How long have you known? Wasn't that business deal of yours almost a month ago?"

"Yes, the business deal that made me almost lose you," he said, as a grim look crossed his face. "I've known about the art since a few days after the purchase, but it took a while to work things out with the Russian authorities whether the art belonged to me or the state."

"And?"

"For now, I'm its custodian," Grant stated matter-of-factly. "We're talking about art stolen from Europe by the Nazis. When the pieces come out, I'm sure people will come forward to claim them. I'm not interested in selling, although Christie's has already given me a call."

I had to pick my jaw off the table. I wiped my lips primly with a napkin. "You'll do the right thing."

Grant had a gleam in his eyes. "Come on, you're curious about the collection I have."

"Oh, I dunno, am I?"

"Blaire," he said chidingly before he returned his attention to his burger, but I saw him sneaking glances at me, the corners of his lips twitching as he tried not to smile.

I stabbed at the poor mussels and continue eating. Finally, I couldn't stand it anymore. "All right! Whose art do you have?"

Grant took his time finishing his burger, and when he'd swallowed the last bite, I was, indeed, ready to stab him with my fork. Not really.

"Well, let's see," he said in all mock suspense. "Definitely Picasso, Renoir, Matisse. Degas, Max Liebermann... the list goes on and on. Baby?" he asked in amusement. "Are you okay?"

"Oh my God. Oh my God," I whispered. "And you kept this from me? How could you?"

"I wanted to be sure that I could bring them Stateside," Grant said. "I didn't want to raise your hopes and then let you down. I also wanted to secure the art gallery first."

"I'm sure you had a lot of offers."

"The Guggenheim called as well."

Good Lord. How did everyone know but me? I lived with the guy. Of course I couldn't complain because I was the fool who tried to avoid him for weeks.

"I've picked one right here in SoHo," Grant continued. "The Prestige's owner is a friend of mine. The artwork arrives tomorrow. Blaire, are you certain you're all right? You're looking a bit pale."

I glared at him. "You're a tease, Grant Thorne."

"Would you like to help him set up in the gallery?"

Containing my excitement took sheer will. I would have shot up from my chair and hugged and kissed him. Instead, I kept my ass planted firmly in my seat and smiled at Grant. "I would love to."

"It's okay to kiss me, you know," he said with a knowing grin.

Shaking my head, I smiled into my drink. This man was too charming. I should be alarmed that I was falling for him all over again, but I wasn't.

For the first time in weeks, my heart lifted with hope. I looked at Grant who had glanced away to get the attention of our waitress.

He gave me hope.

30

THE WATCHER

AT THE CORNER of Spring Street, diagonally across from the brasserie where Grant dined with Blaire, a man stood against a brick building seemingly occupied with his smartphone. He observed the bodyguards standing discreetly away from the couple and yet keeping a watchful eye on the surroundings. This was why he didn't approach any closer. Standing near the intersection where pedestrians came in waves from the Prince Subway station was enough for him to keep a low profile.

Thorne and Ms. Callahan were getting ready to leave. He should too.

He walked away to make his report.

Finding a quiet corner, he swiped his phone to call his contact.

"Yes?" a gruff voice answered.

"Thorne picked up Ms. Callahan from the therapist office. They just finished lunch. It appears they're still very much together."

"Are you certain?"

"That's what I'm picking up on Thorne's side," the watcher said.

"Ms. Callahan appears more reserved, but I think Thorne said something that made her happy."

"Security around her is tight?"

"Very."

"It'll be a problem if she sees the paintings. My sources tell me they will arrive tomorrow. The Prestige Gallery is handling the exhibit."

"What do you want me to do, boss?"

"Are you sure there's no way to grab Paulina—Ms. Callahan?"

"Her guard dogs are alert to her surroundings."

"Any indication they've made you?"

"No, I'm pretty sure they haven't. I change my appearance often."

"Good. I want you to watch the gallery and let me know as soon as the shipment arrives."

"How about Ms. Callahan?"

His employer sighed. "If she sees any of the paintings and recognizes them, we'll have to deal with it then. My people got to her before. I served her to Orlov on a silver platter and he fucked that up."

The watcher understood his boss's frustration. Orlov was supposed to hand Ms. Callahan to him while the ROC, with more than enough manpower, organized a heist of the paintings. But now, that wasn't happening. The ROC was crippled and his boss had a lot of money on the line if he didn't get some paintings back.

"Grant Thorne has thwarted me at every turn," his boss continued. "He doesn't care about the paintings, but this girl, Blaire, means everything to him. She has many uses and it's time I teach Thorne some humility."

"Boss?"

"You watch the gallery and keep me informed if Ms. Callahan shows up. I'll set things in motion, be ready to take her."

31

Grant

THE UNFETTERED VIEW of the Midtown Manhattan skyline from his corner office at 150 Greenwich Street used to give Grant a sense of purpose. He'd worked tirelessly over the past twelve years. So when he'd finally moved Thorne Industries from their rambling office space in New Jersey to the coveted top floors of this building in Manhattan four years before, he felt he'd reached the pinnacle of his success. And yet, as he stood looking down on some of the skyscrapers that exuded financial power, the rush wasn't the same. There was resentment there, that the conquests he'd coveted before were the cause of the danger now facing the people he loved the most. He made his first million before he graduated from Harvard Business School and bought his first tech company by the time he'd gotten his diploma. He'd been accused of corporate raiding, but he only took over when he felt an organization's leadership was incompetent. Did he have to lay people off? Sure, he had, but not without careful consideration. Layoffs hurt company morale and spelled doom for productivity. After restructuring and bringing a business back to profitability, if there were open positions, first priority was given to deserving former employees. Grant was a results-oriented CEO. He didn't care how an employee spent his time as long as he or she did the job and did the job well. That meant he had no time for sloth and people who couldn't carry their weight.

With his success, he had made enemies, and this success had also meant less time with Blaire. It was time to make changes. He'd have to work fewer hours and hire people to take over some of his work. That might make the board nervous, but he didn't give a fuck. The high he'd experienced after each business coup was gone. Blaire had become his new drug and she was one addiction he had no intention of giving up.

The intercom buzzed. "Mr. Lopez is here to see you," Heather informed him.

Rafe was his second-to-last appointment for the day.

"Send him in."

His managing director walked in and Grant noted he didn't look as harried as he did in the past few weeks. He'd let Rafe spearhead the recent property acquisition and, from all reports, Thorne Real Estate was weeks from closing the deal.

"Grant."

"Rafe. You're looking more rested today. I heard things are going well with the Meridian deal."

Rafe blew out a breath and sat on the chair in front of Grant's table. "Yes, we've finally managed to convince the Russian government to sell us the land the structures sit on." The recent rise in real estate interest in Russia was spurred by the relaxing of ordinances regarding property ownership. Russian law dictated that the land and the structure on it were treated as separate legal entities, thereby, making private ownership complicated. For a prime location in Moscow, Grant's company preferred the outright purchase of the land rather than a long-term lease, especially given volatile relations between Moscow and D.C.

"I knew you had this, Lopez," Grant grinned, pleased.

"I don't know how you do it, man," Rafe gave a lopsided smile. "Stay above all the dirty business."

Grant walked away from the wall of windows and perched on the edge of the table. "Who?"

"Who else?"

"Ivan Yashkin," he muttered. The Russian oligarch was a pain in the ass. These new-monied businessmen emerged after the fall of the Soviet Union and rise of Russian privatization and had made Grant wary of doing business in the country. However, having a U.S. Senator for a father had its perks, not because he relied on his father's position of power—although one couldn't argue its advantage —but because of the political and business connections he'd forged. It definitely leveled the playing field for his company to do business in the country. The oligarchy had their influences in the Kremlin; Grant did as well. What his company wouldn't touch was the use of organized crime to influence the decision-making process of the entities they do business with.

"Yup," Rafe confirmed. "He'd been a nuisance player in our bid for the Meridian."

"He really wanted the Galleria Development and, when we won the bid, he released all kinds of bad press about Thorne Industries in the Russian media."

"I never understood why he wanted that development so badly," Grant said. "His interests are energy and technology."

"Maybe he wanted a piece of the real estate market boom."

Grant shrugged and nodded at the binder Rafe was holding. "Those need my signature?"

"Can't wait to get rid of me, boss?"

Grant winced. "I hate it when you call me that."

His friend chuckled. "Well, it's true. You sign my paycheck."

He took the binder from Rafe. "I'll look over these tonight. Now get out of here."

Giving Grant a mock salute, his managing director left the office.

As soon as the door closed, his intercom buzzed again. "Jake Donovan here to see you."

His head of security entered with long, easy strides. Grant had increased pressure on his investigative division and Jake Donovan in the past month to do thorough background checks on his father's associates and especially his security. The senator didn't know this.

"By the look on your face, you have something for me," Grant observed.

Jake gave a brief nod. "Nothing on the senator's personnel. Everyone's got a clean record. We do have a lead on the explosive device."

"And?"

"Gazinef Holdings mines the triptinum ore. It's a subsidiary of YGE."

"You're fucking kidding me," Grant rasped. "Yashkin Global Enterprises owns Gazinef?"

"Yes. There are several companies that make the explosive device, but the blast didn't leave any signature as to whom the bomb maker was. Our only link right now is YGE, which makes me wonder if this isn't partly about your recent face-off on the Galleria deal."

"The Russian oligarchs do have strong links with the Russian mafia. Have you found any communication between Yashkin and the ROC?"

Jake shook his head. "Not through regular channels. I'm looking into his associates. I don't think he'd do his own dirty work."

"This troubles me," Grant said. "I just announced to the whole world that Blaire and I are together again." The picture of he and Blaire hit the tabloid news sites immediately after their lunch that day. "Rafe just informed me that Yashkin is giving him heartburn. What if he'd found a way to go after Blaire again?"

"We're speculating right now. Everything is circumstantial," Jake cautioned and then heaved a sigh. "I've uncovered another piece of information that I think might piss you off."

"What?"

"The paparazzi who hounded you and Ms. Peterson and took those pictures that were posted on the Tattler website? The tip came from Senator Thorne's office."

"Lynch," Grant growled. "How did you find this out?" Gus was a source of friction between the senator and Grant since Blaire's abduction. He wanted the man fired, but his dad and his political strategist had over twenty years of history. Although Lynch had been severely reprimanded, the senator had no intention of firing his aide.

"Phone records," Jake paused. "There are some phone calls from Lynch's phone to Russia, but they were telephone numbers of people working on the senator's legitimate projects."

Grant walked over to his chair and sunk into it. "Lynch is going to blow a gasket when he sees me and Blaire on the web. Blaire's association with the ROC is in the DOJ file. That's going to come out when each one of those assholes go to trial. We'll just have to weather public opinion." She and the U.S. Attorney and U.S. Marshals Service discussed witness protection, but Blaire told them she was done hiding and all the evidence was with the Justice Department anyway. Grant had pulled the U.S. Attorney aside and vowed to protect her with everything he had.

"How do you want me to proceed?" Jake asked.

"Narrow down the list of bomb makers. See if any of them would have been in contact with Yashkin or the ROC lately. Continue to search for a link between Orlov and Yashkin." Grant paused, rubbing a finger across his mouth contemplatively. "Also, Yashkin and Lynch."

"Lynch?"

Grant nodded. "Lynch wants Blaire out of the picture; Orlov wanted Blaire. Yashkin may or may not have a grudge against me. The Galleria deal wasn't the first time our companies have clashed. Lynch is our inside guy; Yashkin provides the bomb. By that time, Lynch's tabloid ruse already had Blaire doubting our relationship. Though I can't believe Lynch would put Mom in danger, he did jump at the chance to paint Blaire as the problem. The men who abducted her could have been either Yashkin or Orlov's."

"Blaire out of the picture serves Lynch's purpose, but what does Yashkin get out of this?"

"I'm not sure. My guess? He needs something from Orlov."

"With Orlov dead and most of the ROC in disarray, I guess he's the loser in this."

Grant smiled grimly. "And from experience, he's not very good at losing."

"Should we re-evaluate our security detail?"

Blaire was going to hate having more men on her, but Grant didn't want to keep her a prisoner in his penthouse either. He'd make damned sure she'd have a normal life as much as possible. Her eyes lit up when he told her she'd be helping in setting up the exhibit. "She's going to be assisting Jeffrey Hawkins with his gallery. I want a man on every exit and inside the gallery with her. I want you to start interviewing additional bodyguards."

"Good idea," Jake said. "Are you going to be explaining the increase in security to her?"

"She's probably gonna say I'm overreacting," Grant sighed. "Am I, Jake?"

"With all the evidence being circumstantial? I'd say yes, sir."

"Well it's a good thing I don't give a fuck."

IT WAS LATE when Grant entered the penthouse. All the lights were off except the under-cabinet lighting in the kitchen. He was about to pour himself some Scotch when he heard it.

The faint cry.

His jaw tightened.

Blaire was having another nightmare and this time he wasn't waiting another second to go to her. He headed down the hallway to her room. He tested the doorknob and it was locked. Grant pulled out the key. He'd always had the key, but his own guilt with his part in Blaire's abduction dictated he give her space. Although one might argue that forcing her to stay with him while he was giving her space defeated its purpose. But he'd had enough. She needed him and she'd pushed him away enough.

"No! Stop ... I don't know..." her sobs tore at his heart and shredded his soul. Long strides ate the distance between the door and her bed and he slid between the covers, gathering her into his arms. She fought him, her fist glanced off his jaw, but he held on to her. Emotions burned his eyes as her keening cry shook him to his core. And then she stopped.

She inhaled him while he held his breath.

"Grant?"

"You were having a nightmare." His voice was gruff.

She tried to push him away, but he held tight.

"Please, Angel," he pleaded. "Let me hold you."

When her body remained stiff, he added. "I need this."

Her answer was a resigned sigh and her body relaxed. Hope flared in his chest. He wasn't giving her a chance to change her mind, so he quickly toed off his shoes.

Grant missed holding her this way so fucking much. He wasn't going to screw up again. He just had to be patient.

32

Blaire

I WOKE up that morning against a hard wall of muscle and smelling the scent of spicy wood and man. Grant's chest was bare and judging from the rough hairs I was feeling against my legs, he had taken off his pants too. I should feel outraged—I was surprised I didn't. I felt comfortable and safe. Cherished.

Gah! I disentangled our limbs and shot off the bed. Even his sleepy groan of protest was sexy. I dashed into the en suite bathroom, locked the door and did my morning routine. As I was brushing my teeth, I realized this was the first morning I had not awakened with sadness.

The guilt came, but Dr. Jones' voice chased it away.

"Liam and your father wouldn't want you to mourn their deaths forever, Blaire. Don't waste their sacrifices by refusing to let go of your grief. Honor them by going after what makes you happy."

Painting made me happy, but I was happiest when I was with Grant. He also had the power to hurt me the most, and I didn't know if I could survive another breakup with him.

There was a knock on my bathroom door.

"Baby, are you all right in there?"

"Yes."

"Well, open up so I can use the bathroom."

"Can't you use the one in your own room?"

No answer.

The room was unusually quiet so maybe he'd left. I felt relief, disappointment and guilt—a very familiar emotion lately. This time it was because I was acting like a bitch when Grant had been nothing but supportive. I tried to argue with myself that he was holding me against my will, but, after that first week when my grief and guilt were at their most overwhelming, I'd never made another effort to leave. Probably because I had to face the U.S. Attorney. Besides, Grant would have found me anyway with the blasted tracker.

When I opened the bathroom door, I was shocked to see Grant lying on the bed against the headboard with one knee cocked lazily. All he had on were his boxer briefs and I couldn't help the heat that bloomed between my thighs.

"It's very presumptuous of you to sleep naked with me," I said, escaping to the closet. I wasn't wearing a bra and my nipples were a treacherous pair, hardening with just a heated gaze from him.

"You know that's the only way I do sleep," his voice was suddenly in my ear and I jumped.

He had me cornered in the closet and my breathing turned erratic.

"How do you manage to do that?"

"Do what?"

"Move so quietly when you're no lightweight."

"Ouch! Are you saying I'm fat?" Grant teased, moving closer as I shrank further into the tiny space.

"What are you doing?" I whispered.

"I don't know anymore," he muttered as his head lowered and pressed his lips to mine. I couldn't help it and parted my own, and we both groaned when our tongues met. One hand gripped my ass while the other gripped my side and I was lifted and crushed against him. His mouth devoured mine in a dominant kiss.

Grant broke off and whispered, "Wrap your legs around me."

Cold water extinguished my libido. I wasn't ready.

He noticed the conflict on my face and grimaced. He lowered me to the floor, but spread his arms, resting one hand at the door of the closet and the other against a wall, caging me in.

"Let me pass," I said.

"No," he gritted. "Not until you tell me why you're still so skittish about us. Why won't you give me another chance?"

"I don't trust you not to freeze me out again," I said. "When things get tough, that's when it's important to communicate, Grant."

His hand cupped my cheek and I welcomed the gesture.

"I loathe that it took almost losing you to learn my lesson," he said huskily. "I shut you out so the Galleria deal could receive my undivided attention. Jake asked me if it was worth losing you over and it wasn't. Not even close. It was my complacency thinking that I could keep you in one compartment of my life while I operated freely in others, but that was selfish."

"I'm not a toy that you can bring out whenever you want to play."

"That wasn't my intention!" he grated, taking his hand from my cheek and slapping it against the door. "There was danger around you and I needed you safe!"

"You didn't text or call me for three days because you were pissed at me for sparring with Tyler."

"I couldn't bring myself to call or text you because there were so many things I wanted to say to you. I wanted to settle our problems face-to-face. Words over text or phone can be misinterpreted and knowing how I say shit sometimes, I didn't want to make matters worse between us. I wanted that Galleria deal over so I can concentrate on us. And then at the ER ..."

"Let's not talk about that anymore," I interrupted.

"Blaire—"

"I didn't hold anything you said at that time against you, Grant. It hurt me, but I understood," I said. "Amelia came first. The senator and your sister needed you."

Something flashed in his eyes and his hands gripped my shoulders. "I handled that wrong," Grant rasped. "Things were shaky between us, and, again, I thought I could keep you locked away to figure things out later while I dealt with my family. Thinking I could deal with you when I felt I was ready without considering your feelings—that arrogance nearly cost me you."

"Am I still in a compartment?" I asked quietly.

"No. You're everything to me. You're my world, Blaire," he declared. "And fuck, I'm not telling you how I feel in a closet," Grant added ruefully.

I gave a nervous laugh even if a web of warmth drew the shattered pieces of my heart together.

His head lowered to brush his lips against mine. "I better leave you alone before I fuck you against the wall of this closet. Not how I envisioned making love to you again after a long time, but there's only so much self-control a man can have."

He backed away, not breaking our gaze. "Jeffrey Hawkins will be waiting for you at The Prestige Gallery at nine. I received word that the crates arrived last night and he'll be unpacking them this morning."

"Are you sure he won't mind me being there?"

"Let's put it this way, Blaire. You're my representative. Those paintings are mine for the time being unless someone files a legitimate claim," Grant said. "I made it clear to Hawkins that if he says or does anything to make you unhappy, I'm pulling the artwork from his gallery."

A distressed look must have crossed my face because Grant's expression softened. "Blaire, I know you don't see this side of me, but I need you to understand that I would do anything to make you happy."

"Yes, but it's making me look like a high-maintenance bitch that has to have all her whims catered to," I protested. I didn't want someone being nice to me because he was scared of Grant.

A corner of his mouth kicked up. "High-maintenance, yes." At my glare, he added. "Bitch, never. Look, consider this part of my courtship."

"This is becoming one expensive courtship," I muttered.

Grant was already at the door, his hand resting on the knob. "What was that they said? Go big or go home?"

I rolled my eyes as he chuckled and left the room.

WILL they or won't they?

 Billionaire Grant Thorne seen cozying up to Blaire Callahan at a popular SoHo Brasserie. The pair appears to be smitten with each other and the reports of physical abuse from a few weeks ago seem to be unfounded. Also, it seems Ms. Callahan has completely forgiven Thorne for his brief affair with his ex Kylie Peterson, rumored to be the reason for their breakup. Is another confirmed bachelor off the market? There are also emerging rumors about Ms. Callahan's background that she's the secret lovechild of the mob boss of the most powerful Bratva in Russia. Senator Thorne's office has no comment as of this time, but our sources say the relationship is causing heartburn for the people running Thorne's reelection bid as well as any future plans for the White House.

"Where do they dig up this garbage?" I muttered into my phone. "Now, I'm a mafia princess?"

"You're definitely causing us heartburn," Andy chuckled. He and I texted everyday and called each other when there was random news or development in the senator's affairs correlated to my former association with the ROC. "I thought I'd need to give Gus CPR this morning."

"How's the senator taking it?"

"He was troubled. I think he's going to talk to Grant this morning to address those rumors. Grant is not accepting any of Gus' calls from what I've heard."

"It's not up to Grant. It's up to the DOJ."

"Do they think the remnants of the ROC will come after you?"

"I'm not a witness for the prosecution in any of the cases. The list of potential witnesses is on a flash drive and the FBI is working on it." I was a safe keeper of the evidence. It was up to forensics, the judge, and the U.S. Attorney to admit or reject any evidence. "Besides, I have enough bodyguards as it is."

Tyler's eyes met mine in the rear-view mirror and crinkled. I was informed this morning that Grant would be expanding my security detail from three to six. Really? Jake was interviewing the new crew today.

Of course, Grant had been rushing out the door this morning and left poor Tyler to explain to me that there might be a Russian oligarch working with Orlov who had a beef against Grant or Thorne Industries. This information nagged at me, but I couldn't put my finger on why.

"Ha, you sure do. The office got the memo from Grant last night. His dad is grumbling that his son had more enemies than he does," Andy sighed. "Val is gonna hate this."

"So how are things going between you and Val?" As much as I disliked Grant's sister, Andy didn't share the same sentiment, so here I was being a good friend.

"Our second date went well," he said. "I think she finally believes I'm not interested in her just to keep her out of trouble."

"I don't think the Senator would do that."

"No, but you're forgetting who I report to."

"And are you, Andy?" I asked. "Did Gus put you up to this?"

"Of course not," he said, offended. "You're forgetting I was your only ally in that office when Gus and your boyfriend ganged up on you."

Old resentments sparked inside me. How could I forget that

meeting that started my distrust in Grant? "I'm sorry, Andy. You're right. However, Grant isn't my boyfriend."

Andy chuckled. "He's going to be more than that if he has his way."

"All right, Spencer, back to work."

"Trying to get rid of me?"

"I'm at the gallery."

"Oh, right. The Prestige, right? You mentioned you'll be curating the artwork."

"Yup."

"Has it arrived?"

"Last night."

"Are you excited?"

"Jeez, I'm hanging up now."

Andy barked a laugh as I ended the call. I tried to hide my smile, but Tyler caught my expression in the mirror. "What?"

"Mr. Thorne doesn't like you talking to him," Tyler said as he pulled into the back alley leading to the rear of the gallery.

"He doesn't like me talking to any man. I'm surprised he's letting me work with Jeffrey Hawkins."

"He thinks Spencer is spying for Gus."

"What are you saying? They're playing bad cop, good cop?"

Tyler's non-answer was answer enough.

Andy was easy to talk to. He was like the younger brother I'd never had. A pang of sadness clutched my heart as I remembered Liam. He was like a protective uncle, surrogate father, and older brother rolled into one. I missed him so much.

33

Blaire

Jeffrey Hawkins was a man of about sixty. He had a head of gray hair that was balding at the crown. A man with a lanky build, he was slightly taller than me. He wore round spectacles that sat on the bridge of a fleshy nose. I took careful note of his appearance because there seemed to be a few men Grant would let near me, and I wondered if his choice of gallery had anything to do with his possessiveness.

Jeff was as scholarly as he looked. He also introduced me to his gallery manager, Sofia Ricci. I couldn't place her age, probably fifty, but she looked like the glamorous movie stars of the gilded age. Full breasts and full hips were sheathed in a tight jersey dress. I guess Jeff wanted to be left alone with the artwork, while Sofia dealt with customers.

"Do you want some coffee, dear?" Sofia asked. Full lips too. I couldn't help staring.

"Uh ..."

"No, Sofia," Jeff said. "You know what I think about drinks and food around all those paintings."

His manager shrugged her elegant shoulders and pivoted on her three-inch heels. She brushed a finger on Tyler's suit. "How about you, handsome?"

"I'll be with her," Tyler nodded to me. "So, no."

Just then, the gallery door jingled and a man in a disheveled suit walked in. His skin was the color of caramel, but for some reason he looked pale. Tyler tensed beside me. I saw Bobby, my other body-guard, follow in behind the newcomer.

Sofia clacked on the tiled floor as she moved to intercept Suit Guy even when his eyes were zeroed in on me.

"May I help you, sir?"

"I have a few questions for Ms. Callahan," Suit Guy said and flashed an agency badge I didn't catch. After passing Sofia, Tyler blocked him.

He flashed his badge again. "Special Agent Wilkes. I'm from the Miami field office. I remember you." He eyed Tyler. "You were with Mr. Thorne that day."

"Tyler?" I asked tentatively.

"You need to call Mr. Thorne's PA and set up an appointment," Tyler gritted out. "You can't ambush Ms. Callahan like this."

"Your boss's office has been giving me the run-around," Wilkes said. "I'm kinda sick of it."

"As far as I know, the case has been transferred to the Boston field office."

"Ah, that's convenient, isn't it?" Wilkes said. "But I'm not here for what happened with the ROC. But I do have questions about Liam Watts."

I couldn't stand behind Tyler anymore, so I walked around him. "Liam is dead, Agent Wilkes. What could you possibly want to know about him?"

The fed smiled, but there was malice in his grin. "A couple of weeks ago, we found the body of a missing FBI agent. He was six months from retirement." The haunted flash in Wilkes' eyes indicated that he knew the guy well. "We have evidence that links Watts to his murder." His eyes sharpened and pinned me with a calculating stare. "Do you know why he killed him, Ms. Callahan?"

The dead guy must be the fed Liam was after who had the keys to the self-storage unit.

Oh, Liam, what did you do?

"I don't think Liam killed him," I replied, doing my best to hold Wilkes' gaze. "But he can't defend himself, can he? He's dead." I repeated, my voice hoarse. "What do you hope to accomplish by pursuing this?"

"The agent's body showed signs that he was tortured for information."

"Sounds like a ROC M.O." I said.

"Ms. Callahan ..."

"You're done," Tyler ordered. "Ms. Callahan has been through enough. I suggest you contact Mr. Thorne's office if you want an audience, but the better option is to drop this if your suspect is Watts. The man is dead. You saw his body."

"No, I didn't," the fed replied.

"What?" Blaire whispered.

"I never saw a body because it never arrived at the medical examiner's office. Some bullshit agency whisked the bodies of Watts and his men away."

"And Orlov?"

Wilkes smiled grimly. "Orlov and his crew are dead-dead. Don't worry about that." He searched my face, reading something in it and sighed. "I guess you know nothing."

I wouldn't say I knew nothing, but I didn't know about Liam's body never getting to the ME's office. They took three weeks to process it. "Maybe it was the Boston Feds."

"It's not," Wilkes said. "I guess I need to pay a visit to his daughter."

He started to turn away, but I called his attention. "Agent Wilkes. Liam had not seen his daughter in six years. The next time she saw him, she had to bury him. Let this go."

Wilkes studied me for long seconds before he inclined his head, walked past Bobby, and left.

I didn't realize my heart was pounding until I leveled my gaze at Tyler. "Could Liam be ...?"

"He had no pulse, Blaire," my bodyguard reminded me. His voice was too gentle, almost as if he pitied me. "You attended his funeral."

I kept my tears at bay and took several breaths to calm my racing heart. I needed to move on. When my composure returned, I looked at Jeff and pasted a smile on my face. "Shall we look at the paintings?"

THE CONTENTS of the first crate lay before us. Six paintings, each secured in a tee-frame and wrapped in polyethylene. Jeff and I were crouched in front of one as he carefully sliced through the tape that secured the plastic.

"Shipping masterpieces internationally has become harder," Jeff said as he reverently peeled the layers of covering from the three-foot by two-foot painting. "It's fortunate Mr. Thorne has the money and connections to make things happen. Otherwise it would have taken months instead of weeks to get these pieces here."

"That long?" I murmured as I turned the artwork on its length.

"Museums plan for a year. Galleries for a couple of months. Most of them have to pass through an airline subcontractor who may have to repack them if the crate tests for explosives." Jeff shuddered at the thought and so did I. "A painting that costs millions could end up ruined with a slice from a box cutter."

"Grant facilitated the transfer?"

"A man of Mr. Thorne's caliber knows the right people and ...Oh my God," Jeff broke off as he peeled the last layer of plastic to reveal the painting underneath. Even without looking at the signature, we knew we were looking at the work of a painting legend. "Marie-Thérèse," the older man breathed. Picasso's muse and mistress during the 1930s. I was not familiar with the name of this painting, but it could be chalked up as the long lost work of the master.

We worked carefully to unwrap the next five paintings. Though Jeff needed to take these pieces under a magnifying glass to certify their authenticity, he told me that he was confident that three of the six were originals from the old masters. Hours passed. Tyler and I took a quick break for lunch while Jeff ate at his office. At two that afternoon, we returned to "The Vault" as Jeff liked to call it—an area separated from the main gallery by heavy curtains that dropped from the fifteen-foot ceiling—where all the paintings yet to be displayed were kept. He had the first Picasso we unwrapped under a lit table and was analyzing the brush strokes. Reproductions were usually flat, while some Giclée prints—fine art created on inkjet printers—may have some dabs of paint by the artist to pass as original work. However, there were also counterfeit paintings and it took a very experienced art dealer to validate its authenticity.

"Shall we uncrate the third box?" I asked. The second crate had contained two Renoirs.

Jeff looked at me distractedly. "Yes. Yes." He reluctantly left the Picasso. Tyler helped us pry the boards off the crates with a crow bar. The first painting from that batch was from an unknown artist. "This collector has odd taste." I could hear the frustration in his voice. We proceeded to the next one. When Jeff lifted the polyethylene to reveal the first half of the painting, I was struck with déjà vu. A familiar landscape of impressionist art stared back at me.

"What do we have here?" Jeff wondered as he removed the plastic veil to uncover the full view of the painting. "The style reminds me of Van Gogh, but the artist has his own unique strokes."

"Sergei," I whispered.

"What was that, dear?" Jeff asked absent-mindedly.

I shook my head as I helped remove the T-frame and when it was done, I looked for the signature. There, in its familiar cursive, it mocked me.

Sergei Kostin.

IN TOTAL, there were twenty-four paintings unearthed from four crates. Half of them could be original works by the old masters and Jeff estimated their worth at more than seven-hundred-million dollars when all was said and done. Some of the priceless paintings were moved to a room secured with an electronic keypad lock.

I found three more paintings by Sergei.

Jeff went out on the floor to answer questions from some customers. I overheard Sofia telling Tyler that the shop's busiest time was between five and seven. Expecting Jeff to be occupied for the next hour and a half, I asked to use his table with the overhead light. It had a swivel arm with a magnifying glass. I was anxious to see what Sergei was hiding underneath. Mounting one of Sergei's paintings, I studied the brush strokes. It was a different medium, not watercolor, but I could almost see what it was trying to mask under layers of pigment.

My gut churned and I wasn't sure if it was from hunger or excitement. Since Grant was working late, Tyler and I decided it was a good time to grab dinner.

"Bravo-niner-niner, you there?"

I turned to look at Tyler and noticed the grin on his face. I'd never heard that call sign before, but I figured he was messing with Bobby.

"Copy. Go ahead," Bobby's slightly amused voice answered.

"We have a situation," Tyler continued speaking through his wrist comm. "Paintpixie needs to be fed or we'll be having a crisis on our hands. Something of the high-sodium variety would be ideal."

I scowled at Tyler as he winked at me.

"Copy that. Hotdogs, chief?"

"Affirmative. Four hotdogs and two Cokes."

"She can eat four?" Bobby chuckled.

"Two are for me, dumbass," Tyler shot back.

I shook my head at their continued banter and turned my attention back on the piece before me. After a few minutes, I heard Bobby tell Tyler that he would meet him at the entrance.

"You'll be okay while I secure the package?" Tyler asked, deadpan.

I waved my arm without looking at him. "Shoo! Go play your spy games."

Tyler's bark of laughter echoed in the Vault. Poor guys. They were so bored being my bodyguards, they were trying to liven things up however they could.

I didn't realize Tyler had been gone for a while until footsteps clicked behind me. It struck me as strange that no aroma of hotdogs hit me, but I was too engrossed in studying Sergei's work to turn around. "You had to use a map to find your way back?" I teased Tyler.

"It's beautiful, isn't it?" an unfamiliar voice said behind me.

I whipped around and saw a man dressed impeccably in a suit. He was tall but not quite six-feet. Thick dark hair was slicked back over his head. He had dark eyes, maybe brown, and a lean build. This man would have blended easily with the rest of Manhattan except for the jagged scar that ran across his right cheek.

"This area is off limits," I told him. What happened to Tyler?

His eyes looked over Sergei's paintings. "My boss wants those four."

"Didn't you hear me?" I hated that my voice grew shrill. "You can't be here. Please leave."

"Don't you want to find out what's underneath those, Paulina?"

Oh my God.

"Who are you?"

His head cocked to the side and I realized he was wearing an earpiece. "Your guard dog is on his way back. We'll meet again."

He disappeared behind the curtains. I ran after him and bumped into a couple. I apologized and searched frantically around the gallery. There were a few customers milling around, but the gallery was so big that it was impossible that he'd taken off so fast. Jeff was talking to an elderly couple in front of a colorful drip work piece. Sofia was assisting another man in a suit regarding a bronze sculpture, but the man I was looking for was nowhere in sight. I looked down the hallway on my right.

"Hey," Tyler said, hurrying toward me. "Homeless guy took a

swing at Bobby and tried to grab the hotdogs … Blaire, what's wrong?" He looked around frowning. "And where's Drew?"

"A man approached me in The Vault."

"What?" Tyler's brows furrowed as he led me back behind the curtains and lowered the hotdogs and drinks. "Just now?"

I nodded. "He just disappeared. I think he went in the direction of the restrooms, but I didn't want to follow."

"I told Drew to keep an eye on you," Tyler said tightly as he drew his gun from behind him and held it low at his side. He spoke into his wrist comm and after a few seconds, he swore, "Drew's not answering his radio. I told Bobby to check on him."

"What's going on?" Jeff asked, alarmed when he saw Tyler's gun. His eyes widened at our hotdogs on the table. "I told you both that food is not allowed—"

"Shut up," Tyler and I said in unison.

"Stay here," my bodyguard told me.

"Nope, I'm coming with you." I withdrew my own Beretta Pico from my ankle holster.

"Why are you both carrying guns?" Jeff asked, following us through the curtains and right to the hallway. Tyler ordered him to stay back. Following behind my bodyguard, we walked past the restrooms and headed to the exit. Tyler bumped his hip into the exit bar with his gun at the ready.

"What the fuck?" he cursed and I got right beside him to see what had unsettled him.

Bobby was crouched down over Drew. He glanced up at us. "He's breathing."

"Call 911!" Tyler ordered as he yanked the door to the gallery open and shoved me back inside. He was talking to me, but I wasn't hearing him because Orlov's words came back to haunt me.

You're lucky I'm not allowed to kill you.

Make sure Marco is dead; we need Paulina alive.

Someone was still after me.

34

Grant

"YOU AND BLAIRE need to make a statement to the press."

"No, we don't." Grant narrowed his gaze at August Lynch who sat across the desk from him. The man had a lot of guts showing up here when he knew Grant wanted him gone from the senator's team and from their lives.

"Senator," Gus looked at his dad who was staring out the window. "Talk some sense into your son. We have a responsibility to your donors to make sure they're not backing a man with links to the Russian mafia."

Marcus Thorne turned around and sighed, looking briefly in Grant's direction. "Grant, as much as I hate to break your rule about not responding to tabloid news, Gus has a point. You know the country is watching U.S. relations with the Kremlin ... the rumors of its involvement in the last presidential election."

"Not to mention your buying up real estate in Moscow is doing nothing to dispel rumors that you have some officials in the Kremlin and the Russian mafia doing favors for you," Gus said.

"The Russian mafia nearly killed my woman," Grant reminded him darkly, although he wouldn't deny or admit to greasing a few palms in the Kremlin to facilitate business transactions. A corporation would never survive in a country where the government was corrupt without a couple of well-placed bribes. It usually spelled safety or doom for his employees and saved them the trouble from the government or the rebels. International business wasn't cut-and-dried, but Grant's awareness of a country's political situation, how to work around the corruption, and how to win the loyalty of the locals were very important to its success. He hated to capitulate to Gus' requests, but he hated to put his father in this untenable position more. "Blaire and I will speak to the DOJ and ask them what we can and can't reveal."

"That's all I ask," the senator said. "Now, your mom is waiting at the hotel and she's been pushing for dinner tonight with you and Blaire. She misses her."

"Not her son?" Grant quirked a brow in amusement. "I'm sure Blaire would love to catch up with her. Let me check—"

There was commotion outside his office and then Jake burst into the room with an angry Morris following.

"You should teach your people manners, Thorne," Gus said.

"I'm sorry, sir—" Morris huffed.

"Last I checked, this was my office," Grant snapped at his father's aide. The look on Jake's face already had him thinking the worst. He jumped up from his chair and was already rounding the table. "Blaire?"

"There was an incident in the gallery. Something's going down."

"What?" Grant grated, already heading out the door with Jake.

"Tyler's call got cut off. Either they're jamming the signal or—"

"Don't fucking say it," he gritted out. "NYPD?"

"Already sent them."

"What do we know?" They got into the elevator.

"We're down a man—Drew."

"How the fuck did this happen?" Shit, his dad. What if this was a coordinated attack? When they got to the ground floor, he called the senator.

"Grant, what the hell is going on?"

"I don't know. Does mom have security at the hotel?"

"Of course."

"Get there and wait for us. As soon as I have information, I'll let you know."

"Be careful, Grant."

"I will."

Blaire

"I'M CALLING JAKE," Tyler said.

Sofia and Jeff walked over to us. "What's going on?"

"You need to close the gallery," I said, trying to remain calm. "Someone attacked our man outside and ..." My words trailed off when I noticed Tyler's pissed-off expression.

"Hello ... Jake ... what the fuck?" He glared at his phone before looking at me. "I can't get a signal."

I turned back to Sofia and Jeff. "Let's get everyone out now." People were starting to notice our huddle and the fact that my body-guard and I were holding guns.

"Blaire, we need to get you out of here." Tyler's demeanor had turned urgent.

"I agree, but let's get the people out of here first."

We heard screeching tires and what sounded like gunshots in the back alley. There were gasps, small sobs, and cursing from the people in the gallery.

More gunshots echoed from outside.

The customers started running for the entrance while Sofia and Jeff sprung into action to lead them out.

Tyler dragged me down the hallway. His gun-hand doing a sweep between the back alley exit and the gallery entrance. When we reached the ladies' room, he pushed me inside, put me in a stall, and ordered me to lock it.

"We don't know if someone's waiting outside to grab you," Tyler told me. "We wait for help here."

"You need to help Bobby and Drew!" I slapped my palm against the closed door.

"No, Blaire," Tyler said, his voice resolute. "My responsibility is to you."

"But Bobby—"

"Is doing his job." The gutturalness of Tyler's tone told me what it was costing him not to help his colleague.

"This is bullshit!" I whisper-yelled. "We need to help them!"

"Shut-up," Tyler hissed.

I was fuming. I wasn't helpless. I could fight. I could shoot, but I couldn't distract Tyler if he wouldn't let me help him, so I kept quiet.

The gunshots had stopped.

Voices filtered from the hallway. They were a bit muffled, but I could decipher their words.

"Let's get the paintings and go."

"How about the girl?"

I watched through the space between the stall's door and frame. Tyler was flat against the wall beside the entrance, his chest rising and falling heavily with both hands on the gun. The door to the bathroom opened a crack and I stepped up onto the rim of the porcelain toilet.

Sirens wailed in the distance.

"Shit! Cops!"

"We need to go. Paintings are priority."

"What about the girl?"

"He may not need her."

The restroom door closed and Tyler's shoulders relaxed a tad as I slowly lowered my feet to the floor. I hadn't said a word and neither had Tyler, but I was sure his mind was busy figuring out what had just happened.

As for me, I had one thought: *Will this mess ever end?*

Grant

AS WAS with every rush hour in New York, traffic was at standstill. The race from lower Manhattan to SoHo took on a snail's pace and each passing second was agony.

"Did you check Church Street?" he demanded of their driver, Zed, while Jake checked the police scanners for information.

"Yes, sir. West Street is the fastest route."

Grant tried Blaire's phone again and still couldn't get through. He wanted to hurl the device out the window. He needed to get to her fast, dammit.

"The jamming signal is affecting cellular activity for a quarter-mile radius," Jake informed him.

When their vehicle hit another red light after barely moving a block, Grant had had enough. They'd be faster on foot with the gallery less than two miles away. He shoved the door open and hopped out. Not waiting for his bodyguard, he took off up West Street.

"Mr. Thorne," Jake growled as he caught up with him. "You can't just take off like that."

"I just did, Donovan" Grant told him, weaving in and out of pedestrians.

"I can't protect you if you disregard all security protocols."

"Fuck the protocols," he muttered as he jogged faster, shouldering past people who cursed at him. He may have shoved a hipster out of the way who had no business moseying at this hour like he was taking a stroll in Central Park. He was single-minded in his determination to get to Blaire, and no one was getting in his way. Jake learned this quickly, kept his mouth shut, and kept pace with him.

Entering the SoHo district, Grant left the main road and crossed over to the side street where the gallery was located. Less traffic—both people and cars, but a few blocks up he saw the strobing lights of four NYPD cruisers. Grant broke into a run, thanking his daily workouts for enabling him to dash up Manhattan without breaking a sweat. If he was sweating for any reason, it wasn't from physical exertion but from anxiety and adrenaline.

The police were getting ready to cordon off the perimeter to keep away spectators.

Air whooshed out of his lungs as dizzying relief slammed him when he spotted Jeff, Blaire, and Tyler talking to a uniform just inside the gallery. He didn't even think, he just approached the shop and was immediately stopped by an officer.

"Sir, you need to stand back."

Grant pointed to Blaire. "That's my girlfriend."

"Hold on." The cop spoke to his shoulder radio. "Hey, Will, guy here says he's Ms. Callahan's boyfriend."

The uniform talking to Blaire craned his neck to look through the glass doors. "Shit, that's Grant Thorne. Let him through."

Grant and Jake were escorted through the gallery threshold. With long purposeful strides, he headed straight for his woman whose face lit up when she spotted him. Her expression did funny things to his chest.

Blaire broke away from the huddle and rushed toward him. He quickened his steps and swept her into his arms, held her tight, and buried his face in the crook of her neck.

"Grant," she breathed. The manner with which she said his name eased the crazy terror that dominated his thoughts during the fifteen-minute sprint through Manhattan.

"Blaire. Oh, Christ, baby," he whispered in her ear. He must be crushing the shit out of her, but he couldn't seem to get close enough. He wanted everyone to disappear so he could be alone with her. "I was so fucking scared," he confessed roughly. He planted quick kisses over her upturned face before capturing her lips in a long searing one. Fear and adrenaline were morphing into a primal need to be inside her. He couldn't stop touching her.

"Ahem." A clearing of the throat brought them out of their haze.

Grant glared at the uniform who interrupted him. "Are you done taking her statement?"

"Mr. Thorne, right?" the officer confirmed. "It appears we've had a daring art heist."

"I see," Grant said. He didn't really care about the art at this point, so he turned to Tyler. "How're Bobby and Drew?"

"Bobby is critical with several GSWs," Tyler said. "Drew has a concussion. He was still unconscious when the ambulance took him away."

"I don't understand," Jeff said. "They took four paintings—not one of them was from the old masters that was worth millions."

Blaire stiffened in his arms and dread swirled in his gut. He sensed she knew something. He tamped down the fierce desire to shake the truth out of her. So help her God, if she'd been keeping something from him again—but he'd already learned his lesson when he shut her out the last time she didn't tell him everything. He accidentally squeezed her too tight as he struggled with his internal conflict.

"Grant," she protested.

He relaxed his grip but continued holding her. The nagging fear that she could be snatched any moment had been festering since she'd first been abducted and, after this incident, it wouldn't surprise him if he'd become psychotic with her safety. Heaven help him, he wanted to chain Blaire to his side so he could personally watch over her.

"Mr. Thorne," the cop said. "We do need to clear this place for the crime scene crew to do their job. The detectives are on their way. I believe the paintings that were stolen belong to you?"

"That's correct, officer. Listen, I need to take Ms. Callahan home. Any questions regarding the paintings can be directed toward Mr. Hawkins. Tyler, stay to answer the questions for the detectives, but once that's done, I want you back at the penthouse."

"Yes, sir."

Grant ushered Blaire toward the gallery entrance, "Donovan, where's the car?"

"Zed parked just up a block."

"Good. Find out which hospital they've taken Bobby and Drew. Send two of our guys to watch over them. We need to find out what happened when they're ready to talk."

"We're going back to the penthouse?" Blaire asked.

"Yes. Dad's in New York with Mom. I need to talk to you first before I call them over." Grant pulled out his phone and swiped a number.

His dad came on the line on the first ring. "Grant, any news?"

"Blaire's fine. I want you guys to come over to the penthouse at ten."

"Two hours from now? Where are you going?"

"I need to talk to Blaire first, and Tyler should have more information by then, but he needs to stay behind to talk to the detectives."

"Does this have something to do with Blaire again?" There was no accusation in his father's tone, just a need to find out the truth.

"I don't know yet, Dad."

"All right," his father replied. "We'll be there at ten." Grant thumbed the call off.

"Amelia and the Senator are in New York?"

"Yes," Grant answered as they exited to curious onlookers. Jake nodded to the other two men who were part of his security detail. Those men remained discreet so in case there were threats coming at Grant and Blaire, they could intervene with an element of surprise.

There were so many questions he needed to ask and, with the way Jake looked at Blaire and then back at Grant, Donovan had the same burning questions. Who were those men? Why did they take those particular paintings? And why the hell did Blaire look like she knew exactly what was going on?

35

Blaire

OXYGEN SEEMED to be in short supply inside the vehicle, or maybe, Grant was holding me too tight. Or maybe the weight of my past was coming back to suffocate me. Art had been my escape. That was the only place I found refuge in the violence of my childhood's checkered past. That one solace was now ruined and I was drowning.

"I can't breathe," I croaked.

Arms that cleaved me to a hard chest loosened and I heard a muttered apology. Grant's hands continued to touch me, as though he was making sure I was there beside him and I was okay. As for me, I'd been transported momentarily to that time with Sergei. I knew the questions would come, and I intended to answer them the best I could remember because I wanted to find out what was happening as well.

I caught Jake's eyes in the rearview mirror. He was riding in the passenger side as Zed drove us back to Grant's penthouse in the Upper East Side. Unlike the suspicious glare the first time he found out my father was the mob's cleaner, there was a thoughtfulness in his gaze. There was concern that was directed at me and that gave me courage to face what was ahead.

"Did you know the men who took the paintings, Blaire?"

"Let's leave the questions until we get her to the penthouse," Grant said sharply.

"No," I said, straightening up in my seat. "It's all right, Grant." I put a placating hand on his thigh and heard a rumble in his throat. "No, I didn't know them, but the paintings they took have a link to my past and something the man in the suit said makes me think they know of that link."

"Wait, what man in a suit?" Grant asked. "And how did he talk to you? Weren't you and Tyler keeping low in the restroom?"

I sighed. Maybe it was better to talk about this in the penthouse. "No. The man approached me—"

"How?" Grant snapped.

"Um, Tyler went to pick up dinner—"

Grant swore. "He fucking left you?"

"Bobby was going to hand him the food at the entrance but a homeless guy attacked Bobby. Tyler radioed Drew to keep an eye on me..." I glanced at Jake—I couldn't read his expression, but the man beside me was about to blow a fuse. "Please don't blame Tyler."

"Oh, I'm not going to blame him," Grant replied in a deceptively soft voice even as his breathing grew shallow. "I'm going to fucking bury him." He grabbed his phone but I managed to knock it out of his hand.

"What the fuck?" Grant glared at me.

"You need to calm down. Tyler is already beating himself over it," I hissed. "He's beating himself up over damned hotdogs for Christ's sake!"

"He shouldn't have left you!" Grant snarled. "That's why we're getting you more security."

"Why do I even carry a gun if I can't be left alone for two seconds? Stop making me into a helpless victim who can't defend herself!" I yelled, untangling myself from him and scooting over to the far side of the seat so I can look at him better. His features were lit by the neon signs of the passing buildings and I witnessed the slackening of his jaw and the alarm in his eyes.

"Blaire," he whispered as he tentatively reached out. "Don't pull away."

"Jesus, Grant, I'm not," I sighed raggedly. "You're just too much sometimes and it's overwhelming." I hugged my upper arms and stared out the window. Out of the corner of my eye, I saw his hand drop which caused a pinch in my chest. I hated hurting him, but I couldn't let him blame or, even worse, fire Tyler. The answer wasn't to lock me away from the world. I was so sick and tired of that. Liam protected me, but he also provided the tools and skills so I could protect myself. Grant needed to see I wasn't a fragile flower. If the past few weeks and especially what that scene at the gallery proved to me was this: I still had a lot of fight left in me and I was ready to take my life back.

"Maybe we should talk about this at the penthouse," Jake suggested.

I could feel Grant's eyes on me, so I nodded.

WHEN JAKE LET us into the penthouse, Grant told him to give us a moment and to let Colette know that we would be having guests at ten. The security detail and the housekeeper had apartments on the floor below the penthouse. When Jake disappeared back into the elevators, Grant asked me if I wanted anything to drink. I shook my head and walked to the fridge to get myself a glass of water while he headed to the bar and poured himself three fingers of Scotch. He tossed that back and turned around to face me.

"This uncertainty ends now," he growled as he stalked toward me, pinning me with his heated gaze.

Startled, I managed to lower my glass on the center island where I was standing when his hands grabbed me and lifted me on the counter. His fingers dug into my hair, tilting my face up before he slammed his mouth on mine. My lips parted and he didn't waste time forcing my tongue to respond to his. I had denied myself the touch of this man for so long, he was like a drink from an oasis in the desert. Clothing ripped and buttons went flying. It was his shirt and I was the aggressor. A satisfied grunt rumbled in his throat and I tried to tear my mouth away, but he wouldn't let me. More buttons went flying and I felt cool air touch my breasts as my sweater laid open. He finally let me up for air only to yank the cup of my bra away, then I was on my back as he fastened his mouth on my nipple. He tormented me there as heat gathered low in my belly. His mouth was needed somewhere else.

"Grant," I moaned. "Isn't someone coming?"

He let go of a nipple with a pop. "You are."

I yanked at his hair to make him look at me. "We can't do this."

"The fuck we can't." Lust and annoyance flared in his eyes.

"I mean, right now," I wheezed. "Later. Fuck me later. When we have more time."

He stilled. "Are you mine?"

"I've always been yours," I stated softly.

He rested his forehead on my belly and muttered something like "About fucking time."

Grant helped me sit up and I glanced around, mortified at the broken glass and the scattering of buttons on the floor. I didn't even hear the glass fall. "Oh, no, we need to clean up."

"Colette will take care of it."

"We can't let her see this mess!"

Grant looked at me with amusement. "I pay my people to be discreet."

"I won't be able to look her in the eyes."

His finger went under my chin, and tilted it up so I was looking at him. "Blaire, we're going to be making love in every corner of this penthouse. We're bound to leave evidence of our fucking behind. Might as well get used to it."

"But—"

"Now, I don't want Donovan to see my woman half-naked. Go get changed and I'll call him up."

He pulled me off the counter and slapped my ass playfully. I glared at him but did as I was told.

"His name is Sergei Kostin."

Grant, Jake, and I were in his penthouse office. I had changed into tights and a tunic sweater. I wanted nothing more than to slip into my flannel pajamas but we were being invaded in an hour. Grant had changed into drawstring sweatpants and a worn-out, long-sleeved Harvard tee. I had the urge to cuddle on his lap and have his strong arms wrap their warmth around me. I missed the intimacy between us. Grant was a force to be reckoned with and I'd been afraid that I was too beaten down to be the woman he needed. His devotion this past month had eased the uncertainties that plagued me about resuming a relationship with him. I wanted to come back to him with a clean slate, but Grant wasn't waiting any longer and, apparently, I didn't want to either.

"He was a painter who came to live with us and was my artistic mentor." I went on to tell them about the summers with Sergei and that last year when I was sixteen and what he had taught me.

Jake stared at me as if he was re-evaluating what he knew about me. As for Grant, his expression was one of bemusement. "Are you telling us you concealed paintings for smuggling?"

"Sergei taught me how to do it. I've never actually done it on stolen work." I felt I needed to qualify that difference.

"A Jackson Pollock, you say?" Grant queried.

"Yup. There are different methods of concealment. The easiest one is to layer the canvas of an existing less valuable painting over the intended one, but most art heists are done by taking the painting off the frame and smuggling them through shipping tubes. Sergei liked to use watercolor since it's easy to wash off. The ones I saw in the gallery, though, used a different medium. I'd probably need the guide of a spectrometer to use a scalpel and solvent to reveal the painting beneath."

"You think they're coming after you?" Grant asked.

I swallowed hard. "The man in the suit asked me if I wanted to find out what was underneath that painting. Depending on its complexity, anyone experienced with restoration can do it."

"Maybe they don't need you for these paintings, but for future heists," Jake speculated. "From what you've told us, you've become Sergei's protégé."

I scowled at Jake as an image of myself chained to a basement with paintings lined up for me to camouflage flashed through my mind. "Geez, I hope not."

"Not gonna happen," Grant assured me, curling his fingers into mine and tugging me to his side. "We've got a tracker on you, remember?"

"Your paranoia is serving me well," I murmured. Then I remembered Orlov's words. Even if I didn't want to add to Grant's problems, I had to tell him everything. "There's something else."

Jake and Grant straightened in alert. I could feel their apprehension. God, I hated doing this to them.

"Lay it on us, Ms. Blaire," Jake invited.

I recounted the Russian Vor's words. "I'm trying to figure it out in my head, but it sounded like he was handing me to someone else after he'd had his revenge on me."

"Sounded like it," Grant stated grimly. The wave of rage coming off him was palpable. "You're thinking what I'm thinking, Donovan?"

"Ivan Yashkin," Jake replied.

"Exactly."

"Who's Ivan Yashkin?" I asked.

"He was my main rival for the Galleria Development," Grant explained. "Rafe and I were baffled with how rabid he'd gone after that property deal when real estate isn't his company's specialty."

"The paintings. That's what he must've been after," Jake said.

"But he left the expensive ones," I said. "We're looking at seven-hundred million dollars."

Grant whistled and cocked his head to the side. "That's more than what the Galleria cost."

"You're sitting on a goldmine, boss," his head of security said.

"I doubt I'll end up keeping most of them," Grant replied. "I'll have to staff up my investigative division just to look into the claims."

There was a rap on the door and Tyler walked in.

He grimaced when he looked at Grant who, I could only imagine, had his glare on. I squeezed his hand.

"I know I messed up, Mr. Thorne," Tyler said, looking at me.

"You sure did," Grant grated out. "You're lucky Blaire stuck up for you or you'd be finding a new job."

Tyler's face reddened as he looked at the floor.

"Don't make the same mistake again," Grant told him.

"What? Getting me hotdogs?" I quipped.

"Blaire this isn't funny. That suit guy could have kidnapped you."

"I would have put up a fight, Grant, and Tyler would have returned by then," I argued. "I'm here. I'm alive. You need Tyler. You're two men down, so can we move on?"

A protracted silence reigned in the room and I could feel Grant's struggle not to go off on Tyler some more. He finally lifted his chin at my bodyguard. "What do you have?"

"There was not much crime scene to process. The thieves were in and out of there in minutes. They wore gloves. Cops found the jammer at the cable box right outside the gallery and I found a hidden camera attached to the curtains."

"What?" All three of us chorused.

"The guy in the suit knew when to approach you, Blaire. He came in when the paintings they stole were uncrated and he knew I wasn't with you," Tyler said. "Anyone could have clipped that camera there. I have a copy of the surveillance footage from today, but my guess is, the camera was placed when we went out to lunch and Jeff was in his office. I talked to Sofia and she said they had a rush of people around noon."

"Did the gallery post any announcement about the forthcoming exhibit, Grant?"

"Yes," he said. "It was posted in the New York Times art section two weeks ago."

"That means we can't base our suspect list on people who knew about the art being there. Is this where you're going with this, Blaire?" Jake asked.

I nodded. "So who knew the Sergei paintings would be in the crates arriving from Russia?"

"Our people in Moscow," Grant said.

"Are they contractors?" I asked.

"Yes. They specialize in shipping valuable art work, but I have trusted people who supervised the entire process from extracting the paintings from the basement of the apartment building to their shipment." Grant looked at Jake. "Can you coordinate with Heather? We need to check the history of ownership on that building for the past twenty years."

"Sergei might have used an alias," I pointed out.

"That's very likely," Grant muttered in agreement.

There was another knock on the door and Colette stepped in, looking very put together even at ten in the evening. "The senator and your mother have arrived, Mr. Thorne."

"Show them into the living room, will you, Colette?" Grant requested. "Tyler, Donovan, give us a minute." He pulled me closer.

When everyone left the room, he turned me slightly so I was facing him. His hands went to my shoulders. "Blaire, I know I don't have a good track record when we're facing my father, but whatever I say in there, please go along with it."

"I don't want to lie."

"We won't be lying. We will be omitting some facts and there isn't enough time to explain why."

I trusted Grant, and yet, I had an odd feeling he was bulldozing me into something.

"Okay."

The triumphant gleam in his eyes made me want to renege on agreeing with his request, but he was already leading me out of the office.

36

Grant

GRANT STOOD by his dad as they watched his mother and Blaire fuss over each other. The women had not seen each other since the accident and Blaire's subsequent abduction, although he knew they communicated regularly through text or phone call. His mother needed to recuperate from the head injury and it was only now that the senator allowed his wife to travel. In that regard, Grant was similar to his father—they were protective of their women.

"I'm glad you're all right," Mom said to Blaire. "When Marcus told me you'd been attacked at the gallery, I feared the worst."

So did I, Grant thought.

"So do we know exactly who we're dealing with?" Gus asked. His father's political advisor was seated on a single sofa, with his right ankle crossed over left knee. He'd been watching Blaire like a hawk and it took all of Grant's self-control not to toss the asshole out of his penthouse.

"We're following up on leads," Grant answered.

"What's the connection to Blaire?" the senator asked.

"She knew the artist whose paintings were stolen. Sergei Kostin," he answered. Gus lowered his leg and leaned forward in his chair. Grant repeated what Blaire had already told him and Jake.

"What would make them leave almost seven-hundred million dollars worth of art behind?" This came from the senator. "Are you certain there's another painting underneath what you've already seen, Blaire?"

"I'm familiar with Sergei's brush strokes where he conceals a certain area," she said. "Sometimes he doesn't even cover the entire original painting but turns it into something else."

"You seem enthralled, my dear," Gus said with candor.

Blaire held his gaze. "Sergei was brilliant, but I don't know the reasons why he chose this life of crime. Our conversations were never personal, and he discouraged my asking about him. If he was born into it, he certainly had enough talent to leave it, but organized crime has a compelling method to make you stay."

"And you know first-hand, of course." Gus gave a disgusted shake of his head at Grant and looked at his father. "Senator, I don't know how you expect our communications staff to put a spin on this. We haven't addressed the rumors that Blaire is the illegitimate daughter of the most powerful Vor of Russia—"

"And we know that's not true," Grant cut in.

"Yes, but do you know that people are speculating why you're having much success in Moscow real estate acquisitions? They say you're using the Russian mafia?"

"Let them speculate," Grant retorted. "I'm not admitting or denying. Next thing you know, they'll have me laundering money."

"Jesus, Grant," the senator muttered.

"There'll always be rumors, Senator," he addressed his father formally since this was a political meeting. "That's why we agreed that I never talk about how I do business, but be assured that I have not broken any laws stateside."

"That's reassuring," Gus shot back.

"Tell me, Lynch," Grant said silkily. "How am I any different from the CIA that is given the go-ahead to break laws in other countries as long as they don't get caught doing it?"

"Okay, that's enough," the senator said. "We're going off course here."

"Maybe you should muzzle your pit bull," Grant suggested.

"And maybe you should reconsider the type of female company you keep," Gus sneered, looking pointedly at Blaire.

Red hazed Grant's vision and he barely heard the women gasp before he realized he had yanked Gus to his feet and his father was between them.

"August," his father growled. "That was out of line. Grant, calm down."

"Apologize to Blaire, you son of a bitch," Grant snarled, his grip tightening on Gus' collar, but Jake and Tyler also jumped in to pull him off his father's aide.

Visibly flustered, Gus attempted to regain his composure by straightening his collar, but he looked in no way apologetic. "That's the second time you've assaulted me because of her. Don't you see how bad she is for you?"

"Lynch!" his father snapped.

"Why you—" Grant's temper skyrocketed again as he struggled to break free from Jake and Tyler.

"But I apologize, Ms. Callahan," Gus directed his gaze at Blaire who was red in the face and obviously affected by Gus' tirade. Grant wanted to march over to her and whisk her away from this political bullshit.

"I was out of line," he continued. "And I am sorry. But I'm appealing to you right now, Blaire, in light of your friendship with the Thorne family, to see how your relationship with Grant is impacting the senator's reputation."

"Oh, shut up, August," Amelia snapped. "There's no truth to the lovechild rumor, so what are we afraid of?"

"Then why are we here, Amelia, trying to diffuse the 'girlfriend situation' when the senator is supposed to be back in DC, going over legislation and preparing for the next Senate Intelligence committee hearing?"

Grant shrugged off Jake and Tyler's hold and walked over to Blaire. He held out his hand, urging her to stand up beside him, his eyes appealing to her questioning ones to trust him. Tightening his fingers around hers, he didn't want her to run away when he spoke his next words.

"Blaire's not my girlfriend." Grant kept his gaze on his mother whose eyes narrowed at him. He smiled before glancing at the woman beside him. Blaire was staring at the area rug, probably feeling hurt and pissed at his announcement when not too long ago he demanded she be his again.

"She's my fiancée." Her head snapped up then, eyes flaring with outrage, and before she could screw up his plans, he silenced her with a kiss. When he released her lips, he cupped her face with both hands so she had nowhere else to look but at him. "I know we were going to keep it a secret for a while longer, baby," he crooned. "But there's no reason to keep it under wraps anymore, not when the National Tattler released that story this morning." Her eyes were shooting sparks of retribution, and Grant had to will his cock not to rise to the challenge just yet by reminding himself that his mother was in the room.

"Well that certainly changes everything," Amelia exclaimed, clapping her hands once in excitement. As if on cue, Colette appeared with a platter of small sandwiches and sweet little cakes and a pot of tea. "Don't you think this calls for a celebration, Colette?"

"It sure does, ma'am," his housekeeper replied demurely before withdrawing back into the kitchen, but Grant caught the satisfied smile on her face.

"I don't see how this changes anything?" Gus sputtered, but Grant knew that he'd defeated his dad's political advisor in his own manipulative game. He'd have to thank Gus later for giving him the opportunity to work his play to his advantage.

"It changes a whole lot actually," the senator said reflectively as he joined his wife who walked over to them.

"You've always been a part of the family, Blaire," his mother said while giving his woman a kiss and squeezing Grant's arm. His dad hugged Blaire and welcomed her to the family as well. Though Grant felt a pinch of guilt in his chest as he met Jake's amused stare, he convinced himself he did the right thing for everyone.

Mom held Blaire's bare ring finger. "I know you wanted to keep this a secret, but I hope you proposed properly, Grant."

He grinned at his mother before surrendering a bemused Blaire to her. Grant walked to his office safe, unlocked the secure cabinet, and withdrew the small box he'd kept there for more than a month. He'd been debating on ways to ask Blaire to marry him, but each carefully composed speech didn't sound like him. He wasn't a man of tender words—he was a man who took what he wanted. He lifted the sparkling diamond from the box and strode back to the living room.

Shit! Blaire had that deer-in-headlights look as his mother went on and on about wedding dresses, flower arrangements, and reception venues. He'd better go rescue her.

"Don't scare my bride-to-be, Mom, when she's just getting used to the idea," he chided. Pulling Blaire back into his arms, he held her left hand and slipped the ring on her finger. "Now, you're mine, Angel," he whispered in her ear. He tried to kiss her lips, but Blaire turned her head toward his mother and he ended up kissing her cheek instead.

"Your son is sooooo possessive." Blaire smiled as if making a joke, but Grant knew better and winced when her fingers pinched the muscle at his side.

"Oh, these Thorne men are," Mom replied conspiratorially.

Gus cleared his throat. "Senator, where do we want to go from here?"

"It's up to Grant and Blaire to announce their engagement," the senator looked pointedly at his son. "The sooner the better."

"I'll have a press release out tomorrow," Grant said smoothly.

"How will this help with the Tattler story?" Blaire asked.

"There's a big difference between a girlfriend and a fiancée," the senator said. "The latter implies commitment. There's nothing worse than uncertainty influencing public opinion. Being Grant's fiancée, you're more or less already family, and there's a suggested permanence that would go a long way in calming my supporters."

"The term girlfriend could be twisted to mean lover, hookup, fling, or even worse," his mother added. "Too much scandal can come from that, but as a fiancée you can only be looked upon as the future Mrs. Thorne and that, my dear, commands respect."

"There'll be questions about Blaire's background," Gus pointed out. "But since she's engaged to Grant, it'll be more accepted when the senator's office throws their support behind her. One caveat. This may fly with our Massachusetts voters, but if you run for higher office, it might cause an issue."

"Family first," the senator replied without hesitation.

Lynch nodded, resignation on his face, even if he tried to remain stoic. "She's not a criminal ... that much we ascertained, unless she hasn't told us everything. She can't choose her family. If you need the senator's office to draft a show of support if the lovechild rumors persist, then we'll get involved. Otherwise, I hope you get your engagement announced as soon as possible."

Grant gave his father's advisor a curt nod. He didn't fully trust August Lynch, but he had bigger matters to settle at that moment. Blaire was staring daggers at him like she wanted to do damage to some parts of his anatomy.

He couldn't wait to get her alone.

37

Blaire

OUR VISITORS HAD LEFT and Jake was updating Grant on the status of Bobby and Drew. I was sitting on the couch and Grant was perched on its arm, his hand never leaving mine ever since he'd slipped the ring on my finger. I was fuming on the inside, but set my outrage aside to listen to Jake.

"Bobby's out of surgery. Two of the bullets were through and through, but one was lodged in his shoulder," Jake explained. "Drew has a concussion due to his fall."

"His fall?" Grant asked.

"The reason he was out for a while was because someone shot him with a tranquilizer."

"It must be the suit guy who approached Blaire," Tyler said. "I was able to radio Drew when the homeless guy attacked Bobby, so it must have happened soon after."

"The hospital will be keeping them both overnight for observation," Jake said. "Bobby will be out of commission for a while; Drew, probably until he's clear of his concussion."

"Make sure Bobby and Drew are covered with what they need," Grant told his man. "Get with Heather to see where their short-term disability is at. The company will cover anything the insurance won't."

"On it, Mr. Thorne."

"Anything else?"

Tyler looked at me, then returned his eyes to Grant. "We had a visit from a Miami FBI agent this morning."

Grant tensed beside me. "Wilkes?"

"Yes," I answered. "So you know him?"

"He was the agent on the scene in Miami. What did he want from you?"

I told him my conversation with the fed.

"Is he trying to say that Liam's death was a cover-up?" Grant asked.

"I don't know anymore." I was afraid to put my hope into words.

"Blaire, don't," Tyler whispered, his expression one of sadness and pity.

"Anyway, I think he's dropping the case," I shrugged.

"I don't want Wilkes showing up unannounced again," Grant said. "Donovan, you still have the number for Liam's crew?"

"Last I heard from any of them was during Watt's funeral in Atlanta. The number's been disconnected. I figured they were using aliases."

Hope reawakened inside me. "Doesn't that sound suspicious?"

"If they've disconnected their number, they don't want to be found," Jake informed me. "Don't buy any more trouble, Blaire."

Jake and I had come a long way since his initial disapproval of me after finding out I was the daughter of a ROC cleaner, but his last statement stung because I knew he was right. Grant had expended so many resources to keep me safe and his family was paying the price. I had to let this go.

"I'm tired," I said, rising and trying to pull my hand out of Grant's, but he wouldn't let me go. This reminded me of another issue—the fact that I was engaged. I glared at my *fiancé* as he got up calmly.

"That'll be all, Tyler, Donovan." His eyes never left mine.

When our security left, we were still staring at each other. His expression was inscrutable, but I was sure mine left no doubt as to what I was feeling.

"*Whatever I say in there, please go along with it?*" I mimicked his exact words from earlier with as much sarcasm as I could muster. "You manipulative son of a bitch."

"That was the right call and you know it," Grant countered. "Even Gus had no objection to it."

I raised a brow. "So our engagement is not real, right? It's just for show?"

His eyes flashed dangerously. "Of course, it's fucking real."

"I don't recall getting asked," I taunted, ignoring the hardening of his jaw.

"Blaire ..." he warned.

Getting on tiptoes, which was really a joke since he still loomed above me, I leaned in. "And I certainly don't recall saying yes!"

"That's it," he muttered. Suddenly, my world went upside down as I found myself tossed over his shoulder.

"Grant!"

"Quiet!"

Oh no, he didn't. I wasn't taking this Neanderthal act. I struggled, twisting and kicking. He swore, clamping both his arms over my legs to prevent injury to him and me.

"Goddammit, woman!" He flipped me on the bed, leaving me sprawled on the mattress and glowering up at him. He stared at me with a mixture of frustration and—amusement? I couldn't tell as he reached behind him and took off his shirt, exposing the ridges of muscle that made my mouth water.

He smirked.

I glared.

"You think sex is going to fix everything?" I hissed even as my eyes hungrily took in his huge cock pressing behind his sweatpants.

"No, but I could sure pound a 'yes' out of you."

"You still haven't asked—Grant!" I yelled as he yanked my leg forward, reaching for the waistband of my leggings and stripped them off with my panties even as I was kicking him. He chuckled. Chuckled!

He went for my tunic, but I managed to land my feet on his chest and kick him off, but I didn't get far when he hooked me around the waist and tossed me back on the mattress. He got on top of me, settling between my legs, his hardness against my needy core. I was so annoyed and so aroused at the same time. I tried to buck him off. My nails bit into his sides and he growled, manacled both my wrists with one hand and pinned them above me. It was then I saw the gleam in his eyes. They were euphoric and triumphant.

"Marry me," he whispered.

"No!" I said.

"Marry me," he repeated and bit my lower lip. I shook my head.

"Marry me, Angel," he mumbled against my throat, before heading lower and releasing my wrists. I didn't answer, but gasped as he bit my nipple through my tunic and bra before pulling away to discard the rest of my clothes. He then resumed his downward journey with his fingers, seeking the heat between my thighs, groaning when he found me wet. He looked up from just above my navel. "You want me." He circled my entrance, reveling in my slickness before slipping his calloused fingers in and out, deliciously abrading the sensitive nerves of my inner walls. "Your pussy doesn't lie, baby." He continued nipping down my pelvis and I inhaled sharply when I felt the first flick of his tongue. With his face buried between my thighs and my legs over his shoulders, Grant devoured my delicate folds. His tongue lashed and dipped at my entrance and then he moved to my clit.

"Yes, there ... there... oh, God," I whimpered as my fingers clutched the sheets and my ankles squirmed on his back.

He flicked his tongue, back and forth, back and forth, building an unbearable pressure and then he sucked the sensitive nub and I exploded on a scream, my back arching at the force of my orgasm.

"Don't stop. Don't stop." Then it became too much until I couldn't breathe. "Stop. Oh God, no more!" I yanked his hair but he only smashed his face further into my core, keeping the pressure on my clit and extending my pleasure.

I was still coming down from my high when he drove into me. My fingers clutched his shoulders as I marveled at his powerful body moving above me, muscles cording in sculpted beauty with the force of his vigorous pounding.

He lowered his head to kiss me roughly. "Marry me, baby."

With my legs hooked under his arms, he spread me wider, giving him unfettered access to slam his cock into me, over and over.

"Grant," I moaned as he hit a particularly sweet spot and I knew I was seconds from coming again. "Fuck me harder."

He changed the angle of his thrusts, keeping me on the brink, not letting me come. His mouth was tight, he was sweating, and straining not to come himself. "Answer me, Angel," he growled. "And it better be the fucking answer I want."

"Harder," I moaned.

His pumping was relentless but it wasn't the rhythm I needed. I reached for my clit, but he grabbed both my hands and pinned them above me once more.

"Make me come, please ..." I begged, anticipating the intensity of release only Grant could give me.

"Say it, Angel," he mumbled, slowing down to a maddening pace.

"Yes," I whispered in surrender.

"Yes, what?"

"Yes, I'll marry you." I barely got the last word out when his lips crashed down on me. His thumb hit my clit and I soared into climax.

My inner muscles gripped his cock and he went feral, pounding deeper, sending me higher until he joined me. He groaned into the crook of my neck as he released inside me. His thrusting slowed and gentled. Then he was kissing my jaw, my cheek, and my lips. When the tremors left us both, he caught my gaze.

"I love you, Blaire." Grant kissed the tip of my nose.

I didn't know why, but my eyes filled with tears and a sob caught in my throat. I laughed to hide the sudden onslaught of emotions. "You kinda did that in reverse, Thorne."

"I know," He grinned crookedly. "We've wasted so much time these past ten months." He pulled out of me, and maneuvered us to sit against the headboard. I was naked and he was still wearing his sweatpants. How was that fair?

"I took too long to tell you how I felt," Grant said. "You took off and then I discovered your secrets in the cabin and I didn't know if you were the same woman I had fallen in love with. When I got you back, I knew nothing had changed and then the whole mess of the past month happened. I only fell deeper in love with you and you had put up a wall between us." Pained eyes looked at me. "Do you know how crazy you made me?"

"I think I have an idea," I murmured, drawing circles on his chest. "You had us engaged when we barely got back together."

"In my mind, we were never broken up," Grant said with arrogance. "I used that time to woo you."

I shook my head, as a burst of laughter exploded from my lips. "You really never do things in order."

"See, if I told you I loved you first, and if I followed the order of things, I would have to wait at least three months without sounding psycho-in-love to ask you to marry me. I wasn't willing to wait that long."

"Hmm ... and this doesn't make you psycho?" I teased.

"I have you where I want you," he smirked. "Naked, on my bed, and wearing my ring."

"Usually, feelings have to be mutual, Grant. Are you sure I love you?"

He scowled down at me. "I couldn't love you this much without you loving me in return."

"That's very presumptive on your part." I was having a hard time keeping a straight face, but his smug expression was annoying. Who wanted to be a foregone conclusion? Not me.

"You love me," he growled, and had me sprawled on my back once again.

"I do love your cock," I said. "And your diabolical tongue."

"Blaire ..." My name was a guttural warning.

"Oh, all right," I smiled. "I guess I love you."

"Guess?" His eyes sparked with amusement this time when he caught on to my teasing.

"I definitely love you, Grant Thorne."

"I know." The smirk was back.

Cocky bastard.

38

Grant

THE FOLLOWING MORNING, Grant went into his penthouse office and closed the door. He knew there was one person who wouldn't be pleased about his engagement to Blaire and he'd rather that someone found out from him before the news broke.

Sighing heavily, he thumbed the number to call his sister.

The phone rang and rang.

"Dammit, Val, pick up," he muttered. He wanted to get this over and done with and he'd be damned before he left her a message.

Just when he thought the call was going to voicemail, his sister answered the phone. "Hello?"

She was breathless.

"Hey, sis. Catch you at a bad time?"

"Nah, it's good. Just came back from my run. Heard Dad and Mom went to see you last night."

"Did they mention anything?"

"Is there anything else I should know besides your girlfriend is a mafia princess?"

"Val," Grant sighed in irritation. "You should know better than to believe that garbage."

His sister snorted a derisive laugh. "It's kind of funny. I like it when Gus gets all huffy and puffy."

If there was one thing he and his sister shared, it was their dislike for the senator's political advisor.

"One would think Dad is the King of England," Val continued. "And everyone in the family needs to fall in line to some royal protocol."

"Gus is probably setting the stage for a possible White House bid."

"That's kind of presumptuous, isn't it?" Val said. "Dad has yet to win his reelection to the senate. Does he even want the presidency?"

"I don't think he does, but there's pressure from the party," Grant speculated. "But knowing Dad, he's going to consider how this is going to affect Mom and us."

"Well," Val snorted. "I should be thankful that you're dating a woman with questionable background. Takes the heat off of me."

Grant bristled at his sister's barb, but she provided him with the perfect opening. "Well, sis, you'll be happy to know I'll be making Blaire an honest woman."

A gouging silence, and then, "Please tell me I misunderstood you and you're not marrying her."

"I plan to have the company's publicist announce our engagement today."

"I can't believe you're bringing that criminal and gold digger into the family! Are you out of your fucking mind?"

His fingers almost crushed his phone. "I couldn't be more clear-headed about this."

"What does she give you, Grant? Sex? You can get that anywhere."

"I actually feel sorry that you think that way. Maybe if you stop dating losers, you'll figure it out." No way in hell was he discussing with his sister how fucking hot sex was when you were crazy in love.

"At least I'm not blind to their faults and can dispatch them when I want to," Val sneered.

"This conversation is going nowhere," Grant muttered. "Consider yourself informed and don't go crying to Mom that I didn't tell you—"

"Yeah, Blaire would look great in orange by the way—"

"Dammit, Val," he snapped. "The next time you call Blaire a criminal or a gold digger, you can lose my number."

"You're picking that bitch over me?"

"You're the bitch, sis." It twisted his heart to say that, but he'd had enough. "I love Blaire, she's going to be my wife, and if you can't get onboard with that, it's your problem, not mine."

Val hung up.

———————

THE DAYS FOLLOWING the announcement of their engagement were a whirlwind of interviews and social appearances. Much to everyone's miscalculation, the interest in Blaire and him didn't die down. Instead, it skyrocketed. Mostly from the female demographic who wanted to romanticize his fiancée's background as a mafia princess and Grant was the knight in shining armor billionaire who rescued her. What baffled his publicist was there was thirty percent who wanted an Italian mafia prince paired with Blaire.

Heather was chuckling when she handed him the latest report from the PR agency. "Looks like you have competition for Blaire's affections."

"What are you talking about?" Grant scowled. The mere idea of someone else vying for his woman's affections made him furious enough to bend a crowbar.

"Luca Morelli just tweeted to his followers for suggestions on how to court Blaire."

"That fucker," Grant growled. Luca Morelli was the head of Mediterranean Shipping Lines, a legitimate enterprise owned by the Morelli crime family. To his knowledge, the man's nose was clean, but everyone knew his brothers ran the Italian mafia.

"Do you want me to tell your publicist to draft a response on your official twitter account?" Heather asked.

"No, I'll handle it myself." He had some past dealings with Morelli and had the man's private number, so Grant called him and told him to fuck off.

Just as Grant suspected, the mafia prince wasn't really serious, but was just a limelight hog with a big ego and apologized for using Grant's engagement to Blaire as a social media stunt.

Other than the thirty percent of women not approving of Grant for Blaire, the rest were enthralled with their love affair. Because of the interest in their relationship, Gus sent Andy to Manhattan to temporarily work out of Grant's office so he'd be available to advise the couple on political etiquette should the need arise, especially since they'd received several dinner invitations from New York politicians like the governor and mayor.

Even if he knew Andy was acting in an official capacity, he didn't like it when he came home to the penthouse to find him spending time with Blaire. He heard their laughter just when the elevator doors opened. Tyler was sitting at the bar, Blaire and Andy were busy pouring over a newspaper.

"Are you sure that's not gossip, Andy?" Blaire laughed.

"It's actually true. That's why there's tension in city hall right now."

His fiancée's eyes lit on Grant and he was gratified to see her jump up from her comfy seating with Andy and greet him at the foyer.

"What are you two gossiping about?" Grant murmured, kissing her on the lips.

"Andy is giving me the inside scoop on city hall," Blaire said. "It's rumored that the mayor's mistress is the city council speaker. He's giving me pointers on how to tactfully navigate the sticky situation for The Prestige exhibit."

"We can just scrap them from the guest list," Grant suggested.

Andy gave a choking sound.

"The mayor is at the top of Jeff's list," Blaire protested.

"Yes, but the art in the exhibit is mine," he said. "I'm not going to have anyone ruin the evening for you. You've been working so hard assisting Jeff in restoring the paintings." The exhibit was six weeks away and Blaire had been helping out in the gallery amidst her therapy visits and meetings with Grant's publicist. She lamented she didn't have enough time for her own art. Grant was pleased that Blaire had shown interest in painting again. She'd been like a ghost finding joy in nothing after her experience at Orlov's hands. Both of them hoped the interest in their engagement would die down enough to cut back on the demands from the publicist.

Andy jumped up from the sofa. "I guess I should be going."

"Are you driving to Boston to see Val?" Blaire asked.

"No, but I'm seeing her Saturday evening."

Blaire inclined her head, a sadness flitted over her face. Grant could curse his sister for her stubbornness. He had not spoken to Val since he issued his ultimatum and it looked like his sister followed his advice to lose his number.

———

THAT SATURDAY, ten days after declaring their engagement, his woman begged him for a weekend lazing around the penthouse. Everyone from politicians to fashion houses wanted a piece of Blaire. At first she was excited, but the thrill faded after the first few nights of endless cocktail and dinner parties. Sometimes they had to squeeze in two events in one evening but that soon got old for his fiancée. Grant was used to the fast-paced nightlife because he usually did it for business, although rarely for pleasure.

"I'm tired of smiling when my feet hurt," Blaire whined as she plopped in front of the kitchen counter and welcomed the mug of coffee Grant set in front of her. "And it's ridiculous the amount of clothes these designers send me. They're sending me size zeros. Do I look like a size zero to you?"

Grant rounded the kitchen counter and hugged her from behind, kissing her temple. "You're a size sexy-as-fuck."

Blaire giggled. "Great answer. Have these people seen my ass?"

"It's a very nice ass."

"Thank you. I'm a six and on my off days I could be an eight. Maybe it's my skinny legs that make me look like a zero."

Grant nipped her ear. "Your legs aren't skinny, they fit around my hips perfectly with enough meat for my fingers to grip." *As I nail you to the wall.*

"Meat?" Blaire cast him a dubious sideways glance. "That's not a sexy description."

He kissed her exposed shoulder. She was wearing a robe, belted loosely over her sleeping tank and shorts. "Hmmm ... did I ruin my chances for morning sex?"

"Grant Thorne, shame on you," Blaire said in mock rebuke. "You woke me at four this morning."

"That was a pre-dawn fuck."

"Not to mention how you fucked me right by the elevators when we arrived at the penthouse last night," his woman grumbled.

"That was a make-up fuck." Grant smiled against her skin.

The night prior, they had a fight. It started with a disagreement regarding the wedding date before they left for the Harvest Gala. The barbs continued on the way to the event, and when they arrived, Grant wanted nothing more than to bundle Blaire back into the vehicle so they could continue their discussion. Instead, his frustration grew and smiling became a chore, so he quit forcing one.

"WOULD YOU PLEASE TRY TO SMILE," Blaire whispered, annoyance drawing her brows together. *"One would think you're facing a death sentence instead of having just gotten engaged."*

Grant bared his teeth. "Better?"

Blaire's jaw turned mulish. "December is too soon. What's wrong with waiting until May?"

"Are your feelings going to change between now and May?" he challenged. "Mine won't."

"That's an unfair question."

"I get the feeling you're hedging—that you're unsure about something."

Blaire looked away uncomfortably.

Grant suppressed the urge to drag her into a deserted hallway and kiss her into submission. He needed a drink. "I'm going to the bar. Want me to get you a glass of cabernet?"

Her expression softened as she glanced at him. "That would be nice."

He gave her a chaste peck on the lips and nodded to the silent auction table. "Why don't you find something for us?"

Grant took that opportunity to give them both a breather, resisting the instinct to glance back and check on her. There was no reason for him to act paranoid. The Diplomatic Security Service was in charge of safeguarding the event because there were several high-profile foreign dignitaries in attendance. Blaire was as safe as she could get.

As he waited his turn at the bar, he mulled over the real reason why he was pushing for a December wedding. It wasn't the date itself, but a tactic to find out what she wasn't telling him. But unlike the uncertainty that hounded him in the beginning of their relationship, he felt an openness in communicating his thoughts without the fear of sending her running. Blaire changed him in a fundamental way as the instinct to shutdown when he got pissed had diminished. Elation expanded in his chest with this self-discovery. His eyes sought her in the room. His gaze narrowed. Well, something else hadn't changed.

His possessiveness.

A man was busy chatting up his fiancée by the auction table. Grant recognized him as an upstate NY state representative who had recently grabbed the headlines. Abandoning the quest for drinks, he made his way back to his woman.

"You were a total caveman," Blaire sighed, bringing his attention back to the present. It took Grant a moment to register that she was referring to the elevator sex. Her eyes flashed as she pushed against his chest. "Oh ... oh... and I had to stop you from going all alpha male at the auction table. You're lucky I saved you from getting hauled off by the Secret Service."

"That punk-ass congressman had his hand on your back. He had no reason to touch you," Grant shot back. "And it's the DSS, baby. The Secret Service protects—"

"Stop," Blaire cut in dryly. "I don't need a lecture on federal security agencies. If I need to know, I'll Google it. My point is I could have handled the situation. I was about to move away when you swooped in like some knight about to rescue a damsel in distress."

"My job is to protect you," he growled. "Besides, all I wanted was to talk to him."

Blaire eyed him dubiously. "Somehow I have a feeling that chat would end up with me bailing you out of jail this morning." She patted his cheek. "Aren't you glad I saved our weekend?" Her eyes twinkled merrily. "We argued about this ad nauseam on the way home last night. Are you plotting another makeup-sex session?"

Grant grinned crookedly and scratched the scruff at his jaw. "Is it working?"

She laughed and went on tiptoes to kiss him. "Thanks for defending my honor."

"Anytime."

"Love you, Mr. Thorne," Blaire said softly as a tender look crossed her face. "Glad you didn't freeze me out despite looking like you were about to lose your mind."

"I'll never shut you out again," Grant promised. "Especially since the make-up sex is so good." His hand slipped inside her robe and stroked her breast.

"Be serious, Grant."

"I am, baby," he said. "I've made huge mistakes in our relationship that caused you so much pain, both physically and mentally—"

"Never blame yourself for what Orlov did."

"It's not about the blame, Angel," he said quietly. "It's about learning from that experience and making sure it doesn't happen again. I was afraid to hurt you with words and yet it was my silence that almost caused me to lose you. This past month, when you were busy finding yourself, fixing yourself, I was doing the same thing," he said. "I was unworthy of you." Blaire opened her mouth to protest but Grant put a finger on her lips. "Let me get this out." When she nodded, he continued, "I'm too selfish to let you go. Val nearly dying fucked me up, but I shouldn't let it define how I dealt with my anger. I'm a grown-ass man. No excuse not to control my temper or the words coming from my mouth around the people I love. Last night, I realized I haven't had the instinct to shut down in a while—"

"A half day."

"What?" His brows drew together.

"When you get angry you have half a day to process your anger, but that's all I'm giving you," Blaire declared. "We talk about the issue no matter how much we want to strangle each other."

He smirked. "Somehow my desire to wring your pretty neck always ends up with me wanting to fuck you."

"That's a problem?" A delicate eyebrow rose.

"That sassy mouth," Grant lowered his head, murmuring against her lips. "Needs to be wrapped around my cock."

She pushed away from his chest to stare up at him. "Agreed?"

"Half a day it is, Angel." He wouldn't need that time. Like he said earlier, Grant had learned his lesson. "Can I ask you something?"

She cast him a wary look.

"I know December was pushing it, but something was bugging me about your aversion to that date."

Blaire muttered under her breath. Something about taking "communication too far."

Grant chuckled. "It goes both ways, baby."

"It's just that I'm still in therapy," she mumbled. "I'm afraid the stress of preparing for a wedding might set me back. And I really, really want to be perfect for you."

Something tugged at the muscles of his chest. "Oh, Blaire, you're nothing but perfect for me," he whispered. "But I understand," he added. "I'll defer to you to set the wedding date, but I'm not waiting longer than May."

She nodded, but was staring at his chest, tracing the lines of the design on his shirt. Her feather-light touch was a direct stimulant to his groin.

"Anything else?" he cleared his throat.

Blaire glanced at him from beneath her lashes. "Maybe you can come with me to my last sessions with Dr. Jones?"

"Name the time. I'll be there," Grant replied without hesitation. He'd been wanting in on some of her therapy appointments, but she hadn't been ready. He was pleased she'd initiated the idea from her end.

"Thank you."

"Blaire?"

"Hmm?"

"I need to fuck you."

Without waiting for her response, he leaned forward and grasped the back of her legs, lifting her and moving forward to where the counter was clear. He set her on top and wedged himself between her thighs.

"Grant ..." Blaire whispered, her hazel eyes heavy-lidded. Oh yeah, she was ready for him.

"Sexy as fuck," he purred. He freed his cock, moved her sleeping shorts to the side and thrust up into her. Mouth, tongue, hands, and cock, he was all over her. He made her come quickly, and not long after, he poured his release into her.

AND THAT WAS how that weekend went. They talked, ate, fucked, and, when they weren't doing any of those things, Blaire caught up with this zombie apocalypse series she was hooked on.

He once thought he'd be happy living a hedonistic lifestyle with Blaire, but he knew that, just like him, she would need balance and time away from him. He could easily smother her with his insatiable need for her and it was fortunate that his business commitments forced him to leave the house. But ever since Blaire's abduction, fear of letting her out of his sight had gotten into the mix. Maybe he needed to talk to a therapist himself because the fear wasn't fading and had only gotten worse.

Grant would think back to this time and realize his psyche was giving him a premonition.

THE CALL CAME late Sunday evening. Blaire was already sleeping and Grant was in his office finishing up a call with his Hong Kong office.

"Grant." His name on his father's gruff, tormented voice was enough to send the blood draining from his face. He held the phone tight.

"What's wrong?" Shit, he hoped Mom was fine.

"It's Valerie."

Grant sighed, relief briefly taking over. "What did she do now?"

"Grant, they took her!"

"What? Who took her?"

"Andy went over to see her and she wasn't at her house. He thought she was just mad at your engagement and took off without telling anyone."

"How do you know someone took her?" Grant asked. "You know Val has a habit of going off on her own when she's upset. And where the hell was her security?"

"They called with their demands," his father's voice grew hoarse. "Her two bodyguards were found dead inside the house."

"Jesus Christ. Do we know who they are? Is it one of those white supremacist groups?"

"No, Grant. It's the people who took the paintings."

Dread unlike any gripped his lungs in a strangle hold, and he knew, just fucking knew, what those fuckers wanted.

Or who.

"They want Blaire for Val," the senator said raggedly.

39

Blaire

SOMETHING WOKE ME. It felt like a light brush on my lips. Grant was leaning over me, his features shadowed in the darkness.

"Grant?"

He twisted and turned on the night lamp, illuminating his ravaged face. Something was terribly wrong. I jacked knifed to a sitting position and put my hand on his arm.

"I didn't mean to wake you, Angel."

"What happened?"

He studied my face, emotions conflicted, until a determined gleam entered his eyes. "The men who took the paintings kidnapped Val."

Oh, no. Words refused to come out of my mouth. I swallowed.

"Dad is meeting me at the office within the hour." He kissed my forehead and got to his feet.

When I realized he was simply leaving, I scrambled off the bed, noting briefly that it was one in the morning. "Wait, Grant!"

I cursed his long legs as I struggled to catch up with him and tugged on his arm. "It's me they want, right?"

"Yeah. Not happening."

He shrugged off my hold and continued stalking down the hallway. I ran past him and confronted him in the kitchen. Jake, Tyler, and two new security guys I didn't recognize were there.

Grant tried to side step me, but I mimicked his movements.

"I don't have time for this, Blaire!" he growled.

"Bull!" I retorted. "Why am I not included in the efforts to get Val back? I'm the one they want."

His face darkened, jaw tightening. "I'm not making the same mistake."

"What are you talking about?"

"I chose my family before and I nearly lost you."

"It's not about choosing. You put a tracker on me—you'll always know where I am."

"No." Tired of trying to side step me, Grant gripped my shoulders and handed me to Jake.

"You know that's the right choice!" I yelled at his retreating back as I fought Jake's hold. "If something happens to Val, you'll resent me. Is that what you want?"

Grant paused, spun on his heel, and prowled back to me. "No. That's not what I want, but if I trade you for Val and I never get you back, I'll hate her forever. I can live with resenting you. I'll even live with Mom and Dad hating me, but don't ever ask me to live without you, Blaire."

"You're not thinking this through." I tried another tact. "I can defend myself. Val can't. I can delay giving them what they want until you all come up with a plan to extract me."

He shook his head, face torn in anguish.

"Grant ..."

"No."

"I don't understand—"

"I won't risk you!" he roared as his breath sawed through his lungs. "My decision is final. Jake is staying with you. I'm taking Tyler with me." It went without saying that Grant didn't trust Tyler not to get compelled by me to go against his wishes. I watched helplessly as Grant got into the elevators with his men and disappeared from our penthouse.

Jake released me.

I lowered my head, shoulders slumping. "You know I'm right, Jake."

"Mr. Thorne is scared of losing you. He thinks he can throw enough money at Val's abductors to render the value of the paintings nil."

"This wasn't his decision to make."

"No, it wasn't."

I raised my tear-filled eyes to Jake. "If we don't get Val back, it'll destroy him."

He nodded. "It will change him, but he'll survive. Losing you, Blaire, will kill him."

40

Blaire

I HAD NEVER FELT AS ISOLATED as I did now. Jake wasn't telling me anything and I was ready to climb the walls. I heard Amelia had been transferred to a secure location, and I was feeling guilty enough to leave her alone. Even Andy wasn't answering my calls or texts. He could blame me all he wanted, but, dammit, he'd always been logical about this. Then I remembered Grant, and how I couldn't reason with him. I was fighting for us—why couldn't he see that? An eternity of resentment wasn't how I envisioned our lives together. That wasn't a life ... that was going to be hell.

My phone buzzed.

Andy calling.

Finally.

"Andy!"

"Hey."

"How are you holding up?"

There was a deep exhale. "I don't know what else to do, Blaire. The senator has shut me out. I think he blames me."

"Why in the world would they blame you? I'm the one those assholes want."

"So Grant wouldn't give you up, huh?" There was bitterness in his tone and even if I understood how he felt, hurt pinched my heart.

"I tried to convince him to give me up."

"Listen," Andy sighed. "I'm kinda drifting right now, hoping the senator or Gus will return my calls. I'm in Manhattan and was wondering if I could crash at your penthouse. I need someone to commiserate with."

"I would love nothing more than someone to talk to, Andy. I'm slowly losing my mind waiting for news."

"You think your guard dogs would let me up?"

"I'll take care of it."

I argued with Jake for five minutes.

"When everybody abandoned me at the ER, Andy was there for me, Jake," I said. "He got shot because of me and needs my support now."

"He's going to mess with your head," Jake responded. "He's going to want you to take Val's place."

"As I should!" I gritted out. "But you're here to stop me. So what's the harm in letting him up?"

Jake glared at me for a second longer before allowing the building guard to let Andy into the elevators.

My friend walked in, looking haggard. Dark circles smudged his under-eyes and his already light complexion had become more pasty. Poor Andy. He was wearing jeans and a sweatshirt, a far cry from the suits and crisp white shirts he wore as part of the senator's staff. His red brown hair couldn't get more mussed up, but it was like he'd been running his fingers through it repeatedly.

"Andy," I whispered. I ignored the fear of rejection and walked up to him and hugged him tightly. He was stiff, but he gave me a token one-arm hug. "I'm sorry."

He sniffed a laugh. "Yeah. You must feel like shit, but I can't hate you, Blaire." His eyes were shifty, as if he wasn't certain he should be here. He eyed Jake and the other bodyguards.

"Come on, let's go to the living room. Have you eaten? Do you want something to drink?"

"I'll have a glass of water if you don't mind." He crashed on one of the couches with his forearm over his eyes.

I was feeling more torn up by the second as I walked into the kitchen to fetch Andy his water. I wished Grant would call soon. It'd been over two hours since he'd left to meet his father in his Lower Manhattan office. Waiting sucked.

Grant

GRANT ARRIVED at Thorne Industries and waited for his father who was already en route from the Manhattan Heliport. The senator was bringing in reinforcements, but he didn't elaborate who or what. This was making him antsy and he wished he'd kept Blaire in a separate unknown location. Even if he knew his dad wouldn't stoop to kidnapping her, the possibility had crossed his mind. There'd been a minute of charged tempers on that first phone call with his dad because Grant wouldn't consider using Blaire as bait.

His office phone buzzed and the night guard announced the arrival of his guests.

"Send them up."

He couldn't sit still, so he got up and walked out of his office, past the reception area, and waited for the elevator car to arrive. It didn't take long. The elevator doors slid open and the senator stepped out flanked by two men as tall as Grant. Both were built—one had light blond buzz-cut hair; the other had dark hair. Both were about forty, but it was hard to tell with the blond one, there was a depth of experience in his ice blue eyes.

"Viktor, Sully," the senator said. "You haven't met my son, Grant.

Grant, this is Viktor Baran and Sully—Gabriel Sullivan," he said flatly, gesturing to each man in turn. "They work for Artemis Guardians Services."

He shook hands with the two men. Grant sized them up, not only as former military, but he'd bet they'd been in special-ops.

"Gentlemen," Grant waved his arm toward his office.

"They specialize in international K & R but offered to help given the circumstances," the senator explained.

"Do you think we can convince Val's kidnappers to take a ransom instead?" Grant didn't waste time in asking.

They'd entered his office and he motioned for them to sit. The sitting area comprised of two sofas and two wingback chairs surrounding a coffee table. The senator sat in one of the chairs; his two companions remained standing. Viktor leaned against the door frame and Sully stood with arms crossed.

"No," Viktor clipped.

"Why can't we just pay for whatever those paintings are worth," Grant said. "I understand there may be more valuable work hidden underneath, but everything has its price."

"Agreed," the blond man said. "However, your net worth is roughly twenty-billion dollars, Mr. Thorne. You're six billion short of what those paintings are worth."

"You're shitting me," Grant whispered.

"I'm not," Viktor responded. "Sully, do you want to explain?"

"Most of the intel is classified," Sully said. "And what I'm about to tell you does not leave this room or this could undermine months of intelligence work."

Grant backed into his desk and perched on the edge. What the hell was going on?

"You're familiar with the Russian oligarchy. You've done business with a few of them and your recent rival for the Galleria Development was Ivan Yashkin," Sully said.

"Go on."

"There'd been a recent shake-up in the oligarchy. Billions of dollars were mishandled and became lost in the infighting. Roughly twenty-six billion were in offshore accounts and were set to be invested in the U.S. with the ultimate goal of destabilizing the financial market."

"Jesus," Grant muttered.

"I'm sure, as a business man, you understand the intricacies of market volatility. They also planned to infiltrate the U.S. banking system via these offshore accounts. It was believed that Sergei Kostin was entrusted the lost account numbers by his brother, the former most powerful mafia boss in Russia."

"What happened to Kostin's brother?"

"He was assassinated. It was a brutal shake-up. The Kremlin, the Oligarchs, and the Russian mafia are this one big happy family until they turn on each other. We believe Kostin was tortured regarding the account numbers and he revealed where the paintings were, however, the interrogation proved too much for his weak heart and he died. Yashkin couldn't get to the building where the paintings were hidden."

"That's where we had an advantage on the bid," Grant said. "There was bad blood between the family that owned the Galleria Development and Yashkin. He'd attempted several hostile takeovers of that family's corporation before. Wait, are you saying the account numbers are hidden under the paintings?"

"Correct."

"Blaire mentioned some technology that can scan through the pigments."

"Yes, but since they'd kidnapped the senator's daughter, it appears that method had failed. They need someone who's familiar with Kostin's technique to get to it."

Sully's phone beeped and he excused himself to take a call.

"How did they find out about Blaire?"

"We're not sure," Viktor said. "Kostin must have talked about Paulina Antonova and Yashkin had strong ties to Orlov. I think they were aware that Kostin had taken to Paulina and had built her up as an unwitting protégé."

Sully returned. "That was our analyst. He's sending me a dossier on the men we think got to Valerie. This is also the reason why we didn't bring any of the senator's staff with him." He handed the tablet to the senator. His father looked at the screen and paled. "Oh, Christ, Valerie." His father's fingers shook as he rubbed his temple while reading through the information just received.

Viktor must have received the same transmission and handed his own device to Grant.

His eyes zeroed in on the picture staring up at him and absorbed the supporting intel. His blood turned to ice. "Son of a bitch!"

Blaire

SOMEONE'S PHONE rang and I heard Jake answer. There were seconds of silence and then I heard him inhale sharply. "We're at homestead Charlie, Mr. Thorne." I wracked my brain for what that meant. I was about to walk out the kitchen when I heard quick movements and then...

"Drop it!" Jake yelled before I saw him go down. One of my bodyguards rushed me toward the elevator.

"What's going on?" I shrieked.

He got dropped as well, dragging me down with him. I pushed his body off and sat up, confused. Andy approached me with a lazy stride, his right hand holding a weird looking gun.

"What did you do?"

"Your bodyguards are lucky I like them better than Val's," Andy said, stopping three feet in front of me.

My heart tried to reject what my mind was telling me, but all my interactions with Andy suddenly made sense. "You set me up."

"Not really. You weren't my job at first. I was simply insurance— my boss had bigger plans for me." His eyes turned hard. "You screwed that up because you kept turning up like a bad penny."

"I trusted you!"

"We'll have a heart-to-heart later, sweetheart." He raised his gun and shot me with no hesitation. The searing prick in my stomach instantaneously dimmed my vision and turned my muscles to Jell-O. I collapsed on the floor unable to move. His image blurred as he crouched in front of me and spoke in this slo-mo voice I couldn't make out. He stood and dragged my body into the elevator. Afterward, there was nothing.

41

Grant

"HOMESTEAD CHARLIE."

"Fuck!"

"That doesn't sound good," Viktor commented as Grant sprinted for the elevators, phone in his ear.

"Tyler, bring the car around." He punched the button to call the car before turning to his companions. "Homestead Charlie is a threat code similar to Defcon 3. Donovan ended the call immediately and I think it's because Andy was already there."

"What do we do?" the senator asked no one in particular. All four of them got into the elevator.

"We're heading to the penthouse," Grant said. "Donovan will call once he has the situation handled." That was the optimal result. As soon as they cleared the elevator, he brought up his phone app that contained the tracking software. "I'm getting a faulty read. Blaire's blinking in and out of the penthouse."

"The tracking device made specifically for the BloodTrak serum is more accurate," Viktor said who was looking over Grant's shoulder.

He caught a troubled look on the blond man's face, but it quickly disappeared and Viktor's face was once again unreadable.

Tyler was already waiting for them in the Escalade and all four of them climbed in.

"Sully and I will ride with you for now," Viktor informed him. "Our vehicles and my men are on the way."

Grant didn't respond but reached for the tracking device in the glove compartment and turned it on. "Signal is weak, but, from the coordinates, it looks like she's in the basement." They'd been in the car for a few minutes when Blaire's signal blinked out. "Shit, this couldn't be right? She disappeared."

"How could that be?" the senator queried. "The BloodTrak serum is fool-proof."

"Not anymore," Sully countered.

Grant turned in his seat and glared at the two AGS men. "Explain. And don't tell me it's classified."

"But it is," Viktor replied. "Even the senator doesn't know about it."

"Well, I suggest you de-classify it pretty quick," his dad snapped.

Viktor regarded the senator for a second before speaking. "Since the attack on your wife when the explosive device was identified, the CIA stepped up its probe against YGE and Yashkin's other associates," he said. "We've uncovered a company that fronts as an energy research laboratory that's actually manufacturing counter-measures against U.S.-made advanced military weapons. Among those was the hack of the BloodTrak serum."

"Yes, but how would Andy know that's the tracker we used on Blaire?" Grant said. "We've kept the information confidential from Dad and his staff until now."

"Would Blaire have mentioned it to Andy in passing?" Sully asked. "We couldn't access both their cell phone records."

Grant smiled grimly. "Blaire's phone is secured, but no, I don't know if she's mentioned it to that son of a bitch."

"It doesn't matter. Spencer would be aware of this serum and could use a specialized tracking wand to confirm it's active," Viktor replied.

He was about to ask another question when Tyler cut in to ask if he should park on the street or the garage. Grant instructed him to go directly to the basement. Parking in their designated area, Blaire's signal still had not resurfaced.

"We need to split up," Viktor said. "Sully, go with Tyler. Mr. Thorne, hand Tyler the tracking device. Let's go to your penthouse."

Grant got into the elevator with his dad and Viktor. He swiped his keycard and punched the level for the penthouse. It was the slowest elevator ride in his life. The car stopped at the lobby and Grant wanted to smash his fist into the elevator panel. A person who was coming in from a morning run was about to hop on, but he blocked the man.

Grant glared at the runner. "Take the next one," he snarled and repeatedly punched the arrow buttons to close the doors.

The senator stared at the floor and shook his head. Viktor cleared his throat. Grant stared ahead at the lit elevator numbers willing them to ascend faster. His mind raced with a thousand questions, but couldn't find the words to voice a coherent one. When they reached the penthouse level, Grant re-swiped his access card to open the doors. He stepped out first, cursing when he saw one of the body-guards sprawled at the foyer. He refused to be paralyzed by fear. Blaire needed him to be stronger than ever. He bent over and felt for a pulse while Viktor and his dad went to check on Jake and his third man. His bodyguard was alive. He left everyone to check the rooms even if his instincts screamed at him that Blaire was gone. He returned to the kitchen where his father met him.

"We need to call for an ambulance," the senator said.

"No," Viktor said. "The AGS is involved now and we want to keep this under the radar if possible. I'm sure Spencer and his cronies are monitoring first responder channels. I'll get someone here."

Grant watched Viktor call that someone on his smartphone. He remembered his father mentioning how the CIA couldn't operate in the homeland without local law enforcement taking the lead. As the

AGS boss made arrangements for medical service to be brought in, Sully and Tyler emerged from the elevators. His bodyguard shook his head to indicate that they hadn't found anything, while Sully approached Viktor.

"You trust them?" Grant nodded to the two men while helping his dad transfer Jake to the couch. The AGS guys were standing at the edge of the living room by the picture window, presumably to stay out of earshot.

"They're the best, son," the senator confirmed. "If anyone could get Val and Blaire back it's AGS. If they think it's hopeless, we're screwed." His father searched his face. "How are you holding up?"

"Hanging on," Grant admitted. "I can't afford to lose my shit now." He looked at Viktor and Sully again. "I want to be in on every opportunity to find Blaire and Val. I'm not letting anyone tell me I can't."

"You and I are too close to this," the senator said. "We need to let them take the lead."

"And they will," he agreed. "But I'm not going to be idly standing by waiting for news."

"What happened in Miami, Grant?" his father asked suddenly. He never told the senator that he'd shot and killed someone to save Blaire, but he admitted his and his crew's part in the Orlov takedown to the feds assigned by the DOJ to handle the ROC case.

"The good guys won, Dad," Grant stated simply.

And they were going to win again.

Viktor's EMTs arrived. Grant learned that the AGS top man had contacts in most of the major cities when certain services were required. Much like what happened to Drew, his men had suffered mild concussions from their falls and needed to be given an intravenous solution to counteract the effects of the tranquilizer.

Grant went to his office and started loading cartridges into the magazines of his Sigs. Sully walked in and surveyed the arsenal on his desk.

"Looks like you're preparing for war."

"I want to be ready," he muttered.

"You can't come with us when the time comes."

He looked up and fixed the other man with a raptor stare. "You think you can stop me?"

"You don't want to get in the way. When we get a lock on Blaire's position, it'll be a quick surgical mission. In and out. That's what we do."

A muscle ticked at his jaw. Grant lowered the bullets and the magazine. His hands were shaking from cold rage. "They took her from me, Sully. I want to kill every last one of them."

Sully sighed and perched at the edge of his desk. "Believe me, man. I know exactly how you feel."

Grant's brows furrowed and he lifted his gaze to see a haunted look cross Sully's face. The man wasn't lying; he'd been through this before.

"My wife, Beatrice ... she was taken by our enemies to send her father and me a message," Sully swallowed hard. "They tortured her, cut her up, and then dumped her in front of my house."

"Jesus," Grant whispered.

"The waiting was agony, but that moment when they dropped her off, when I didn't know whether she was alive or dead ... it was the worst fucking feeling in my life," Sully said. "I got her back, but it changed me. We'll get Blaire back, Grant, but that's not gonna be the end of the fight."

Grant already understood what Sully meant, but he let the man speak.

"You've lost her once when she was captured by Orlov," the other man continued. "The fear of losing her made you put a tracker on her? Am I right?"

"Yeah."

"You'll be a basket case for a while. You'll be afraid to let her out of your sight. Not for a single moment if you have a choice."

"I'm fucking fine with that."

Sully grinned. "I know you are. I see men like you all the time.

We're fiercely protective of our women." He paused. "Welcome to the club."

Grant didn't know if Sully made him feel better or worse, but it was of some comfort that the other man understood what was at stake. Grant didn't give a damn about the twenty-six billion dollars, he'd give up everything he owned if he could get Blaire and Val back. Money could be made. Blaire and his sister were irreplaceable.

Before Grant could respond, Tyler walked in. "We have a lock on Blaire." His man was confused. "Several locks."

Sully swore viciously and called for Viktor. He came into Grant's office with the senator.

"Just what we feared would happen."

Viktor swallowed a curse. "I'll get Tim and MDI on it."

"What's going on?" the senator asked.

"Why is the tracker showing twenty-five locations for Blaire?" Grant asked.

The AGS boss looked grim. "What I think ... Yashkin has developed an anti-serum that would momentarily mask the signal. Spencer would have injected it into Blaire, then he'd have extracted enough blood to float three carrier devices."

"Carrier devices?" the senator repeated.

Viktor nodded. "Recent technology. Just discovered two months ago. It mimics the host's blood frequency. Equipped with a booster and redirectors, it can keep the blood viable for three days relaying signals."

"That's some serious crazy shit, Baran," Grant muttered. "So one of those signals is Blaire and the others are decoys? Can you crack it?"

"That's why we need my analyst, Tim. MDI is the manufacturer of the BloodTrak serum."

"You think they'll give you access to proprietary information?" Grant asked, knowing the importance of intellectual property.

"Oh, they will," Viktor said arrogantly. "It's a blow to their ego to have their technology hacked, besides the CEO of MDI is sort of my brother-in-law."

Despite the gravity of the situation, Grant lips tipped up in a faint smile. The way these two men seemed unfazed by the obstacles coming at them inspired confidence in their ability and that went a long way in stabilizing his emotions enough for him to function and see reason.

"Seems like a good idea to invest in military contractors," Grant murmured. His father shot him a disapproving look. Being the Vice Chairman of the Senate Intelligence Committee would put them in a clear conflict of interest.

Viktor chuckled briefly. "That'll put you at the top of your game if protecting your woman is your priority. Although, I warn you, our types don't play nice with men in suits of non-military background."

"I'm a fast learner," Grant replied.

42

Blaire

"WAKE UP!"

I didn't want to open my eyes. My lids felt like lead and the voice was like a bee buzzing in my ear. I tried to shift my position on the bed. My eyes popped open. The mattress creaked too much.

"Wake up, Blaire."

"Valerie?" I finally recognized the voice and sat up. Grant's sister was sitting on the edge of a twin-sized cot. Her eyes filled with relief.

"Oh, thank God, you're okay," she cried and hugged me. I wasn't sure if I had entered an alternate universe so I surveyed my surroundings, noting the tall crates and boxes and wide-open space. We were in a warehouse and there was a man off to one side holding a rifle. And then I recalled everything. Val kidnapped. Grant leaving the penthouse. Andy coming by and faking his misery when he was the mastermind who'd betrayed us all. Plus, the bastard tranq'd me.

"Just a bit groggy," I replied, grimacing at the cottony feel of my mouth. "Did they hurt you, Val?"

"No."

"Do you know where we are?" I whispered.

"Hey!" Our guard called. "No whispering or I'll separate you two bitches."

"Charming," I muttered. "Where's Andy?"

"He's around somewhere," Val said, her voice turning hard. "I can't believe I fell for his boyish act."

"We all did," I said and lowered my voice again. "Do you know how many guards—"

The guard growled and stalked toward us. He yanked Valerie off the bed as she gasped in outrage. I jumped off the bed, got between them, and rammed my fist into the man's face. He let go of Val and was about to backhand me when footsteps came running.

"Rex!" Andy scowled at his man. Beside the senator's fake aide, stood Suit-Guy from the gallery. He had a laptop under his arm. But my eyes momentarily locked on Rex. He looked familiar.

"Good, you're awake, Blaire. We can't waste time," Andy stated. He motioned for Suit-Guy to get situated at a desk that had several wires attached to computer equipment. "I believe you met Eric at the gallery?" I turned to Eric who gave me a mock salute.

On another table were the paintings. They'd been cut from their frames and laid stacked on top of each other. Above the table was a swivel lamp and magnifying glass. Beside it was what I suspected was a spectrometer. "Do you need anything right now? Are you hungry?"

"All right," I stood back and swept my arms out helplessly. "You all have to tell me what I'm supposed to find underneath that."

"Numbers, Blaire," Andy said impatiently. "We tried to leave you out of it, but Kostin concealed the numbers very well, it's hard to separate the pigments. You'll have to go in there manually." He scowled at me. "Don't give me that look."

He stalked over to Val, yanked her arm, twisted it behind her, and held her in front of him. "We don't have time. Your damned tracker is causing us problems and it's not like we can cut it out of you. I'll hurt Valerie if I have to." He jerked the arm behind Val higher, but Grant's sister, although in pain, wasn't giving Andy the satisfaction.

Brave girl. Now if I could figure out how many people we were up against and plot our escape.

"Release her and I'll get started," I said. "I need a scalpel, solvent, a bowl of water, and clean rags. Think you can get me those?"

"Do you really need the scalpel?" Andy asked, pushing Val off to the side. There was a hurt look on her face, but I couldn't analyze what she was feeling at the moment, although, it would wreck me if Grant had used me the way Andy had used her. Hopefully, she wasn't in too deep with him yet.

"Do you really want those numbers?" I countered. Ugh, I wanted to punch him in the face. To think I thought his boyishness was adorable. Now he made my skin crawl. That two-faced bastard.

He came back moments later with a box cutter. "This is all I have."

"It's not ideal, but it will do," I returned coolly then settled in front of the desk and got to work.

THREE HOURS LATER, my back and eyes were killing me. The solvent had also nauseated me. My fingers were tired from maneuvering the box cutter. I was miserable, but I had uncovered the two bank account numbers they needed. I had passed the paintings through the scanner and noted that each painting hid four account numbers.

I wasn't sure what Suit-Guy, Eric, was doing with the account numbers, but he confirmed the money in them, and it sounded like they were distributing it to different accounts.

"You need to work faster," Andy murmured close to my ear while his hands massaged my shoulders.

"Take your hands off me."

His fingers disappeared and he plopped down on a chair beside me. "You know, Blaire, I really liked you."

"Lot of good it did me—you still sold me out," I muttered as I scraped some paint off a section to reveal a 2. A thought occurred to me. "Did you put the bomb under the car, Andy?"

Val gasped.

"Rex was the senator's driver that day, wasn't he?" I asked. "He didn't have a beard then." It had finally clicked where I had seen him. "He told you I was secure in that Bentley and wouldn't get killed in that rollover, but you didn't care about Amelia."

"Orlov couldn't get to you, so he asked my boss for some help. We needed you alive and it was the perfect setup to alienate you from them."

"You fucking bastard!" Grant's sister leapt up from the cot, but Rex turned the rifle at her.

"Wow! And then you marched me out to the slaughter," I derided.

"You're a survivor though. You've ruined my chances for greater things."

I sat up straight and cracked my neck from side-to-side. "What do you mean?"

"Blaire, do you think I wasted years going to law school, years building my reputation as a political advisor, just to be a thief? No. The plan was to infiltrate the administration of the next president. Then you proved to be too difficult to abduct because your damned boyfriend was too paranoid. There was a change of strategy. It wasn't my preference, but my backer was making it worth my while."

"You work for the Russians? Are you a spy for the Kremlin?"

Andy burst out laughing. "No, I don't work for the Kremlin."

He did not deny working for the Russians.

A large clanging gate slid open somewhere and a rush of footsteps echoed through the warehouse. Two men appeared, both armed with carbines.

"One of the carriers is down," one of them said. "It's being hacked."

"By whom?"

"We're not sure, chief. But the location markers are down to seventeen. What do you want to do?"

"If we try to move out of the tracker's range, they'll locate us before we reach a safe house. BloodTrak is using satellites, so there's no guarantee they won't find us." Andy glanced at Valerie. "We'll send a message. What do you think, sweetheart? Shall we see who's more important? Will your daddy stop me from chopping off your finger? Or maybe we should go straight for the jugular?"

Val's eyes widened in terror and I wanted to kick Andy's ass.

"You wouldn't," Val said, her chin trembled but she tilted it up in defiance.

Andy smirked, before he turned to Eric. "Get the webcam up and make sure our IP redirectors are activated."

"Andy, don't do this," I appealed to my former friend. "I'll get this done faster."

"You're not even halfway done, Blaire," Andy told me. "I'm buying you more time, sweetie." His smile was maniacal as he considered Val. "I'll do this side-show in another area."

"No!" I shouted.

"Rex." Andy tilted his head in my direction and his guard pointed his carbine at me. He then grabbed Val's arm, but she yanked out of his hold and refused to budge. It took three men to pull her past a section of stacked crates.

"Get to work," Rex ordered.

"You can tell Andy I'm not going to—"

Rex swung the butt of his rifle toward me and smacked me at the tip of my chin. Pain erupted on the whole side of my face as my eyes watered. Refusing to let him see my tears, I turned back to the paintings and grabbed the cutter and solvent.

I tried to block out Val's cries and struggles on the other side of the rows of boxes, but I couldn't.

"Shut up!" I heard Eric shout. His outburst was followed by the sound of flesh hitting flesh and Val suddenly stopped crying.

"That was harsh, Eric, but thanks," Andy said. "She was getting on my last nerve and I would have shot her."

Asshole.

"Do we have contact yet? Good." Andy paused. "Ah, Senator."

"You sick son of a bitch. What have you done to my daughter?"

"Oh, you mean, this daughter?"

"Daddy ..." Val croaked.

"Oh my God, what have you done to her? I'll kill you, Spencer."

"She's been a handful," Andy said.

"Where's Blaire?" *Grant!*

"She's busy earning us billions. Don't worry—she's still in one piece," Andy said. "Now, I want you all to back off. We have no use for the women. Once Blaire gives us what we need, we'll let them go."

"Your word is shit, Spencer. You work for Yashkin," Grant growled.

"Stop hacking the carriers," Andy warned.

"Chief, we lost another one. We're down to nine locations," Eric said.

"Damn it, I'm warning you, Senator."

"No!"

Val screamed.

I clenched my fist around the cutter and spun around. Rex didn't see me coming because his attention was on the drama unfolding on the other side of the crates. I jumped on his back just as he was about to turn toward me. With my left hand covering his mouth, I sank the cutter into his neck and jerked it up. Valerie was still screaming and her father was yelling, so no one heard us hit the floor. Blood pooled like a river around us. My body and mind went into survival-attack mode with a single focus. I heard Liam's voice in my head.

Fight.

I grabbed Rex's carbine, checked the magazine, grabbed his extra ones, and went to get Valerie.

43

Grant

"No!" the senator yelled.

That motherfucker had one of his men hold Val down, while the other started to cut a finger.

"Stop it! All right!"

Andy's face filled the screen while Val was crying hysterically in the background. "Now, Senator." He threatened.

"Grant, please," his father turned to him. Grant was conflicted. He had just received an update from Viktor that his analyst was close to isolating the carriers. The AGS men took a chopper out and were hovering around the location dots that were within a twenty-mile radius of each other, so as soon as the real coordinates were identified they could quickly respond. In his mind, Val could survive with one less finger if that meant they could be saved.

"Maybe I should just slit your baby girl's throat," his father's former aide said silkily.

"Chief, they've got us!" One of Andy's men shouted.

"You just killed your daughter." A cruel sneer twisted Andy's face.

"Stop!" the senator lunged at the monitor.

A loud cracking noise was heard from the screen. The man holding Val fell over, and Andy and two other men ran for cover leaving Val sitting stunned in her chair. Gunshots? Who was shooting?

"What...?" the senator whispered. Grant's mind raced, trying to figure out what was going on. Viktor and his men couldn't have gotten there this quickly.

"Dammit, Val, get over here!"

Blaire!

44

Blaire

CURSING Grant's sister to the high heavens, I left the cover of the stacked crates and ran toward her. With my carbine set in fully automatic, I shot in the direction where Andy, Eric, and their other man disappeared and grabbed Val.

"Come on," I shouted and wished to God she'd snap out of her daze.

"Oh my God, Blaire, you're bleeding. You're bleeding!"

"Not my blood," I muttered.

When a bullet kicked up concrete beside her feet, I turned my weapon and fired in the direction where the shot came from. Val was a crying mess and if I didn't calm her down, she'd get us both killed. My own courage was hanging by a thread, and if I thought about our situation too much, I would doom us both. I fisted Val's shirt and dragged her behind the metal containers.

To her credit she was trying to stop the sobs rising up from her throat. "I need you to suck it up," I growled, glancing around the crates to check our immediate surroundings. "Can you do that, Val?"

"You got us into this mess," she blurted out.

Good Lord. "You can go back to hating me later," I told her. "Right now, we need to work together to get out of this mess." A bullet ricocheted off our steel hiding place. She jumped but didn't scream. "Are you with me, Val?"

She pressed her lips together and nodded.

"Okay. You saw that open gate on our left?" It was serendipitous that the two men who reported the tracking hack left the warehouse gates open

"Yes."

"We're going to weave through these crates, but when I tell you to run, you run like hell. Don't look back. Don't see if I'm following you. They'll try not to shoot me because they need me for the paintings, but they *are* going to kill you. Understand?"

Val scowled at me.

"Ready?"

Again, she nodded.

"Go!"

We ran between a series of shipping crates. Sporadic gunfire followed us. When we had to break cover, I had to blast the carbine at full auto. The gate seemed too far away, but I was running for my life —thinking that next second would be my last with each second lasting an eternity. I reloaded magazines in the middle of our sprint to freedom and, during that moment, a bullet nicked my arm. I cried out, feeling the burn, but, thank God, Val listened to me and continued running. We made it to the exit and that was when I noticed that it locked from outside.

"Help me push this!" I yelled. This should buy us some time. There were side doors and folding gates all around the warehouse, but I was hoping they'd have trouble opening those. We sealed the sliding gates and I threaded a chain with the padlock to secure it.

The sun was shining high in the sky and I took a moment to look around. The warehouse was in the middle of farmlands. The driveway and parking lot were not paved. There were several parked vehicles—newer SUVs, an older model pickup truck, and a Jeep. I quickly checked the SUVs; they were locked. The Jeep didn't have the keys, so that left the truck. It wasn't quite vintage, but it was a model before transponders were installed in cars that prevented hot wiring. I just hoped it didn't run like a clunker.

The pickup was unlocked. I handed the carbine to Val. "Here. Make yourself useful. It's set on full-auto... just press the trigger." Luckily, this was the version of the carbine that didn't have a lot of kickback so I didn't bother warning her of it. Recoil was worse when anticipated. The steering column cover came off and exposed the housing of the wiring. "Shoot anything that moves!" I yelled over my shoulder. Twisting the black wire to the ignition wire together, I started flicking the starter wire to the battery one. The engine sputtered and came to life just as Val screamed "Motherfuckers!" and sprayed the warehouse with bullets.

I pulled her to the front of the pickup. "Can you drive?"

Her eyes were bright from her adrenaline rush. "Oh my God!" she answered.

"Val, can you drive?" I shouted to get her back in the moment.

Her grin was cocky. "I've got a few speeding tickets."

Fantastic.

"Keep your head down. Get to the driver's side. Close your door. Open mine. Go!" I grabbed the carbine from her and shot at Andy and his men trying to make their way toward us. I circled the hood and dove into the passenger seat.

"The steering is locked," she muttered.

"Shit. Hold on." I removed the ignition wiring harness to reveal the pin, then used the butt of the carbine to knock off the lock cylinder. "Pull the pin!"

"It's free!" Val answered.

A shot broke through the rear of the pick up and went through the windshield.

"Floor it!" I screamed and we shot forward.

We sped through dirt and gravel, bouncing like a rickety ride in an amusement park. The shocks on the pickup should've been replaced long ago, but at least we were getting out of that hellhole. I spied a main road up ahead at the same time I noticed the Jeep and the SUV in pursuit. Another shot through the rear windshield caused the cracks to spread like a spider web. Using the butt of my carbine again, I chipped at the glass until the whole section fell away, giving me a good vantage point against our pursuers.

"Left or right!" Val yelled.

"It doesn't matter!" I shouted. "Choose!"

She swerved left, barely slowing down and I slammed against my door. Val cackled with euphoria. I wondered if we would survive the chase only to crash in a ball of fire.

"Keep your head as low as possible," I reminded her as I saw the Jeep follow our turn. I sighted the tire of the Jeep and was about to squeeze the trigger when the pickup veered right. "Keep it steady!"

Val mumbled something in return. My pulse was pounding in my ears as I fired again. Missed. I tried again and kicked up pavement far from my target. Sounds receded into a vacuum until all I heard was my erratic breathing. *Okay, Blaire. Focus! It's now or never.* I took a couple of cleansing breaths then aimed again. I inhaled, held my breath, pulled my belly button to my spine, and squeezed the trigger. The Jeep careened to one side and then the other until it spun one hundred and eighty degrees and stopped at the shoulder facing the opposite direction. The black SUV following it avoided a collision by inches.

"Okay, okay," I told myself. "One more. Hold it together, Blaire." I tuned everything out, but the blunt rhythm of a chopper invaded my consciousness. "What the—?"

"Choppers!" Val yelled.

I looked to the front of the vehicle and sure enough, I saw three helicopters closing in fast. Shit, were they for us or for them? Just then, our tire burst or it got hit by a bullet.

"Oh, no! Oh no!" Grant's sister tried her best to control the vehicle. She had the presence of mind not to slam on the brakes, and, after a harrowing swerve toward an oncoming vehicle, she righted it back in our lane, letting it crawl to a stop. Another bullet bounced on the top of the pickup.

"Keep down."

But then something happened, the Black SUV made a u-turn and started driving away from us. Two of the choppers flew over us and went in pursuit while another was landing on the open farmland right beside us. The powerful rotors flattened the grass around it. Two men jumped down.

"Stay inside," I ordered as I hopped out and pointed the barrel at the approaching figures. They removed their helmets and I was almost certain they were on our side. One had striking white blond hair. The dark-haired man reminded me of Grant.

"It's Viktor Baran!" Val shouted over the noise of the choppers as she scrambled out of the pickup from my side. She pushed the barrel of my rifle down. "They're the good guys, Blaire. I've seen him at Dad's committee hearings."

I pressed my lips together, still doubtful.

"These men are incorruptible, trust me." She was grinning like an idiot. I had no chance to second-guess her because they were upon us. Their clear paratrooper goggles did nothing to mask the baffled look on their faces.

"Did you ladies just shoot your way out of there?" the dark-haired guy asked. His eyes were gleaming with awe and amusement.

"Blaire was amazing. She's like the female version of Rambo," Val gushed.

I squirmed under the intense scrutiny of both men. "And Val drove like a maniac."

"Louise," Val corrected. "I'm Louise to your Thelma."

Uhm, did Grant's sister just become my BFF?

The blond guy introduced himself. "I'm Viktor Baran. This is Gabriel Sullivan. We're here to take you home."

45

Grant

GRANT STOOD AT THE HELIPORT. That day was a wake-up call. A day of admitting that power, position, and money couldn't do a damn thing to ensure the safety of his woman. There were always people more powerful and loftier than he was, and those with more money than he had. That day was indeed a lesson in humility. It was people who mattered. It was his faith and trust in people of strength and integrity that would bring his woman back. As the cold wind of the Hudson River whipped his trench coat around him, the words of Viktor Baran replayed in his head. Grant had wanted in on the rescue mission, but the lead guardian was firmly against it.

"*Mr. Thorne, I understand what you're going through. Most of us have experienced it. We understand how important it is for you to be there for Ms. Callahan, but we're a rapid response team. We conduct our missions with surgical precision. We put hours into training to be the best and function as a unit. We trust the other to have our back. We can read each other's moves without hesitation. For the safety of my men and the success of this mission, we can't babysit a civilian. You want Blaire and Val back—you have to trust us to do our fucking job."*

And that was the end of it. Grant had no reason to be stupid. He checked his ego at the door of his penthouse. He stood beside his dad with his hands shoved in his pockets. He found it the only effective way to keep from pacing the heliport like a deranged madman.

Details had been coming in, but they were sketchy. Apparently, Blaire and Val had escaped and were found speeding down Route Nine in Columbia County.

The BlackHawk appeared in the horizon and his father patted him on the shoulder in a gesture of mutual reassurance. Their agonizing wait was almost over. As the chopper descended, the blades kicked up stinging mist from the river, but he refused to back away. Everything seemed to happen in slow motion like a dream. It was hypnotic. The rhythmic sound of the engine, the rotation of the blades, the chopper landing, and its door sliding open. Grant's pulse and breathing quickened as two Guardians hopped off and helped the women step out.

Then he saw her face.

His Blaire.

She had a blanket wrapped around her. She looked so lost and her face was pinched as she struggled in those first few steps. And then she saw him and a glow of happiness lit her face, her stunning smile filling his chest with a riot of emotions.

His Blaire.

She ran toward him while his long strides shortened the distance between them. He caught her in his arms and lifted her up. Hazel eyes brimming with tears stared down at him and he lowered her slowly and kissed her with all the desperation and anguish of the past day and replaced them with all the love, yearning, and joy of her return.

"Teddy!" Val shouted and his sister leapt into his arms. Not letting go of Blaire with his left arm, he hugged Val with his right and planted a kiss on top of her head. And then a miracle of miracles happened. Val grinned at Blaire.

The senator came over to greet Blaire and took her momentarily from his arms. Grant spied Sully and Viktor observing the happy reunion. Leaving the women with the senator, he walked over to the Guardians and extended his arm to shake hands with both men.

"Thanks for getting my girls back," Grant said gruffly.

"They almost didn't need us," Viktor gave a crooked grin. "Your fiancée kicked ass."

"Can't wait to hear all about it at the debrief," Sully said. "Your office or the penthouse?"

"Penthouse," Grant said. "I want them to feel comfortable."

Both men nodded.

Grant turned around and headed back to his woman and hugged her tightly. "Love you so much, Angel."

She stood on tiptoes, kissed him and mouthed, "Love you, too."

———

BLAIRE AND VAL finished their debriefing with Sully. Grant was still reeling from what he'd heard, but he couldn't be prouder of his woman and sister. He didn't think he could fall more in love with Blaire, but he just did. His woman was a badass. Sully smirked at him as the Guardian packed up the recording equipment. Blaire glanced helplessly over her shoulder as Val dragged her out of the room. His sister wanted to make Blaire her specialty drink.

"Wow," was all Grant said.

"Your fiancée should consider a career change. The Guardians would welcome her."

"Not fucking likely."

Sully chuckled. "It was kinda embarrassing when our cavalry arrived. We hardly did anything. Our crew chased and rounded up Spencer and his men and retrieved the paintings. Not a single shot was fired."

Grant felt a corner of his mouth tip up. "I'm glad she has her old fire back. You heard what happened down in Miami?"

Sully nodded.

"Orlov beat the fight out of her and then she lost her best friend."

"She just needed that catalyst," Sully said. "And your sister was it."

"I'm so proud of Val, too," Grant said. "She has been spoiled all her life and she pulled through when it counted."

"Adversity brings out the best or worst in people. The best won."

They both fell silent for a few seconds in silent agreement.

Grant exhaled a weary sigh. "What will happen now?"

"Well, the senator and Viktor are in a meeting with the FBI and DOJ. We're finding ourselves in a gray area. Legally, Viktor can't hold Spencer and his crew, so they're going to charge them with grand larceny, kidnapping, and conspiracy to murder Amelia Thorne."

"And the paintings?"

The other man eyed him warily. "We'll need Blaire to recover the account numbers."

"What will happen to the money?" Grant demanded. "I want it out of our lives as soon as possible."

"Our analyst will work on securing the accounts. That money is a culmination of thirty years of organized crime. Drugs, prostitution, arms trafficking—you name it. The agency will freeze the money or put it to better use."

"And Yashkin?" The mastermind of it all.

The other man smiled enigmatically. "Don't worry about him."

They walked out of his office and saw the joviality in the living room. Val was snuggled up against their mother. Blaire was talking to Jake and Tyler, while Colette was busy fluttering about in the kitchen.

"I'm sure you can't wait to get back to your family," Sully said, extending his hand. "It was a pleasure, Mr. Thorne. We'll be in touch regarding the paintings and if we have any more questions."

He gripped the Guardian's hand firmly. "Thanks, Sullivan. For everything."

"ALONE AT LAST," Grant murmured into Blaire's ear as the last of their bodyguards entered the elevators. His parents and Val left ten minutes before midnight. It had been a stressful, emotional, long-ass twenty-four hours, and he was ready to put the day behind him.

"Hmm," Blaire hummed, leaning back against him and resting her hands on his arms that were wrapped around her.

"Although I'd say," Grant said. "I'm a bit hurt."

Blaire's suppressed laugh made him grin like an idiot. She turned in his arms and looked up at him. "What has offended you this time?"

"I'm no longer Val's favorite person," he teased. "She couldn't stop gushing about 'Blaire this' and 'Blaire that' as if you were the second coming of Christ."

"The novelty will pass," she patted his arm as if reassuring a child. "You'll be her favorite person again, but I hope we've bonded over our shared ordeal for it to be lasting."

Grant snorted. "Well, I hope you won't need something this intense for future bonding." He kissed the tip of her nose. "My heart couldn't take it." His mouth found her lips and they shared slow drugging kisses. After the adrenaline and intensity of the day, he wanted to make slow love to her. They rocked back and forth like lovers in a slow dance with him expertly moving them closer to the bedroom. He lifted his lips a fraction. "Thanks for saving my sister."

"She drove the getaway car. In that moment, we worked as a team. We saved each other."

The events of the day suddenly overwhelmed him with need, and, with a growl, he pressed her against the wall, snaked his hand under her skirt and found her wet behind her panties. Groaning his approval, his button and zipper were opened in a flash. "I can't wait to have you. I wanted to go slow, but, fuck, I need to be inside you now." He freed his cock, lifted her up, pushed the scrap of lace aside and surged inside her.

"Grant, the bedroom is right there," Blaire gasped as her legs struggled to find purchase around him.

"Don't care," he buried his face in the glorious skein of her hair as he thrust in deliberate measured strokes, savoring the tight, wet pussy and fighting against the urge to take her hard. She'd experienced too much violence that day, she needed a calmer pace, so he loved her with a gentleness he hadn't used before.

"Grant," she whimpered. "I need more."

"No, Angel, let me give you this," he raised his head to gaze at her. Their breaths mingled as he teased her with the smooth glide of his cock as he rocked her against the wall. He moved inside her for long minutes, the build to their climax slow, until they came together in a sigh of emotions. Faith overcoming uncertainty, courage overcoming fear, and love overcoming all.

46

Blaire

IT WAS early November and the leaves turned bright yellow and burnt orange. The grass had lost its vibrant green and had begun to fade to brown. Fall's sunlight dappled the marble gravestone with specks of gold. I wasn't sure why I was there. It had only been a few weeks since Liam's funeral, but the doubt Agent Wilkes planted in my head compelled me to visit Atlanta.

The stark letters on the headstone slashed my heart, but it held together because I was stronger. I sat beside the plot and stretched out my legs, picking at the twigs and leaves that had littered across it.

"Well," I said gruffly. "Here I am checking to see if you're still dead." My voice cracked. "I would hate you because you put me through such grief, but I would forgive you in a heartbeat if you'd just show up right now." I took a few moments to suppress a rising sob. "Anyway"—I held up my ring as if to show him—"I'm getting married this spring. I know, I know, you told me not to be easy, but have you met Grant?" I snickered as if it was an inside joke. "Truth is, I love him, Liam, and he loves me. He can be too much and crazy protective." I let out an irritated breath. "All right psycho protective, but after everything I put him through, I can't blame him. If he'd been in the same danger I was, I would be a nutcase too." The sun moved and I closed my eyes, tilting my face up and enjoyed the warmth on my skin for a minute. I lowered my head and cracked my eyes open. "You'd be proud of me. I was afraid I'd lost the will to live after the number Orlov did on me, but all I needed was time and Grant's love to show me I had a lot of fight left in me. The thing with Orlov was only the tip of the iceberg. So many things have happened since then, but the gist of it is ... your girl is scott-free."

Footsteps sounded behind me.

"*My* girl."

I smiled and turned to look at Grant. He accompanied me to the graveyard. I'd asked him to give me a few minutes alone with Liam. He walked over to me now and held out his hand. "Ready to go, baby?"

"Yes." I smiled as he pulled me into his embrace. With his arms still wrapped around me, he stared at Liam's headstone. "I'll protect her with my life, Liam. Count on it."

It was a bittersweet visit. Liam made it possible for me to have a full, normal life with Grant. I wouldn't let my friend down.

As Grant and I cleared the cemetery gates, I looked at the man I loved and looked forward to days and years ahead of us.

Thank you, my friend.

47

CAM MURPHY

FOR A FEW DAYS NOW, Cam had blended into the shadows of Chester Square in London. It was an affluent neighborhood decked with rowhouses made of warm-hued limestone in an Italian baroque style. Arched entrances were lit with cast-iron lanterns. But he wasn't here to admire the architecture; he was here for one of its residents.

Ivan Yashkin was a man of habit. He rarely left his house nowadays because he'd made enemies everywhere. He'd gone from one of the most powerful men in Russia to one of its most maligned. He took money from the mob and other Kremlin bureaucrats, thinking he'd have twenty-six billion to buffer the investments he'd made for them. He was one of the masterminds who wanted the U.S. financial market to crash but, without the money from those lost accounts, he had no buffer, the investments tanked, and he lost everything.

Still, Cam considered him a threat. With this third chance for a new life, he would clean up the loose ends he'd left with his last one. He was no longer Liam Watts nor was he Lucas Myers. Leaving Liam behind was necessary. He'd tortured and eventually killed a dirty FBI agent who had the final pieces of evidence necessary to bring down Orlov and the ROC. In his rush to get Blaire back, he'd become sloppy. He'd realized his mistake too late and a tenacious FBI agent—a friend of the one he had killed—had linked all his aliases together. But Liam had been offered a second chance by AGS and, by extension, the CIA. The agency couldn't actively operate in the homeland so they strategically placed some of their agents undercover with local first responders. What happened to Amelia Thorne had exposed the missing piece in the AGS investigation into the shakeup of the oligarchy and its plot against the United States. One of his crew during the Orlov sting was working for Viktor Baran—the AGS top man. He'd been given a shot of a life-saving drug by another undercover agent who worked as an EMT, the same one who covered him with a white sheet, so no one would notice any signs of life until the scene was completely processed. The drug jump-started his heart but kept it at an almost undetectable rate while preserving organ function. It was rarely used because agents have come back with no brain activity or brain-damaged. Luckily, as far as Cam was concerned, he was mentally stable, if not a bit homicidal.

From there he was whisked by a fake coroner and kept at a CIA medical facility; all paperwork and records doctored to show that he had died. The only regret he had was that his daughter buried a body that wasn't his, but it was for the best. He also regretted putting Blaire through agonizing grief. He'd been conflicted, wanting to let her know that he was alive, but Blaire had come back from her experience from Orlov a stronger woman. And maybe, just maybe, letting his broken wren fly was the right thing to do. He'd been teaching her survival skills for two years, preparing her for a life without him. Maybe Liam was holding her back in a co-dependent way and he needed to cut the ties.

So he kept away.

Movement at the front door of one of the row houses caught his attention. His prey had emerged.

Ivan Yashkin would die today.

INTERNATIONAL BUSINESS WIRE

 Ivan Yashkin, CEO and owner of Yashkin Global Enterprises, died in a freak car explosion while leaving his home in Chester Square. London authorities are still investigating the cause of the incident. Witnesses report they heard a boom and saw a vehicle go up in flames at the corner of Elizabeth Street and Chester Row. Foul play is suspected. YGE is a Russian energy company specializing in the exploration, production, refinement, marketing, and distribution of oil and gas with subsidiaries involved in mining and speculative research in technology. There'd been rumors of recent financial difficulties stemming from charges of fraud and money laundering.

EPILOGUE

Grant

GRANT PULLED the Escalade in front of Blaire's log cabin. Thanksgiving was in four days and they'd decided to spend some time together locked away from the world before they joined his family in their Vail mountain home.

He could feel Blaire's excitement and anxiety. It was like a homecoming of sorts for her. She hopped out of the car and stared at her house.

"Go on inside," Grant urged. "I'll bring the stuff in."

She shot him a dazzling smile before moving up the steps. He walked to the rear of the vehicle and lifted the tailgate of the SUV. This week was about them. It was easy to head out into parts unknown, but this place held a special meaning. They'd come without bodyguards. They'd left the luxury of their Manhattan and Boston residences behind. They were simply Grant and Blaire.

He lifted their suitcase and her little carry-on and loped to the cabin. The news frenzy about their engagement had died down, but their wedding next spring was sure to ramp up interest again. Blaire suggested eloping, much to the horror of his mother. He didn't want to put too much pressure on his woman, but Grant wanted to have a big wedding. He'd admit to male pride. He wanted to declare to the world that Blaire was his.

Possessiveness surged through his veins as he dropped the suitcases to the floor. Every muscle and pulse was already responding to the idea that they were alone, no one could hear her when he made her scream with pleasure and he could fuck her to his cock's content without their security intruding. He was already in full predator mode by the time Blaire switched the circuit breakers on and returned from the kitchen to the living room where he stood motionless.

"Well, I'm glad your brief stint in B&E didn't mess up this place," Blaire teased, still unaware that he'd already gone through several filthy images in his head of how he wanted to fuck her. Lately, she'd been wearing dresses that hit mid-thigh. She called this particular one a tunic dress. Grant called them easy-access clothes. Her tall soft boots that came up above her knees only added to the sexiness. His mouth was already salivating at the thought of spreading her open and burying his face between her thighs. His dick hardened behind his jeans, but anticipation was half the pleasure, so he watched her some more as she made her way to the farm table. She crouched beside it to straighten the tassel of the rug. When she stood and turned to look at him, her eyes widened, and her lips parted on an inhale. She finally realized she was about to get ravished.

"Uh ..."

He stalked toward her. "No morning sex and it was a six-hour plane ride, baby. You know me enough by now that I aim to be buried inside you first chance I get."

"Grant ..." she whispered on a shaky laugh. "The place needs some dusting and airing out."

He crowded her against the kitchen wall, his hands slipping under her dress.

"Later," he murmured against her lips as his fingers went behind her panties. "Your pussy needs some eating." He delved into her tight heat, groaning at how her slick inner muscles gripped him. "Fuck, you *are* ready." He dropped to his knees, his hands sliding up the back of her thighs squeezing the globes of her ass, before he gripped the edges of her panties and tore them down. He heard her gasp and he smiled against the dress right above her pussy. He inhaled her arousal through the fabric. Grant slid a hand back down her left leg and lifted it over his shoulder, and with the other, he tossed her skirt up and dove right in.

She cried out as her back arched, forcing her pelvis out and practically shoving her core into his mouth. He growled in approval and devoured her wanton offering. Blaire moaned, burying her hands in his hair as her juices gushed right onto his greedy tongue. When she came down from her high, he stood up and released his aching cock. He hoisted her into his arms and without further warning, plunged inside her.

He pounded her mercilessly against the wall. Grant had tempered his lovemaking those past few weeks, giving Blaire and him a chance to experience their love without the desperation and angst brought about from nearly losing her twice. This time his need was brought about by the instinct to possess, to claim, and to mark. He rooted deeply and she squirmed and gasped.

"Oh!" she whimpered.

He growled, pulled out, and thrust in hard.

"Ah! I'm gonna come again," she cried out. When her muscles clenched around his dick, Grant lost his mind and started rutting like a beast, grunting, snarling, his thrusting sliding her up and down the wall.

She screamed and pulled his hair as he continued moving inside her. He came and groaned into her neck, staying embedded inside her while keeping her pinned until the last tremors of his release left him.

"I love wall fucks," she murmured against his ear.

He smiled against her skin.

Blaire

AFTER GRANT spectacularly fucked me against the wall, he lowered my legs to the floor and held me steady. I didn't think I could hold myself up for a good few minutes. He led me to the couch, stripped off the cover, sat, and pulled me across his lap. He continued nuzzling my neck as we recovered from our carnal activity. This vigorous coming together was long overdue. Grant seemed to know when I needed gentle and he definitely knew when I needed him to take me with fierce possession.

"Too rough?" he murmured. There was no remorse in his voice.

"I can handle it."

"Good. You don't know how much I want to tear you apart."

I shuddered. My back felt a bit raw and I could still feel him inside me. Pulling away from nibbling my neck, his blue eyes locked on mine.

"I want you to skip your next birth control shot."

"Why?" I asked, bewildered.

"Dreaming of you heavy with my kid," he said. "Turns me the fuck on like anything." His hands lowered to my belly. "Need to get started with our family, Angel."

"Uhh, we're getting married in May. I don't want to worry on whether I'll fit into my wedding gown."

"Eloping has its merits," he grumbled.

"Told ya."

"Still," his eyes took on a proprietary gleam. "It'll all be worth it when I finally put that ring on your finger for all the world to see."

I sighed. "You're such a freaking caveman."

"Get used to it," he murmured, attacking my neck again. I settled contentedly into my man. All wrapped up and cuddled on his lap was the best place in the world to be. One would say we'd gone through the most extreme situations as a couple, but we came out of them stronger and more committed to each other. Grant still had a problem letting me out of his sight. I felt his anxiety every morning when he left for work. He texted me often and called me at least twice a day. I wondered how he ever got any work done. I had a few more therapy sessions with Dr. Jones and Grant was coming with me to the remaining ones, but I think he should go see a therapist on his own as well.

My eyes started to wander around the cabin and something, or some things, caught my eyes above the fireplace mantle in the living room. Disentangling myself from my man who muttered in protest, I walked to the unfamiliar objects.

My breath caught.

Five miniature wood sculptures of a wren lay before me. They were arranged in different stages of flight. The first had its wings tucked to its side and the last had its wings fully spread in flight.

"What are these?" Grant murmured as I picked the last one and caressed the intricate grooves carved into the wood.

My heart pushed into my throat, clogging my words.

"Blaire?" he whispered, brows drawing in concern.

Eyes filling with tears, my lips trembled but I managed to smile. I took a deep inhale, then exhaling, I said, "Liam."

The End

ACKNOWLEDGMENTS

My thanks to Christina Trevaskis of Book Matchmaker for letting my words take flight. Your guidance through every stage of the manuscript, from first draft to last, gave me the confidence to write with inspiration.

Much praise to my editor, Kristan Roetker of Edit LLC—your understanding of my characters and story polished the book to my ultimate vision.

To Laurie and Ms. D, I can't thank you enough for your valuable insights that helped me enrich the story.

To the community of bloggers and readers, I am eternally grateful for your support.

And lastly, to S—greatest husband ever. Thanks for taking care of me and Loki while I get lost in the world of my characters.

CONNECT WITH THE AUTHOR

Find me at:
Facebook: Victoria Paige Books
Website: victoriapaigebooks.com
Email: victoriapaigebooks@gmail.com

ALSO BY VICTORIA PAIGE

Guardians

Fire and Ice

Silver Fire

Smoke and Shadows

Always

It's Always Been You

Always Been Mine

A Love For Always

Misty Grove

Fighting Chance

Saving Grace

Standalone

Deadly Obsession

* Most series books can be read as standalone.

Made in the USA
Las Vegas, NV
30 August 2021